A Secret Daughter from Ireland

BOOKS BY ANN O'LOUGHLIN

The Irish House
My Only Daughter
Her Husband's Secret
Secrets of an Irish House
Escape to the Irish Village
A Letter from Ireland

A Secret Daughter from Ireland

Ann O'Loughlin

bookouture

Published by Bookouture in 2025

An imprint of Storyfire Ltd.
Carmelite House
50 Victoria Embankment
London EC4Y 0DZ

www.bookouture.com

The authorised representative in the EEA is Hachette Ireland
8 Castlecourt Centre
Dublin 15 D15 XTP3
Ireland
(email: info@hbgi.ie)

ISBN: 978-1-83618-912-1
eBook ISBN: 978-1-83618-911-4

To John, Roshan and Zia xxx

ONE

MAY 2024

'What's left? Tell me, what the hell do I do now?' Becky buried her head in her hands. How could their lives have gone so spectacularly wrong in such a short space of time?

She felt the light touch of Jen's hand on her shoulder.

'I'm still here, Mom.'

Becky's heart constricted. Shame seared through her that she had almost forgotten about Jen. After all, it was just the two of them now against the world.

Exhausted, Becky slumped down on the sofa, finding a strange comfort in the cold feel of the leather pressing into her back. Shutting her eyes, she attempted to block out her friend Sadie's voice.

'Darling, we need a drink. It has all been such a nightmare,' Sadie said as she rummaged through the kitchen cupboards for a bottle of alcohol. Becky couldn't help smiling; her friend was brash and so loud, but she had also been her rock this past week.

'Try Hilda's study,' Becky said, wincing as Sadie continued to open and shut cabinet doors. Reaching into the Trader Joe's carrier bag, Becky carefully took out the pewter urn containing her mother's ashes. Hilda would be so cross at the indignity of being transported in a supermarket carrier bag, and she didn't know whether to laugh or cry at the absurdity of the situation.

'Where will we put Granny?' Jen asked.

'I don't know. She wouldn't want to go on display like an ornament,' Becky said quietly.

Sadie pulled a bottle of whiskey triumphantly from a cupboard under the kitchen sink, and sloshed a measure into a tumbler. 'Get that down you, and let me park Hilda in the study,' she said, taking the urn before Becky had time to reply.

Jen jumped up. 'Granny Hilda can stay in my room,' she said, whipping the canister from Sadie's hands, and heading for her room.

Becky wanted to bolt after her, but stopped herself; best to let Jen be. A din of loud music emanated from her daughter's bedroom. Becky took deep breaths, and tried to calm down as she sat in the semi-darkness, the lights from the buildings all around flooding into the apartment, creating crazy shapes on the floor. If Hilda were here, she would complain that it was silly to sit in the dark, and that Becky looked as if she were snooping on their neighbours. She missed her mother so much. The feeling of loss outweighed her anger at the mess left behind.

All of those who had attended the memorial service for Hilda, offering to support Becky and Jen, had slipped away so quickly and easily. All they had left were Hilda's ashes, and a mountain of debts.

'Does Jen know?' Sadie asked, flopping down opposite Becky and switching on a table lamp.

'Doesn't everybody? Hilda left us with a shitload of bank debt, but Jen insists there's been some mistake, that Granny Hilda was an amazing businesswoman who would never run up millions in debt. Last week, I would have said the same thing.'

'You'll get through it, darling; you have to,' Sadie said, reaching across to refill her glass.

'I have to sell everything,' Becky said, her voice shaking.

'Not the apartment surely.'

Becky nodded. Three days after the memorial service, she had called into the family attorney. He had been polite and firm – the news devastating.

Anger and frustration coursed through Becky now to think Hilda had risked everything on an extension of their dress design business to the West Coast, and had not even bothered to discuss it with her.

'This apartment, the small place on Rhode Island too, they're all already on the market.'

'But, darling, surely the loans died with Hilda.'

Becky, choking with tears, got up, and started to pace the hardwood floor. 'Apparently, I was a co-signatory on these ginormous loans. They're my responsibility now.'

Sadie was about to say something, but stopped when Becky suddenly threw her hands in the air. 'What does it matter? Our investors have pulled out. The Hilda White brand of Manhattan is no more. Somebody suggested I should bring back the staff and create a capsule collection, but apparently without Hilda, nobody wants to know us. I hardly have the heart for it now, anyway.'

'That's so shit,' Sadie said.

Becky walked to the window, and stared at the building across the way. In the apartment below them, a woman was sitting down to eat dinner alone, while in another room, a child played on a games console.

'I know it sounds dumb, but I don't even remember signing any of the loan stuff. I guess I was the creative one in the partnership, and happy to let Mom carry the load,' she said, turning away from the window.

Sadie didn't say anything.

'It sounds pathetic, like I'm making excuses, doesn't it?' Becky said.

'A little.'

'But Hilda looked after the business side of things. I just turned up every day and designed dresses.'

Sadie put down her glass carefully on the walnut coffee table. 'Let me put on my attorney hat for a moment. Ignorance is never a defence. Unfortunately, debts only get bigger with time, and if you don't show a readiness to take steps to deal with the matter, you could find yourself in front of a judge.'

Becky paced round and round the room like a clockwork toy. 'You mean I'm saddled with this debt? But I don't even understand how it got to this. Mom was always so careful.'

'This is a fine city apartment; here's hoping with this and the Rhode Island property you might be able to wipe the slate clean.'

Becky's mouth dried up. Her head was spinning, and she couldn't even muster one word. It was never meant to end like this. She knew if her mother was here, she would throw her eyes upwards, and declare the situation preposterous. She so needed Hilda's courage right now.

That they had to leave this loft they loved on East 11th Street was a blow too far. Becky stopped the frantic pacing, and looked down the narrow corridor which ran the length of the apartment.

At the far end was Hilda's office. At this time of the evening, Hilda would usually have been at her large mahogany desk, a whiskey in a crystal glass at her elbow as she pored over spreadsheets. When she'd needed Becky's signature, she would call her.

Becky shook herself, and looked directly at Sadie.

'I have to get out of Manhattan,' she said.

'What?'

'We're going to Ireland.'

'Where?' Sadie asked, frowning.

'Ireland,' Becky said, taking a white envelope and a large key from the corridor bookcase. 'The night I found Hilda after she had the heart attack, she was clutching this envelope which contained the key and details of a house in Ireland, along with the legal documents showing she owned the property. I never even heard about this place; why would she have a house in Ireland and not tell me? I need to go there.'

Sadie frowned.

'I know I'm not making much sense,' Becky said.

'Heck, darling, you're making as much sense as the talking cookie jar on the kitchen counter. Why on earth do you think you and Jen should move so far away?'

Becky took a deep breath.

'I'm not going to be happy until I have some answers.'

'But you don't know anybody in Ireland. This is so fricking nuts!' Sadie cried.

'My mind is made up,' Becky said firmly.

'You're a respected designer; you'll get work in this city. You can get over all this,' Sadie said.

Becky pulled her hands down her face. 'Sadie, please trust me on this. This is not just about Mom; I have to get away.'

'OK, darling, but does it have to be so far away?'

Becky didn't answer but held up the key so Sadie could examine it.

'That seems more like a jailer's key than a house key. Seriously, girl, this is crazy,' Sadie said.

'There's nothing here for me, or for us any more.'

'Darling, you've been through hell. Give yourself time before making any big life plans. Real estate is always good to have, and better to offload. Sell the damn place; use the money to set yourself and Jen up,' Sadie said impatiently.

Becky stopped to examine the display of photographs on the corridor wall. There were nearly a dozen framed press cuttings and photographs of an elegantly dressed Hilda at numerous glittering events on the Manhattan social circuit over the years.

Feeling alone and helpless, a part of Becky wanted to pull the pictures from the wall, and hear the glass shatter across the floor. A bigger part of her desperately wanted Hilda to reappear, and sort out this mess.

'Maybe an adventure will be good for me and Jen,' she said uncertainly.

Sadie clicked her tongue to show her disapproval. 'Listen to your words, girl. It's crazy talk. You don't want to go there and neither does Jen right now.'

Becky slapped her hands over her ears. Her eyes blurred with tears.

'Tell me, why haven't I heard of this place before? I thought Mom told me everything. I have to find out why she was keeping it a secret, and if it was important to her.'

'Are you sure this isn't the grief talking? That you're looking for signs that are simply not there?'

'Please stop. We're not in court; I don't need to be cross-examined,' Becky said.

'But, darling, you're not making much sense.'

Becky pulled a photograph from the envelope. 'This is the house. Look at it,' she said fiercely.

Sadie picked up the photograph and examined it closely. A large Georgian house, painted ice pink, with long windows over two floors at the front and a wide door with a stained-glass fan-light and side lights. Swathes of wisteria and Virginia creeper covered the façade. Two giant lawns at the front overlooked the ocean, and apple blossom trees lined the sides of the property with more blossom trees in the middle of the grass. Flowers intermingled with lavender were planted either side of the centre path on both sides. Granite steps led up from the front gate to the path through the lawns and the front door.

'Turn it around to see what it says,' Becky said urgently as Sadie read it aloud.

Coolnamona House, Orchid Bay, Coolnamona, Co Wicklow.

'That's Hilda's handwriting too,' Becky said.

'I don't know, Hilda could have just bought the place without even viewing. Maybe it was only ever meant to be an investment property,' Sadie said. Becky laughed nervously.

She didn't know why, but she felt drawn to this big house. There were so many questions flooding her brain right now, and she had this nagging feeling that it was only in the house overlooking Orchid Bay at Coolnamona that she would find any answers.

'Come to Ireland with us, even just for a short visit,' Becky said, her tone softer now.

Sadie took a slug of her whiskey before speaking. 'To Ireland? Me? No. That's not happening. I have a very big court case coming up. I won't even have a weekend off after next week,' she said.

'I just don't know how I'm going to sell the idea to Jen, particularly if you don't come along,' Becky said despondently.

'Jen is just a kid; she doesn't have a say. But I'm telling you, this is a foolish idea. What is the point of dragging yourself and Jen all the way over there and away from—?'

'We don't have a home any more,' Becky groaned.

'But you know nothing of this Coolnamona House. You hardly know where it is.'

Becky tugged at her long brown hair, like she always did when she was stressed. 'I have just lost Mom; I'm at sea. Can't you let me steer for port at Orchid Bay in this storm?'

'Which makes so much sense,' Sadie muttered.

Becky got up, and walked over to a small table beside the French doors. Picking up a photograph of herself and her mother, she smiled. She was just five years old on her first day at kindergarten. Becky was making a face, but Hilda was beaming.

She remembered her mother had always been by her side; they'd laughed that they were two tough Brooklyn women, together against the rest of the world.

'Everything was so simple when it was just the two of us against everyone else. I never expected her to keep anything from me.'

'It's just a house, some interesting real estate. Let's face it, you could do with the extra bucks right now,' Sadie said.

Becky examined the picture of the house again, and sighed. 'My mother attached significance to the smallest things. She would never have been the owner of a house anywhere without it being important to her life. This place, Coolnamona House, meant something to her, and I need to find out why. It's all I can think about right now.'

'Haven't you ever heard of not making big decisions at a time of crisis in your life?'

'It just feels right; otherwise I will regret not going there,' Becky said firmly.

Sadie sighed loudly, but didn't speak.

'We fly out in two days; I only stayed this long to collect Hilda's ashes,' Becky said.

'Please reconsider, darling. This is too drastic.'

Becky shook her head. 'What's left here for us? We're surrounded by sadness.'

'And you figure your situation will be any better over there, where you know nobody?'

Becky banged down her glass so hard on the coffee table, some whiskey plopped out. 'I don't have a choice, Sadie, can't you see that?'

'Not true, darling.'

Becky rapped the coffee table hard with her knuckles. 'You're my best friend, Sadie, but you don't know everything. Please believe me when I say I have my reasons, and I definitely have no choice. There is no other way out.'

TWO

Becky swallowed hard, and tried to stay calm as she drove on the narrow road hugging Orchid Bay, and up the cliff lane to the village of Coolnamona.

Her hands trembling, she gripped the wheel tight as she turned onto the wide main street. The house was somewhere near here with a view across the bay and the Irish Sea. She shivered.

So much had changed in their lives in the space of two weeks. Back then, Becky thought the worst thing she would have to do was tell Jen her favourite person in the whole world had died. Becky shuddered to think back on the moment. Jen was silent for several minutes as if she'd forgotten to react, but when she remembered, she moaned; a sorrowful type of keening that turned into heart-wrenching sobs and screams as she collapsed deep into Becky's arms.

Becky had held her daughter for hours, the two of them curled together on the long leather sofa in the sitting room which Hilda had always complained was too chilly. She had wool throws arranged on the armrests, and they unfolded them, wrapping them around themselves because it reminded them of Hilda.

They sat surrounded by the silence of death, and didn't even bother to move when the phone rang. When the evening sunlight peeked through the windows, they watched the patterns on the wooden parquet floor, and they wondered how they would survive without Hilda. As darkness crept across the loft, and the lights of the buildings spotted across the floors, Becky took the pillows from Hilda's bed, and they curled up together, breathing in the smell of Hilda White, which was a mixture of expensive Chanel perfume and her favourite rose geranium oil.

And now, Becky had moved her seventeen-year-old daughter, still smarting with the pain of grief, to this small town on the east coast of Ireland. Sadie was right; it was fucking crazy, and she had made a huge mistake. It was too early in the morning, and Coolnamona appeared so quiet. Becky's head was thumping, because she knew there was no going back. There was nothing left for them in New York. They had put the contents of the apartment in storage including all of Hilda's clothes and possessions, which Becky had not the heart to sort through. They packed two cases each, and that was their baggage, along with their hearts, still heavy with grief.

She had just lost Hilda, the only person she could possibly confide in. Hilda would have known what to do, giving her the strength to fight back, but now she was running away to a place where she knew nobody. Her shoulders tensed, and she wanted to throw up.

Jen, when Becky had told her the plan to move to Ireland, had shouted no, and locked herself in her bedroom. When she'd pleaded with her, Jen had refused to listen. Becky had pounded on the bedroom door, but Jen had flung her schoolbooks all over the place.

Becky eventually had to call Sadie over to the apartment to help talk her daughter out of her room. Sadie, in her business suit and stiletto heels, had said she hadn't a lot of time but she'd brokered a deal between mother and daughter, where Jen would give Ireland the summer months. At the end of August, it was agreed they would review what they would do next, and a decision for the future would be made together.

This had to work, Becky thought. Every part of her was screaming 'big mistake' right now, but there was no going back; this small town of Coolnamona by the Irish Sea was their only chance to take stock, and move towards a new chapter of their lives. Becky knew too it was her only hope to claw back some of her own life in a place where nobody would find her.

'Mom, where are we? Is this it?' Jen whispered, taking out her phone and checking the time.

'We'll be there soon. We'll have a big backyard, too.'

'Whatever. I'm going back to sleep.'

Becky looked at Jen slumped in the front seat, her long hair hiding her face.

If she could only turn back time. There was no point thinking like this; their old life was in the past; their hearts broken and their brains fogged with grief. She had to be strong for Jen. All they had was each other and precious memories, but right this minute, even the recollection of good times past was too painful.

A high white van came up close behind her car. Anxiously, Becky eyed the driver as the van zigzagged behind her, attempting to overtake. She had nowhere to go. Her head began to pound as fear surged through her. For a moment, she thought she had been followed. This was more than feeling vulnerable in a strange place. She reminded herself that nobody but Sadie knew she was here. Quickly, she pulled the car into the side, her hands shaking so much, she had to release her grip of the wheel. The driver waved thanks. Becky, her stomach still churning, smiled as relief washed over her that there was an innocent explanation for the van pulling up so close. She chided herself that she had been afraid of a white van pulling too near in this small rural Irish town, but this is the way it would be, until she could feel safe again.

She drove up the street past small shops, a bank, a post office, a delicatessen and a number of shops that were boarded up and vacant. A large, grey, stone building was set back with a number of granite steps up to a wooden door painted a maroon colour. A small sign said: *Coolnamona Courthouse 1884.*

She continued past a big supermarket, where the delivery driver was already unloading cardboard boxes. There was nobody else about, except for a dog, which was stubbornly lying in the middle of the street further on.

Becky slowed down, hoping it would move to one side. She saw the dog open one eye, and wag its tail, before stretching out all four paws, like it was on the softest bed. She made to move around it, but it suddenly jumped up, barking loudly, the sound of the woofing hitting off the buildings, and echoing down the lanes.

Panic searing through her, Becky frantically looked all around. It was stupid to get so agitated about a dog. She beeped; the dog stopped barking, and looked straight at her before deliberately positioning himself in front of the car bumper.

'Mom, what's happening?' Jen said, sitting up straight and yawning.

'It's the dog, he won't let me pass.'

'He's so cute,' Jen said, raising her phone to film it.

'Jen, that's not helping.'

'Mom, it's hilarious! He'll move along soon.'

'Not before he has woken up the whole town,' Becky said, hitting the car horn again.

'Chill, Mom; this is so funny,' Jen said, making Becky want to scream. Tears welled up in her. She had intended to slip into this town quietly. Not like this, blaring her car horn, and being made a fool of by a dog.

A door opened, and a woman in her dressing gown ran out onto the road, shouting at the dog. The golden labrador, without a backward glance, ambled slowly back to the house.

Becky thought the woman looked cross, her hair tied up in a bun on top of her head, her dressing gown stretched tight around her. She saw her throw her hands up in the air, and march over to the car.

Nervously, Becky wound down her window, and smiled weakly. 'I'm very sorry. I didn't know what to do.'

'That stupid dog of mine does this all the time. Everyone around here knows to drive slowly up to him, and he'll eventually move. He's a stubborn bugger, and when it goes past his feeding time he always does something for attention. Old Ronnie doesn't believe in lie-ins. I guess it was his lucky day that you came along; you're helping a cranky old dog get his way.' The woman stopped when she saw Becky's face.

Becky tried to hide her tears, but the woman leaned closer.

'Sweetheart, it's OK. This is all that stupid dog's fault. Park up, and come in and have a cup of tea.'

Becky smiled. 'I have to get along. We're staying in the village.'

The woman clapped her hands. 'You have a bit to go if you're looking for the new housing estate. It's at the far side of town.'

'Seaview Terrace? I think it's near here.'

'Drive up a good bit of Main Street, and take a right after Spring's Restaurant. Which house?'

'Number three.'

'The old Reilly house?'

'I think so,' Becky stuttered.

'Wow, I was good friends with Regina. I miss her so much. I never introduced myself. I'm Mary Ryan, but for some reason, everybody around here calls me Maisie. Now, you have to come in for that cuppa.'

Becky hesitated.

Maisie reached in the window, and gripped Becky's hand tight.

'I can see you want to get to your house. Maybe I will call up later in the morning when you have found your bearings.'

'I would like that,' Becky said.

She was about to put up the window, when Maisie leaned closer.

'The place needs a bit of work, but don't let it get you down. It's a fine property. It was once the centre of life in this town. Regina and Pat were loved around here.'

Becky drove up the main street past a few boutiques and a restaurant with a burgundy and gold façade, and which was called Spring's Restaurant of Coolnamona. A man was watering petunias in the restaurant window boxes.

'Mom, is this it?'

'It's early in the morning yet; I bet it will be buzzing later,' Becky said, trying to sound convincing.

'I'm not getting out of the car,' Jen muttered.

'We have been through this. We will give it a few months,' Becky replied, turning the car right onto a narrow lane, where grass was growing down the middle. 'It will be an adventure.'

Jen guffawed loudly. 'Climbing Everest is an adventure; moving to this flyshit on the map, where we know nobody, is just gross,' she snapped, before curling up into a ball and squeezing her eyes shut.

Becky lightly tapped her daughter's knee, but Jen turned away, and tightened up.

'It will work out, it has to,' Becky whispered, but her daughter didn't respond.

She drove down the lane past the first two houses. The third house was bigger and wider than the others with what looked like an extra wing to one side. The front garden was huge, but it was overgrown with brambles and nettles, and lots of tall purple-pink flowers, which Becky knew must be weeds. All the same, she thought it looked pretty in the morning light.

Nervously, Becky stopped the car, and got out. The structure was the same as the photograph, but this was a property that had not been loved in a long time.

The front gate was half open, and she stepped onto the steps and the gravel path, which was stuck with weeds. What must have once been lawn on either side, was a mess of brambles, nettles and rubbish as far as the front door.

An apple tree, its branches spread across the path, was blocking her way.

Delicately stepping over the branches, she kicked loose gravel aside, a flurry of wasps rising up, making her rush on. A yellow rose bush was pushing out onto the rest of the path. The splash of colour gladdened Becky's heart. A row of lavender stubbornly bloomed, the aroma filling the air as she scraped past, making the bees cross and loud.

She stopped when she got to the door. It must have once been imposing with its brass handle and a keyhole big enough for the large key in her pocket. The stained-glass fan-light overhead was a myriad of colours, but streaked with dead insects and dust.

Becky ran her hand along the door. The paint was peeling in places and dust, built up over the years, had settled in waves across the front, and into crevices, where spiders had spooled strong webs.

Rummaging for the key, she heard Jen call out.

'I'm at the front door. Come up the path,' she replied.

'You don't seriously expect us to live here?' Jen said, pushing an apple tree branch out of her way and kicking stray stones on the path, making them skitter across the grass.

'It needs a bit of work,' Becky said uncertainly as she pushed the key into the lock.

'Mom, you're so crazy.'

'Maybe that's not such a bad thing right now,' Becky said as she attempted to turn the key.

'This can't be it. Granny Hilda wouldn't expect us to stay in this dump.'

Becky smiled. 'It just needs a tidy-up.'

'Mom, have you looked around? I'm not staying here.'

'I admit it is a bit different to the photo, but once we get inside, it will be better,' Becky said, not quite believing her own words. She tried to turn the key in the lock, but it wouldn't budge. 'You try, the key is stuck,' she said.

'Euww, too many spiders. I'm not going near that door. Mom, can we just go home?'

Becky pulled her daughter into a tight hug. 'Sweetheart, this is home.'

'Only until the end of August, and it can't really be home without Granny Hilda,' Jen said, pulling away.

'I know the situation is shit, but we have to make the best of it. There are no other options.'

'We could have stayed in the States.'

Becky stepped back, and looked her daughter in the eye. 'You know this was the only option.'

'Can't we sell this dump, and move back home? I doubt Granny Hilda meant us to come all the way over here.'

Becky took the key, and tried it again.

'Let's just give it a go,' Becky said, her voice low and tired. She pushed the door with her shoulder, hoping to divert Jen away from why they had to flee Manhattan.

'I'm going back to the car,' Jen whimpered, her lips trembling.

Becky followed, trying to keep up. 'It's a blip. Maybe when

the shops downtown open, we can get something like oil for the lock.'

'Downtown? What downtown?' Jen shouted.

'Sweetheart, we have to make the best of things.'

'Why?'

'Granny would want us to.'

Becky stepped back as Jen turned around to face her.

'Granny Hilda wouldn't have even walked up the driveway to the house, it all looks so crap.'

'Jen, please give me a break,' Becky said, her voice low in defeat.

Jen hesitated as Becky looked towards the sea, taking deep breaths in an attempt to calm down.

'Can we just leave?' Jen asked.

Becky nodded, and they turned back down the path, pushing nettles and brambles out of their way.

'It looks nothing like the photo either,' Jen muttered.

Exasperated, Becky tugged the car door too fiercely, and it hit the stone wall.

'Nice one, Mom. The car hire company are going to love you.' Jen sniggered.

Becky got into the car beside her daughter. 'You're not the only one missing Hilda, sweetie,' she said wearily.

'I just want to go home.'

'I know but we agreed to give it a few months at least, and hopefully, afterwards we will be able to get on with our lives as best we can without Granny.'

Jen slumped against her mother, her breathing fast, tears pumping through her.

'Let's go. I saw somebody at the fancy-looking restaurant; he should be able to help us,' Becky said, trying desperately to sound upbeat.

Just as they were about to drive away, a woman appeared at the gate next door.

'Can I help you? Are you looking for anyone?' she asked as she pushed her bicycle out onto the road.

'No, we're good, thank you,' Becky said.

'Do we really have to stay here?' Jen whispered, curling up on the front seat, and pretending to go back to sleep.

Becky looked at the house from here. It was imposing, and at one time must have been quite a grand place overlooking the sea. She wished she knew why Hilda was the owner. In her heart, she was hoping her mother would sashay up the lane, and explain everything. Hilda would have loved this town, and would have taken delight in dressing up to the nines to make sure everybody noticed her. Becky smiled at the thought of Hilda White of Brooklyn, and latterly Manhattan, New York descending on this sleepy place. She needed to solve the mystery as to why Hilda, that Manhattan cheerleader, should ever buy a property in a sleepy place like this, so far from everything and everyone they knew.

Becky knew it appeared mad to haul Jen to Coolnamona on a whim, but if she didn't unravel the mystery of Coolnamona House, she didn't see how they could pick up the threads of their lives. Exhaustion washed over her, but she pushed herself beyond it, and smiled brightly at Jen.

'Everything will work out, honey,' Becky said a little too brightly.

Jen made a face, and turned away.

THREE

Jen continued to fake being asleep, so Becky let her be, quietly got out of the car, and gently shut the door behind her. Maybe on the second run, things might look better at Coolnamona House.

Climbing the stone steps again, she stopped at a flat rock halfway up the front garden. It looked as if it had been placed there specifically so a person could pause to sit, and admire the view of Orchid Bay. If this were just a holiday, it would be a perfect location. The sun was sparkling across the sea where a small boat was chugging through the wave ripples. It looked as if it were steering a course to round the headland, probably moving on to the next town, which Becky could just make out in the distance.

At the small horseshoe harbour, yachts and smaller sailing boats were moored beside fishing trawlers. A number of people were out walking their dogs on the path beside the harbour wall. Others at the far side of the harbour were hiking up the steep cliff path to the top of the headland, where a big grey house with long narrow chimney pots was huddled against the wind whipping across the sea. It was as pretty as a picture, and yet her heart was heavy. This was all too much for her; she had lost Hilda so suddenly, and she didn't want to think about what had happened just a week before. It was overwhelming. Her brain fogged over, and she wanted to scream loud and long, letting her pain be carried across the land and out to sea.

Jumping up from the rock, she felt like running to the car and driving back to the airport, but instead, she gritted her teeth until the waves of anxiety abated, and the sick feeling in the pit of her stomach lessened. She should go back to the main street, and find somewhere to buy oil for the lock.

As Becky got back in the car, Jen stirred. She was about to move off, when Maisie, with Ronnie in tow, came up the lane.

'I'm glad I didn't miss you. I thought you should have some company going into that cold house,' she said after flagging down the car.

Becky stepped out onto the lane. 'Thank you for being so kind, it's all a little overwhelming.'

'Well, don't you worry, Maisie is here now. You can rely on me.'

'That's so nice of you, but...'

Maisie leaned closer to Becky. 'Between you, me and the wall, I wouldn't spend so much time with your near neighbour, Iris Jones. She will be in and out of your house like a yo-yo. She's some class of an artist left over from the hippy era, that one is.'

'Is that a bad thing?'

Maisie guffawed out loud. 'I can see you will need my help. You have a lot to learn.'

Flustered, Becky said she had to go and get some oil for the lock.

'I'll wait here for you,' Maisie said.

'Please don't. I'm sure you've more interesting things to do.'

'Not exactly.'

'Thank you so much for your help. You have a nice day,'

Becky said, quickly getting back into her car. She was anxious not to get caught in a web of gossip in her first hour in Coolnamona.

She drove off, leaving Maisie scowling on the lane.

'I don't think I like her, but I love her dog,' Jen murmured, before turning away to snooze some more.

'Me too,' Becky said.

As she pulled up outside Spring's Restaurant, the man she had seen watering the flowers waved.

When she got out of the car, he approached Becky, and said they weren't open.

'Pardon me, but I wonder can you help? We can't get into our house. The key won't turn in the lock and—'

She saw him shrug, and walk back into the restaurant. When he returned, he was carrying a small oil can.

'Are you down at Seaview Terrace? I can come and have a look, if you like.'

'How did you know?' she stuttered.

'Maisie rang me with the news.'

'Oh.'

'Don't worry, I'm not a serial killer, just being neighbourly.'

Becky blushed, and she hoped he didn't notice.

'I wasn't thinking that. If I can borrow the oil, I'm sure we can manage on our own.'

'Drive back, I will just lock up here, and follow you.'

Embarrassed, and feeling nervous, Becky did as she was told.

She had just parked outside the house when a jeep pulled in behind her.

'I didn't realise it was Regina's house. Maisie was very mysterious,' he said as he smartly climbed the steps, and walked up the path, barely pushing the brambles and nettles out of his way.

At the door, he doused the lock with oil, and dipped the key in the oil can before shoving it in the lock.

'We should leave it a few minutes to sink in,' he said, before offering Becky his hand, and introducing himself. 'Ben Evans, restaurant proprietor, chef and general dogsbody.'

'Thank you for helping us, Mr Evans,' she said quietly.

'Please, call me Ben. Are you just visitors or have you a connection to the house?' he asked.

Becky hesitated.

'I don't mean to pry, but this was a big house around here at one time, and you will find everybody is interested.'

She extended her hand. 'Becky White from New York, the new owner. I'm here with my daughter, Jen.'

He shook her hand and smiled. 'I noticed the friendly teenager in the front. I have the male version at home.'

Despite herself, she giggled. She liked this tall man who seemed so gentle and kind, and yet his broad shoulders, huge hands and shoulder-length hair made him appear almost bearlike.

'How long will it take before the oil works?' she asked.

'Hopefully, not too long. The house has been vacant a while. I'm not sure if ye will be able to stay here straight away.'

'We can clean out one room; take it from there.'

Becky stumbled and Ben put his hand out to steady her.

'Are you all right?' he asked gently.

'Jet lag,' she said feebly.

'Why don't you two come back to mine, have a bite to eat and get some sleep? In the meantime, I will get working on the lock.'

She looked at him, taking in his unruly mop of black hair and his soft grey eyes which were full of concern.

She wanted to trust him, but she felt vulnerable and alone.

'We're good, thank you,' she said quietly.

'Promise again, I'm not a serial killer,' he said kindly.

'We're good. We'll work something out,' she said firmly. These days, she didn't feel she could trust anyone.

He looked all around him. 'At this hour of the morning, in this small town, not very likely. Why don't you drive down the lane after me to the restaurant? I have a small apartment you can use, and we'll take it from there.'

Embarrassed, Becky didn't know what to do. 'OK,' she whispered, feeling anxious and guilty at the same time at not trusting this kind stranger.

'Let's get going,' he said, and Becky followed him to where her car was parked.

She drove behind him to the restaurant where they parked one behind the other on the main street.

'You can use the Airbnb over the restaurant if you want a rest. There are two bedrooms, a kitchen, and a balcony off the sitting room overlooking my garden. You're welcome to walk in the garden, if you wish.' Becky traipsed up the stairs after him into a bright airy room.

'This is lovely. How much do you charge?'

'You're OK, and if you want to stay on, we can work something out. There's a supermarket up the road, but you will find the basics in the fridge and the cupboards. The bakery on the left up the road is quite good, but the owner is elderly, so he only opens in the morning.'

Becky called Jen upstairs.

'This place is cool. Is there Wi-Fi?' Jen asked.

Ben laughed. 'Of course. Now, I will leave you to it. Try and get some rest.'

Jen disappeared into the front bedroom, and said she was going to crash. Becky stepped out on the balcony. She gasped when she saw the garden, which on one side was awash with wild flowers, cornflowers and poppies and clumps of yellow flowers she could not identify. Along the other side were raised beds which were filled with vegetables interspersed with roses and sweet peas.

She took a blanket, and wrapped it around herself before sitting into a comfy wicker chair. Loneliness gripped her, and she hoped beyond anything she had made the right decision to drag them here.

It was the late morning when Becky woke up just as Jen stepped out on the balcony.

'Can we stay here Mom, please? It's so nice. They have a proper coffee machine and lots of different pods. Do you want a cup?'

'No, and we have our own house. We need to stay there.'

'Mom, I'm not going back to that dump, all right?'

'That's OK for now, but we're staying at Coolnamona House tonight.'

Jen pretended not to hear, and turned away, slapping on her earphones.

Becky loitered in the doorway in the hope that Jen would change her mind. But feeling silly, she gave up. She stopped to throw water on her face before going downstairs, and letting herself out onto the street.

To clear her head, she decided to walk to the house. She felt herself calm down as she headed past a discount shop where the owner was putting out baskets of sale items, and a delicatessen where a woman in bright pink trousers and T-shirt, and wearing a red apron, was writing the day's lunch specials on the window with a marker.

She lingered to watch.

'It's roast beef sandwiches today. Any time after 12.30 p.m. but don't leave it too late. We sell out fast,' the woman said in a sing-song voice.

'Thanks,' Becky said as she made to continue on her way.

'You think I'm just all talk. If you're around, call by; we usually have a queue down the street and around the corner.'

'You should open a coffee shop so people can sit and dine,' Becky said.

'No space, I'm afraid, and people like to pick up their roll, and drive back to the office.'

'There are offices around here?'

The woman laughed, throwing her head back so her long black hair flowed out behind her. 'I know we look a sleepy little spot, but there is a big American pharmaceuticals factory out the Ballymoney Road. That's why we have the housing estates too; it has been a huge boost for the town. We would be long gone, but for it. You're American?'

'Yes.'

'Are you with the big plant?'

'Oh no, my daughter and I are here for a while. We have a house at Seaview Terrace.'

The woman put out her hand, and caught Becky's. 'Welcome, I am Edith Hannigan.'

'Becky, nice to meet you.'

'Where on Seaview Terrace are you?'

'The house with the disgraceful garden.'

'The old Reilly house? You will have your work cut out for you there. I didn't know they were looking for tenants.'

Becky grinned, not sure how to answer.

The woman stepped closer. 'Do you want me to hold a roll for you?'

'Could you hold two? I can pay you now,' Becky said, pulling a twenty-euro note from her pocket.

'Don't be silly; put away your money. Call it a moving-in present. It's as good as done. Are you renting or did you buy the place?'

'I'm the new owner,' Becky said, surprised by herself, and how proud that statement made her feel. She smiled gratefully at Edith, before continuing on her way past a number of residential houses and a cobbler's until she reached the lane down to the sea.

Even from here, the Reilly house looked dilapidated and unloved, the front garden a mess and unkempt. She saw the neighbour park her bicycle outside the house next door, and disappear into her garden.

Becky hung back on the road, so she wouldn't be seen. This next bit she wanted to do without interruption, and she didn't want to contend with any neighbours at this stage. It was time to come to terms with Hilda's secret house on her own. When she got as far as the gate, Becky pushed it gently so it didn't creak and alert her neighbour. Ben, she noticed, had slashed away some of the briars and brambles blocking the path. Dipping under the apple tree, she liked when the branches brushed against her head and the bees buzzed louder.

At the door, she stopped. Maybe she could sell the house, and return to the States; take a place in a quiet village in upstate New York or even Connecticut or Rhode Island, but she had to find out why her mother owned this property. And why here? Gripping the key, she turned it in the lock without much effort. Pressing against the door, she felt it give way, the seal uncracking. She leaned against the door, letting it swing back.

The sun was shining outside, but when Becky stepped into the hall, the air was cold, and she shivered. It was as if she were going back in time. The long hallway was covered in a floral-patterned carpet; a mahogany console table contained an empty vase and a leather visitor book. She tipped up the cover, and read the last entry dating back five years. *Thank you for such a lovely afternoon tea in your splendid front garden by the sea. We will be back, Rose and Chuck, Texas, USA.*

Becky quickly let the cover drop into place. She had a strange feeling, like she was intruding on somebody's life, or breaking in, and prying where she shouldn't.

An old weather-beaten wooden sign was propped up

against the wall. Becky read the words out loud: *The Café over Orchid Bay*. Tracing her finger along the outline of each letter, she thought the name sounded romantic.

Stepping across the hall, she turned the brass knob on a cream door into a room with three long windows in a row looking out over the front garden. A rambling rose was pushed up against the glass; shutters were only on one window, the others hanging off their hinges. Dust sheets were thrown across the furniture and on what must be a painting over the marble fireplace. Another painting and framed photographs on the wall were covered with pages from a broadsheet newspaper.

The fireplace was the only thing in the room not under cover. Ornate white marble with a wide grate, tiled inserts and a high mantelpiece, she ran her fingers along the top. It was caked in dirt, and she pulled her hand away, wiping it off on her jeans.

Tentatively, she pulled the sheet above the mantelpiece, the white fabric billowing in a cloud of dust before falling at her feet.

Standing back, she took in the full-length portrait. It was of a woman in a ball gown looking directly at the artist. Her eyes were sad, but she was smiling as if she were obeying orders. She was wearing a blush-pink tulle gown. A boned, sleeveless bodice was nipped in at the waist. The skirt flowed out in tiers of gathered tulle in a bell-shaped skirt which was longer at the back. The pink gown complemented the woman's russet-red hair which tumbled down to her bare shoulders.

Becky sat mesmerised. It was only when she concentrated on the lace edging that she saw the small brass plaque which read: *Regina wearing Dior*.

Becky smiled that she had come all this way to a small village in Ireland for her first glimpse of this stunning Dior gown. Regina looked so young, her cheeks a blush pink like the dress. How Hilda would have adored this. She had two vintage

Dior gowns and had worn one to the Met Gala last year. Did Hilda know this dress was here?

Becky stepped closer to examine the detailing in the gown. It was the Eugénie ball gown, she was sure of it. She had heard Hilda talk about such a dress. There was a fitted sleeveless bodice with lace details on a sweetheart neckline, which Becky thought emphasised the long slender neck of the wearer in the painting, but the skirt was a confection of tulle and lace in layers of ruffles which gave an air of innocence and expectation.

Becky stood back to take in the length of the painting. There was something hypnotic about Regina's sad eyes. She wanted to know more about this woman, who seemed in the first bloom of youth. She wanted to know her story. She looked about as young as Jen was right now. Jen should be looking forward to a summer in the city, but she was here in Coolna-mona. Anxiety flowed through Becky, who suddenly felt over-whelmed that they had taken on too much. She sat down on the couch, which was still covered in a dust sheet. Maybe she should just treat this as a holiday, and stop playing detective. She could pretend, too, that Hilda had not left them, and was looking after things back home. That would give her the head-space she needed.

When there was a knock on the front door, Becky leapt up. She froze, hoping the caller would go away. When she heard somebody call hello, she sank back down onto the couch.

'Hi there, I have brought you over some tea and fresh scones as a welcome,' the person said loudly as Becky heard her step into the hall. Becky got up, and opened the sitting room door a little. The woman, wearing white palazzo pants, a red button-through jacket and a multicoloured scarf knotted at her neck, was placing a tray down on the console table. She beamed when she saw Becky.

'I don't mean to intrude, but I thought you might appreciate a cuppa and fruit scones, fresh out of the oven. There is butter and jam here for you too,' she said.

'Thank you, this is very kind of you.'

'Not at all. What are neighbours for? Now, I will get out of your way. I am Iris Jones by the way, I am the house to your left. Drop by any time.'

Becky thought Iris looked the artistic type, but she instinctively liked her. Iris tipped Becky gently on the arm as she left. Turning around at the front door, she flashed a smile.

'It's great to think there will be life in the old house again. I hope we can be good neighbours. See you soon.'

Becky nodded, and smiled. Examining the scones, she realised she was very hungry. Pouring the tea, and slathering butter on a bun, she went back to the sitting room.

Pulling the dust sheet off with one hand, she sat down on the navy velvet couch. Only a short while ago, she was planning the autumn collection, and trying to decide on a weekend order from Whole Foods. Shit, she had forgotten to officially call off that Sunday lunch. Their life had imploded, and here she was now in another country, and she hardly knew what day it was. Her own life had been ripped apart, and she had lost Hilda too. Her only hope now was to make a go of it here in Coolnamona.

She closed her eyes, listening to the creeping silence of the house. Strange to be surrounded by such stillness, and not feel uncomfortable. Back home there was quiet too, but a different sort because even inside the apartment, there was the ever-present feeling of being at the centre of a big city. Straining, she thought she heard the faraway sound of the sea, and she wanted to rush, and open all the windows, but she knew she should get back to Jen. Stopping briefly in the hall, Becky looked all around her. They could make something of this house, she was sure; it had been vacant a while, but there was nothing a lot of elbow grease, as Hilda would say, couldn't sort out. Placing the mug back on the tray, she stepped out into the front garden, pulling the front door shut behind her.

Flitting down the path, she squeezed through a gap left because the gate had not closed properly, and hurried down the lane. When she turned onto the main street, people were gathering outside the delicatessen. Edith, her hair now tied back in a tight bun, called out to her when she saw her walk past.

'You haven't forgotten I have two rolls for you?' she said, sounding disappointed.

Becky crept into the shop, and took the two wrapped rolls from the counter.

'Thank you,' she said quietly. 'If there is ever anything I can do.'

'I'm sure we will think of something.' Edith guffawed as she moved down the line to other customers.

Becky continued up the street. When she opened their apartment door, she stopped to compose herself, before walking in to see Jen.

'I've got lunch for us, and I met our neighbour; such a nice lady.'

Jen didn't say anything.

'You have to try this food, it's really good. It's from that trendy delicatessen. There was a line down the street.'

Jen took a bite.

'Good, isn't it?' Becky asked.

'OK, I suppose.' Jen shrugged.

She looked at her daughter tucking into her beef baguette, and smiled. 'We need to buy some gear so we can camp out at the house.'

'Can't we just stay here?'

'Camping out at Coolnamona House might be fun.'

'Fat chance in that dump. It's probably crawling with bugs.'

Becky sighed. 'Jen, give me a break. We need to stay in our own home.'

'Our home is in Manhattan or have you forgotten?'

'Sweetheart, you know we had to leave New York,' Becky said, reaching out to her daughter.

Jen pulled away. 'Wrong, Mom. You wanted to leave; I had to.'

Becky turned away to hide her tears. She'd had to leave Manhattan; fear had pushed her out, and now they were faced with the near impossible task of starting over again. Soon, the little bit of money she had would be gone. She had taken a huge risk bringing them to Coolnamona, but it was better than the risk of staying in Manhattan. All she could hope for now was that trouble would not follow them here.

FOUR

'This place is like a 1950s movie set,' Jen whispered as they wandered through Coolnamona House. Becky wasn't quite sure whether that was a compliment or not.

'Who is that?' Jen asked, pointing to the portrait over the fireplace.

'The previous owner of the house, Regina Reilly, when she was eighteen years of age.'

Jen moved closer. 'I know this dress. Granny Hilda showed me a picture once. It's vintage Dior. She said she wanted to buy it for me. She was always on the lookout for it.'

'You never mentioned that before; though I knew she hankered over that particular design.'

'She had one of those studio photographs. A famous actress back then wore it on the set of a movie. Granny said it was her mission to find it for me by the time I was eighteen, and I could accompany her to the Met Gala. I guess I'll never get there now.'

When Becky saw her daughter's shoulders slump, she suggested they go upstairs.

Jen slowly followed her.

'Isn't that so weird about the dress?' she said as they reached the first landing.

Becky was about to answer, but Jen was distracted by the stairs going higher.

'I didn't know there were three floors. Can I sleep on the top floor?' she asked, already running up the stairs.

Becky diverted into the wide front bedroom with three long windows, identical to the one in the sitting room, overlooking Orchid Bay. She gasped; Jen was right, everything looked amazing from the top floors.

She took in the room; it was as if time had stood still here. The walls were covered in pink wallpaper embossed with cream-coloured roses, the edges of the petals picked out in silver. The furniture was solid mahogany. Becky stood at the extravagant dressing table which had three large oval mirrors. Perfume bottles and jewellery boxes competed for space in what was now a surface covered with a thick layer of dust.

Something had skittered across the mirrors, and over a large jewellery box, leaving a trail in the thickness of the dirt. The dressing table stool was slightly pushed back as if somebody had just got up, and expected to return. Becky stepped away, afraid of disturbing anything. She was so aware that she was rifling through Regina's possessions. Should she go out, and lock the room or should she sit down, and examine everything?

A dressing gown was hanging on the back of the door and a pair of sheepskin slippers had been neatly set together to one side of the bed. On the bedside table was a book about American dress designers, the bookmark sticking out of page thirty-five. Idly, she picked up the book, and opened it at the marked page: Christian Dior. Hilda would so approve. Putting back the book, she walked to the windows and pulled back the net curtains to let in more light.

Sunshine filled the room, and she knew this had to be her bedroom. The sun rays flashed off the curtains and across the bed, which no longer had a mattress, but was covered in a light pink candlewick bedspread. A large mahogany wardrobe with inlaid satinwood took over the wall near the door. Gently, she unlocked a door and peered in.

It was stuffed with long dresses and gowns. Some had special zip covers and others were protected by old sheets or plastic refuse sacks.

She took out the first dress which was partially covered by a plastic bag. Pulling away the plastic, sapphire-blue silk unfurled to the ground. Holding it up to herself, Becky stood in front of the full-length antique mirror. A simple long-sleeved dress with a side train which fell off in pleats from the left shoulder; she looked for the designer label, but was surprised when there was none.

She wanted to try it on, but was too nervous. She could imagine wearing it with high strappy sandals and her long auburn hair in a messy bun. Swaying in front of the mirror, the swish of the silk as it fell around her cut through the silence. Her shoulders flopped. When would she ever have an opportunity again to dress up, and be carefree and happy? Quickly, she bundled the dress back into the wardrobe.

She heard Jen on the stairs, and she called her to come into the bedroom.

'Gross, I don't know how you could even think of sleeping in this room. Mom, it feels haunted.'

'It has the best view in the world, and all I have to do is give the room a thorough clear-out and clean.'

'You're not seriously going to sleep on that bed? She might have died there.'

'The mahogany bed is beautiful, and a new mattress could be here in a day or two.'

'Come see my room. It's huge, and I have views to the front and back.'

'Awesome,' Becky said, following her up to the top landing.

Jen's room was empty except for a wardrobe and an old armchair that looked as if it had been left there because nobody could find anywhere else to put it.

'I need a new bed, and a desk for writing and stuff.'

'We will order online tonight.'

'Something nice; I don't want cheap stuff,' Jen said, and Becky smiled, glad that her daughter was finally interested.

'You should come and see the vintage dress collection in my room,' she said, but Jen pouted.

'I've had enough. I'm going to sit in the back garden.'

Becky didn't let on her disappointment, but went back downstairs to her bedroom. There, she sat at the dressing table, and gazed in the mirror.

She looked exhausted, and she should definitely have gone to the hairdressers before making the trip. She smiled. It was a Saturday, and that was usually the day she and Jen got their nails done. She looked down at her hands now; her nails were uneven and dry, and there was a smudge of pink left on her ring finger, because she had found it too hard to scrape off.

Hilda would not approve. She always said if you did not present well, how could you expect anyone to take you seriously? Becky doubted if anyone around here would notice if she had her nails painted or her hair blow-dried.

She pulled open a wide drawer, and gasped.

Inside were a series of what appeared to be jewellery boxes, oblong boxes of various colours and probably holding necklaces.

Becky picked out a red velvet box, and snapped it open. Inside was a pearl necklace, a double row of light cream pearls with golden and silver overtones. Cultured saltwater pearls; the writing on the inside of the box said: *Rosita Cultured Pearls*.

Delicately, she lifted the necklace out, and held it up to her throat.

Hilda would have adored it, she thought, but it was a little fussy for her own taste. It was a short necklace and Hilda, no doubt, could have told her a lot about the pearls by examining them and their threading. Carefully, she replaced them in the box, and picked out another.

This was more her style; a heavy antique T-bar necklace in gold. She put on the piece, and saw that it sat well on her. She was admiring the choker when she noticed the house was very quiet. She called out Jen's name, and peeped out the window in case she was in the front garden. Walking to the landing, she checked the back garden, taking in for the first time the long plot which was set out in potato drills.

Becky made her way downstairs, stopping to straighten a small painting on the landing wall.

'Jen, this isn't funny. Where are you?' she called out.

She texted, but there was no reply.

Stepping through to the kitchen, she filled and switched on the kettle, hoping Jen would suddenly appear. When the kettle had long since boiled and there still was no sign, Becky tentatively stepped out into the back garden, past the old patio and the wooden furniture that looked warped and decrepit. Anxiety laced with fear coursed through her. She tried to tell herself it was OK, but worry made her tremble.

When she saw the gate on the side wall open, and Jen appeared, she wanted to get cross, but pretended not to be too bothered.

'Where were you? I was calling,' Becky said, bending down to examine the potato drills.

'I was next door.'

'Where?'

'Iris invited me in. She's really nice; she's an artist. She says I can go with her when she goes around the countryside painting.'

'We don't know her very well.'

'Mom, she's cool.'

'I don't know, sweetheart. You need to make friends your own age.'

Jen turned away towards the kitchen.

Becky retreated to the front garden rather than have a silly row with her daughter. Sitting down, she breathed in the heavy scent of the flowers.

Hilda had loved her roses. She had a farm upstate that delivered a huge bunch of roses to their apartment every Friday. There were different colours every week, and she said it was the best start to a weekend. She missed Hilda and her funny ways so much. She always made a big deal of placing her roses in a wide-bottomed vase beside her reading chair so she was surrounded by the sweet aroma as she did one of her favourite things.

When Hilda died, Becky rang the farm, and asked for enough roses, white and pink, to cover her coffin. The farmer had driven to Manhattan himself with the roses in boxes on the back of his pickup. He insisted on staying to arrange not only the coffin roses, but also the bouquets for inside the funeral home. He refused payment, too. Becky thought the farm's earnings must have been drastically reduced because Hilda, their regular and eccentric customer, had died.

A creaking sound behind her made Becky jump. A part of the side fence swung back, and Iris stepped into the garden.

'Oh, I didn't mean to startle you. Your girl left her jacket in my house, and well, we know what all these things cost, I didn't want ye to think it was missing and...' Iris stopped talking when she saw Becky doing her best to hide her fear.

'I'm so sorry. When Regina lived here, I always used this old door or the gate in the back garden. You don't mind, do you?'

'I didn't know it was there.'

'It made sense to install it rather than have the bother of traipsing up and down our gardens,' Iris said, her voice nervous.

'You've been kind to my daughter, thank you.'

'She's a wonderful young woman.'

'Good to hear. I see a lot of her grumpy teenage moods.'

Iris laughed out loud. 'Teenagers always behave badly at home. Send her my way, and I will keep her occupied. She wants to come on my painting trips. I told her we have to cycle ten to fifteen miles, but even that didn't put her off.'

'I don't know.'

'Of course you don't. You don't know me, and no doubt Maisie Ryan has been talking.'

'Nothing like that.'

Iris reached out, and put her hand on Becky's shoulder. 'Best to widen your circle, and move away from Maisie. Don't get me wrong, she's a decent sort when she wants to be, but she relishes gossip. Remember, if the woman is telling you about everyone else in the village, she is also telling them about you.'

'I don't have time for any of this. We just want to settle in.'

Iris took Becky's hand in hers. 'It is very nice to see the house occupied after so long.'

Becky noticed that her grip was strong, and she immediately liked Iris a little more, which was probably helped by the fact that she was wearing sunglasses and bright yellow wellingtons on a dull day.

'I was going to have a drink, can I offer you one?' Becky asked.

'If it's something alcoholic, I'm in,' Iris said, following Becky into the house.

Becky led her to the kitchen.

She reached for the kettle, but Iris tapped her on the shoulder.

'Get out two glasses, girl. It's time for the strong stuff. I'll be back in a minute,' she said, rushing down the hall.

Becky went to the sink, and threw cold water on her cheeks. Holding her face up to the sun, she pulled a paper towel from the roll, and dabbed her face dry. Grabbing two tumblers, she walked to the sitting room and stood in front of the painting waiting for Iris to return.

There was a mysterious something about that painting that intrigued her. Regina unnerved her, and yet she felt completely at home in her house. It was strange that she should feel so conflicted by Regina, but so comfortable in her home.

When Iris came back, she was carrying a bottle of whiskey.

'Isn't it too early?' Becky stuttered.

'Nonsense, girl. A shot of whiskey is good at any o'clock. It won't be long in the glass anyway.' Iris chuckled as she poured a generous measure into each glass.

They sat on the blue velvet couch, sipping their drinks.

After a few moments, Iris put down her glass on the armrest, and turned to Becky.

'I know we have just met, but my shoulder is a lot better than Maisie's. Don't let her worm her way into your life. There's a phrase around these parts: tell Maisie, tell a phone.'

Becky took a gulp of her whiskey, and let it burn down her throat.

Whiskey had been Hilda's night-time favourite.

Iris gently prodded her. 'I can see the weight of the world on your shoulders, and it's in Jen's eyes too.'

Becky shook her head.

'Drink up, dear. You don't have to tell me anything right now, but I'm here for you. That door in the front garden opens both ways,' Iris said.

Becky nodded, and let Iris hold her hand.

'I will leave the bottle, and whenever you feel like it, we can sit together again. Myself and Regina never let a bottle last more than ten days. I found I did all the talking in this house. When she came to mine, she did all the unburdening. It worked for us.'

'This house and staying here seems to be a tough gig,' Becky muttered.

Iris threw her head back, and snorted loudly.

'Coolnamona is a bit of a cesspit of gossip, but there are a few of us good ones left; just give it time. Now, I must be off,' she said, making for the door.

She was halfway through, when she turned back.

'Tell Jen she can come on a painting trip with me in the morning. Ben has a loan of a bike for her.'

'Are you sure?'

'Dear, I wouldn't make the offer if I didn't mean it. We should be back by five.'

The door shut, and Becky heard Iris scurry up her gravel path to her front door.

She wandered into the sitting room. With a neighbour like Iris, just maybe they could make this work, she thought.

FIVE

Becky had barely slept, and her back hurt like hell. They had put a foil ground sheet over the old floor in the sitting room, and pumped up a thin air mattress, putting sleeping bags on top – and her back still felt like a board.

Last night, Jen had a wobble, and begged to be allowed to return to the States on her own, saying she could stay with Sadie. When Becky refused to relent, Jen had put in her earbuds, and ignored her mother. She was still wearing them now, her playlist on a loop as she slept. Easing her legs out of the sleeping bag, Becky got up, and tiptoed out of the room, pulling on her jeans in the hall.

Opening the front door, she peeped out. The early morning air was chilly, so she pulled her cardigan tight around her.

There was nobody about. A thrush scuttled under a rose bush and a blackbird screeched a warning call before disappearing high into the apple tree. A black and white cat ran across the road and up the steps of Coolnamona House, but when it saw Becky it halted, before changing course, and darting under a neighbour's hedge.

Hesitating, and not wanting to leave Jen alone, Becky

turned to go back inside. She closed the door gently, letting the harsh morning light filter through the fan-light. It cast designs across the walls, hitting the mirror, and dazzling her eyes. She didn't know exactly why, but she felt at ease in this house. The stillness wrapped itself around her. At Coolnamona House, she somehow felt at home.

For a while yesterday they had such fun exploring the house, and getting their camping gear set up. Becky had eased the last shutter off the windows in the sitting room, and tugged the sheets off the furniture, puffs of dust clouding the air.

There were two well-worn leather armchairs either side of the fireplace. In the corner was a mahogany and glass china cabinet full of what looked like old crystal. Jen opened one of the glass doors, and took out one of a set of five delicate vintage champagne glasses. Holding it up to the light, she examined the elegant rose-like flowers etched into the glass, and she made Becky promise that one day they would be happy, and sip the finest champagne from these glasses.

As Jen held the glass up, it caught the light as she twirled the stem, making different colours shaft across as if through a prism. 'Granny Hilda would have liked to drink from a glass like this,' she said, and they had laughed, thinking of Hilda, and how she always carried a crystal glass in her handbag because life was too short to waste it drinking from plastic or paper cups.

When there was a loud noise in the front garden, Becky at first didn't know what to do. She managed to peek out the door's glass side panel. A woman in a red coat was using an umbrella to thrash stray brambles and any branches out of her way as she marched up the path. Becky stayed close to the hall wall as the woman got as far as the front door, banging on it several times with the umbrella handle, the sharp sound reverberating through the house. Becky shrank back as the woman impa-tiently thumped on the door one last time, before stomping into the hall almost falling over Becky.

'Ma'am, excuse me, ma'am, you can't just barge in here,' Becky said loudly.

The woman, who took off her headscarf, and was making her way to the kitchen, swung around. 'Who the hell says?' she said, fixing her stare on Becky.

'Pardon me, but I am the owner of this property, and you're trespassing,' Becky said.

'The Yank tells me I'm trespassing. What a bloody cheek! This was my sister's house, and who the hell are you anyway?'

Becky clenched and unclenched her fists as she stepped further down the hall. 'I am Becky White from the States.'

'And that is supposed to mean something to me?'

Becky swallowed hard. 'Maybe you knew my mother, Hilda White of New York.'

'Hilda White of New York, what a lot of nonsense!' the woman said.

She stamped into the sitting room, and ignoring Jen, who was sitting up rubbing her eyes, she pointed to the portrait of Regina Reilly over the mantelpiece.

'White of New York means nothing to me. We're Reillys. My sister Regina owned this house. It has nothing to do with anyone in New York. Now, I suggest you leave before this gets ugly, and I have to call the police.'

Becky stared at the woman who was wearing a ruby-red mackintosh, a black scarf knotted around her neck. Her grey hair looked as if it had been freshly permed, and Becky thought she could smell hairspray as if she had recently been at the hairdressers.

'Would you like to sit down?' she asked quietly.

The woman turned around so fiercely the umbrella whacked Jen's feet.

'Who the hell do you think you are, asking me do I want to sit down in my own sister's house and my family home?'

Becky shook her head. 'There must be some confusion. Maybe we can talk this through?'

The woman squared up in front of Becky, who realised she was tall and had the same haughty nose as the woman in the painting.

'Mom, what is going on?' Jen pleaded, her voice scared.

'It's a misunderstanding. It's OK, sweetie,' Becky said, her voice high-pitched with alarm.

'Damn right it's a bloody misunderstanding. You need to get out of this house, if you know what's good for you,' the woman shrieked.

'You don't understand. I am the rightful owner of this house, and my daughter and I have moved in.'

'Really,' the woman said so fiercely her spittle sprayed into the air. She walked over to the fireplace, trampled across the air mattress, and gripped the portrait frame.

'I'm not going without this,' she shouted.

Becky put her hands out to stop the old lady as Iris stepped into the hall and hovered at the sitting room doorway.

'Please, I know this is upsetting for you, but you can't come in here and take things off the walls,' Becky said.

'Things? So that is all this is to you? I will have you know this is a portrait commissioned for my sister's eighteenth birthday.'

'But she owns it, Bella, and you must leave immediately,' a voice boomed from the hall.

Bella scowled fiercely. 'Iris Jones, sticking your nose in as usual.'

'Why don't you tell her yourself and Regina had not talked in a long time? She would turn in her grave to think you had that painting,' Iris said, marching into the sitting room.

'Iris Jones, you have no right to be here. What is any of this to you?' Bella said.

Iris moved into the sitting room. 'Because Regina Reilly was my best friend, and she asked me to make sure this house was left intact after her death. You know you are barred from entry. You're not getting in to steal the family silver.'

'That's a lie. You tried to influence her. You wanted this house all for yourself.'

'That's a whole load of bullshit, Bella, and you know it. I suggest you leave before I call Regina's solicitors.'

Bella snatched up her umbrella which had fallen to the side of the armchair. Pushing past Becky, she leaned in so close to her, Becky could feel her breath.

'This isn't finished. This was never your house to buy; it's not your house, and I will fight you every step of the way. If you think you can walk in here and take over, you have another thing coming. Regina Reilly was my sister, and that means something.'

With that, she plodded out the front door, using her umbrella to thrash any plant that got in her way, and leaving a trail of battered lavender stalks on the ground after her.

'Mom, who was that?' Jen sobbed.

'Well, now you have met the wicked witch. In just twenty-four hours, you have created quite a stir. I rather imagine Bella heard about you when she was getting her curls tightened yesterday afternoon.' Iris suddenly stopped when she noticed Becky's face had turned grey, and she was shaking. 'Oh dear, you're terrified,' she said, taking Becky's hand, and leading her to sit on the couch.

'Who is that person?' Becky stuttered.

'All will be revealed, but first you need a good shot of whiskey, my dear,' Iris said, opening the china cabinet and rummaging through the bottom shelf. She pulled out a bottle of whiskey and two crystal tumbler glasses.

'Let's get this in you,' she said.

'What about me?' Jen said.

'You're young and tough; it's different,' Iris said.

Becky knocked the whiskey back in one go. 'Can you please tell me what this is all about?'

Iris gulped her drink, and sat down. She was silent for a moment before starting her story.

'Regina and Bella grew up in this house, but their parents were exceptionally strict. Bella married a man they didn't approve of, and they cut her out of the will. The house was left to Regina, who was also married and had a baby girl. Unfortunately, Bella's husband died in a train accident and Regina took her in. A few years later, Regina's husband passed away. The two sisters were back to being the Reillys once more. Everything was fine until Regina's daughter grew up and something happened. Regina said Bella interfered where she wasn't wanted, and Regina's daughter moved away to England. The girl never came back, not even to visit. The sisters had a huge row after Laura left, and Regina threw her sister out of the house, and never spoke to her again.'

Jen shrugged, and put her earphones back on.

'What was the row about?' Becky asked.

Regina never talked about it. I know Bella tried every Christmas to get her sister to communicate with her, but Regina was steadfast. She said she could never talk to Bella.

'She made me promise that I would keep all her things here in the house when she was gone, and keep Bella away.'

'Something terrible must have happened between them. I can't believe I'm caught in the middle of it.' Becky got up, and stood in front of the portrait. 'Regina Reilly sounds scary.'

'I knew her as a sweet, gentle lady, but we all have the capacity for rage. So, reveal all. What are you guys doing here?'

'My mother passed away, and it turned out she owned this house. I'd never heard of the place until then.'

'I'm not much help, I'm afraid. Regina and I were the best of friends, but we didn't push each other to reveal everything. She had her secrets, and I have mine.'

'Sounds mysterious.'

'What a compliment! When you have been around for as long as I, mysterious is not the first thing that comes to anyone's mind.'

'I never thought of it like that. I should get my attorney to email over all the documentation in case anyone else comes knocking.'

Iris chuckled. 'Bella is all bark and very little bite. She will go home now, and hit the bottle; that's her usual modus operandi.'

Becky wasn't so sure. What had drawn Hilda to this place, and did she know any of the backstory? Surely, she didn't, because if she had, she would have been bursting to talk about it. Becky shifted uncomfortably. Maybe she didn't know her own mother as much as she thought she did.

'Bella sounds like a lost soul,' she said, her voice low.

'Well she can stay lost. Don't you be worrying about her.'

'Does she live in Coolnamona?'

'Unfortunately, not far from here. She has rooms over the old bakery.' Iris suddenly got up. 'Change of subject: tell me your plans for this place, if I'm not being too pushy, and please tell me why the hell you're camping out? You could have stayed at mine.'

'We're OK. The bed mattresses and bedding are ordered, and will be here in a day or two, and as for plans, I have no idea at the moment.'

'Well I hope for one, you revive The Café over Orchid Bay. That establishment is sorely missed around here.'

'I know nothing about running a café, but I need to find some way of keeping a roof over our heads so who knows?' Becky muttered.

Iris rubbed her hands together. 'I'm only speaking my mind, but you think I'm a nosy parker, don't you?' she said.

'No, it's just everything is so different. I feel a bit at sea. I don't know what I'm doing or even why I came here.'

'I'm sure all will become clear in time. Now, in the interests of full transparency, as the politicians like to say, and I know we don't know each other very well, but I have a confession to make.'

'I'm not sure I want to hear this.'

'Dear, I must be honest with you.'

'I don't understand.'

Iris paused for effect, before continuing her story. 'Regina arranged for a modest stipend to be sent to me every month, to pay me for the upkeep of this house after her death. I also had to arrange to keep the front and back gardens looking well.'

Becky stared at Iris from under her eyelids. 'You did such a good job of it.'

'I deserve that. The truth is I did very well until the start of this year, but then I became ill, and I was just recovering when I fell and broke my hip. It necessitated a hip operation. I managed to get dust sheets on everything, and do a bit of light hoovering so the inside was kept up, but the gardens were beyond me. I gave Ben permission to set up a veg garden in the back, but the front became a jungle. Now, I feel so bad about it all.'

'I'm sure you did your best.'

Linking her arm, Becky asked Iris to walk the ground floor with her. Iris smiled indulgently and said they should start in the dining room at the other side of the hall, where a large mahogany table which seated twelve was taking up too much space.

'I told Regina she should flog it, but she was totally resistant to change.'

The chairs needed covering, Becky thought, and the room needed a refresh, but there wasn't anything here that worried her. She liked the big table. They had a large round table in the loft apartment, too – Hilda had insisted on it. She said it helped with the flow of conversation.

In the kitchen, she took in the large Aga, the free-standing dresser and various tables with crockery pots and pans on them.

'Regina was going to get a new kitchen. She had it ordered. It was the only room she was willing to update. Maybe the company will oblige because she had paid for it. I have their name; they're just in the next town.'

'Was Regina's death sudden?'

Iris shook her head.

'It's hard to believe even now, but the silly woman had taken to wearing ball gowns all over the house, and she tripped over the hem of a particularly long one with a train. I was always telling her to be careful. She hit her head off the tiled section inside the front door.'

'Oh my God, I had no idea.'

'I probably shouldn't be telling you, but don't worry, even if Regina came back as a ghost, she wouldn't be capable of doing a bad thing. There was only good in Regina.'

'Why was she wearing a ball gown?'

'Loneliness can make a person do strange things; it brought her comfort to remember a time past. She was very beautiful in her youth, and wearing her designer dresses kept her young.'

'I recognise the Dior dress in the painting.'

Iris laughed out loud. 'That would make Regina so happy to hear. She was a brilliant seamstress and she was an expert at copying all the great designers. Dior was her favourite, and that dress in the painting was very special to her.'

'She was very talented; dress designing is my world, and I wouldn't dream of trying to emulate the great masters. Regina was a wonder with the needle; her eye for detail, perfect.'

Iris smiled. 'It's only a pity that it is this small place and maybe as far as Bray which saw her talent. When she was young, her parents stymied all talk of her moving away and studying, but I think in her mind, she travelled the world.'

'She sounds like such an interesting lady.'

Iris took down a framed photograph from the mantelpiece over the Aga. 'That was her a few years before her death, standing in the front garden and café. It was very different then, though thankfully the house hasn't changed much.'

'It was Regina who ran a café here?'

'Yes, she always said it kept her young.'

'Do you really think I could get that kitchen she ordered?'

'Dan Williams owes me a favour, and he drank enough at the café here. Hopefully, we can twist his arm.'

'A house like this needs a proper kitchen,' Becky said.

'Now, I had better get to the deli or I will miss out on my morning croissant. Can I bring one back for you?'

'No, I'm good, thank you.'

Iris left by the back door, telling Becky not to be a stranger. Becky watched her walk down the back garden to a makeshift gap in the wall between the two properties, where a wrought iron gate, which looked like it had been taken from a graveyard, was open.

Becky wandered up the hall, and seeing Jen busy scrolling on her phone, she went out into the front garden. There was something hauntingly beautiful about the bay from this angle. Morning sunshine dappled across the calm sea water, and in the distance she heard the chug of a fishing boat as it made its way back to port. A dog broke free from its owner, tearing down by the harbour wall, and jumped into the sea. Becky stood transfixed, and she smiled, slightly bemused that such a simple scene should make her heart warm and fuzzy. But just as quickly it disappeared, and worry took over.

Becky thought she may have come to this place overlooking Orchid Bay hoping for an uncomplicated life, but somehow she didn't think that was going to happen, only a life complicated in a very different way. If she could only be guaranteed that they could make a go of it here, that her past would not creep up on them and cause trouble, maybe she could begin to settle into this small place over Orchid Bay, and start to trust the world once again. She wandered down the path to close her front gate. When would she ever have the place looking as good as the house in the photograph? Maybe she had taken on too much here, especially without Hilda, but she had nowhere else to go. Fear prickled up her back when she thought about why she had to get out of Manhattan. She checked right and left to see if there was anyone on the lane. Relief washed over her, and she smiled that the only disturbance was from the crows sitting high in the oak tree at the entrance to the lane. She had to make it work here, she thought firmly, but she had no idea how she was going to do that.

<h1 style="text-align:center">SIX</h1>

Over the next few nights, Becky and Jen continued to camp in the sitting room. They had settled into a routine of sorts, where Jen helped around the house in the mornings but took the afternoons off, often wandering down to the harbour and the sea.

This morning, Becky was upstairs trying to move her bed frame to a better spot when there was a knock on the front door.

Afraid Bella had decided to return for round two, she waited to hear another knock, but Jen bolted downstairs, and she had to follow her.

She was talking to a young man in the hall.

As Becky reached the first landing, Jen flashed her a smile. The happy look on her daughter's face threw her.

'This is Brian, Mom. He looks after the garden at the back.'

'Excuse me?' Becky said.

The boy who looked as if he was around Jen's age or maybe a little older stepped forward.

'Brian Evans. You know my dad, Ben.'

'Oh yes, how can we help you?' Becky said.

'My dad sent me up to get some spuds and scallions for tonight's menu. He said it would be all right.'

'Of course, you can go out through the kitchen,' Becky said.

Jen offered to show him the way.

He laughed, and said he had been looking after the garden for a few years, but he usually entered through the back entrance. Becky heard them walk outside, and she ducked back to the first-floor landing window to spy on them. She had previously only glanced that way, but now she noticed the drills of potatoes, vegetable boxes and raised beds for herbs and strawberries. Brian picked a strawberry, handing it to Jen. Becky slowly pulled the sash window up an inch. She heard the lilt of Brian's voice and Jen's laughter, and she realised she hadn't heard her daughter so happy in a long while.

Going back into the bedroom, she decided to open the windows there too. Regina wasn't a very tidy person; there were necklaces and scarves hanging from the notches at the side of each mirror of the dressing table, and clothes were scattered all over the floor.

As she pulled up the bottom window frames to let in the air, she saw Iris get on her bike and cycle down the lane, a big straw bag and her easel tied to the back of the bike.

From here too, Becky could see across the bay out to sea. The house on the cliff looked beautiful in the morning sunshine, its white windows and doors highlighted against the grey stone walls. She thought it looked as if the house was closed up, the shutters drawn, and she wished she had binoculars to have a closer look. On the bay, a few children were learning how to kayak, and a huddle of people were doing their daily yoga exercises beside the harbour wall. Becky leaned out the window, and breathed in the fresh air. She loved this house, and she loved Orchid Bay; she had to trust everything else would work out.

Jen loitered in the doorway. 'Mom, Brian asked did I want to hang out with him. He works in the restaurant with his dad, but his shift doesn't start until four.'

'I guess it would be OK,' Becky said, and Jen ran and kissed her on the cheek.

'I will be back before four, promise.'

'Is he waiting for you?'

'We agreed to meet at the corner; I didn't know if I was allowed.'

'Just don't do anything silly, and don't get into the water. You don't know about the tide and currents around here.'

'I won't,' Jen shouted as she ran down the stairs, and out the front door.

Becky stood at the window watching Jen skip down the steps. At the gate, she stopped to talk to somebody who was hidden from view, and pointed at the front door. Becky's heart thumped, sure Bella had returned.

She was wondering how she should react when Ronnie, the golden labrador bounded into the garden, nosed around for a sunny spot, and lay out. Maisie, carrying a basket, made her way up the steps and path, and Becky breathed a sigh of relief. When she looked up and spied Becky at the bedroom window, Maisie waved enthusiastically, and pointed to the front door.

Maisie was already in the hall when Becky got downstairs.

'It gladdens my heart to see you in the old place. Regina would be happy to see life around Coolnamona House again.'

'Thank you, we're just getting to grips with things.'

Maisie put down the basket on the console table. 'I heard you had a visit from Bella. I think that's my fault. I was getting my hair done in Bray and she was beside me,' she said as she twirled around so Becky could admire her hairdo. 'I was sure she knew that somebody had moved into the house. Please forgive me.'

'There's nothing to forgive.'

'Oh, I hear she became quite cross. Did you call the police? Who came to your rescue?'

Becky looked at Maisie's expectant face, and she immediately became more guarded. 'Nothing like that. If you will excuse me, I have to be getting on with things,' Becky said brusquely.

Maisie eyed her up and down. 'Well, I wouldn't want to be stopping you going about your business. You want to watch Bella. If you need any help, you know where I am,' she said in her marbles-in-the-mouth tone.

'Thank you. Let me give you your basket before you go.'

'I just made some brown bread and a few fruit scones,' Maisie said, putting up her hand to prevent Becky removing them from the basket.

'You keep it for now, it will give me an excuse to come back,' she said, as she stuck her head into the sitting room to have a gawk. 'You can move that old painting over the fireplace for starters. Regina always did have notions above her station.'

Becky reached for the handle of the front door, and yanked it open for Maisie, but her guest continued to linger.

'I will come back another time when you can spare me a few more minutes. Was that your daughter I saw with the Evans lad?'

'Yes, he's a very nice young man.'

'If you say so. You do know he's only here for the holidays? His father lets him stay in Dublin during the school term, even though there are trains from Bray. Of course, there's no mother in the boy's life, and I always say for a house to be a home, there has to be a mother and a father, don't you think?'

She stared at Becky, who looked away, afraid of what she would say if she answered.

'There is no woman's touch there either,' Maisie said.

'I'm not sure if we should be having this conversation,' Becky said stiffly.

'Nonsense, everybody around here feels the same. Ben Evans is working night and day; no wonder he wants his son staying away for most of the year. You know he was once a police detective and he threw it all up.'

Becky shuffled uncomfortably. 'I don't really know an awful lot about Brian and his father,' she said.

'Well, if he continues to see your daughter, you'll probably get to know them better than the rest of us. Anyway, I'm holding you up,' Maisie said, and whistled for the dog, who reluctantly stood up.

'Call down someday; we can sit out in the garden and have a good chat. The whole of Coolnamona is dying to hear what you intend to do with the place and why you came here.'

'I guess they will know, when I know,' Becky said, making Maisie frown.

Becky watched her walk down the path and the granite steps before turning at the gate to wave. Not sure what to make of the visit, she closed the front door, and went upstairs to Regina's bedroom. Sitting down at the dressing table, she picked up a gold bangle from a tray which held some earrings and what looked like a marcasite ring. She snapped the bangle over her narrow wrist. It glinted in the sunshine, but she slipped it off almost immediately. As she replaced it on the tray, she noticed the engraving along the inside: *To Laura, with all my love forever*.

Another name, and another person she didn't know. Honestly, she felt she should have been provided with a cast of characters for Coolnamona and Coolnamona House along with the keys. She came here thinking it would be a simple life, and it had already become stressful and complicated. Regina Reilly was a mystery. She seemed to have been so lucky in so many ways, and yet Becky felt a sadness about this life she was only beginning to find out about.

She needed to get out of the house. Grabbing her jacket, she rushed down the stairs, and out the front door, letting it bang behind her. She took the steep path down to the harbour. It was time she got to know Orchid Bay. A man out walking his dog said hello, and Becky smiled, her step more relaxed now as she rounded the bend which opened up to the wide vista of the bay. An ice cream van had parked at the entrance to the harbour, and Becky stopped to look at what was on offer.

'Have a 99; it's the most popular,' the owner said.

'What's a 99?'

The man and the children queueing behind her laughed, and she took a five-euro note from her jeans pocket.

The ice cream man whipped a spiral of ice cream onto a wafer cone, stuck a chocolate flake on top with a half spoon of sprinkles and lashings of raspberry sauce.

Becky, trying to keep up with the melting ice cream, licked all around the cone before heading off down the harbour wall. She walked for a while past the boats moored at one side, and the sea wall on the other. When she got to the end of the harbour wall, she climbed up to look out to sea.

A woman in a rowing boat waved to her, and she waved back, feeling a little silly to be doing so. Hurriedly, she turned back, and diverted down to the shingle beach to crunch across the stones to the seafront café, where she ordered a cappuccino, and sat outside in the sunshine.

'Having a day off, I see,' a voice from the next table said.

Becky turned around to see Edith from the delicatessen.

'Don't tell anyone you saw me here; it's my guilty secret. The coffee on offer is not as good as my place, but you can't beat being so close to the water,' Edith said, glancing to her left and right.

'Who would I be telling?' Becky snorted, making the other woman giggle.

'Can I come and join you? You can be my cover, and if anyone sees me, I can say you invited me to sit and chat.'

'Surely people aren't that bothered?'

'I take it you have met Maisie.'

Becky threw her eyes to the sky. 'Maybe now, I understand.'

'It's my day off today; I suppose I can do what I like.'

'I should say so.'

Edith sipped her coffee. 'Can I tell you something?'

'I guess.'

'I want to tell you a secret.'

'I don't know why you would trust me. We hardly know each other.'

'Exactly why I want to tell you.'

'Oh.'

Becky waited, but Edith didn't say anything. She kept staring out to sea.

They sat in silence for a few moments, and Becky thought Edith had decided against her disclosure until she heard her clear her throat.

'Becky, I have cancer. I got the results back today, and it's not good.'

Becky gasped, not sure what to say, but Edith continued to talk.

'I thought I would scream and rant, but when I was told I had to get my affairs in order, I just shrugged and said OK. Stupid response, I suppose, but really I have nothing to do, nothing I want to do, only sit by the sea.'

'I am so sorry to hear this,' Becky stammered.

'No, I don't want your sympathy. I just wanted to tell you because I'm not going to tell Claire, my wife and business part-ner, just yet. You see, the deli was her dream, and she won't be able to run it without me. I don't want to burst her bubble. We're doing really well, and she's so proud of the deli.'

'Claire is hardly going to care about any of that now.'

'I don't know how to tell her,' Edith said, her voice watery with tears.

'You're not being fair on Claire.'

Edith dipped her head.

'I'm sorry. It really isn't my place to make a comment. It's your life,' Becky said hurriedly.

'And my death. Do you really think I am being unfair?'

'I recently lost my mother. It happened so fast. She was alive in the morning and dead by the evening. How I wish we'd had time to talk, and I'd had time to show her how much I loved her. I missed out on that; her death hurts all the more for it.'

Edith stood up. 'You're a funny one, Becky, and I think you might be right, but I will wait a while until I get my own head around it, before I tell Claire. She's an emotional person. I have to be ready for it.'

'Best of luck with it. If you need to talk again, you know where to find me.'

'Will you keep my secret?'

'Of course, I don't really have anyone to tell anyway.'

Edith put her hand out and shook Becky's. 'I like you, Becky White. I wish I had time to get to know you better.'

'Me too.'

Becky sat and watched Edith stroll across the shingle beach. Sipping her cappuccino, she scanned across the sea to the horizon. She wished she could talk out her own problems with a compassionate stranger; the weight of her own secret was almost too heavy to bear. She kept her eyes on the sea, finding comfort in the waves that kept on rolling in a wide convoy towards shore. Who was she kidding? How could she even begin to tell anyone what happened?

SEVEN

'Sweetheart, I was hoping you would help around the house today. We are almost two weeks in and there is still so much to be done,' Becky said as Jen sat, and ate a bowl of cereal.

Jen made a face. 'Do I have to?'

'You can sort through all the old dresses in the big closet. That should be fun.'

'You have a strange idea of fun,' Jen said, and Becky smiled because she knew by her daughter's tone, she would help.

Jen was upstairs for about half an hour when she called out to Becky, who was deep-cleaning the kitchen.

'Mom, come upstairs. You have to see this,' Jen yelled urgently.

Exasperated, Becky threw down her scrubbing brush, and peeled off her plastic gloves. 'All right, give me a minute.'

She was halfway up the stairs when Jen appeared on the landing.

'I can't believe it. It's the dress Granny Hilda was looking for. This is so weird,' she said holding up a blush-pink lace dress, and twirling so that the skirt fanned out a little.

Becky gasped.

'Isn't it the most wonderful dress in the world? Look how it shimmers when I move,' Jen said excitedly.

Becky walked up to the landing, and stroked the delicate tulle and lace.

'It's the dress in the painting. Where did you get this?'

'You know that closet in the back room you said to clear out? It was at the very back, wrapped in a sheet and lots of tissue paper.'

Becky picked up the skirt, and examined it carefully. 'So much intricate work. This dress must have cost a fortune.'

'Can I try it on?' Jen asked.

Becky looked at her daughter's bright, happy face; her eyes shining; the delicate pink of the dress complementing her long brown hair.

'It's our dress now. So if you want to put it on, go right ahead.'

'Granny Hilda would be amazed that we found a dress like this in Coolnamona.'

Becky eyed the dress up and down. Hilda would've been ecstatic at this discovery. Loneliness crawled through her as she thought how much her mother would have enjoyed this moment. As she bunched the fabric, and sniffed at it, Becky thought how much she missed working with luxury fabrics, and how when she became immersed in a design, all her other troubles seemed to fade away.

'We should air it; it smells so musty. There's an old washing line in the back garden. We could hang it up there,' Becky said.

Jen leaned closer, and smelled the dress. 'Euww, stale and old,' she said, quickly pushing it away.

'Sweetheart, it's a vintage dress and it has probably been in the closet for a long time. Let's get it outside. Careful walking down the stairs with it,' she said. Gathering up the skirt, she let the silk lightly touch her cheek. She was back in her Manhattan design studio at the most exciting stage of the design process when she chose the fabric. Quickly bunching up the skirt under her arm, she instructed Jen to hold the bodice as they tramped down the steps.

It took the two of them to get it on the line so it wasn't trailing on the ground. Afterwards, they sat on the old bench at the back door, watching the dress sparkle in the sunshine, lightly lifting and billowing in the breeze coming in from the Irish Sea.

'This is so weird,' Jen said as she took a picture of the dress, and uploaded it on Snapchat.

Becky stretched out her legs, and held her face up to the sunshine.

'Just one of those coincidences, I guess,' she said.

'Mom, it is more than a coincidence; it has to be,' Jen whispered.

Becky giggled. 'If you say so,' she said in the best imitation she could muster of Hilda's voice.

Jen joined in the giggling. 'I hated when Granny said that. Now I wish I could hear it one last time,' Jen whispered.

Becky hugged her tight. 'Let's get this gown on you,' she said gently, pulling Jen up to help her check on the dress. 'It smells of the sea now; so much better.'

'I wish Granny Hilda could see this. She would be so happy,' Jen said, but her face suddenly changed. 'I won't ever get to the Met Gala now, will I?' she said glumly.

There was a loud creaking noise from past the raised vegetable beds in the middle of the garden, and somebody pushed the old side door in the garden wall. Iris waved.

'I hope you don't mind. I saw the dress out on the line, and couldn't resist coming over to have a gawk,' Iris said, loitering around the door in case she got a bad reception.

Becky gestured to Iris to join them beside the dress which was swinging lightly in the breeze.

'Funny you should decide to do this now. In the summer

months, Regina got out all her ball gowns, and gave them a good airing. It was quite a sight. She could fit four evening gowns in one go on the line. It was sad too; those dresses never got a proper day out or event. They were surely designed for more.'

'Strange behaviour,' Becky said.

'It got stranger. I told you Regina started wearing these long dresses on a daily basis. People began to talk, said she must be losing her mind, but they didn't understand someone like Regina. Wearing those dresses, she told me, was her way of coping with the loneliness of old age. By the time she had glammed up, half the morning was gone.'

'Please don't tell me she wore this beauty around the house,' Jen said.

Iris shook her head. 'This confection of a dress, she said, was one of a kind, only to be worn on a special occasion.'

Jen carefully took it from the washing line. 'How did somebody in Coolnamona afford such a designer ball gown?' she asked.

Iris chuckled. 'Maisie is convinced Regina was a millionaire, but the answer is very simple.' She paused for effect as both Jen and Becky listened intently. 'Regina would be so thrilled that two women from New York admired her work.'

'What do you mean?' Becky asked.

'Regina was an extremely talented designer, not that she got to show off her talent other than in Coolnamona, and at the county hunt ball. She loved to cut out photographs from magazines, and if she liked the outfit, she made it herself. She didn't have a pattern, she just had her good eye and whatever description was given of the dress at the time.'

'You're kidding. How could she have made this dress? Look at the seams on the bodice and all that lace, where did she get it?' Becky said.

Iris threw back her head, and laughed. 'She most certainly did make it.'

'But she was so young.'

'Great talent is never confined by age, dear,' Iris guffawed.

She took the dress from Jen, and ran her hand across the skirt.

'Mr Dior's dress caused quite a stir back in the day. Olivia de Havilland wore a version in lilac, but Regina was set on replicating the blush pink as much as possible. Go and try it on, girl,' she said kindly, handing it back to Jen.

'Regina told me she stole off on the train to Dublin, and used all the money she had managed to squirrel away to buy as near as she could to the lace the great designer had used. She showed me a photograph of the Dior design, and I have to say, Regina's is frothier, more feminine in my opinion.'

Jen checked the neckline. 'I don't believe it. If Granny Hilda had seen this, she would have paid a fortune for it.' She pulled at the dress, searching for the label. She read it out. 'After Dior by Regina.'

'It's an embroidered label. She even made that,' Iris said.

'But where did she wear these dresses?'

Iris shrugged. 'She said it was the challenge and the fun of making something beautiful. It took her away from her life here in Coolnamona. It was her dream life, I suppose.'

She reached out, and rubbed Jen lightly on the cheek. 'This is your dress now, Jen. Regina would be delighted to know the new owners appreciated her hard work.'

Jen carefully placed the dress over her arm, and skipped off to the kitchen to try it on.

'She has settled in well,' Iris said.

'Today anyway.'

'I think a certain young man might have something to do with that.'

'She's still so young, though.'

'You're never too young for love, Becky. Look at the way it's making Jen smile. She's quite a beauty when she does.'

'We haven't had a lot to smile about of late.'

'Well, you lot being here is making a few of us beam, and it has set Maisie going big time.'

'What do you mean?'

'She has only started a rumour that you intend to knock the house down, and look for planning permission to build luxury apartments overlooking the sea.'

'What? That's a ridiculous idea.'

Maisie always loves to have a bit of hot gossip, and when there is none, she's well known for making it up.'

'She seemed so nice at first.'

'You know she sent Bella your way?'

'She told me. I don't want this interfering with our time here. How do I nip it in the bud?'

'Gone way past that, I'm afraid.'

There was a loud noise from the kitchen as Jen hit a stainless steel saucepan with a spoon.

'Announcing Jen White wearing After Dior by Regina,' she said, before stepping out into the yard.

'A beauty queen for sure. That dress fits like a glove,' Iris said as Jen twirled about the yard as if she were a ballet dancer.

The tulle and lace skirt fanned around her, and Becky squealed with delight.

'You look so beautiful, but it needs something at the neck – a delicate necklace,' Becky said.

'My mother, the dress designer,' Jen said, nervously patting her bare neck.

Iris put her hand out, and invited Jen to dance. The two of them waltzed across the rough ground of the yard, Jen holding up the hem of her dress so it didn't trail in the dirt.

When they stopped, Jen looked expectantly at her mother.

'Do you think you and I one day could go somewhere fancy, where I could wear a dress like this?'

'I hope so, but maybe not in Coolnamona,' Becky replied, and they all laughed.

When Jen had gone to change back into her jeans and T-shirt, Becky sat down on the bench beside Iris.

'You're finding it difficult finding your feet here,' Iris said.

Becky shrugged.

'Can't leave the big city behind even for a little while?'

'I thought if we came here that somehow I would see a path through the mess since my mother died. I was wrong. I thought we spoke the same language, watched much the same programmes on TV, but it's beginning to feel more and more like I am in a foreign country.'

'Give yourself time. Sure you're only here a wet week or two. Rome wasn't built in a day, and there wasn't, I'm sure, the likes of Maisie or Bella to contend with either.'

'Thankfully, Bella has not returned.'

'That one is waiting in the long grass. Mark my words.'

Becky shivered.

'To be honest, I don't even know what we're doing here. I seem to be spending every minute trying to get the house up to scratch.'

Iris jumped up, and pulled at Becky's hand. 'Sounds like you need help getting out of that rut you have settled nicely in.'

'I'm sorry. I'm just having a moan. Since Mom died, it's been non-stop with bad news about debts, and I have to find a new way to make some sort of living.'

'You'll think of something.'

'I had better. Most of my savings were used up getting us here. I doubt, though, anyone in Coolnamona would want handmade designer pieces; it looks like the only customer is long since gone.'

'Snap out of it, young lady. You're coming with me,' Iris said, getting up from the seat.

'I don't know... I have so much to do.'

Iris turned around, her hands on her hips. 'All that will wait, Becky. Everything about you says you need time to stop and stare.'

'Hmph.'

'You may mock, but I'm not taking no for an answer.'

'I should change,' Becky said, looking down at her stained jeans and her T-shirt which was smudged with a long smear of grease across the front.

'Girl, get over yourself, and come on,' Iris said impatiently.

She led the way through the kitchen and hall, and out to the front garden, calling up the stairs to Jen on the way that they wouldn't be long.

When she got to the front gate, she turned left.

'This is my favourite path over the headland. We like to keep it overgrown so the tourists stay to the more conventional paths, but this leads, not to the harbour, but a sandy cove. It's almost like our private beach.'

'I didn't know.'

'Of course you didn't, which is why it's handy to have Iris next door,' she said as she picked up a stick leaning against the gap in the stone wall.

Becky followed as Iris thrashed brambles out of the way, and gently lifted fern leaves from their path.

'This is the only spot you'll see the ferns; the path gets too exposed later on,' she said as they tramped out of the copse onto the headland which overlooked the bay and further out across the Irish Sea.

'They are planning a wind farm out there, so soon we won't be able to see Wales on a good day,' Iris said, using her stick to sweep across the length of the horizon.

'It's so peaceful,' Becky said.

'Exactly. You need to let your brain rest. Forget all the questions, and you'll find answers will come in their own time.'

Suddenly, Iris threw the stick to one side and with her arms flung out, she twirled, her head thrown back, and shouted, her words swept away with the wind. Becky stepped back out of the way, anxiety rising in her that Iris might topple over. When she stopped, Iris staggered, and looked at Becky.

'Come on girl, do it.'

Becky dithered, making Iris click her tongue impatiently.

'Let go of that angst building up inside you. You'll feel better.'

Becky shook her head. 'I'm not like you, Iris. I can't let go like that.'

'Dear, we all have to learn to let go. You'll feel so much better.'

'Maybe another time.'

Iris stepped back, and looked at Becky.

'You're young, you can say that. For me, time has a different meaning. But let's stop being maudlin,' she said, taking Becky's hand, and leading her to a flat rock. 'This is a good spot to sit, and contemplate the sea.'

'I haven't fully stopped to look at the ocean since I arrived. I have seen it, but I don't think I have stood still for any length of time,' Becky muttered.

'That's your first mistake. Follow the rhythm of the sea; let it guide you.'

'I'm a city gal. I don't do this sort of thing.'

'There is always a first time. Now, close your eyes.'

Becky did as she was bid.

The warm sunshine tingled across her face as the sound of the sea surrounded her. Slowly, she began to decipher the different water sounds, and not just the noise of the sea, but the waves as they first thudded against the sandy beach, throwing up spray; then the water as it circled around the rocks at the bottom of the cliff. She thought she could hear the drag back across the stones on that shingle part of the shore, and the sound of the breaking waves further on as the sea pushed against the sharp rocks jutting out of the water at the base of the cliff. A bee buzzed nearby, but she didn't open her eyes. It passed close, and she knew it was burrowing and nuzzling up the bells of the wild pink foxgloves all around them, and she took comfort in that. A light breeze curled around her, gently caressing her, and she felt her face relax.

'I have been running for so long. I even brought my mother's ashes here with us, because I haven't a clue what to do with them. I am hopeless,' she whispered.

'I know, but you're in Coolnamona now,' Iris said softly.

'I just wish I knew what I should do here,' Becky said, opening her eyes.

'Maybe you're trying too hard, girl. The answers to deep held questions never come on demand, but have a habit of stealing up on us. Why don't you set up a café? Carry on the tradition?'

'That sounds like a lot of hassle and stress.'

'Not really. Everything you need is locked up in the back shed. A bit of elbow grease and help, especially from Ben, and you'll be grand.'

'I'm not sure I'm that brave.'

'Nonsense, girl, you won't know until you try it,' Iris said.

They got up, and walked side by side on the path which had widened out. Every now and again they stopped to take in the view.

'You must tell me more about Regina,' Becky said.

'She was a beautiful woman, but I only knew her when she was full of sadness. She was near the end of her life, and she had little peace. We were friends, but she never truly let me in. Regina was full of secrets, and they died with her.'

'It sounds so sad.'

'I suppose it does, but we had a lot of laughs together too. I think our friendship worked because we never put pressure on each other.'

At that moment, they heard somebody come along the path ahead of them.

Ben waved when he saw them.

'I didn't think anybody came this way any more,' he said as he reached them.

'I was showing Becky here our secret pathways off the beaten track,' Iris said.

'Yes, as the summer moves on you'll be glad of this respite from the deluge of tourists,' he said, before nodding goodbye to the two ladies, and continuing on his way.

When he was practically out of sight, Iris turned to Becky. 'That man is a good catch. You couldn't ask for more. A man who cooks and is handsome and nice,' she said as they turned back towards Seaview Terrace.

'I think I have enough going on in my life right now,' Becky said firmly.

'Nonsense, girl, there is always time to let love come calling,' Iris boomed, and Becky worried that her voice had carried so far, Ben might have heard her.

EIGHT

It was early, and there was still a sharp chill to the air. Becky pulled on a cardigan before leaving the house. It was the first week in June, and Becky knew that soon, Orchid Bay would come to life under the warm rays of the morning sunshine.

She was wandering down Main Street, past the delicatessen, when Edith gestured for her to step in.

Tentatively, Becky moved inside to the counter.

'How are you doing?'

'Not so good. I need your help. Do you have time to talk? I can take a break in ten minutes.'

'Sure,' she said, her eyes showing surprise.

'Please, Becky, I know this is off-kilter, and we don't even know each other really, but you're the only person I want to talk to. I need you.'

'Hey, is that the American I have heard so much about?' a woman shouted from the back.

Becky stepped back.

The woman, wearing a white apron and a hairnet, wiped her hands on a tea-towel before introducing herself. 'Hi, I'm Claire, Edith's partner.'

Becky took her hand, and smiled faintly.

'Edith here tells me you are an important addition to our town. Welcome,' she said.

'Thank you, Edith has been very kind. I really like your place and what you're doing here. Your baguettes are delicious.'

'It's been a lot of hard work, but we finally feel we're getting there.'

Edith said she was taking her break. 'Becky here is going to show me the house. I will be back shortly.'

'OK, not more than half an hour. There's a conference out at the American plant, and I was told to expect even longer lines today, and more calls for takeout too.'

Becky smiled at Claire as Edith took off her apron, and left it on the counter. She followed her out the door, not exactly sure where they were going.

'Are you sure you want to lie to Claire?' Becky said.

'We're going to have a look at your house.'

'We are?'

'Yeah, of course,' Edith said, quickening her pace until they got as far as the lane.

'You know we can talk on the street,' Becky said.

'I need to sit down, and I may cry, so I have to get in where nobody will see me.'

Becky looked all around her. 'There's nobody about; we could sit somewhere,' she suggested.

'No, let's head for Coolnamona House,' Edith said hurriedly.

'You're of course welcome inside, but I don't understand all this mystery. Have things got worse?'

Edith gripped Becky's arm. 'Let's get inside, Becky, please.'

Becky opened the gate, and led the way up the three stone steps and the path to the front door.

'We can sit in the front room. I have started to paint it so sorry about the mess,' she said as she unlocked the door.

Edith followed her into the sitting room. 'I often wondered about this room. When the café was open, it was always locked. Everybody said Regina liked to keep it private because it was her writing room.'

'Writing room?'

'Yeah, she liked to pen letters. Sometimes, she came to our delicatessen and the café, and sat at the outside tables, writing. I asked her once why, when she ran the best café in town, she came to ours.'

'What was her answer?'

'It was sad really; she said that sometimes the four walls of Coolnamona House came in around her, and she needed to break free.'

'What was she writing?'

'Letters, she said, to a person who probably would never read them. She said it was just her random thoughts, and that she often, at the end of the month, reread them before throwing them on the fire. She liked to sit, and watch her words burn.'

'There's something so sad about that. Why write all those letters just to burn them?'

'There was always a mysterious air and loneliness about Regina. It's as if she ran the café to surround herself with others, so she wouldn't have to spend time with her own thoughts. I didn't know her very well, but I'm not sure anybody did.'

'I just wish I could find out more about her. I'm also thinking I may have to resurrect the café to help keep the roof over our heads.'

'It always was the favourite café in town. You could do worse than to reopen it,' Edith said before glancing at her watch, and taking a deep breath.

Becky reached out, and grasped Edith's hand. 'OK, enough about me. How are you?'

'Not good, turns out this tumour of mine is inoperable. They have decided that we will try some chemotherapy, but if it works it will just give me a little longer. It's not a solution or a life-saver, just a way of staying around a tad longer.'

Becky gripped Edith tighter. 'I am so sorry.'

'I know, now I have to tell Claire, and you have to help me.'

Becky stuttered, 'OK,' but she felt uncertain and over-whelmed.

Edith either not noticing or ignoring Becky's reaction continued. 'I was stupid. I thought I would get a few years, and I could fight my battle and hide it from Claire until the time was right. Who was I kidding? When is the time right to deliver devastating news?'

'I think you need to tell her as soon as possible,' Becky whispered.

'I know that now. The doctors say even with the chemo-therapy, I have six to nine months at best, and at worst, three months.'

Becky, attempting to hide the shock on her face, got up and stood at the fireplace. 'What do you need from me, Edith?' she asked quietly.

'Tell me, what do I do? Do I walk out on Claire and leave her running the delicatessen? Do I engineer a huge row and go away and...'

Becky put her hands up to stop Edith talking. 'What are you thinking of? Do you love Claire?'

Edith took another deep breath. 'More than anyone or anything. I'm not afraid of dying, but I hate what it is going to do to Claire. She is my sun and my stars, and I would do anything rather than put her through the pain she's going to feel if I have to tell her.'

'She deserves to know the truth,' Becky said.

Edith put her head in her hands. 'I can't do it. I can't tell her, see the pain in her face, see the fear in her eyes. I can't do it. I don't know how to do it.'

'And you think to walk out on her after an engineered row is the right thing to do? That's not fair on someone you say you love.'

Edith jumped up, and made for the door. 'I don't know why I'm even talking to you. You don't understand.'

Becky blocked her way. 'I lost my mother a short while ago. It was sudden and brutal. What I wouldn't give to be able to talk to her one last time. If you truly love Claire, you will give her that chance. All we can hope for at the end is that we have been fair to the ones we love, and that we have loved them completely. You owe yourself that in particular.'

Edith collapsed back onto the velvet couch. 'But she will devote herself to me, and look after me, and her whole business will slip away.'

Becky shook her head. 'I worked so hard in my mother's business. It all died with her, and we were left with nothing, only debts. Despite all that crap afterwards, I love her so much, and I would give anything to be able to tell her that. Don't deprive Claire of that opportunity to love you, and be by your side. That would be the greatest disservice to yourself, to Claire and to your love.'

Becky turned away, unable to speak any more.

Edith took a cushion, and held it to her face. Her shoulders shook as she cried. Becky wiped away her own tears, and sat beside Edith, placing her hand on her back.

'Let me walk back to the deli with you. I can serve, and I will call in my daughter. We can take over while you two talk.'

'Would you do that for me?'

'Let's go, or we will be late,' Becky said, taking Edith by the hand. In the hall, she reached for a box of tissues, and tugged a bunch out, handing them to Edith.

Edith blew her nose, and looked at herself in the mirror. 'Who am I kidding? I look like shit.'

'Claire is not going to even notice. I'll text Jen; she can meet us outside the deli.'

They walked on in silence until they were near the deli-catessen when Edith stopped on the street.

'Becky, can you go in and get Claire? I can't walk in there.'

'OK.'

Becky clenched her fists, marched through the door and up to the counter.

'Where is she? I already have five orders ready for collection and ten more in by phone and soon the hordes of Genghis Khan will be queueing down the street,' Claire shouted.

Becky swallowed hard. 'Edith is outside, and she would like to talk to you. I'll look after things here with some help from my daughter while you two chat.'

'Run things here?'

'Take the orders, wrap the rolls, hand them out. We can handle the till; we won't pocket any bucks.'

Claire knocked on the counter, and leaning close to Becky, whispered urgently, 'What the hell is going on? Is she breaking up with me?'

Shocked, Becky stepped back. 'I'm just the messenger. Can you please go out to her? She is right outside.'

'This could be the busiest day of the year. What is she doing to us? This is about the row Edith and I had this morning, isn't it? Tell her it's forgotten, but today has to be about the business. I need her here.'

Becky reached over, and touched Claire on the wrist. 'Just go out, and talk to Edith, please.'

She saw fear flash across Claire's eyes.

'We have got it here; take as long as you like,' she whispered as Claire, her lip quivering, slipped by her.

Becky tidied up the counter, and took some calls, and tried not to look out the window at Edith and Claire who were chatting on the other side of the street. After a while, Jen stuck her head around the door .

'What's going on? Those two are hugging and crying, and everybody is looking at them.'

Becky gestured to Jen to join her. 'I guess it's good to talk.'

'Or not. They are bawling their eyes out now,' Jen said.

The phone rang, and Becky answered it, writing down an order.

'OK, time to get working, Jen. There are two hundred rolls here, five different fillings, and from what everybody says, they will all be gone in the next two hours.'

'Can I do the phone, and you wrap the orders?' Jen said.

For the next two hours mother and daughter worked side by side. People queueing were surprised to see the American visitors helping out, and many asked why, but Becky just smiled, and said she was grateful to get the opportunity. When she saw Maisie at the end of the queue, she hoped she would be out of rolls by the time she got to the counter.

'I'm not here to buy anything, but to offer my help. Do you need another pair of hands behind the counter? I'm only too happy to assist. Have Edith and Claire got bad news? Somebody said they were crying.'

'We have it covered, and Claire and Edith will be back shortly,' Becky said, noting the frown that came across Maisie's brow.

Claire appeared at the doorway, but when she saw Maisie, she slipped around the back out of view. Becky told Jen to hold the fort, and she walked in the back.

'You have been a good friend, Becky. Edith has told me everything.'

'If you want us to help out again, we are more than happy.'

'Thank you. We have decided to close the deli immediately. Edith is more important than anything to me. We've commitments and orders to fulfil, but after that, we shut down.'

'Are you OK with closing down?' Becky asked, and she worried that she had been too forthright.

'None of this is anything without Edith. I want us to spend every minute we can together. I don't want to be here, when I can be with Edith. We have a small place by the sea on the west coast. We will go there, and spend precious time together.'

'I wish you both well.'

'Thank you, but I must ask you to keep this to yourself. We need to be together and in peace right now. We need to deal with our own fears and get on with our own shaky plans.'

'Don't worry,' Becky said as she took her jacket from the hook on the back door and walked through the front to collect Jen. When they got outside, Jen said she was going back to the restaurant to meet up with Brian.

Becky hadn't the heart to stop her, and instead, watched her daughter saunter up the street, her head stuck in her phone. Feeling lonely, Becky headed for Coolnamona House. It was as if when she felt down, she was drawn to the house overlooking Orchid Bay. Regina may have needed to bolt from these four walls from time to time, but Becky found they gave her a sense of place.

She was in the kitchen when there was a knock at the door. Afraid it was Maisie, she tiptoed to the sitting room, and peeped out the window. Edith and Claire were standing outside.

Becky opened the door quickly, and ushered them both inside.

'We won't sit down. Claire said I had to come back and thank you, and she's right. I put a lot on you, Becky, and you've been a star.'

'That's OK. I'm glad I could help.'

Claire nudged Edith in the side.

'We know you're trying to find out about Regina and the house, so Claire said I should tell you that Regina once told me she kept her best letters in a special hiding place.'

'Did she say where?'

'What do you think? She only let out that piece of information because she was upset as she had just seen Bella on the street. It was so sad; they never made up before she died,' Edith said as Claire put her arm around her, and said they had to go.

As they walked out the door, Edith turned back to look at Becky. 'I am so glad you're here at Coolnamona House, Becky. Everything will work out for you, and for us,' she said.

Becky hugged Edith tight, and then she stood in the doorway watching the two women make their way slowly down the path.

When they had moved out of sight, she went back into the sitting room to gaze at the portrait. What had happened to the once beautiful young Regina, that she ended up a sad and lonely woman writing letters that only strangers would read if they were ever found?

NINE

Becky wasn't sure what to do. The van carrying the two mattresses had blocked the lane leading up to the terrace of houses. She waited at the front door for the delivery men to come and speak to her, but then she saw Maisie chatting to the driver.

'They want to leave the mattresses in the garden,' Maisie said as she walked up the path.

'They won't carry them into the house? But we have been waiting so long for these,' Becky said, her exasperation making her voice high-pitched.

'Apparently, they have another three deliveries and are already behind, and the helper has to knock off at lunchtime as his wife is in hospital having a baby.'

'Oh.'

The men got out, and started to pull one mattress from the van.

'We can leave them inside the gate if that's all right,' one said.

'I suppose it will have to be,' Becky replied, her voice tense.

'You'll do no such thing. The woman has paid for delivery,

and that is to the bedroom,' a loud voice boomed from down the lane.

Becky turned around to see Bella standing to the side of the van, a deep scowl on her face.

'Can you get along and clear the way for them?' she said to Becky as if it were the most natural thing in the world that she was standing directing operations at Coolnamona House.

Becky called out to Jen to direct the delivery men upstairs. She stood beside Bella and Maisie as they saw the men struggle up the path, huffing and puffing under the weight of the first mattress.

'Shouldn't we help?' Becky asked.

'After they tried to con you, and leave them behind the garden wall? Are you mad?'

After a little while, Jen opened the top window, and called out that both mattresses were in situ. The delivery men came thundering down the stairs, and loitered for a few moments on the front path. Uncomfortable, Becky scrabbled in her pockets for change, but Bella put a hand out to stop her.

'Gentlemen, you should move your van. You can't block the road up forever,' she said.

When the van had left, Bella turned to Becky. 'Do you think we could talk in private?'

Maisie coughed, and said she had called down to see if she could help with the moving in.

'Very kind of you, I'm sure,' Bella sniped, and Becky mumbled something about not needing help.

Maisie turned on her heel, and walked quickly away.

'We certainly don't need her earwigging on our conversation,' Bella said as she made her way up the garden path with Becky following behind.

Becky hung back to see what would happen at the front door.

'Well, are you going to let me in or do I have to beg?' Bella said.

Becky brushed past her, leading the way to the sitting room. 'What can I do for you?' she asked.

Bella looked around the room. 'You kept all the furniture and the layout, I see.'

'It was already beautifully furnished.'

'Mmm,' Bella said as she sat down on the couch.

Becky sat opposite on the leather wingback chair.

'I think we may have got off on the wrong foot,' Bella said.

'I don't know what you mean. Was it when you came into my home shouting and threatening legal action?'

Bella moved uncomfortably on the sofa. 'I am a passionate person; what can I say?'

'You could apologise.'

Bella gave Becky a withering look. 'Well, if it will speed things up. I'm sorry for my behaviour the other day.'

Becky swallowed hard. 'So what really brings you here?'

'I have been hearing a lot about your plans for Coolnamona House.'

'I didn't know I had any.'

Bella perched on the edge of the sofa, and clutched her handbag. 'It would be best to scotch any rumours that aren't true. Are you really going to reinstate the café?'

Becky laughed. 'The rumour mill really has been working overtime.'

'You mean Maisie, and yes, she is dining out on you at the moment. You're quite the celebrity.'

'I hadn't realised.'

They sat in silence for a few moments, neither knowing what to say next. Becky concentrated on the painting, examining Regina's face in the hope that it would give her confidence. The old clock on the hall table chimed, and she thought she saw Bella flinch a little in surprise.

Swallowing hard, she decided she had to be the one to break the heavy silence, punctuated only by the rhythmic tick-tock of the clock.

'Can we get to the point, and you tell me why exactly you're here?' she said firmly. Her voice was stiff, but she made sure Bella did not see her dig her nails into the palms of her hands or notice that her knees had begun to shake.

Bella gave Becky a steely look.

'I did not behave well when I was last here. I am not that type of person. Brawling is not something I approve of. However, out of courtesy, I decided on this occasion to come here personally to tell you that I have instructed a solicitor with a view to taking legal proceedings so this house can return to the Reilly family.'

'The house is legally mine. I have the papers.'

'Darling, anyone these days can produce documents, but they have to stand up in court. You can't come here, and insist that our family home is suddenly yours.'

'If this is going to court, I don't think we should be talking about it.'

'Have it your way, but I warn you that my next visit to Cool-namona House will be to take up residence in my family home.'

Becky stood up. 'Let me see you out.'

'You should take what I say seriously.'

'I will instruct my attorney. Why don't you leave details of your—'

'Solicitor,' Bella said sharply as she handed a business card to Becky.

'My attorney will be in touch.'

Bella looked around the sitting room. 'This was always my favourite room. Attorney, isn't that some mouthful? I'm beginning to feel like I'm in a movie.' Bella chortled.

Becky swept back the front door. 'Ms Reilly, thank you for stopping by.'

'Carter is my married name,' Bella said as she stepped out into the garden.

Becky quickly closed it behind her. Fear and anger surged through her. She was sure of one thing: nobody was going to wrestle this house from her. She had lost so much already and so had Jen. Nobody was going to push her out of Coolnamona House ever, and certainly not before she had unravelled the mystery as to why Hilda had owned this place.

Iris stuck her head around the kitchen door. 'I didn't want to interrupt. Tell us all, did you send her off with a bee in her bonnet?'

Becky's face crumpled. 'She's going to take me to court. I can't afford a legal battle.'

In three strides, Iris was at her side, pulling Becky into a tight hug.

'That one hasn't a leg to stand on. She hasn't two pennies to rub together either. Hold tough, because she's only trying to frighten you.'

'She has succeeded in that,' Becky gasped.

Iris led her to the sitting room. 'Time for our shot of whiskey. Let's talk this through.'

Becky, her hands clenched in tight fists, punched a cushion Jen had thrown there that morning.

'Why is that woman so against me?'

Iris poured the whiskey, and handed a glass to Becky.

'I only moved to the area ten years ago, but Regina herself told me this story. It might help. I think it all goes back to Regina's daughter, Laura.

'I saw a gold bangle upstairs inscribed to Laura.'

'All I know is whatever Bella said or did, Laura left Coolnamona House for London and never came back. She was the same age as Regina was in that painting. There was some row, and she walked out with just the clothes she had on her back. It might explain the bangle left behind.'

'And she never returned?'

'No.'

'I couldn't imagine my life without Jen.'

'I am not sure Regina was ever the same afterwards. I don't know the ins and outs. Regina was a kind, gentle woman who clearly had a large burden to carry.'

Becky pointed to the painting.

'When I first saw this portrait, I thought she was such a lucky young woman. Now, I'm not so sure. Bella thought I was setting up a café.'

'That's Maisie and her rumours. You could do worse. The café was very popular with locals and visitors alike.'

'But where did she seat everybody?'

'Outside in the summer, and in the dining room in the winter. In the winter months it was only a few locals in for a cup of tea in front of the fire in the dining room.'

'Sounds nice.'

'It was, and of course they served the famous Reilly recipe homemade scones. She only closed the café shortly before she died. Anyway, I had better rush off, I have been told that there's a beautiful rose bush in flower up at the grey house on the hill. It is a lovely day to sit outside and paint.'

'Is that house lived in at all?'

'Been shuttered and locked up for decades now. I don't know a lot about it. Some say it's haunted, but that sounds like a Maisie story to me.'

'It must be the best property in the locality.'

Iris laughed. 'Believe it or not, but Regina Reilly's home, when she ran the café on the front lawns, was once regarded as the best property in the district. The grey house is pummelled by winds all the time. Even on a good day, there's a breeze on top of that cliff that could skin a cat. Coolnamona House has the aspect, the space and was once quite perfect. Now, I must be off.'

At the same time, Jen called from the front door, and said she was going to the restaurant.

Becky waited until everybody had left before putting on her long cardigan and canvas walking shoes. Pulling the front door shut behind her, she set off on the secret path to the top of the cliff.

Her head down, and her shoulders hunched to avoid the brambles, she tramped along at a steady pace. Breathing in the smell of the sea, and listening to the waves fall and pull back on the shore, she already felt better. She stopped to sit on the flat rock. The sun sparkled across the wide expanse of water highlighting small ruffles of waves as they made their way to shore. A fishing boat cut through the water, and she envied those on board their freedom. She thought she had run away too, but the worry and anxiety of her situation just hitched a ride along with her. She wanted to shout at Hilda to come back to show her the way. There was nothing for them in the States, and they were strangers here in this beautiful place beside the sea.

When she saw Ben come up the path, she dithered. Anxiety rose in her when she realised she was on her own. It was too late to turn back so she quickened her pace in the hope that she could just pass by.

'So, the magic of the place has got to you as well,' he said, and Becky nodded as she stepped around Ben.

'Oh, I have disturbed you. I'm very sorry,' he said, his face showing concern.

She hesitated. 'No, I'm just a little homesick for the city,' she sighed.

'Really, and there was I thinking a visit from Bella had you running scared.'

'You heard what happened?'

'Jen told Brian. I came looking for you.'

She didn't want this man to be so nice. It would be so much easier if she could brush him off, but there was something about him. She wanted to get to know him better, but she didn't think she was able to do that right now; not after what had happened in Manhattan.

'That's kind of you, but I think I can handle it,' she said primly.

He took a step back, making her regret her hasty reply.

'I am out of my depth. I shouldn't have snapped at you. I have a lot on my mind.'

'That's OK. By any chance, do you fancy a bit of a stretch? If you're up for a longer walk, there's a steep path down to the sandy beach. Brian said the seals were there this morning.'

'OK.'

She followed Ben as they walked on the narrow path until they got to a section which dipped down steeply.

'Don't worry, I'm right in front of you. If you find yourself going too fast, just shout out,' he said.

Becky found it exhilarating, concentrating on every step she was taking as they slipped down towards the sea. At the bottom, Ben turned around, and held out his hand so she could jump from the last step to the sand below.

She landed, her feet sinking into the sand, the warm grains filling up her shoes.

Ben reached over, and helped her to a rock to sit down.

'That path is not for the faint-hearted, but it's so worth it,' he said as he kicked off his runners, and strolled to the water's edge.

Stepping out of her canvas shoes, Becky followed him.

He rolled up his trousers, and waded into the sea. He called out for the seal, and Becky thought he was nuts shouting across the waves, expecting a seal to respond.

'The old seal that hangs around these waters likes company,' he explained, making her laugh.

'You think because I'm American, I'll believe any old crap.'

'While that may be the case, the seal does respond to the

human voice, but she probably won't appear now because it would prove me right.'

Becky scanned the water as far as the horizon. 'Nothing there. So there goes your theory.'

'She obviously got a better offer,' he said, throwing his hands in the air, before hollering loudly again for the seal.

'You might as well give up, I just don't believe you.' She laughed.

He made a face as if he were very disappointed, and they continued to paddle, the sunshine shimmering across the water and dazzling their eyes.

When they got to the end of the little cove, Ben pointed to another set of steps leading back up the cliff.

'That will bring us back near the town, and we can get you home from there,' he said.

'Is the restaurant not open this evening?' she asked.

'Yes, but all the prep is done, and I have left the setting up of the tables to Brian and Jen. Are you OK about Jen helping out?'

'Working for a wage, I hope?'

'Of course, I wouldn't have it any other way.'

She was about to respond, when he told her to look back to the sea.

'It's the old seal, a bit late for our rendezvous.'

She could barely see the head of the seal as it bobbed in the water, and rolled onto its back.

'I think she's showing off,' Ben said.

Becky grinned, and they continued across the field until they linked up to the road leading into the village.

TEN

Becky was supposed to be cleaning out the old shed so they could store their new bicycles, but she had become distracted.

She wandered out to the garden and sat down. Opening the large cookery book where a label had been stuck over the front cover – *Café Essentials and Other Things* – she began to read.

A few handwritten pages were stuck over the photographs beside the recipes.

Becky read the first note.

I never thought that I could run a business, but when I set up the café, it just happened. Running the café has saved my life. It has been hard, and it has been fun, and without it, I don't know where I would be.

Becky pulled over a stool, and put her feet up as she turned the page. These had to be Regina's notes, she thought, excitedly reading the next one.

Scones and the Reilly recipe are a huge hit. Yesterday, a family came in and sat down, and ordered two scones each, and pots of

*coffee and orange squash for the kids. The local newspaper said
it was some bigwig in the rock and roll business, but to me it
was just another group who left this place well fed. Now, if it
had been one of the old-time movie stars, I would have had a
better chance of recognising him.*

Another page had a note on Ben Evans.

*He runs a great restaurant, but I wish he would open later. I
notice the days he opens from four o'clock, my business falls off.
He says we are not in competition, but I'm not so sure. The
other evening, I had two groups who were sitting at my tables,
and suddenly they changed their minds and were gone. Maisie
said afterwards she saw them sitting outside Ben's restaurant.
She said he was running a specially discounted set menu and,
sure, weren't they better having a three-course meal than some
buns and tea? Maisie can be very cheeky and rather nasty,
though in this case, she had a point.*

Becky heard Jen calling from the house.
'Mom, I'm off out with Brian.'
She stood up. 'You're pretty sweet on him, aren't you?'
'Shut up, Mom. He's OK, I guess.'
'I just want more information.'
'Granny told me you had boyfriends at my age, and you
wouldn't even give her a name, and she never met them until
your heart was broken, and you came running home.'
'It's just Brian is a little older than you, and I thought it
might be nice for you to meet girls your own age. There is a
youth club in the village on Friday nights.'
'Youth clubs are for losers. See you later.' As she went down
the hall, Jen called out, 'If a package comes for me, it's Brian's.'
'What do you mean?'
Jen stopped and swivelled around to face her mother. 'Brian

has sent off for a DNA test kit. He's adopted, so he's hoping to trace his birth parents or family.'

'Does Ben know?'

'No, he doesn't want to upset him, but he wants to know if there are any matches out there. I told him he could use this address.'

'I'm not sure he should be sending a sample to a DNA bank. Who knows what they will do with it?'

'Mom, it will be fine. If a package comes for me, please don't open it because it's for Brian.'

'You've given out our address already.'

'I thought you wouldn't mind.'

'OK, I just hope Ben isn't unhappy about it.'

'He doesn't need to know, not unless Brian finds some relatives, I guess.'

'I doubt if it will come to anything. They are only after his money. But I think he owes it to Ben to tell him,' Becky said as Jen left by the front door.

Becky, feeling a sense of defeat that only dealing with a teenager can bring on, went back to Regina's book.

Picking it up, it slipped from her hands and she made to grab it. A folded piece of paper popped out from between the pages and floated across the ground.

Becky scooped it up, and sat down to read.

Coolnamona House

My Darling Laura,

I don't even know if you will ever read this, but a part of me hopes that someday you will come to Coolnamona House, and you will find this letter and the others I have written to you. This letter is an amalgam of all the letters I have ever penned to you. There were so many words I put on the page, but I have burned a lot of them. These words are all I have left, along with the love I have held in my heart for you, Laura, all these years.

I have written you so many letters. Some I have kept, but mainly I sit, and watch them burn in the grate. It is all I can do at this stage. I have spent all my savings and all this time looking for you, and I have to now accept that I may never meet you again.

I was this week given bad news about my health. Dementia is creeping up on me. I don't have long and that matters little, but it matters because it leaves less time for me to hope you may walk up the path to Coolnamona House, stop to look at the view of Orchid Bay, and come in, and collapse on the couch. These are the simple pleasures I yearn for as I sit in this big, draughty house surrounded by the deafening sound of silence.

I have so many regrets, and the notes I have kept for you will state them clearly in black and white. I listened to those I should not have, and I pushed you away. I will forever regret my actions. I have only one dream, one hope, and that is to see you again, listen to your chatter, and sit with you here under the portrait, and catch up. I can picture you and Bella coming bustling in without being asked, and plonking down, demanding tea in my best tea-set. Wouldn't the three of us have such a grand time? But for now, these are the foolish imaginings of an old woman, who before she meets her maker, wants to earn the forgiveness of those she has hurt the most.

Darling Laura, I can never give you back the years you had to stay away from Coolnamona House and Orchid Bay, but you must know this one thing: I will love you forever. It was my privilege to be your mother, and my greatest grief to lose you.

Mam

XX

Becky sat back, and closed her eyes. The sun was shining but she was trembling, and she couldn't stop. In an attempt to regain her composure, she opened up the book, and began to read a handwritten note titled: *Why I Set Up the Café.*

I was so lonely when Laura left. I thought I had right on my side, but nothing compares to a daughter's love. To be righteous is such a lonely desert. There is nothing to comfort late at night as darkness clouds around me, or in the morning when a long, lonely day stretches ahead of me without any intermission. I wasn't made to pine away, be smothered by loneliness, so I did the only thing I could do; I baked my scones, biscuits and little cakes, and made tea and coffee, and people came, and sat outside, and I felt needed. After a few weeks, the carpenter in Bray made up my sign, and it was a proud moment when I put it up outside the door.

The Café over Orchid Bay gave me back a life; not the same life I had so carelessly thrown away, but some sort of life. It gave me a reason to get up every morning; a reason to look forward every night.

The café gave me a reason to go on. It became very popular with locals and tourists, and I felt I was part of the wider Coolnamona family.

Becky closed the book, and went back to the shed where wooden tables and chairs were stacked along with bags labelled 'tea-towels' and 'tablecloths', and stacks of crockery bearing the motif: *The Café over Orchid Bay.*

When she heard a step in the backyard, she stopped what she was doing. Leaning against a stack of chairs, she told herself she was OK. Her mouth went dry, and she felt pain shoot through her body. She swallowed hard. She strained to listen as the footsteps moved towards the shed. Crouching down, she felt the pain of her nails digging into the palms of her hands.

When she heard Ben's voice calling out her name, relief flooded through her.

'Give me a minute,' she called out as she attempted to calm down before stepping out into the yard. 'I was just looking at all this café stuff. I think it is time I used it,' she said.

'How exactly?'

'Set up a small café on the front lawns.'

'Following in Regina's footsteps.'

'I suppose I am.'

'Sounds good, but can I pull you away from your planning for a while? I was going to ask you, and Brian is asking Jen, of course, if ye wanted to go for a picnic at around noon. Myself and Brian are planning to drive into the Wicklow Mountains. It might be nice for you two to get away from Coolnamona.'

'That's so kind of you.'

'Good stuff. I'll see you in a while,' he said.

A few moments later she heard Jen on the stairs, rushing to her room presumably to change and lash on lots of make-up.

Becky had no idea what to wear either, she thought, looking down at her jeans which were scuffed with grass marks from when she had knelt down to pull rubbish out from under the rose bush. She went upstairs to have a quick wash, and get changed.

She had few clothes to choose from, but picked her nicest designer white shirt and a fresh pair of jeans. She slicked some lipstick on her lips, and brushed her hair back into a ponytail before grabbing a pink sweater from her case. She was making for the door when she decided to run back, and borrow some of the house jewellery. She smiled thinking fashionista Sadie would definitely approve. She always said jewellery made an outfit.

Opening up the drawer, she picked the T-bar necklace, and thought it gave an understated elegance to her outfit. Downstairs, she sat on the last step of the stairs, and changed into her canvas shoes.

Jen, who had changed into her best jeans and a short tank top, came downstairs.

'Brian said he and his dad go up into the mountains as often as they can. He says it is the most beautiful place in the world, but I don't know.'

Becky hugged her daughter. 'I'm sure we will find out, but it will have to be bloody good to beat Orchid Bay.'

She was surprised when Jen agreed.

Becky locked up the house, and they set off down the lane to the main street. On their way to the restaurant, they stopped to read a notice on the delicatessen window.

DUE TO ILLNESS, WE HAVE MADE THE DIFFICULT DECISION TO CLOSE THE STORE. WE WANT TO THANK ALL OUR LOYAL CUSTOMERS AND WISH YOU ALL WELL. EDITH AND CLAIRE. IN OUR ABSENCE PLEASE CONSIDER SPRING'S RESTAURANT OR THE CAFÉ OVER ORCHID BAY.

Becky wiped away a tear. The Café over Orchid Bay seemed like such a good idea, and she felt emotional that Edith and Claire appeared to think so too.

Brian was loading up the boot of the car when they arrived at the restaurant.

'Wow, you guys are taking this picnic thing seriously,' Becky said.

'It's Dad, he insists. Mum always loved a picnic, and he wants to continue the tradition of going up the mountains. These days it brings us closer to her, too.'

'That's cute,' Jen said, and the two of them wandered off together.

Becky mulled over what Brian had said. She felt faintly jealous that Ben still loved his wife so much he went on picnics to the mountains to feel close to her. She waited by the car, not sure if she should go around the back to Ben's living quarters.

She had been there a few minutes, when Ben came around the corner carrying a stack of rugs.

'Your daughter has distracted my son, and we nearly left without these,' he said, calling over his shoulder for Brian and Jen to come along.

Becky sat in the front of the jeep with Ben. Not sure of what to say, she thanked him for including herself and Jen.

'We love a mountain picnic. It's a time to stop and stare. I find I need to do it every few weeks. Even in winter, I head for the mountains with a flask of hot chocolate or coffee, go for a walk, clear the head, and enjoy the peace of having the clouds at almost touching distance and the mountains surrounding me,' he said.

'Awesome,' she said, before going quiet as they headed up the mountain towards Roundwood, on narrow roads past houses and villages, until they got deep into the mountains.

Even Jen looked up from her phone as they passed along the mountain roads. Above them, the stony peaks reached for the sky, while below them, the paths swept down to an inky-black lake, which reflected the mountains on the other side as they slipped off this way and that.

The purple heather stretched as far as they could see. In places, banks of foxgloves swayed in the light zephyr travelling inland from the sea, and touching off the mountains.

Becky could sense the stress of the last few weeks melt away as they climbed higher and higher. She felt light-headed to think they were somehow higher than the clouds.

Ben pulled into a parking spot.

'We will have to walk a bit, but it will be worth it for the views,' he said.

'I don't see how it can get better than this,' Becky said as they divided up the gear between them.

'We have a flat rock that we always sit on overlooking the lake,' Ben said as he led the way along a narrow rough path up the mountain.

Butterflies rose up from the swathes of heather, disappearing into the sky.

'Don't stray off the track. The ground is boggy around here, and we don't want you to sink into the mud,' Brian said, and Jen gripped his hand.

They came to a crossroads of sorts, where they could stand side by side.

'We always have an argument which path to take, but Dad insists it is the left one, and we walk halfway down, and have to come back to take the path going straight on and the next left,' Brian said with a friendly resignation.

'Well, let's cut out all those steps, and go straight on,' Becky said.

'Spoken with a lot of common sense,' Ben said, letting her lead the way.

She liked that, and could imagine she was the only one on the mountain, the narrow path stretching ahead of her towards the clouds. She was in her own world, watching the bees, butterflies and the clouds, almost within touching distance, as their party coasted along under the sky, when Ben called out to her.

'That is how people get lost on the mountain. You missed the left turn.' He laughed.

When she swivelled around, the others were waiting for her, and Becky blushed in embarrassment.

'I didn't even notice it. Where is it?'

'It's OK, Dad misses it every time,' Brian said.

They set off down the path, a happy group chatting and laughing until they reached the massive flat rock.

'It's like somebody put it here so we could sit and be on top of the world,' Jen said as Brian helped her climb up.

Ben told everybody to wait as he threw out rugs and cushions to sit on, and Becky opened up the hamper.

'You went to a lot of bother. Is that quiche?'

'Made this morning, and three salads because I wasn't sure what everyone would eat. There is cold non-alcoholic beer, because alcohol and the walk down the mountain won't fit together,' Ben said.

'All sounds good to me,' she said.

Jen looked in the basket. 'Oh, there's strawberry cheesecake for dessert. My favourite.'

'Don't tell me you whipped that up this morning as well,' Becky said.

'No, that was last night's job.'

'Lucky we agreed to come along then.' Becky laughed.

Brian and Jen took their food further along the path and sat on a smaller flat rock.

'Those two are getting on just fine,' Ben said.

'Aren't they a little young?'

'I was that age when I met my wife, but you hardly want to hear that.'

'It's OK. It's nice that Jen has made a friend here.'

'It's good for Brian too. He lost his mum eighteen months ago, and it hasn't been easy.'

'I'm so sorry. That must be so tough. Brian mentioned you come here to remember her.'

'We scattered Rachel's ashes here because she loved to come here for picnics.'

He fell silent, and Becky didn't know what to do. She was ashamed that she had felt jealous earlier. Rachel was a very lucky woman to have had a man like Ben by her side.

After a few moments, Ben turned to her. 'Have I ruined the moment?'

'No, I just think it is so sad and romantic that you come back here. You must have loved Rachel so much.'

'I did, and I do. Brian is the reason I keep going. She told me I was to go out, and live my life when she was gone. Said she would come back and haunt me if I didn't.'

'Sounds like a sensible woman.'

Ben laughed out loud. 'That's not a word I would use to describe her.'

Brian looked over at them, and waved.

'I think he likes that you're laughing,' Becky said.

Ben gazed at her. 'I hope you do open a café. It will be a great meeting place for the village once again.'

'Not competition?'

'Please! That's the only Regina tradition I don't want resurrected. Her feud with me and my restaurant...' He laughed and took Becky's hand. 'Seriously, I will help in any way I can, and I can tell you if you two hadn't come with us, we would have argued all the way up the mountain, sat here in silence and been sad before going back down the mountain in a huff, and feeling sorry we bothered at all. Thank you for a lovely afternoon.'

'If it is any consolation to you, Jen and I have been sparring since her granny died. We had to leave New York to come to Coolnamona, where we are desperately trying to find our feet.' She stopped, and looked at Ben directly. 'It has been a really good day, and I have definitely decided to reopen The Café over Orchid Bay. I so value your support. The mountains gave me that opportunity to think more clearly, and I thank you for that.'

'Any time,' he said.

'It means a lot to us to have your support and friendship,' she said.

'Always,' he said.

Becky so wanted to believe him, but what if he knew the real reason she'd fled New York? Her head throbbed with a tension headache, and she wondered, would she ever feel completely free again?

ELEVEN

There was a loud banging on the door. Becky looked out her bedroom window, but she couldn't make out who it was.

'Who is calling before 8 a.m.?' Jen said as she came onto the landing.

'Stay here. It's probably Bella again with another threat for us to get out of the house,' Becky said urgently as the person thumped on the front door again.

Slowly, Becky went down the stairs. She could hear the person outside, muttering and cursing.

Pulling back the bolts, she heard the snarky comment, 'About time.'

Becky froze for a moment until she realised the voice was so familiar. Hurriedly, she pulled back the door as Sadie fell into the hall.

'Darling, I thought I was going to have to break in.'

'Sadie, what are you doing here?'

'Didn't you get my phone message? I left a long drawn out explanation. Shit, maybe I rang your US phone. You don't use it here, do you?'

'No, I moved over to a network here. I sent you my number.'

Sadie, her long black hair in a ponytail, shrugged her shoulders. 'Oh well, am I dumb or what? I'm here now; say welcome.'

'Welcome,' Becky said, pulling her friend into a hug.

'What brings you here? I thought you had that court case,' she muttered in her friend's ear.

'Long story. First, I need coffee. I don't want any decaffeinated crap either,' Sadie said, wriggling free.

Becky glanced outside where a taxi driver was waiting with Sadie's cases. 'You got a cab from Dublin Airport?'

'Of course. I don't do public transport, and I forgot my driver's licence.'

'You came in a hurry, but you managed to pack three cases.'

'Darling, can you pay the cab driver? I don't have any of those euros.'

Becky grabbed her purse. She was lucky she just had enough to cover the fare, but that would leave her well short when she had to go to the supermarket later.

'I promise I will pay you back as soon as I get over the jet lag. I'm good for it,' Sadie said, taking in the decor. 'What a cute place you have here, though you're going to have to improve on the kerbside appeal.'

Jen came thundering down the stairs, and flung herself at Sadie.

'Whoa, girl! High heels. I will topple over,' Sadie said as she enthusiastically hugged Jen back.

'How long are you staying with us?' Jen asked.

A frown appeared on Sadie's face. 'My plans are fluid. For as long as you will have me, I guess.'

'It will be good to have an American girlfriend here,' Becky said, leading Sadie down to the kitchen.

'Oh, rustic vibes, very different to back home,' Sadie said as she sat down on an old painted wooden chair.

Jen boiled the kettle, and made a mug of instant coffee. She handed it to Sadie.

'We always have our coffee in the front garden. I'm hoping to see Wales this morning,' Jen said.

'I have no idea what that means, but it sounds fun,' Sadie said, and they all headed back out the front door.

'What has happened? You're always far too busy to leave New York,' Becky said after a while.

'For another time, please,' Sadie said, staring pointedly at Becky.

'The realtor emailed. There's an offer in on the apartment. Is that you?'

'Chance would be a fine thing.' Sadie harrumphed as she got up off the bench to join Jen on the rock. 'You should clear this garden. The view is stunning. You really should make the most of it,' she said loudly.

'There used to be a café here at one time, tables on the front lawn. I am going to revive the concept,' Becky said.

'It's going to take a lot of hard labour to get to that stage, darling, but if anyone can do it, it's Becky White,' Sadie said, turning around to look across the overgrown garden.

'OK, but we have another pair of hands now that you're here.' Becky laughed.

'Not with this beautiful set of nails, darling,' Sadie said.

'I have missed you, Sadie. I could do with your attitude around here.'

'Well, I'm here whether you like it or not.'

'I guess Coolnamona won't know what hit it.' Becky laughed as she threw the last of her coffee into the base of a rose bush. 'Let's get inside and pick a room for you. I'll need to order a bed.'

'A camp bed will do.'

'You need to be comfortable.'

Sadie caught up with her friend in the hall. 'Don't look now, but there is what looks like a fashion icon from the 1950s on your driveway.'

Wearing a blue summer dress cinched in with a belt at the waist and a wide straw hat, Becky thought Bella looked quite stylish, if a little out of place.

'Whoa, who is this Coolnamona fashionista?' Sadie said looking over Becky's shoulder.

'Trouble. A lot of it.'

'Remember, you've got backup,' Sadie said, and Becky shivered. The last thing she wanted was these two women slugging it out.

'If you don't mind, I would like to talk to Bella on my own,' Becky called out, and Sadie backed away to loiter around the kitchen.

Becky waited at the front door for Bella, who stopped to take in the sea view as she made her way up the path.

'I had forgotten it's such a beautiful vista,' she said as she reached the front door.

Picking up on her tone, Becky invited her inside.

'Are you sure?' Bella asked nervously.

'I would rather we could sit like civilised human beings, and talk things through,' Becky said primly, leading the way to the sitting room, where she stood at the fireplace.

'I suppose you're expecting me to apologise again,' Bella said as she sat into the far corner of the sofa.

'That's entirely up to you.'

'I have behaved badly and for that, I am sorry as I have already stated, but it doesn't mean I am giving up on my ancestral home, do you understand?'

Becky stepped back, and looked at Bella. She didn't know why, but she felt sorry for this old lady. However, for the moment, she had to hide any feelings of sympathy from her guest. 'Is that why you're here, to warn me off again?'

'No, I was hoping we could reach an amicable agreement.'

Becky folded her arms. 'Either you're joking or you think I'm a pushover.'

Bella took off her hat, and tidied her hair with her hand before fiddling with the hat rim. 'I don't joke about something so serious.'

'You don't even know me. Why would you think I'm a pushover?'

'I don't know, because you're a stranger in these parts, I guess.'

'At least that's honest.'

Bella stared at the portrait. 'She had it all for so long. Anyway' – Bella pulled herself out of the couch, and fished into her straw handbag – 'for you,' she said, handing Becky a sealed envelope.

Becky made to open it, but Bella stretched out a hand to stop her.

'It's from my solicitor to give you notice of our intention to challenge your ownership of this property. I don't know who sold you the house, but it wasn't theirs to sell. A court will have to decide all this. I am afraid you've got yourself mixed up in a messy will business, which will only come right when I have possession of my family home.'

Becky shook her head. 'I will get my attorney to correspond with your solicitor. This can be cleared up quite easily.'

'I wouldn't be so sure,' Bella said, standing up. 'I hope you're not taking in paying guests. The other residents of the terrace won't like it. This has always been an upmarket address. There is no place for a boarding house here.'

'I have a visitor from the States, not a paying guest.'

'Miss Ryan says...'

'Who?'

'Maisie, of course. She says you won't stop until you have knocked down Coolnamona House.'

'That's ridiculous.'

'You would say that.'

Becky opened the sitting room door wide, and looked Bella

straight in the eye. 'You have delivered your letter. It's time you left,' she said firmly and tossed the letter on the armchair.

'You heard the lady,' Sadie said loudly, stomping up the hall, her stilettos digging into the carpet.

'I see you have called in reinforcements. Probably a wise move. You'll need all the friends you can muster,' Bella said.

Becky waved her out. 'Let's not have a repeat performance, and instead leave it to the attorneys.'

Bella stopped, and eyed Sadie up and down before going out the front door. 'Enjoy your vacation, people, because that's all it can be,' she said, before making her way down the path.

'Such friendly folk around here,' Sadie remarked.

'I think she's a sad and troubled figure. I just hope her attorney can talk sense into her.'

'You're far too nice for your own good, Becky. Tell me, are all the locals as colourful?'

'Bella has her reasons. Maybe we can clear it all up.'

'Forever the optimist. Lawyers love will cases, Becks. The reason is simple: they drag on and the costs mount.'

Becky's face crumpled, and Sadie grabbed her into a hug.

'You have an attorney onside now – try not to worry. I feel the need to get out and down to that enticing harbour for a walk. Let's go visit this awesome bay,' Sadie said.

Becky looked down at Sadie's stilettos. 'I have a nice pair of sneakers you can borrow...'

Sadie made a face. 'But my bottom only looks good when it has an uplift, if you get my drift.'

Becky took her by the elbow to the front garden rock. 'Look down there, that's the path that curls down to the sea. That's where we will be walking.'

'They don't do a shuttle?' Sadie asked.

Becky burst out laughing. 'Sadie, this is the countryside, the Irish countryside. There is barely a proper public transport system between towns and cities. We could take the car, if you really want.'

'No, I can walk it.' Sadie shook herself, enthusiastically flexing her muscles. 'I came here for adventure. I can wear sneakers, and trek to the bay.'

'Well done, let's get you kitted out.'

Becky owned a good pair of sneakers and the old runners she wore every day. Sadie immediately grabbed the brilliant white new shoes, and accepted a pair of Jen's designer socks.

When she was ready, they set off down the cliff path to the harbour.

Sadie made a big deal of breathing in the air, and stopping every ten steps to gaze out to sea.

Becky asked her a few times if she was OK. Sadie smiled enigmatically, and said she would be eventually, and Becky knew not to press her friend further at the moment.

When they got to the harbour, they wandered past the fishing boats and yachts to a small shingle beach where Sadie kicked off her shoes and socks, and ran on her tiptoes into the sea.

'Bloody cold, but good. Come and join me,' she shouted.

Becky laughed, and said there was no way she was going barefoot across pebbles and stones.

She saw a man approach them. Feeling nervous, she backed away until she realised it was Ben walking across the shingle strand in his bare feet.

'Push yourself to do it once, and you'll love it. I guarantee it,' he said.

Blushing, Becky demurred. 'I would make a fool of myself howling like a kid.'

Sadie picked her way across the stones. 'Is anybody going to introduce me?' she asked.

Becky and Ben turned to face Sadie at the same time.

'You guys make a cute couple,' she said.

'Oh, we're not...' Ben stammered.

'Ben has given Jen a summer job, and his son is her boyfriend,' Becky said.

'Very complicated, but that need not be a problem,' Sadie said, introducing herself and holding out her hand to Ben.

When he shook it, she giggled. 'Nice firm handshake, a good sign,' she said.

Feeling uncomfortable, Becky said they had to be off.

'Oh, do we have to climb that hill? The jet lag is beginning to kick in,' Sadie said, batting her eyelashes at Ben.

'I can give you both a lift. I just have to collect some boxes of fish from one of the fishermen. I can give you the keys; the jeep's parked in front of the ice cream shop,' he said, handing the bunch of keys to Becky.

The two women watched him walk across the shingle and onto the harbour path.

'Why didn't you tell me about handsome?' Sadie snapped.

'There's nothing to tell. He has been very nice to us,' Becky said.

'I'm sure he has,' Sadie said, play-punching her friend in the arm.

'Sadie, stop. You know nothing,' Becky said, and Sadie gave her an odd look.

TWELVE

Becky sat down, and ripped open the envelope Bella had given her. It appeared to be a standard legal letter putting her on notice that there were proceedings in place in relation to the property, 3 Seaview Terrace, which was the ancestral home of Bella Reilly, now Bella Carter, and until those court proceedings had been concluded, no right existed to sell the property or otherwise dispose of the property.

She didn't know what to do. She had rushed over to Ireland thinking she could leave all her problems behind, and now there was this. She was reluctant to ask Sadie for help as she wasn't sure she could cope with her friend's outrage.

Jumping up, she headed to the kitchen where she filled a saucepan with washing-up liquid and hot water. She needed a distraction, and the freshly painted sitting room seemed a good place to start.

She began with the mantelpiece, squeezing out the cloth several times before dragging it across the top, the flannel turning from grey to dark as she cut through the dust and dirt.

There was something satisfying about getting the colour of the marble up, seeing the white glisten in the sunshine. Her head down, she scrubbed and polished until the marble gleamed. Tentatively, she ran a dry cloth as far up the frame of the painting as she could.

'You need to get it professionally cleaned, but that would cost a fortune,' Iris said as she strolled into the room.

She continued as Becky turned around to greet her. 'Regina said she should never have had an open fire all those years, but she loved sitting here under her portrait as a young woman, and feeling the heat from a log fire.'

'I didn't hear you knocking,' Becky said.

'No, because I was cheeky enough to come straight in. I didn't think you would mind.'

'I don't. Bella came around this morning.'

'Did she give you one of her legal letters?'

'How did you know?'

'She's very quick to fire off the nasty legal missives.'

Becky dropped the wet cloth back in the saucepan of water. 'It sounds as if she really means business.'

Iris flopped down on the leather armchair laughing, but immediately jumped back up. 'Euw, the chair is wet. Have you washed it?'

'I wiped a cloth over it, yes.'

Iris shook out her skirt, and sat on the sofa. 'Show me the letter Bella gave you.'

Becky hesitated.

'Look, I'm trying to help. If you want me to butt out, just say so.' The frustration in Iris's voice was clear.

Becky reached into her jeans pocket, and pulled out the letter.

Iris turned it over in her hands. 'Almost identical to the one she gave me, and absolutely nothing has happened. I had a friend of mine in the Law Society look up the solicitor named in the letterhead. He was struck off years ago. I think Bella worked as his secretary at one stage, and must have kept the headed notepaper.'

'Is the letter not for real?' Becky asked, her eyes wide, her forehead furrowed.

'No, it's Bella trying to push you out the door.'

'But surely she knows I will get legal advice. I don't scare that easily.'

Iris shrugged. 'Does Bella even care? I blame Regina. Whatever happened, she should never have let it fester and stay between two sisters. I think they both suffered as a result, and that is why she is behaving so oddly now. She can't bear to think of this house going out of the Reilly family.'

Becky sat down beside Iris. 'This is all so weird and so sad.'

'It is that,' Iris said quietly.

'But what am I going to do about Bella?'

'What can you do? Only tell her that she will have to go elsewhere with her scam.'

'But it's not really a scam, is it?'

Iris shook her head. 'It's an old woman with no family, and only a dominant bad memory to haunt her,' she said.

'It's more like a cry for help.' Becky leaned over, and put her head in her hands. 'I thought it would be free and easy coming here, staying a few months. This is more than I can handle right now.'

'Bella will give up after a while.'

'Am I the only one who finds Bella's situation so depressing? What do we do? Wait for her to crawl away, her tail between her legs, rather than trying to help her?'

'Sweetheart, she won't take our help. You have to know, the Reillys were a big family around here once. Bella is too proud to take help from anybody.'

'Do you think she is down on her luck? She always seems so well dressed and turned out.'

Iris smiled. 'When she lived here with Regina, they sewed

together and had so much fun making the designer dresses. Bella dressing well is no indicator of how she really is.'

'I feel so bad for her.'

'She is not your responsibility, Becky. You have enough to be doing to get this place liveable for you and your daughter, and now a guest for the next few months.'

'I suppose.'

Iris reached into her bag, and took out a rolled-up page. 'I had a chat with our kitchen man, and he said this is the plan Regina submitted. He can supply it straight away because he had all the cabinets and everything done when she died. It was custom-made so he has not been able to sell it on. If you want any changes, they will cost extra.'

Becky pulled over the small coffee table, which was stored against a side wall, and spread out the page.

'Regina wanted a wooden kitchen painted a duck-egg blue with a wooden counter. Is that good for you?' Iris asked.

'Sounds perfect for the space.'

'That's my girl. The kitchen man said he can install it on Thursday and spray-paint straight away. You're good to go with the café after that.'

Becky beamed at Iris. 'Thank you, I don't know what I would do without you.'

'You would do just fine with Ben Evans lurking in the background.' Iris snorted.

'Ben has been very good to us, but I'm not looking for anyone in my life right now. Does that answer the question you never asked?'

Iris threw back her head, and laughed. 'Becky, my dear, don't you know that is when love creeps up on you, when you're not looking for it? Two perfectly nice people getting together. It would be lovely.'

'I didn't know you were a hopeless romantic.'

'What is there in life, if there isn't love?'

Sadie, who had been out sitting in the backyard, wandered in. 'Sorry to interrupt, but I need to lie down,' she said.

'It's the jet lag. I saw you fast sleep in the garden. The spiders were hopping when I stole past,' Iris said.

'Not an image I want to dwell on. I had too much champagne on the flight. I treated myself to first class,' Sadie said.

Iris giggled. 'I can see we're going to have our work cut out with Ms Manhattan,' she said as she got up to leave. 'Call me if ye need any help, and don't forget the new kitchen is installed on Thursday this week,' Iris said as she made her way out the front door.

'Perfect, I hope we're getting a proper coffee machine too,' Sadie muttered.

Becky shook her head. 'Come on. I'll have to sort a bedroom for you. But if you don't mind sleeping in my bed for the moment, I just have to make it up with fresh bed linen.'

'Lead the way,' Sadie said, yawning.

'You can pick out your room too, and we will try to fashion some sort of bed for you. How long are you planning on staying?'

Sadie didn't answer, and strolled instead into Becky's room on the first landing.

'Hang on, and I will get your fresh sheets,' Becky said.

Sadie threw herself on the bed. 'Don't bother, I just need to sleep.'

'Rest, but we must have a proper talk later,' Becky said. She was leaving the room, and turned to say something else, but Sadie was already asleep. Picking up a dressing gown from a hook on the back door, she draped it over her friend. As Becky made her way downstairs, she heard Sadie's loud snoring. She groaned, and thought they would have to find an out-of-the-way bedroom for her or she would keep them awake every night.

Grabbing her keys, she decided to go for a walk around town. She needed to clear her head. At the top of the lane, instead of turning left down towards Ben's restaurant, she set off right down the main street past an old building that once was a bank, but was now some sort of thrift shop. Next, were three boutiques which looked as if the displays in the windows had not been changed in quite a while. There was a small newsagent's and a pub, which also had a funeral director's sign over the door. Becky stopped to look at a cat curled up asleep on the windowsill. At the end of the road, there were two boarded-up shops and a little bakery.

Sunshine Bakery was closed. Becky remembered it only ever opened until lunchtime, and she had just missed it. She could see an elderly woman wiping down the glass display cabinets and a man gathering up steel trays. When the woman caught her eye, she waved, and walked to the door to open it.

Embarrassed, Becky stepped back.

'Have you just missed us? We still have some brown bread if that takes your fancy,' the woman said.

Becky nodded, and followed her into the bakery shop. 'That would be neat, thank you.'

'Are you the American in Regina's house?' the man asked.

'Yes.'

'It's always nice to see new people coming into town. You know our opening hours?' he asked gently.

'Yes, I apologise. I am still trying to get accustomed to the way things are done around here.'

'Don't be worrying. Everybody knows to knock on the window, and you can do the same,' the woman, who introduced herself as Heather, said as she wrapped a loaf of brown bread in brown paper.

'We have a few eclairs left. Would you like to take them home? They are lovely as something sweet after dinner,' Heather said, placing them in a box before Becky had time to say anything.

Becky rummaged in her pockets for money to pay.

'I was told Bella Reilly, I mean Carter, lives near here,' she said.

Heather, who was counting out the change, stopped. 'Poor Bella. She's afraid you're going to tear down Coolnamona House. You're not, are you?'

'I don't know where that idea came from, but I certainly am not. It's such a fine place.'

Heather handed Becky her change. 'It has a special place in Bella's heart; she can't help worrying. You should get to know her. She's some character.'

'I have met her already.'

'Oh that's good,' Heather said, leading Becky to the door, and unlocking it.

'The intercom for the apartment is on the right. I think she's at home,' she said.

Becky stepped out onto the street. She moved her hand to press the intercom, but quickly pulled it away.

What would she say to Bella? Maybe this was a bad idea.

Heather came out to take in the street sign. 'What are you waiting for? Just press the button,' she said, reaching over, and pushing the buzzer before Becky had time to stop her.

'I didn't want to disturb her.'

'Nonsense, girl, she'll love the company. Bella gets fierce lonely at times. Myself and Dan are lucky, we have each other.'

A voice said, 'Hello, who is it?'

'It's the American living in Regina's house here to see you,' Heather said.

Bella told them to wait downstairs.

'The place must be a mess. She doesn't like to be shown up,' Heather said by way of explanation.

When she came downstairs, Bella had a light blue cardigan on over her summer dress.

Heather slipped back inside the shop.

'I'm surprised to see you here. Do you mind if we walk into the little park across the way?' Bella said, leading the way.

Becky followed Bella for a little while, past the herbaceous borders, until she picked a wooden seat overlooking a small pond.

'I didn't know this was here,' Becky said.

'It's not your fine vista of the sea, but it does me. Why did you come this side?'

'I know that letter you gave me is not real.'

Bella did not say anything, but concentrated on the ducks swimming and quacking their way across the pond towards them.

'I usually bring them bread. They like me for that,' she said.

'I'm sorry about your family home and your sister.'

'Are you?' Bella said despondently.

'I thought maybe you would like to come to the house for a visit, and maybe pick something you like, that means a lot to you.'

Bella looked straight ahead. 'They are only things. I miss my family.'

Becky reached over, and gently stroked her wrinkled hand. 'I know you don't know us, but maybe we could become friends.'

Bella pulled her hand away. 'After what I said to you?'

'You were upset.'

'I still am.'

'Oh.'

'It's nice of you to come here.'

'Maybe you could visit us at the house? We're getting a kitchen in at the end of the week, and we will be more ready to receive guests.'

'Is that the kitchen Regina was planning?'

'Yes, the man is honouring the contract.'

'Iris probably said she would kill him if he didn't.'

'Maybe.'

The two of them giggled.

'How about Sunday? I could call down to you after mass,' Bella said.

'What time would that be?'

'I like to go to an early mass, but this Sunday, I will go to the eleven o'clock mass, and call to you after.'

'That sounds good,' Becky said, and she saw a faint smile creep across Bella's lips.

'I'm sorry about the letter. I can get a bit foolish living on my own, and not having a significant other to rein me in.'

'Don't worry, it happens to us all.'

Bella got up. 'Honestly, I don't know why you would pick Coolnamona over New York. If I ever got as far as there, I would never leave.'

Becky laughed, and said she had better get back.

She was a few feet away, when Bella called out to her. 'Thank you for taking the bother to come by, and I'm looking forward to Sunday. Let's pray it's the priest who says the quick mass.'

Becky waved to her, and set off for Coolnamona House, her step and her heart a little lighter.

THIRTEEN

A crash downstairs woke Becky up. She lay on the bed, her heart pounding, listening, afraid of a step on the stairs. Why was this happening? Had trouble followed her here? Her head hurt, and her body tensed as she made out a footfall on the wooden floorboards in the hall followed by the creak of the sitting room door as it was flung open.

Afraid to turn on a light, she attempted to reach for her phone, but couldn't locate it. Slowly, she sat up to look at the old-fashioned alarm clock with the illuminated face on the dressing table. It was three o'clock in the morning.

Gingerly, she put her feet out on the floor, and grabbed her phone, but her clumsy fingers missed, and it fell with a thud. Becky froze. The noise downstairs appeared more muffled now. Gathering all the strength she could muster, Becky moved across the bedroom floor, and listened again at the door. There was another loud crash and the sound of somebody cursing as if the intruder had fallen over the coffee table. She heard the smashing of glass, and thought it must be the vase of roses she had placed on the table earlier. Harnessing her fear to propel herself forward, she pulled the bedroom door back and stepped out on the landing, and shouted, 'The cops are on their way! Get out of my house!'

Her hands shaking, Becky switched on the landing light.

The sitting room door was open, and somebody was rummaging in the cabinet.

'Sadie, is that you?'

'Becks, I can't find the whiskey. Where do you keep your alcohol stash?'

Becky ran down the last few stairs. 'What the fricking hell are you doing?'

'Is there a liquor store open, do you think?'

Becky grabbed Sadie by the elbow. 'I thought there was an intruder.'

'Lighten up, darling. Help me find the whiskey.'

'Sadie, this isn't funny. I thought...' Becky couldn't finish the sentence. She collapsed on the couch, pulling her knees up, and sinking her head into her lap.

'Hey, sweetheart, this is a bit of an overreaction, don't you think?'

'Shut up, Sadie, you know nothing.'

'Hey, hey, easy girl. What's wrong?'

'Quieten down or you will wake Jen,' Becky snapped.

'I'm sorry, Becks. I couldn't sleep, and I came looking for a drink. What's the big deal?'

'Didn't you have enough champagne earlier?'

'I need to drink some more, OK?'

Sadie rummaged in the cabinet again until she found the bottle of whiskey. She poured a measure into a glass, and handed it to Becky. 'Drink up. I think your need is greater than mine.'

Becky took the glass, and gulped the whiskey in one go. She held out her glass for another.

Sadie reluctantly tipped more whiskey into the glass. 'What's wrong? I have never seen you like this,' she said.

Becky didn't say anything.

Sadie sat beside her on the couch. 'Becks, please tell me what's up.'

Becky shook her head. 'I can't.'

'Is this about Hilda?'

'I thought if I came here, I would be able to sort out the shit in my head,' Becky moaned, and turned away. 'I'm afraid of what you might think of me,' she sighed.

Sadie pulled at her friend's shoulder. 'Surely you know me better than that, darling.'

'I'm sorry. I don't know what to think any more,' Becky whispered.

Sadie wrapped her arms around her friend, and hugged her tight. 'You don't have to talk about anything if you don't want. Just know, you're not alone.'

Becky sobbed, garbled words spilling out of her. She gripped Sadie's hands.

'Hey, slow down, darling. Let's do this right,' Sadie said, reaching for the bottle of whiskey, and pouring some more. 'Iris insists whiskey is the best way to start a serious conversation. So shoot, darling,' she said.

Becky dropped her head, and began to sob.

'Darling, you're home. Cry all you like,' Sadie said, putting her arm around her friend's shoulders.

Becky slugged her whiskey before she started to speak, her eyes fixed on the portrait of Regina over the mantelpiece. 'I'm ashamed, Sadie. I don't know where to start.'

'Darling, I'm always on your side. I'm listening. Just start at the beginning,' Sadie whispered, continuing to hold her friend close.

'There was this guy at work. He was only an intern, and he seemed to be constantly at my elbow offering to help, bringing me coffee and asking questions. I thought he was overly pushy, but I put it down to enthusiasm at the start. He never left the office in the evening until Hilda did, and I think she liked that. Jen and I giggled that he was so smarmy, and we ribbed Hilda a bit about him. We all thought he was good for a laugh and quite harmless.'

Becky stopped, tears flowing down her face.

'It was the weekend before Hilda died. She had gone to Boston, and Jen was on a trip to Washington with her school. I needed to catch up on a lot of work so I went into the office. I was there on a Saturday evening when this guy turned up. He said he had been passing and saw the lights and came to see what was wrong. I was annoyed at the doorman for letting him in, and I told him to go home. I remember thinking he was one eager beaver.

'As it got later, I wasn't worried I was in the building on my own. I liked it when the place was quiet. It's when I did my best work.'

Becky paused, and shook her head.

Sadie pushed a bunch of tissues into her hands. 'You don't have to tell me the detail if you don't want,' she said.

Becky turned to her. 'I have to tell you. It's eating me up inside.' Swallowing hard, she continued her story. 'I was on the way out of the building, and going to my car. I was in the elevator. When it stopped at the basement garage, the intern pushed his way in. He must have been waiting for me.'

'Who is this bastard?' Sadie shouted.

Becky stopped. 'I can't say his name.'

'OK, he's a proper bastard anyway. Continue,' Sadie said gently.

'He pushed me against the wall, and pressed the top-floor button, but stopped the elevator between floors. Becky moved closer to Sadie, who gently stroked her hair. 'I had nowhere to go. He caught the bun at the back of my head, and yanked me onto my tiptoes. He said it was time I learned a lesson. I pleaded with him to stop, but that only made him angrier.'

Becky burrowed into Sadie, making her pyjama top damp. 'He snarled in my ear that if I didn't want to be killed, I would' – she stopped to blow her nose on a tissue – 'take it with a smile, and keep my mouth shut later.'

Sadie gripped her friend as tight as she continued.

'He raped me, Sadie, and when he was finished he told me to tidy myself up. As the elevator went down he warned me if I ever said anything, he would find me.'

Sadie gasped in shock. 'Please tell me you called the cops.'

'I don't know how I got to the car. I managed to drive to a hospital in Long Island. My friend, a nurse, did a rape kit. I needed time to think. I wanted to discuss it with Hilda, but she was out of town. The day she came back, I was on the way to tell her when she had the heart attack. I guess after that, I didn't know what to do.'

'Darling, you could have told me.'

'I just needed to get out of Manhattan. I had to take Jen away to keep her safe.'

'And my bull in a china shop routine scared you big time. I'm so sorry, darling,' Sadie said.

Becky doubled up, sobbing. 'What if he comes after me, Sadie, or does something to Jen?'

'Darling, he's not going to find you in Coolnamona. I had the address, and it was still difficult to locate this place. I'm sorry to have scared you so. But what about the cops? Are you going to inform them?'

'It's too late now, I guess.'

'Nonsense, you did the rape kit. Don't let the bastard get away with it.'

Becky stood up. 'I can't talk about this any more. Can we please change the subject? Now, it's your turn. Please tell me why you rushed all the way to Coolnamona.'

Sadie cleared her throat. 'Becks, can I stay a while? I have lost my job and my reputation. My name is mud in

Manhattan legal circles. I badly need some time and space right now.'

'Of course, but whatever has happened, it surely isn't that bad.'

'It's worse. My home was a company lease; I have lost that too.'

'But why? What is behind all this?'

Sadie stretched out her legs, and knocked back some more whiskey. 'I saw irregularities in a client account; millions of dollars had been siphoned off. I brought it to the attention of my boss. She brought it up to the fourth floor, and we were both fired.'

'That can't be right.'

'It's not, but I'm a small fish in a sea of sharks.'

'Can't you lodge a complaint somewhere?'

'Like you did?'

'That's not fair.'

Sadie began picking the broken vase glass from the floor. 'I am ashamed to say they offered me a settlement, and I took it: four million dollars. Mind you, they also gave me three days to leave the company apartment. I had to hand back the company car.'

'You know you can stay here as long as you like.'

'Thank you, but when it is time for me to leave, just say so.'

'I think we both need Coolnamona House now, and we're happy to have you here for as long as you want,' Becky said, holding up her glass. 'To friendship, and being there for each other,' she added.

They clinked, and sipped their whiskey, each caught up in her own thoughts.

After a few minutes, Sadie turned to Becky. 'Thank you. I had nobody else to turn to, especially when my career fell apart.'

'You listened, and I'm grateful for that, but promise me, no more prowling around the house in the dark.'

'Promise,' Sadie said.

Becky curled up on the couch, and put her head on Sadie's shoulder. 'You're the best friend,' she said.

'Right back at you. We're broken, but together that will make us stronger,' Sadie said.

FOURTEEN

Sadie, wearing an old pair of gardening gloves and holding shears, was standing in the hall when Becky came downstairs the next morning.

'What's going on, you guys? It's so early.'

'It's time to attack the front garden, get it café-ready. Jen is helping out too,' Sadie said excitedly.

Becky groaned, and walked back to the kitchen.

Sadie ran after her. 'Embrace the adventure. A perfect distraction for us, and it will be such fun. We can run the café together. I can bake, and well, you can make coffee and do the business side and—'

Becky swivelled around. 'Does it have to be this morning? I don't feel so good.'

'Where is your sense of fun, Becks?'

'Mom, please, it will give us something to do, and we need an incentive to get this place cleaned up.'

'Sounds like I'm outnumbered. What are you doing with those garden shears, Sadie?'

'Waiting for instructions. Brian is helping us out, but he has to pick peas in the back garden first.'

'He's just going to pop back to the restaurant with the peas. Once he returns, we'll get going on the front,' Jen said.

Becky stared at her. 'What about the spiders?'

'Nobody cares, Mom. Can we just get on with it?' Jen said sharply.

'Brian is going to bring back more gloves, and some more shears and a wheelbarrow so we can all pitch in,' Sadie said.

'I don't know what people in the town will make of all this,' Becky said.

Sadie laughed out loud. 'Who cares? As long as they come along for tea and cookies.'

Becky shivered, but Sadie gave her a hug.

'Have your coffee first. Come out when you're ready, and we will put you to work,' Sadie said as she headed out the front door.

Becky sat down at the kitchen table. Hilda always complained she let Sadie boss her too much, and she was right. She got up, and put two slices of brown bread in the toaster, and stood over it waiting for the bread to pop up. She could hear Jen and Sadie chatting loudly at the front of the house. She felt a stab of jealousy that they were so easy in each other's company. Buttering her toast, she was transported back to the Manhattan apartment and one of the last Second Wednesday Club evenings. Hilda was a little cross because Sadie had turned up unannounced, kicked off her heels, and sat on the couch as if she intended to stay for a very long time. She'd hinted that she had plans, but Sadie had blithely ignored her, and continued to chat about nothing in particular.

Hilda had let out a few deep sighs, but Jen loved having Sadie there. Becky had enjoyed seeing her mother squirm a little before storming off in a huff saying she had work to do. Poor Hilda. Neither Sadie nor Jen noticed until ten minutes later when Jen asked where Granny had got to.

'Your mom sure is high-maintenance,' Sadie said, and they had giggled, and opened a bottle of wine.

Now Becky felt the outsider, and it hurt.

When the front door opened, Iris called Becky's name out loud. 'I have joined the gardening group, but we're all waiting for you to tell us what to do,' she said as she walked to the kitchen.

Becky jumped up from her chair, and stood at the sink rinsing her plate and mug.

'Is there something wrong?' Iris asked.

'No, I'll be there in a minute.'

Iris turned on her heel. 'You had better hurry on or your friend will have let all your secrets slip.' She laughed.

Becky leaned against the sink, and Iris moved towards her.

'Don't mind me. I was only having a laugh. Have I put my foot in it?'

Becky pulled a paper towel from the roller, and wiped her hands. 'I'm just being silly.'

'We're all guilty of being silly at times,' Iris said kindly, and continued towards the front door.

Becky kicked off her slippers, and stepped into her shoes before going out to the others. Sadie was using a slash hook to cut a bank of brambles, and Jen was helping Brian pull out a big patch of nettles near the boundary wall.

'This is better than any workout. Have you heard lovely Ben is going to invite us all to dinner in his restaurant soon?' Sadie said as she stopped to rub her back.

'Is he sure? It will be so much work,' Becky said.

Brian, who was tying up refuse sacks full of old cans, said his father wanted to try out different recipes, and he always picked his tasters.

'I prefer it just as an invitation. I don't like the idea of being put to work,' Sadie said.

'Anything Ben cooks is divine. We're honoured,' Iris said

stiffly, and everybody went back to their work. 'There's plenty more to be done. Let's get on with it,' she said, pointing to clumps of weeds on the path.

'Brian says he will be serving up, and Ben will be in the kitchen. It is ideal for a Second Wednesday Club meeting,' Jen said.

Becky shook her head. 'I don't know. I don't think we can match Hilda's Second Wednesday Club, and it might be too soon.'

Jen scowled, and marched off.

Becky went to follow, but Iris put a hand on her shoulder. 'Let me. Sometimes an independent voice can get through to a teenager,' she said as she followed Jen into the house.

Becky took a shovel, and began to hack at a patch of dandelions. 'Such a vibrant colour, and yet so unwelcome,' she grumbled.

Sadie stuck her head out from behind a rose bush where she was tying back loose branches to a bamboo stick. 'Jen just wants to build a bridge between her old and new lives. I can't see how Hilda would have objected. She would have loved a free meal in a restaurant.'

Becky laughed. 'Aren't we all trying to reconcile the old and new life? I bet you never tried to tame a rose bush before.'

Sadie giggled. 'True, except for a stroll through the rose garden, and a delivery from the florist once a month. I don't know why I ever preferred white roses. I think it was to match the decor, which seems so dumb right now.'

Becky threw the dandelions on a heap, and moved further down the path. 'We're never going to get this place looking like the garden in the picture. You know we're only kidding ourselves,' she said.

Sadie followed her. 'Becky, what's wrong? If it's me being here, I can move out. Ask Ben tonight about the Airbnb. I can pay for it.'

Becky shrugged. 'It's not that, Sadie. I'm just tired, I guess.'

'Becky, my life is shit, and that's why I came here. Your life is shit, but you have a lifeboat right here at Coolnamona, if you choose to take part.'

'Very philosophical all of a sudden. I think I preferred the Sadie whose solution to everything was a glass of wine.'

'That Sadie has disappeared.'

'Oh.'

'My problem, not yours,' Sadie said quickly, picking up the shears, and moving on to the apple tree.

'Whoa, not so quickly with the shears,' Ben called out as he came up the path.

'But it's sticking out. Can't we just move it a few feet to the left?'

Ben, who was carrying a tray of takeaway coffees, handed them out. 'Brian said you would need help, and he's right.'

'It's a crazy idea, isn't it?' Becky said.

'No, but why don't you embrace the garden? That's what Regina did. She had a seat around the apple tree where people with takeaway coffees could sit in the shade without the formality of a table, and those who wanted to get to the tables walked across the grass.'

Becky rested her shovel against the rock. 'Do you think this café idea is a bad idea? It's not like I have a choice. I have to start bringing in money somehow.'

Ben shrugged. 'I think if you're wavering, don't do it, but if you really want to set up a café, go ahead. This café was always the most popular in town, not because of the tea and cakes, but because of the view and Regina herself. There is a certain passion required.'

Sadie elbowed Becky. 'I just have to work on her, but we'll get there. Stop trying to dig up the past, and look to the future.'

Ben stared at her. 'Not exactly what I was going to say, but it'll do.'

Jen and Iris returned hand in hand, making Becky feel a slight sting of jealousy.

'Mom, you'll never guess. Iris came up with such an amazing idea. She says the sketches I have done, we should frame them, and put them up in the hall, like an exhibition. "An American in Coolnamona" is what I can call it. It's going to be so great.'

Becky made to say something, but Sadie stepped on her toe.

'This is such fun, and exactly what we need,' she said, and Jen beamed.

Becky took a deep breath. 'Well, let's get working. If we're to open any time soon, we have a lot to do,' she said.

Iris rubbed her hands in delight as Sadie got up on the rock, clapping loudly to get everyone's attention. 'Being bossy is my specialty, so here it is. Brian and Jen, you're in charge of the furniture stored in the back garden shed, and you need to get it sanded down and painted over the next few days. Pick a nice bright colour that will stand out here in the front garden.

'Ben, you go and get us a coffee machine and supplies, and help Becky pick what she needs to get the kitchen up to scratch.

'Iris, you're in charge of the sitting room and hall.'

'But what about the front garden? Aren't we going to have tables here?' Becky asked.

'Darlings, we need to put all our energy into the food and the ambience. We're not made for weeding, so let's get a landscape company in,' Sadie said.

Becky laughed. 'I don't have money for that sort of thing, and I wouldn't know what to tell them to do.'

'Which is why you have me. I may not know a rose from a petunia, but I know how things should look. So...' Sadie stopped, and looked directly at the others. 'Let's get to work.'

Iris stepped forward. 'Apologies if I'm speaking out of turn, but what exactly will you be doing?' she said.

Sadie smiled. 'Painting my nails and micromanaging,' she

said quickly, but she burst out laughing when she saw the faces of the others. 'Oh come on, do any of you really believe that?'

Becky stepped forward. 'Sadie, I can't afford to pay for a landscaping company.'

Sadie put her arm around her friend. 'You have taken me in when I needed it most. This is the least I can do, along with getting old Regina cleaned up, and micromanaging of course. Now, everybody knows what they have to do, so let's get going.'

Ben clapped, and said Sadie should have a job on the town council, before turning to Becky. 'I can bring you to the whole-saler now, if you like.'

Becky hesitated.

Sadie pulled her aside. 'I have revved some money to you. Just go and buy what we need.'

'But I can't keep taking your money.'

Sadie squeezed her arm. 'It's doing me good seeing my money being used like this. Indulge me, please.'

'Are you OK, Sadie?'

'Perfectly sane if that is what you mean. Now hurry up because that man has to get back to his kitchen by early after-noon so he can work on the menu for tonight.'

When Becky hesitated, Sadie put her hand up. 'Don't worry. We're all good here,' she said.

'We will be back before three,' Ben said as he led the way down the path. Becky grabbed her phone from the hall table and followed, glad to be getting away from Coolnamona House for a while.

FIFTEEN

'What do you mean, you have invited Bella into the house? Regina would not have approved at all,' Iris said, her voice strained and cross.

Becky poured a mug of coffee, and handed it to Iris, hoping it would disturb her flow.

'You know you're inviting the snake on top of us. You'll have to hide everything away. Mark my words. She will bring a big bag, and steal all you have.'

Becky pushed the sugar bowl towards Iris, who shovelled three spoons into her coffee.

'You're making me overload with sugar with this news.'

'She strikes me as a lonely old woman, and I don't see anything wrong in inviting her to this house. Could you by any chance have misjudged Bella?'

'After what she tried to do, this is madness,' Iris retorted.

Becky wanted to tell Iris it was none of her business, but instead she pushed a plate of homemade cookies in her direction. Iris took one, and bit in to it.

'Nice, did you make these?'

'I did,' Sadie said as she came in the door from the garden.

'Good old-fashioned American choc chip cookies. My grand-ma's recipe.'

'Well, I'm a fan. Be sure to have these in the café,' Iris said.

'I just do the baking to earn my keep around here.' Sadie laughed.

Iris turned to her. 'Have you heard who's coming for tea on Sunday?'

Sadie hesitated. 'It's none of my business, I'm only a guest in this house.'

'I realise I'm being an interfering busybody...' Iris paused, but when nobody interrupted to protest, she continued, 'But I'm worried, Becky, you're being too kind, and it will come back to bite you.'

'Why don't you come along on Sunday as well?' Becky said quickly.

'Bella won't want me here.'

Becky took a sip of her coffee before slowly replacing her mug on the table. 'It's time we put all this animosity between the two of you to bed. Bella, I'm sure, will be on her best behaviour, and I know you won't let the side down.'

Iris pushed her mug further in towards the middle of the table.

'I think it's too much to ask, and I respectfully decline your kind invitation. I must be getting on,' she said.

Iris had just left when Jen hurtled down the stairs.

'Where's Iris? I am supposed to go out on her boat this morning. We're hoping to sketch together.'

'She left. She wasn't happy about me inviting Bella for tea on Sunday.'

'Didn't you invite Iris?'

'Of course I did, but that seemed to do more harm than good,' Becky said.

Sadie reached over, and took the remainder of Iris's choc chip cookie from her plate. 'The ladies around here are so sensitive. In Manhattan, we would just slug it out on the day,' she remarked.

'Mom, go after Iris,' Jen pleaded.

'And say what exactly?'

'I don't know, but I got a day off the restaurant specially for this trip, and I don't want to spend it cleaning up this place, which is all we seem to do around here.'

Becky didn't answer, but instead walked out the front with her coffee. She sat on the rock looking out over Orchid Bay.

She had solved one problem, and created another. Iris had been a constant in their lives since they had arrived, and she couldn't bear if they weren't friends. Jen adored her, and she suspected Iris had stepped into the shoes left vacant by Hilda.

Hilda always said that Jen needed the guiding hand of an older female figure and being her grandmother was her most important job on earth.

'I did a good job with you, sweet Becks; we must do the same for Jen,' she always said.

When the gate sounded, she made to get up, but Iris called out to her.

'Stay where you are, Becky. I will come sit beside you.'

Becky moved over on the rock to make room. 'I have made an ass of myself. I shouldn't have walked out like that, and I have to stop preaching. This isn't Regina's house any more, and I have to respect that,' Iris said in such a rush that she was almost out of breath when she was finished.

'It's OK,' Becky said quietly.

Iris slapped her hands on her knees. 'It's not OK. I have to respect you as the new owner of Coolnamona House, and quit the "Regina wouldn't have done this" nonsense.'

'Maybe you do, but I know you two were good friends.'

'The best.'

'That is probably why you and Bella are at loggerheads. You replaced her in Regina's life.'

'I never thought of it that way.'

'Will you come on Sunday? It's only some tea or coffee and Sadie's cookies in the sitting room.'

'I suppose I could drop in. Who knows? Bella might be on her best behaviour. We might actually get on.'

'Did you know her when she lived at Coolnamona House?'

'No, but I have heard they did everything together. Back then, Regina and Bella didn't need to talk to anyone else. They had the café and their dress designing.' Iris picked at a bloom on the white butterfly bush nearby as she continued. 'From what I have heard, one morning Bella suddenly left, and the café wasn't open.'

'What exactly happened?'

'Regina never spoke directly about it. She hinted Bella had done something that was unforgivable, but she would never elaborate. I tried a few times to be a sort of peacemaker, but Regina wouldn't budge down through the years.'

'It's all such a long time ago, Iris. Maybe it's time to build a bridge.'

'Possibly, but first I would like to bring the three of you out in my boat. It is a beautiful day to sail around Orchid Bay, and I thought Jen and I could get some sketching done. She can draw Coolnamona House in all its splendour overlooking the bay. The terrace looks magnificent from the sea.'

Becky dithered.

'You think I'm mad, and you're worried I only have a little tub, and I will put you all in danger.'

Becky blushed.

Iris tugged her arm. 'Come over this side,' she instructed, guiding Becky to the right rock, and pointing down to the harbour.

'Do you see the yacht with the blue and white flag?'

'Yes.'

'There she is. I have a rowing boat as well. I waved to you a while back from the little boat.'

'I didn't realise that was you.'

'I like the rowing boat. The yacht is a lot of bother to take out on the water, but for a small group it's ideal. You're wondering how someone like me owns a yacht, aren't you?'

'Yeah, I think I am.'

'My husband loved to sail, and I couldn't bear to get rid of it when he died about twenty years ago. It's why I came to live here in Orchid Bay. This was our holiday home. I moved here permanently, and keep the yacht and rowing boat at the harbour. When I came here, I was younger and fitter. These days, I have a local lad who helps me bring out the yacht, and pushes the rowing boat out to sea for me. I assure you, you will be perfectly safe.'

'I wasn't thinking anything else.'

'Of course you were, and why not?' Iris laughed as she made her way back to the side door.

'I'll call back in an hour, and tell Ms Manhattan to wear her flats and sensible clothes for going on the high seas. Even on a warm day, it can get cold out on the Irish Sea.'

An hour later, they were sitting on the flat rock waiting for Iris when she appeared through the side door wearing bright white palazzo trousers and a striped blue and white top along with a straw hat and sunglasses. She was carrying a large artist's pad.

'Please tell me we are driving down to the harbour. I have this picnic basket and a bottle of bubbly,' Sadie said.

Iris looked at Becky. 'When she puts it like that, I'm happy to offer Ms Manhattan a ride. You guys follow us,' Iris said.

They all piled in the cars, and drove around the long way towards the harbour. They parked as near as possible to the jetty, and Iris led the way to her yacht, where a man, his hands in his pockets, was waiting.

'Danny, these are the Yanks I have been telling you about. We will go out far enough to be able to get a full view of the harbour, and a good gawk of Seaview Terrace.'

Jen skipped through the yacht, which had two cabins and a bathroom, and a wide deck where seating had been arranged. Iris offered everyone except Jen a beer as Danny took the wheel and manoeuvred out of the harbour.

'It's not very fancy, but we always loved this boat. There is something special about being on the sea,' Iris said.

Danny called out that he was dropping anchor.

'You ladies who like champagne in the afternoon can have your drink, while Jen and I get going on our sketching,' Iris said.

Becky let Sadie open the champagne, and they sat back with their glasses enjoying the cool sea breeze and the sunshine on their faces. After a little while, Becky changed places to be beside Jen. She quickly moved her pastel stick over the sketch pad as she drew Seaview Terrace, where Coolnamona House stood proud. From here, Becky thought the house looked beautiful and imposing, and there was no hint of all the work that still needed to be done to it.

'Pretty impressive, don't you think?' Iris said, pointing to Jen's sketch.

'Can I please bring it home and frame it?' Becky asked, but Jen made a face, and said it wasn't good enough.

'It's just a quick sketch, nothing special. It needs more work,' she said.

Sadie swiped at Jen's head. 'Let your mother revel in your talent, darling. It makes her happy.'

'All right, you can keep it,' Jen murmured.

Iris disappeared downstairs, and came back with another bottle of champagne. 'Now, let's toast the beauty of Orchid Bay,' she said.

'Not for Jen,' Becky said.

'She can have a sip just for the toast,' Iris said, and Becky relented.

Iris raised her glass. 'To your time in Ireland and the beautiful Orchid Bay,' she said, and they all clinked glasses.

Jen sipped the champagne, and grimaced. 'Euww, champagne is gross,' she said, and they all laughed.

'Worked like a charm,' Iris whispered to Becky, who nodded, and grinned.

Iris and Jen went back to their sketching while Sadie and Becky moved to the other end of the boat.

'It feels so good out here,' Sadie said.

'Far from the madding crowd.'

'I so needed this, Becks.'

'So did I,' she said.

Iris called out to Danny to turn for home. They all sat engrossed in their own thoughts as the yacht bobbed across the waves towards Orchid Bay harbour.

SIXTEEN

Becky, unable to sleep, was up before seven on Sunday morning. She pulled on a hoodie and jeans, and slipped out the front door. Standing out in the front garden, she stood still as a robin landed on the top branch of the butterfly bush, and let out a throaty melody. Soon, other birds joined in. She closed her eyes, and twirled slowly around letting the birdsong take over. Staggering to a halt, she tiptoed through the garden and out onto the lane. It was a crisp, dry morning. From here, the sound of the waves as they gently rolled to shore at Orchid Bay drifted through the air.

Heading down the steep path to the harbour, she thought this was the best time at Coolnamona, when she could stop and stare, and not worry about anything in particular. She had told Sadie about the attack, and she wasn't entirely sure how she felt about that. Sadie was also taking over the setting up of the café, and Becky felt overwhelmed. For now, she needed to let her brain rest, and trust that they were safe. In time, she could heal, but she was still so angry at herself that the creep who attacked her had reduced her to a shivering wreck. Waves of anger rose through her, and she set off walking quickly to try and shake it off.

At the shingle beach, she gathered up a fistful of stones and threw them all together in the water.

'Whoa, you'll have the fish running for cover,' Ben said as he came up behind her.

Becky twisted around to find him, his earphones in, running on the spot. 'You jog this early in the morning?'

'In the summer it's the best time of the day. The only people I meet are the fishermen bringing in their catch, which means I get first choice.' He stopped, and scrutinised Becky closely. 'Is there something wrong?'

'Maybe. I was just searching for some quiet time.'

He took a step back, and raised his hands. 'I apologise. It's none of my business, but if I can help...'

'It's not something I can talk about.'

'Well, If you need a break, I have a flask of coffee. I'll be circling back to the sea café outside deck in about ten minutes. They don't open until much later, so we can sit, have my really good brew, and we can talk about the weather,' he said as he took off across the beach. She watched him leave. It would be so nice to linger over a coffee with Ben, but she couldn't, not just now.

Her head down, she started the long walk up the steep hill to Coolnamona House.

This morning she didn't really want to talk to anybody, not even to Ben. She needed to get the house ready for Bella's visit, and she may have to bake the cookies if Sadie didn't surface on time.

When she got in the front door, Becky heard the sound of trays being put in the oven and Sadie, muttering to herself, banging the oven doors shut.

'Easy, those ovens are new. Why are you up so early?' Becky said, checking the oven doors.

'Too much going around in my head,' Sadie said with resignation.

Becky, yawning, sat down at the table. 'I could have followed the recipe, made the cookies.'

Sadie tipped a bag of chocolate chips into her next mix. 'I'll go mad if I sit around doing nothing. This takes my mind off all the bad times. We need a three-tier cake stand for presentation. Is there one in the house?'

'Yeah, somewhere. There are spare china sets and crockery in an old bedroom. I can get Jen to have a look later.'

Sadie wrapped her choc chip mix in cellophane, and put it in the fridge. She pulled down another steel bowl.

'You're not making more, are you?'

'I thought white chocolate and cranberry. Ben gave me some cranberries.'

'Do we need two flavours? Bella will hardly eat that much,' Becky said.

'We can't have this woman thinking we can only do choc chip cookies. We need to impress her. She's coming back to her ancestral home. It's a big deal.'

'I just hope she behaves.'

'I have a feeling she'll be a sweetheart. She's not going to turn nasty until she has us in her pocket.'

'Sadie, you're too suspicious.'

'OK, I have trust issues,' Sadie said, taking the choc chip dough from the fridge and beginning to roll it out using an empty wine bottle.

'Darling, you need to buy a rolling pin,' she said, and Becky giggled.

'And you should leave your cookie dough longer to chill,' she said.

When Sadie had cut out the shapes, and placed them on a tray, Becky put them in the oven, and gently closed the doors.

She told Sadie to sit down, and grabbing a bottle of prosecco from the wine rack, she opened it.

'We have to wait for the other dough to chill. We might as well sit and have a little bubbly,' she said.

'Bubbly is not going to solve either of our problems, and there's hardly anything to celebrate,' Sadie said.

'No, but it will help us cope, and that's all we can hope for right now.'

'Being here is doing me good. I realise there are nice people and some very handsome men in the world too. It's just going to take time. Pity Ben's heart is taken,' Sadie said.

'He's still so in love with his dead wife. They were childhood sweethearts.'

'I was talking about you.'

'What do you mean?'

'I have seen the way you look at him, and the way he looks at you. It's so sweet.'

'Don't be silly, Sadie,' Becky said a bit too quickly.

'I'm just saying it's good, that's all. It restores my faith, and all that.' She refilled their glasses. 'I have been thinking about your situation, Becky. All the right tests were done in hospital. You have the evidence. When you feel stronger, you can go after the bastard who attacked you.'

Becky went to the fridge, and checked on the dough. 'I don't want to talk about it Sadie, please,' she snapped.

'Maybe not today, but eventually you're going to have to confront it, and decide what you're going to do.'

Becky slapped the table hard with her right hand. 'Please, Sadie, I love you, but this is something I have to handle on my own,' she said firmly, before going off to tidy up the sitting room.

Sadie called out to her as she left. 'You're not on your own, darling. I'm with you, and every woman we know will also be behind you.'

Becky mumbled thank you, before disappearing down the hall.

'Whenever you want to talk more, I'm here,' Sadie said louder.

Becky whipped around. 'I know. Now can we please get ready for our guest. Considering we are trying to make an impression, are we going to use mugs?' she said in a desperate attempt to turn the conversation.

'I saw a lovely china tea-set. I'll wash it and it will give us a fancy edge,' Sadie said.

They both jumped when there was a knock at the back door.

'I know I'm early, but I knew you two were up and about, and I thought you might need some help,' Iris said as she bustled in.

'I was just debating whether we should use the tea-set in the top cupboard,' Becky said.

Iris beamed with delight. 'Get rid of the goddamn awful mugs. A beverage is always better from a nice china cup.'

Becky stood on a chair, took the cups and saucers down, and handed them to Iris.

'I don't know what Bella will think of this set. It was Regina's favourite,' Iris said, carefully placing the cups and saucers in the sink.

'What intrigue! It's just a few cups and saucers.' Sadie laughed.

Iris guffawed out loud. 'Don't you know every china set has a history? And this one had a special place in the Reilly family.'

'Of course it did. Why am I not surprised?' Sadie said.

'Don't you want to hear the story?'

'Go on, we have plenty of time, and it's not as if we have anything else to be doing,' Sadie said as she made some tea, and plonked some mugs on the table.

Iris, ignoring Sadie's barbed tone, smiled sweetly.

'I don't mind slumming it with a mug, dear. Now let me tell you about this china tea-set.'

Becky picked up one of the cups which was decorated in blue-grey leaves with a rim of gold. 'Very stylish.'

'Regina got it as a wedding present. It was her prized possession. She never used it, but had it on display in her china cabinet in the sitting room. It was the good set that was never used, but twice a year, Regina took it down, and washed it in warm soapy water, taking care to buff it dry before putting it back in the cabinet.

'All very good, but Bella will be here shortly,' Sadie said.

'Another time, I guess,' Iris said, looking a bit put out as the others scuttled off to get the last jobs done.

Before noon, Bella made her way up the front steps. She was wearing a purple suit with a pearl choker at her neck.

'Have I come too early? I have been very bold, and skipped mass. It's the old priest and he takes an age, so I thought strike me down with lightning, but I would just prefer the company of these nice American women and even Iris Jones.'

'We're all ready. So nice of you to come,' Becky said.

She led the way into the sitting room, where Iris and Sadie were sitting on the armchairs at the fireplace.

Taking in the coffee table where the china tea-set was laid out beside a cake stand full of fresh cookies, Bella beamed with delight.

'It's like the good old days of the café when the dining room was almost like a snug.'

Bella chose Earl Grey tea, and Becky went off to make a pot. Jen sneaked down the stairs, and into the kitchen beside her.

'You don't need me here, do you?' she asked.

'Why? Where do you have to be at this hour of the day?'

'Brian has the day off, so we're going into the city.'

Becky sighed. 'Come in, and spend a little time.'

'Mom, I don't even know this woman, give me a break.'

Becky swung around. 'Why so cross? And what is wrong with showing some manners?'

Jen scowled, and said she had to get dressed.

'Please say hello before you go,' Becky said stiffly, as she made her way back to the sitting room.

'Of course.'

Becky wanted to say it wasn't good enough, but she bit her lip.

Bella didn't take milk or sugar in her tea. 'I don't want to spoil the Earl Grey. An ordinary tea might be different,' she said as she watched Iris heap three spoons of sugar and a slosh of milk into her cup. 'I see you have the sugar bowl out. I presume Iris has told you the story.'

'We await that pleasure,' Sadie said.

'Those were the days when Regina had a heart,' Bella said, cocking an eye towards the portrait.

In an effort to steer her away from anything controversial, Becky asked Bella about the café.

'When I was involved, it really was one of the best times of my life. Coolnamona House was always buzzing. It was the centre of the village, and everybody dropped in for a cuppa. I made my special scones every morning, and Regina made an apple cake like no other. We even got a mention in one of the national newspapers once, and a few celebrities from time to time who were visiting Orchid Bay walked up the hill to spend a bit of time taking in the sea view over a cuppa.

'Before the café, people rarely walked up the hill from Orchid Bay, and sure, look at it now, sometimes you can't get through Main Street, there are so many visitors about.'

'The café sounds like a lot of fun,' Sadie said.

Bella laughed. 'It was a lot of bloody hard work, but I think it kept us young. There's nothing worse than having a whole day stretching ahead, and only yourself for company.'

They all fell silent for a while until Iris reached for a cookie, picking a cranberry and white chocolate biscuit. She bit in, and smacked her lips. 'Bella, these cookies are delish. You should try one.'

Bella chose a choc chip cookie, and broke it in half. 'They are a little large for me, but they look very tasty,' she said.

Sadie and Becky watched as she at first nibbled at the biscuit, but then took a bigger bite.

After she placed the cookie on the saucer to the side of her cup, she looked from one woman to the other. 'I am normally incredibly fussy. I never eat anyone else's baking, even from the bakery below where I live, but I have to say I have never tasted a biscuit as good as this one.'

Sadie clapped in excitement.

Bella sipped her tea, before continuing. 'In fact, I would hazard a guess that you could sell a lot of these biscuits if you put your mind to it,' she said.

'Maybe, but it's just a hobby, and a very good way of dealing with stress at the moment,' Sadie muttered.

'You have a talent. Use it, girl.' Iris guffawed.

Trying to move the spotlight from Sadie, who she knew didn't want to face a cross-examination about her sources of stress, Becky said she would like to try Bella's scones.

'I would be delighted to drop some down to you. I bake fresh every morning,' Bella said.

At that moment, Jen stuck her head in the door, calling out hello and goodbye very quickly.

Becky jumped up, and followed her to the front door. 'What was that, young lady?'

Jen shrugged her shoulders. 'There's no satisfying you, Mom. I might be late back.'

'Hang on, I thought you and Brian had work at the restaurant tonight.'

'We got time off. Now I have to dip,' Jen said, bolting down the path.

'That is a lady in a rush. It must be a young man who has caught her attention,' Bella said as Becky rejoined them in the sitting room.

Iris made polite conversation, but after forty minutes deliberately put down her cup and saucer on the coffee table, and said she had to go.

'I hope you don't consider me rude, but the light is so good today, I have to get out and paint,' she said.

Surprised, Becky asked could she not stay longer.

'I think you may be able to talk more freely without me. The situation suits all of us,' Iris said.

Turning to Bella, she addressed her directly. 'I have enjoyed talking to you, Bella. I hope relations from now on can be cordial.'

Bella smiled sweetly. 'Let's see how we go, Iris Jones. I have learned never to expect too much.'

Iris bowed regally, and said she had to rush off. 'The light is so important to us artists, and today is such a good day,' she said, sweeping out of the sitting room.

Sadie slipped out of the room with her, and Becky watched the two of them chatting as they walked down the garden path.

'It looks like it's just the two of us. Maybe this is what you want,' Bella said softly.

'I didn't engineer it, but I would like if we could have a chat without any of the legal threats.'

Bella put down her cup and saucer, and Becky feared she was getting ready to leave.

'I am exhausted by all the gossip around Coolnamona House. Are you really going ahead with the café?'

'Yes, we plan to open next week.'

'I look forward to sitting in the café once again,' Bella said wistfully.

Becky pointed to the portrait. 'Your sister, I think, was a powerhouse, but she seems to have been so lonely in her last years.'

'Yes, but there is nothing unusual about that. You won't have experienced it yet, but we're all lonely in our twilight years, even when we're surrounded by family. Loneliness is the affliction of the old, after all.'

'Could I ask you a little about Regina?'

'Haven't you heard enough about the two of us? It's all quite boring. Regina was a woman who could hold a grudge for a long time. There were so many occasions I banged on the front door with my umbrella, and the only words she said to me were "go to hell".

'The good lady would be turning in her grave to think I was sitting here, sipping tea from her best tea-set in her favourite room. You know the two of us at one time used to sit in this very room, and put the world to rights. It was my favourite time of the day. Coming back here has been great, but also painful and exhilarating.'

'This house is so beautiful; every room is special.'

Bella put her head back, and laughed. 'Special like the Reillys.'

'I was told Regina wrote a lot of letters, but I have only found one,' Becky said.

'I'm surprised you found any. Regina spent the whole time writing letters. To, well, I'm not going to say; that was her business. But as far as I know she destroyed them soon afterwards, threw them in behind the fire. She said in years to come she didn't want people reading her ramblings.' Bella stood up. 'I have said too much. I need to get along. Thank you, Becky, for your hospitality and your kindness. I don't know if we will ever be bosom pals, but this is a good first step.'

Becky stood up. 'I know you love this house, Bella, and I was wondering is there anything from here you would like to take back to your place?'

'That is very kind, but I doubt you mean the portrait of my sister over the mantelpiece.'

'That portrait is part of Coolnamona House.'

'I know. They never got a portrait of me done. I had already been banished from the family by our mother by then, so I missed my chance. I'm a few years older than Regina. We had an artist staying here at the house, and this is how he paid for his lodgings. My sin was falling in love, which sounds rather ridiculous now.'

Becky moved from one foot to the other, not sure what was going to happen next.

'There's nothing here, Becky, that I want or need, but maybe let me come and visit again some time. I could bring scones. Ye can't be eating those cookies all the time.'

'I would like that, and I am glad we have had a chance to talk.'

'Me too, thank you.'

She was in the hall when Becky called her back.

'Bella, there's a lot of jewellery upstairs, necklaces in velvet boxes, really beautiful pieces. Maybe one has meaning for you. I would be happy to gift one to you.'

'Regina would not like me to be wearing her jewellery. I couldn't possibly. All is changed now, and that jewellery was never meant for me. It's all yours now. Your Jen, in time, may appreciate it.'

Becky saw Bella's lip quiver, and she wanted to drag her

upstairs, and make her pick a piece, but she knew she couldn't do that.

Bella reached over, and kissed Becky on the cheek. Becky felt a rush of warmth to the old lady and hoped that this was the start of some sort of friendship between them.

'This visit has meant so much to me,' Bella said before heading down the front path, stopping at the rock on the way to stand, and look out over Orchid Bay.

SEVENTEEN

Becky was in the sitting room snoozing on the couch when Sadie returned. She jumped when Sadie spoke.

'Have you no respect for when somebody is napping?' she asked, pretending to be annoyed. She smiled at her friend. 'I think our little tea party went well, don't you?'

'Yes, nobody shouted, and nobody was insulted. That's a plus, I guess. Enough of that. I've an idea about the painting I want to share with you.'

'You're not going to suggest I sell it, are you?'

'No, I have enough demons at the moment without Regina haunting me as well.' Sadie sat on the couch, her eyes on the portrait. 'I don't know an awful lot about art, but that painting looks plain grubby. You say that's a pink dress, but from here it looks grey.'

'I know, but I don't have that kind of money right now to get it professionally cleaned.'

'Surely we can do something. Maybe give it a wipe with a damp cloth or at least dust it off?'

'Wouldn't we damage it?'

'Let's try a sample,' Sadie said, jumping up, and darting to the kitchen, where she put a clean cloth under the hot tap, before squeezing the water out.

'It's an oil painting, not a watercolour. What's the worst that could happen?' Sadie said.

Becky looked uncertain. 'I'm not so sure. If I as much as move that painting, I feel Regina will definitely haunt me.'

Sadie reached up, and lightly pulled the cloth over a corner of the canvas. 'Wow, look at the dirt,' she said, dragging the cloth down the side of the gown's skirt.

'Sadie, I'm so worried. We should stop,' Becky said.

'Live a little dangerously, darling. I have a delicate touch.'

Becky pulled up the window frames to let a breeze through the room as Sadie brought over a stool to reach higher up.

'Please don't touch her face. I'm sick to my stomach that there will be a big wet spot on her cheeks that we can't dry.'

'That's what hair dryers are for.'

'Shit, Sadie, stop, I can't stand this,' Becky said, kicking the stool so Sadie jumped off.

'I get the impression you don't trust me, but look at the results, sensational. Imagine if it was professionally cleaned,' Sadie said.

'That's not likely to happen in my lifetime.'

'You're not charging me rent, and I would like to help. I will arrange for it to be taken away to be cleaned.'

'It will cost a fortune.'

'And I have a fortune, darling. You have been so good to me, Becks. Why don't you let me pay for the professional cleaning of the old lady in the picture?'

Becky giggled. 'Do you mean it?'

'I have bucks and nothing at the moment to spend it on, so it will be my pleasure, and I am going to be paying my way around here, starting with rent.'

'You don't have to do that. Bringing Regina back to life is more than enough,' Becky said.

Sadie pouted. 'I'm not altogether sure if we want that exactly, considering what we've heard about her. Come on, help me get this work of art off the wall. I expect to have found somebody to collect it by the morning.'

Becky and Sadie eased the painting down, and were about to carry it to the hall when Sadie appeared to change her mind. 'Can we finish this later? I'm suddenly so tired. I'm not a natural for the early morning club,' she said, helping Becky lean the painting against the wall in the hall.

When Sadie left, Becky wondered what was wrong with her friend, but she was at the same time glad to be on her own. She got old newspaper sheets and placed them about the mantelpiece and got the tin of dragonfly-blue paint.

She had seen a small room in a magazine painted this colour, and she had ordered the paint online. Iris said she should have shopped local, and nobody in the area would thank her for putting the Coolnamona hardware store out of business.

'How will they know if you don't tell them?' Becky said.

Iris had waltzed off in a huff making Becky and Jen giggle. It was a fun night painting the walls, she thought, and they had ordered pizza on Just Eat, which Jen said was probably against the law in Coolnamona too.

She should clean down the chimney breast, but she couldn't be bothered. Pulling in Ben's stepladder from the back garden, she started at the top, and worked slowly downwards. She had the top half of the chimney breast done when she decided to take a break. Carefully, she moved down one step on the stepladder, but was distracted when Ronnie, the labrador, panting and wagging his tail, ran into the house. Losing her balance, she pushed against the wall to save herself from falling, as Maisie knocked on the open front door.

'I'm so sorry. Ronnie is cheeky. He automatically thinks people will love him.' There was a crash as the dog's tail knocked a candle and its holder from the coffee table. 'I do apologise. That tail of his can be lethal. I don't have a coffee table in my house for that reason,' Maisie said as she scooted the dog out into the front garden.

'It's all right. It's not broken,' Becky said as she picked up the candle from the floor.

'Oh my God, what have you done to the painting?' Maisie shrieked.

Becky looked at her in alarm.

'Oh shit, it's leaning against the wall in the hall,' Becky said, getting to the door in two strides.

The dog was sitting on the front step, the painting untouched.

Relief washed over Becky as Maisie came up behind her.

'You're not getting rid of it, are you?'

Becky shook her head. 'No, nothing like that. I'm just painting the chimney breast.'

'Bella will take it off your hands, she will.'

'But I'm not getting rid of it. Is there something you wanted?'

Maisie looked taken aback. 'Can't a neighbour drop in, or do I need an invitation to tea?'

'Of course not. I just got a fright. I would never forgive myself if that painting got damaged.'

'I brought you some of my scones,' Maisie said, handing over a basket with a tea-towel covering the baked goods.

'That is so kind of you.'

'Well, I thought Bella surely offered to bake some for you, so I thought I would get in before her. You'll need someone to provide the scones if you open up the café.'

Becky snorted. 'We've not decided on a menu yet.'

Maisie tapped her lightly on the arm. 'If you say so. Now, I must be off.'

'Do stay. I was going to take a break anyway and have some coffee,' Becky said, ushering Maisie into the kitchen.

'Oh, I hadn't seen the new kitchen. Very nice. But then Regina always had very good taste,' she said, sitting down at the table.

Becky chose to ignore the dig, and switched on the kettle.

'Are you a mug or teacup person?' she asked.

'Oh, don't fuss over me, I'll drink from a beaker,' Maisie said, reaching out to tidy up a pile of napkins on the table. 'I have never seen so many napkins,' she said pointedly.

Becky made a mug of instant coffee, and handed it to Maisie. She pushed a plate of cookies towards her.

'I have heard about these biscuits,' Maisie said, breaking off a small piece, and putting it in her mouth. 'Mmm, everything they said is true. Delicious. Your Sadie has a talent.'

Becky smiled. 'Can I wrap up some for you to take home?'

'Oh, that would be lovely. Can I have one of each flavour?'

'Of course,' Becky said, grabbing a small box and piling the cookies in.

Maisie stood up. 'I suppose that's my cue to leave. Thank you, Becky, and let me know how you like the scones,' she said, taking the box and making her way down the hall where Ronnie was lying out on the wooden floor fast asleep.

Becky held onto the painting before they woke up the dog, and got him out the door.

Maisie was an awful busybody, but Becky thought – maybe she was a fool to think it – there was also something quite endearing about her too. Iris would tell her she was an idiot, but she couldn't dislike Maisie Ryan.

Afraid for the painting if she left it in the hall any longer, and with no date or time for the collection, she decided to quickly finish the chimney breast so she could get the portrait back up there as soon as possible.

An hour later, she was tidying away her painting equipment and the old newspaper, when Sadie returned.

'I have a recommendation for somebody who can clean the painting, but he's on holiday and won't be back until next month,' she said.

'This wall should be dry soon. We can get the painting back up then.'

'Looking good,' Sadie said.

'Did it help talking with Iris?'

'OK, so I slipped out to her place; did me better than any nap. We had a laugh, and we saw Maisie come in here, so we drank, and laughed some more.'

'Maisie is harmless. I think she's lonely.'

Sadie laughed out loud. 'Now that you have saved Bella, you've picked another wounded chicken to look after.'

'Unkind.'

'We all love you for it, Becks. Now let's get this painting back in place before it falls over. I nearly crashed into it when I came in the front door.'

'I'm not sure if the wall is fully dry.'

'If we ease it up and get it in place, it won't matter much if the wall is still a bit damp.'

Reluctantly, Becky went to the hall, and made to pick up her side of the painting, but she lost her grip, and it slipped to the floor.

'Easy, what happened?' Sadie said, picking up the painting which had fallen over, landing on its front.

'Oh shit, have I damaged it? Take a look and tell me how bad it is.'

'If I didn't know better, I would have thought this place has got under your skin, and Regina has got inside your head,' Sadie murmured as she carefully picked the painting from the floor, and stood it back up against the wall.

'Face intact, dress intact. Hell, what is this?' Sadie said, bending down to peer at one side of the painting.

'Shit, I knew it. How bad is it?' Becky pleaded, her eyes clenched shut because she couldn't bear it if she had done anything to the portrait of Regina.

'You'll need to help me with this,' Sadie said.

Becky opened her eyes to see Sadie attempting to tug at a piece of paper from underneath the frame.

'What is it?'

'I don't know. The knock must have dislodged it. It's some sort of envelope, I think.'

'Careful, we don't want to break the frame.'

'It's lodged between the canvas and the backing at the corner.'

Becky gently eased the envelope through a slit. She was excited but also reluctant and wary of opening up the past. This was Regina's secret and she felt a little nervous of it.

'Oh go on, open it. What a mystery! Finally some excitement at Coolnamona House.'

Becky turned the envelope over in her hands. 'I don't know. This doesn't feel right somehow.'

Sadie made a grab for the envelope, but Becky swung away from her.

'Just give me a bit of time. This has been a helluva day. I'd like to have a think about it.'

Sadie sighed loudly. 'Always the spoilsport. What is there to think about?'

'I don't know. It's a letter. It just feels weird.'

'Becky, you're overthinking it. Can we at least pour a whiskey?'

Sadie carried the bottle of whiskey to the kitchen, where she sloshed a measure into two mugs. They sat at the table eyeing the envelope, where Becky had left it propped against a glass.

'Just give me a little time,' she said.

Sadie squeezed her hand. 'Take all the time in the world, darling. No pressure.'

EIGHTEEN

Becky didn't know what she should do with the envelope. She went upstairs to her bedroom, and sat at the dressing table. She didn't know why, but here, surrounded by all the little things that mattered to Regina, she felt at home. When she was young, she used to go into Hilda's bedroom and sit at her dressing table, which was just as messy as this one. She loved to open the top drawer where Hilda kept her jewellery. There was one piece which she tried on every time. It was a silver chain interspersed with little pearls with a single large pear-shaped amethyst stone. Becky liked to hold up the amethyst necklace high, and gently move the chain across her fingers so the big rock swung, flashing in the sunlight. On her eighteenth birthday, when Hilda invited her to pick a piece of jewellery for herself from the drawer, Becky had chosen the amethyst. Hilda seemed pleased with her choice, and told her she must keep it and give it to her daughter one day. It was the only piece of jewellery she had brought to Ireland from Hilda's collection.

She was being silly and reticent about the letter, when she owned everything in this house, but she knew it was because she felt the soul of Regina in every room. The envelope may have been left there by the artist, but she doubted it very much. It was ridiculous to procrastinate like this. She stole downstairs, hoping Sadie wouldn't hear her.

Picking up the envelope from the kitchen table, she went into the sitting room, and sat on the velvet sofa within sight of the painting. Carefully, she eased the envelope open. A number of different coloured notes fell out as she pulled what appeared to be a letter from the envelope.

Gathering up the notes, she placed them on the sofa cushion while she opened the two-page letter to read it.

My Darling Laura,

I have wrestled with whether to compile these letters or notes for you. Words are only words on a page, after all. I need to reach into your heart, and tell you how sorry I am for all that has happened between us.

Every day, I sit down and write to you, but I never seem to get it right. I throw these letters on the fire, and watch the flames eat my words.

I pray that someday I will find you, Laura. That I can look you in the eyes, and ask for your forgiveness.

Remember, when you were about seven years old and we used to walk to the harbour every Sunday and have an ice cream cone at Orchid Bay? We walked hand in hand, and it was non-stop chatter from you.

Every Sunday in the summer, I made sure you had a new dress. Remember the straight speckled purple dress and the deep purple zigzag we ran down the long front seams? You loved it, and kept tracing the zigzag braid the length of your dress. Or the time I made you the dress with the gathered skirt and the bunched tulle underskirt to make sure the dress kicked out in the right places?

You felt like a ballerina, and on that Sunday you spent the whole time on your tiptoes. I have always been so proud of you, Laura.

It is my burden to bear now that maybe I did not show that enough ever, and when our love was tested, I failed you.

If I could change what happened, I would give everything up to do so. I love Coolnamona House, but I would give up all this in a heartbeat to have you back. But Coolnamona House is all I have, and I am hoping that it is this place that will bring you back to me.

I worry that it will be too late or you may never come back, but know no matter what, I love you to the stars and back.

Life is full of expectation and regrets. The only constant is the love we feel in our hearts. The love in my heart for you grows every day. Please read all these notes and understand my heart yearns for you.

Every day, I wake up, and think today might be the day I get to meet my Laura again. Know I love you so much.

All my love,

Mam

XX

Becky replaced the letter and the notes in the envelope. She felt such sadness for the beautiful girl in the portrait and the lonely old woman who walked around this house in ball gowns hoping against hope that her daughter would return. Her heart hurting, she pushed the envelope into an old teapot in the china cabinet before stepping out into the front garden to sit quietly on the bench. What would Hilda make of all this? She wished Hilda had left her letters, to guide her through these days at Coolnamona. Feeling overwhelmed, she yearned to be in Manhattan, sitting in the loft apartment, and listening to the sounds of the city. She wanted to stroll around Greenwich Village, visit her favourite deli and the quirky little street-side café, where she liked to sit and watch well-dressed women push their little carts with their pampered pooches inside. She would sip an iced coffee and stretch her legs, and watch the world go by. Here in Coolnamona, she would never get time alone; somebody would stop to chat or pass a comment or stop to have an exchange about the weather. There were days like today when she wanted to escape all the things that Coolnamona had to offer, all the things that she also loved about the place.

When she heard the gate being pushed open, she shrank back, hoping the caller would not spy her, and instead, see the closed front door. She heard the step on the gravel, and she wondered if she could slip out the side door before being detected.

'Are you hiding from me?' Ben said as he peered around the pink rose bush.

Becky smiled. 'You're the last person I would hide from. I just needed quiet time.'

Ben put out his hand, and pulled her up from the seat. 'Which is why I'm here. Do you want to get out of Coolnamona, and head for the mountains?'

'Have you time?'

He twirled her around. 'We will make time.'

'I have a lot of things to do.'

'So do I, but don't you ever just take time out for yourself?'

'I don't know when I did that last. You know, when we lived in Manhattan, I was always working. Even on holiday there were things to be done. Now, it's all about this house. There isn't much me time here either.'

He shook his head. 'You need to go back to the mountains, to get that exhilarating feeling that you could touch the clouds if you stretched out your hand. You also need the best medicine there is: a good laugh,' he said.

'I don't think I can; I have so much to do here at the house,' she said.

'Let's just go; if you overthink it, you'll find something to do. I have everything in the jeep: spare jacket and rugs.'

Becky, laughing, let him lead her along the path.

'I even brought a little picnic,' he said as they got in the jeep, giggling and laughing like two kids bunking off school.

Ben turned left into the main street, instructing Becky to duck when he saw Maisie out walking her dog. 'The last thing we need is gossip,' he said, raising his hand, and saluting Maisie as he drove past her and Ronnie.

Becky looked at Ben as she settled back into the seat. He was a tall, broad man with an unruly mop of hair, but there was a kindness about his face that made her trust him. It was hard to imagine he had ever been a detective, because somehow, being a chef with a light touch suited him better.

They drove up the narrow roads into the mountains, past low-lying stone cottages and small farm holdings, through tiny villages, until Ben steered onto a very narrow road, hugging the mountain on one side, the land at the other side a sheer drop down.

The mountains towered above them, pushing the clouds out of the way. Becky gazed out the window, every part of her body relaxing in this world where the brown and green hills looked as if they were playing beach ball with the clouds.

Ben rolled down the windows, the fresh, cool breeze filling the jeep and lifting Becky's hair. She pushed it behind her ears, and held it down, but when Ben offered to close the windows, she said no.

He burrowed in his glove box, and found a scarf, which he gave to her to tie back her hair.

'Why would you have that in the car?' She laughed.

'Maisie left it there,' he said.

When Becky didn't answer, he guffawed out loud. 'Give me some credit, Becky. Is it weird for you if I say it belonged to my late wife?' He stopped talking when he saw her face. 'The optics aren't good, are they?' he said doubtfully.

'It's a little—'

'Creepy,' he interrupted.

'Your words,' she said.

He pulled into the side of the road. Becky got out. Drinking in the clear air, she set off to a viewing point, her stride purposeful.

The sun sparkled across the mountains, picking out the lines on the far hills, where attempts had been made to sow potato drills in ancient times, and skipped across the dark waters of the lake below them. A bird of prey flew over their heads so close that Becky could hear its ear-piercing cry as it fanned out its wide wings, before dropping down and gliding across the lake water.

Becky gasped in delight.

'I told you I would bring you high in the sky,' Ben said, catching up with her.

She closed her eyes, listening to the sound of the wind whistling across the mountains, curling around the rocks and skimming across the bog, and she felt its energy all round her. There was a perfume in the air which made her want to stay there forever. She felt complete.

'I never knew this could be so wonderful,' she said, opening her eyes to find him looking at her, and beaming a wide smile.

They walked together until the terrain flattened out, and there was a rock where they could sit, their knees bunched up to watch the light as it played hide-and-seek in the far-off mountains.

After a while, Ben cleared his throat, and began to talk. 'I should never have offered you Rachel's scarf. I'm sorry.'

'It's OK.'

'No, it's not OK. I should have been more sensitive. I guess I kept it in my jeep because...' His voice trailed off.

'I understand.'

'Thank you,' he said quietly.

'Do you want to tell me about Rachel?' she said.

'We were the best of friends, and then we fell in love. She was my rock, and I hope I was hers. She doted on Brian, wanted to see him grow into a man, but that wasn't to be.'

'What happened?'

Ben fixed his gaze far away as he answered her question. 'She was taken from us slowly over two years. It started with a lump in her breast and...'

He stopped but she didn't try to fill the silence. Instead, she closed her eyes, again listening to the wind as it crackled over the plastic bag which was sitting on top of the picnic basket.

'Are you sure you want to hear about this?' he said.

'Only if you are comfortable telling me.'

He shifted on the rock, and pulled at a tuft of grass, turning the blades between his fingers.

'We got good news at first. She had a mastectomy, and while that was tough enough, it turned out that the bloody cancer had returned after about nine months. This time it was in her lungs and they tried everything. Rachel would have done anything to stay with us longer. All she wanted was time, but cancer dashes hopes and is unrelenting,' he said, his voice cracking.

She placed her hand on his back, and rubbed gently.

'It was a stupid mistake with the scarf. I am so sorry,' he whispered.

'What comes across is you loved each other very much. You were very lucky,' she said.

'I suppose we were.' He jumped off the rock, and held out his hand to Becky. 'Do you fancy walking to the top of the mound over there? The view is even more breathtaking.'

She readily agreed, glad of the change of subject. They tramped up the mountain, Ben turning around to help Becky when the going got tough. The wind was stronger here, and when they got to the top of the mound, Ben put his arm around her as he called out the landmarks that could be seen.

'I didn't think it could get better, but it has,' she whispered, and he hugged her shoulders tighter.

They stood like that for a few minutes, lost in their own thoughts. She leaned against him, and she felt him adjust his footing to make her more comfortable.

'Will we go back?' he said quietly.

'I don't know if I ever want to leave these mountains,' she said, and he kissed her gently on the top of her head, before releasing her.

They didn't talk, but concentrated on their steps as they made their way down the mountain to where Ben had left the picnic basket.

'It's simple fare, just quiche and salad and a thermos of coffee,' he said.

'Sounds good. The mountain air has made me hungry,' she said, helping him to unwrap the food.

He poured the coffee, and they began to eat.

'Your turn. Tell me about yourself,' he said.

Surprised, Becky stuttered that there wasn't much to tell. She was a single mum, and Hilda had left her Coolnamona House after her sudden and tragic death. Ben reached over and put his hand on her shoulder.

'Well, I'm so glad she did, and if you are not comfortable giving away all your secrets, that's fine,' he said, throwing the last of his coffee away, before beginning to pack up.

She did the same, and later they walked back to the jeep.

They didn't need to talk on the way back to Coolnamona.

He stopped the jeep a little up the lane from Coolnamona House.

'Thank you for a perfect day,' she said.

'I'm sorry. I promised to make you laugh, and I didn't manage it,' he said.

'That's OK, I had a good time,' she said.

He reached over to kiss her, but she pulled away.

'I'm sorry, I'm just not ready,' she said.

'Thank you for a lovely day. I'm sorry if I've overstepped the mark,' he whispered.

'It was a lovely day. It's not your fault. I'm going to go now,' she said.

He nodded, and Becky wandered slowly down the lane to Coolnamona House.

NINETEEN

For the next few days, they worked inside and out getting everything in order for the opening of the café. Sadie took charge. The landscape company came, and over two days tidied up the garden. Becky insisted that the old apple tree and cherry blossom stayed, and they had custom-made benches fitted around them. She allowed the butterfly bush to be moved along with one scraggly overgrown rose bush down the side. When the idea of artificial grass was mooted, she shot it down, because she knew that the lawns with the drifts of buttercups, daisies and clover were something everyone would find special.

'This is a cottage garden, not just a yard,' she said, and the men working there cut paths snaking through the wild flowers from one table to another. The main path was covered in tiny pink-gold stones, and the outside of the house was restored to light pink along with the garden walls, which were also topped in white to match the front door and windows.

A small plaque was placed at the lookout rock to remind everyone that Regina liked to sit there, and take in Orchid Bay and Wales on a clear day.

Becky had a sign made for the wrought iron gate saying

COOLNAMONA HOUSE, and Ben, early one morning, secured it in place. At first, Becky felt a little awkward around him but he smiled brightly making her feel at ease. Iris, in her dressing gown, came out onto the road to join Becky in admiring Ben's work.

'It's like the good old days, but better,' Iris said with approval.

'We have Sadie to thank for the idea. Where is she? She said she was following me outside,' Becky said.

Sadie waved from the front door, pointing to her phone.

'The sign for the café is next,' Ben said.

Becky twiddled a strand of her long hair around her finger. This was all becoming so real. The lettering on the old sign had been refreshed, and Sadie had insisted on a hint of gold around the edge of each letter, which she said gave it a shabby chic look. They had found hooks embedded in the walls over the front door. Becky knew once that sign went up, she had to open the café.

'Part of me wants to enjoy the house like this, but Sadie will have none of it. She says it's an adventure, but opening up to the public terrifies me.'

'Can't be more terrifying than Maisie. Did you notice she always walks her dog this way these days? Poor old Ronnie is a lazy git. He's looking unhappy. He has never been walked so much.' Iris laughed.

'Maisie just wants to be part of things. You should invite her to the opening,' Ben said.

'You wouldn't be suggesting that if you knew the way she talks about you,' Iris muttered.

'I have heard every word back, and yes, she has to be invited. To exclude her will make her bitter and nasty. At the moment, Maisie is just a silly gossip,' Ben said firmly.

'A party! We have to have a party!' Iris exclaimed, pretending to ignore what Ben had said.

Becky tugged hard on her hair. 'Don't you think this is stressful enough? It will be a soft opening for us, and hopefully people will spread the word.'

'You really are one for hiding your light under a bushel,' Iris said before turning into her own gate.

Becky invited Ben in for tea. They could hear Sadie on the phone in the sitting room, talking quickly.

'Iris is right. A party would be a very good idea, and put you on the map,' he said.

'What map? It is more than I can cope with right now,' she said.

She saw him stand at the sink looking out into the back garden. 'I think it's going to go very well, and soon you will want the back garden for more tables and chairs.'

'I doubt if that day will come, and if it does, they can sit among the potato drills.' Becky giggled.

She did not realise Sadie had slipped into the room, and was hunched over the table.

Ben sat down, and immediately jumped up again. 'Should I leave?' he asked.

Sadie, her eyes red from crying, quietly indicated for him to stay.

'Did you get bad news?' Becky asked, pushing a mug of tea in front of her, and handing another to Ben.

Sadie shook her head.

'Maybe I should leave,' Ben said, his voice full of concern.

Sadie looked at him directly. 'I need your advice. Can you stay?'

'I can, but it's hardly chef stuff you want to talk about.'

'Becky said you were once a police detective?'

'Yes, but honestly, Sadie, if this is anything to do with the police, you need to call them. Has something happened?'

Sadie gestured to Becky. 'You tell him what happened.'

'Are you sure?'

'Yes, the abridged version, please,' Sadie said, putting her head in her hands.

Becky cleared her throat. 'Sadie was fired from her Manhattan job as a commercial lawyer because she found the senior partners were stealing money from the client accounts.'

'And now they want me to come back and give evidence. Seemingly, it's a lot bigger than they thought and is spread right across the organisation, and a pension fund has been decimated,' Sadie said.

'And what do you need from me?' Ben asked kindly.

'I don't really know. I guess I'm scared. My boss went to Mexico, and she refuses to return to even make a statement.'

'So you're the only hope?' Ben said.

'I don't know if I can do it. I took a settlement. I will be ripped to shreds in court about that.'

Becky moved to comfort Sadie, but she began to cry again. 'This is so shit. I feel like the one who did wrong, not those bastards in their corner offices,' she said.

'It might be the case if you help police and give a statement, that your former bosses will plead guilty,' Ben said.

Sadie scrunched her hands into tight fists. 'There's more. There's a civil suit over the pension fund, and seemingly, I'm their star witness as well.'

'But that means you could be helping people claw back some of their losses,' Becky said.

Sadie got up from the table so fast, her chair toppled over. 'That all sounds great. I am Mother fricking Teresa. What will happen when they hear about my big pay-off?'

Ben stood up beside Sadie, and put his hand on her arm. 'You asked for advice, so I'm going to give it, but please sit down,' he said, setting her chair up for her.

Sadie, wiping away her tears, sat back down. 'Shoot,' she said.

Ben clasped his hands in front of him. 'Sadie, you have to do what is right, and providing you did nothing wrong, you won't have much to worry about.'

Sadie stared at Ben. 'The important word there is "much". I don't know what these people will do to exonerate themselves. They may try to pin everything on me.'

'You will need a lawyer to look after your own interests. Can you get somebody you trust?' Ben asked.

'I guess. You think I should go back there?' Sadie said.

'Only you can decide that, but if you don't, you may regret that you let a chance to bring these people to justice and do the right thing by those who lost their life savings and pension pots,' he said.

'You have a way of persuading a person,' Sadie said.

'Have a little think about it. You don't have to decide straight away,' Becky said.

Sadie got up from the table again. 'Decision is made. Ben is right. If I want to move on with my life, I have to do this.'

'What about being a lawyer?'

Sadie shrugged. 'I would love to say doing the right thing is more important, but hell, I don't know. Maybe it's time to find a new career path anyway. I'm going to have to leave shortly. But, what about the café? I don't want to leave you in the lurch.'

'We will manage. You're coming back, are you?'

Becky sounded casual, but inside, her stomach was churning, She wanted to scream to Sadie that they could not do any of this without her.

Ben said he had to get back home, and Sadie said she would stroll out with him, that she needed to go for a walk to try and sort her head out. Becky watched her go out the front door, and head down the path. She was afraid for Sadie if she returned to Manhattan, but she knew she had to do what she thought was right.

Becky, unable to work, went to the china cabinet, and pulled out Regina's letter from the teapot.

She had promised herself that when she felt agitated or the world seemed too much, she would read one of Regina's notes. The words of a woman who finally had a chance to look back over her life surely mattered. She picked out a note written on blue paper and sat on the velvet couch to read it.

Dear Laura,

I guess every old person has a desire at some stage to try to warn the younger generation of all the pitfalls.

I only know one thing: that family and friendship are the most important components of life.

I can say that because I botched it the first time round, and now it looks like I will never get a second chance. I ruined everything with you, Laura. I was pigheaded, too afraid of what people thought of us and not near mindful enough of you and your needs.

What I wouldn't give to hold you in my arms, and stroke your long silky hair again, my sweetheart, or to sit on the velvet couch and just be together in front of the fire, glancing at fashion magazines. Remember how we loved to do that?

Unfortunately, I also messed things up with Bella, and every time she came looking for a reconciliation, I turned my back on her. This has been another hard-earned life lesson. I should have forgiven you, and I should have forgiven Bella.

All she ever did was put your best interests at heart. I know that now, and I wish I could walk down the street, and knock on the door to tell her, but my stupid pride is still getting in the way, and it will be the death of me.

I don't know what lessons are to be learned in all this, but I do know that as a result of my actions, I have moved into old age a lonely woman, and I don't wish that for anyone else.

Today, I will dress in my favourite After Dior creation: grey as befits my mood. I will walk from room to room in the hope that I have forgotten that you are not all here at home. I know I will find cold rooms smelling of damp, but the anticipation will keep me going until loneliness finds me again, and I am left devastated. Don't pity me, Laura, but please, if you ever get to read this, remember the good times, and please, find a way in your heart to forgive me.

All my love,

Mam

XX

Upset, Becky put down the note. She wanted to shout at the young woman in the portrait to run and never stop, to see the world beyond Orchid Bay.

When Sadie came in beside her, Becky didn't move.

'I hope you're not crying over me,' Sadie said.

'Bloody Regina stuff,' Becky said, handing her friend the note.

'It's from that envelope,' she said by way of explanation.

They sat in silence as Sadie read the note. 'Powerful stuff,' she said, dabbing her eyes with a paper tissue.

'It is so sad that Laura never got a chance to forgive her mother.'

'Becks, life is like that.'

'Sometimes I wish it were different.'

'Don't we all. Now, my news. I fly out early next week. All the arrangements are made. I want you to do one thing for me.'

'Anything.'

'Please can we open the café before I leave for New York? I would feel so much better to know everything is up and running here.'

'It will be a bit of a rush.'

'It will be fun.'

Becky reached over, and hugged her friend. 'I'm so proud of you, but also so afraid for you.'

'Don't be. This is something I have to do if I'm ever to be at peace. You just keep this café going,' Sadie said.

'Are you sure you are strong enough to do this?'

Sadie smiled at Becky. 'I have backup, and here she is,' she said.

'And I will get on a plane for the first time too,' Iris said as she walked into the room.

Becky swung around. 'You know about this?'

'Sadie told me over too many whiskeys in a short space of time. We women have to stick together, and sitting and chatting is better than any old walk, ' Iris said.

Becky threw her arms out, and Sadie and Iris curled into a hug.

'You're not on your own. We are all behind you,' Iris said.

TWENTY

'I'm bushed, do I have to go tonight?' Sadie asked.

'I think you should. The invite is to all of us,' Becky said.

'It's only a tasting menu. He won't even miss me.'

'Ben particularly wants the input of the New York palette,' Iris said as she walked into the sitting room. 'And get off that couch, you're way too dusty to be sitting on the good velvet sofa which has been freshly cleaned.' She clipped Sadie gently around the ears.

'All right, but I'm so tired. Are we dressing up?'

'We should. Knowing Ben, he will have gone to a lot of bother, and it is a chance to let our hair down before Sadie and Iris fly out, and before the café opening,' Becky said.

'OK, so how dressed up should we go? I don't have anything formal. Will posh casual do?' Sadie asked.

Iris clicked her tongue impatiently. 'We need to make an effort. You do know Ben hasn't had any friends over for dinner or a tasting menu since Rachel died?'

'Oh gosh, his wife. You know how to put on the pressure,' Becky groaned.

'Tell me more,' Sadie said.

Iris sighed. 'It was such a love story. They met when they were schoolkids, and got married as soon as they could. He was a garda, a detective, but he was injured on duty, and had to leave the force. He was devastated, but took up his second passion, and trained to be a chef. Rachel worked every hour she could while he did the training. It was the proudest day when they opened that restaurant on Main Street. Ben could have had a job anywhere, he was so good. They had even lived in Paris for a while, when he worked under a bigwig chef there.'

'Now I'm looking forward to this tasting menu,' Sadie said, grabbing the others, and pointing to the kitchen. 'Let's sit and have a cuppa while we hear the rest of this story,' she suggested.

Becky switched on the kettle, and got the mugs while the others sat at the table.

'I'm in the mood for a romantic story. This place has made me soft, drinking cups of tea and storytelling,' Sadie said.

'Only thing is, this has a sad ending,' Becky interrupted.

'Talk of ruining the punchline,' Sadie said, getting up to rinse the teapot with boiling water before making the tea, and pouring it into the three mugs.

'I think this story might finally have another chapter,' Iris said.

'What do you mean?'

Iris took the mug of tea when it was handed to her, but didn't drink from it. 'Have you ever heard of sitting quietly and listening? Now, where was I? Rachel and Ben were a good fit. She was great front of house, and he was a wizard in the kitchen.'

'How did they get business in a small place like this?' Sadie said.

'The Dublin set love Ben. The newspapers are always ringing him up, and writing up pieces on the restaurant. He's a good-looker, which helps. The hacks love the former cop story-line. They wanted to write about him and Rachel, particularly when she died. He turned them all away, said his personal life was not going to feature in any media. I am surprised he let on anything to you, Becky. Ben is usually very guarded,' Iris said.

'Oh, I think our Becky might have a special in there, and Jen too, of course, with Brian,' Sadie said.

'Wouldn't that just be nice and dandy?' Iris laughed, and Becky grumbled at them to be quiet as she twisted away quickly so they wouldn't realise she was blushing.

Sadie looked at her watch, and said she had to have time to clean up and put on her face. 'I'm thinking posh casual,' she said.

'Your posh casual is everybody else's good wear,' Becky commented.

Jen ran into the kitchen. 'I know what we can do. We can wear some of the designer dresses from upstairs,' she said.

'What designer dresses?' Sadie muttered.

'But won't we have to air them out?' Becky asked.

'We can put them on a refresh cycle in my dryer,' Iris said, rubbing her hands together in excitement.

'Hey, I'm in the dark here. Somebody tell me what's going on?' Sadie exclaimed.

Jen pulled her from the chair. 'Come on upstairs. I'll show you.'

'Lead the way. I want to have a look at these dresses, and somebody please tell me how couture collectables made it all the way to Coolnamona. Pardon me, but it's hardly the cultural or design centre of the world.' Sadie laughed.

Iris, pretending to be insulted, told Sadie to step back to allow her upstairs first. 'This may not be Paris, but in Coolnamona we clean up good,' she said stiffly.

Becky tapped her friend on the shoulder, and told her to follow.

Upstairs, Jen had already taken a number of dresses out of the wardrobe, and had them hanging at the open window. 'So we can get a start on airing them. I also found some nice wool wraps for us too,' she said.

Wandering further into the back room, Sadie whistled as she looked around. Jen was beaming with excitement. 'I thought there's no point going all ball gown; it would only frighten the chef. However, there are these fantastic sheath dresses. I wanted to wear the gold, but Sadie and Mom can fight over the blue and black. You will both look good in either of these creations,' she said.

'Oh, this must be silk,' Sadie squealed, running her hand across the blue dress. This will be perfect with my stilettos, but what shoes are you wearing, Becky?'

'I can't walk in high shoes. I'm sticking to my flats. My new canvas ones will do just fine.'

'Don't you really know how to dress up, darling? Nobody would ever mistake you for the top dress designer you are,' Sadie said, throwing her eyes to the ceiling in a dramatic fashion.

'Becky has a lovely figure that can carry off any style,' Iris said in her stern voice, making the others giggle.

'Who wore these dresses?' Sadie asked.

'No idea, I have never seen this style. Regina loved her ball gowns,' Iris said.

Becky, Jen and Sadie began to peel off their clothes, and change into their dresses. Iris pretended to be looking out the window until Jen called her to turn around.

'I have an outfit for you too,' she said.

Iris whipped around quickly. 'I hope, dear, you're not expecting me to fit into a mini.'

Jen laughed heartily, and pulled a three-piece outfit from behind her dress.

'Oh my God, you don't expect me to wear that? It's like a painting,' Iris said, gently touching the lamé fabric of the straight skirt. 'It glows, like a giant painting of blue and pink flowers with a gold hue. And that jacket is nipped in at the waist. It's all a bit much for me,' she said, her voice trailing as she stopped and looked at the pink silk blouse with light ruffles at the neck.

'Is there something wrong?' Jen asked.

'Regina wore that blouse for our afternoon tea every Sunday. I never knew it was part of a suit.'

'You have the figure for it, Iris. Please wear it. I bet when you put it on, you'll feel a million dollars,' Sadie said.

'Let's see. I might be too old for it, but I will take it away, and all the others, and bring them back refreshed at six. We are due at Ben's at seven,' she said, her face bright with excitement.

Two hours later, Becky was sitting in the back garden, when Iris tiptoed through the gate. Becky had wandered outside to get away from the others as Sadie did Jen's make-up. She watched as Iris, carrying the other dresses over her arm, tottered on her high-heeled gold strappy sandals up the garden path.

When she got closer, Becky noticed she was wearing matching gold earrings and a gold rope necklace at her neck.

'You look as if you should be attending a bistro in Paris rather than Coolnamona,' Becky said.

'And I feel it. Your Jen has a way of making a woman feel good. Now, here are all your dresses and don't forget to put on the slap. You could do with a slick of lipstick, at least, and a little jewellery. Regina has left plenty for you to choose from. I'll wait in the sitting room,' she said, hanging up the sheath dresses on the hooks at the back door.

When Becky got as far as her bedroom, she thought Iris had a point. Reaching into the drawer, she pulled out the nine-strand pearl choker. She snapped it on, and bundled her hair into a messy bun. What was she doing? This wasn't her. Pulling off the choker, she brushed out her hair.

When she stepped out onto the landing, Sadie was fixing her hair in front of the wall mirror. 'Your daughter looks amazing. She's going to be a real heartbreaker, that girl.'

'I hope you didn't put too much make-up on her; she's too young. I want her to enjoy these days, not spend her time chasing boys.'

'Listen to yourself, Becky. Remember how we were at her age.'

Becky didn't answer, but continued down the stairs.

Iris was sipping a whiskey as she reclined on the velvet couch in the sitting room, and studied the painting. 'This room is looking so good. You gals are doing an amazing job,' she said. She gave out a low whistle when she saw the others dressed up. 'Don't you look the biz. Where's Maisie now?' she said.

They wandered down the front path single file, but linked arms on the lane and ambled along, chatting together until they got to the main street. When they passed the boarded-up delicatessen, Iris stopped the party.

'Have ye heard the latest from Edith?'

'Who's Edith?' Sadie asked.

'Only the nicest person in the place, and today I got the news that she has cancer, and it's very bad. She hasn't long left, weeks, days, who knows? They want to do it alone, and we have to respect that.'

'Is that why they closed down the deli?' Jen asked.

'I suppose so. Nobody really knows. They just upped and left when all we wanted to do was look after her,' Iris said.

'Maybe Edith just needed time to get her head around it, and for the two of them to spend precious time together,' Becky said.

'It's a pity she didn't want us to gather round and help, that's all I'm saying,' Iris said sadly.

They walked on in silence to the restaurant.

Brian was sitting at the outside tables when they came down the street. Jen skipped on ahead to be with him.

'They look good together,' Sadie whispered, but Becky pretended not to hear.

As they got closer, Brian gestured to them to go around the back.

'We are getting the royal treatment tonight, the entire restaurant to ourselves,' Iris said.

They wandered down to a side door where Brian had moved to wait for them.

'Dad is up to ninety in the kitchen so why don't I pour some prosecco? We can sit in the garden until he's ready to serve,' he said.

'This is so wonderful. Coolnamona House has a lot of catching up to do,' Sadie said.

'It's nothing that a lot of hard work won't sort,' Iris said.

Jen went off to help Brian in the kitchen. After a few moments, Ben, wiping his hands on a tea-towel, came out.

'Ladies, thank you all for coming tonight. I probably should have explained that I intend going to the beach for a picnic.'

'What? But we are all glammed up,' Iris said.

Ben shook his head. 'You all look so amazing, but the plan is to cook the fish down on the shingle beach. We will bring everything with us, including my latest dessert, a Sicilian lemon cheesecake.'

'What are you talking about, man? I can hardly walk on the level tarmac road in this get-up, never mind dance across the shingle beach.' Iris sniffed.

Ben shifted uncomfortably. 'OK, to tell the truth, my big industrial oven has given up the ghost, so I have had to think outside the box. It will be nice to go down to the sea. I can guarantee the food will taste even better in the fresh sea air.'

'Couldn't we use the barbecue here in the garden?' Sadie asked.

Ben looked put out. 'How about I carry any of you who can't walk on the shingle beach? Brian has set up everything. I will bring you down in the car.'

'Thank goodness for that small mercy,' Iris grumbled.

'I may have the footwear, but I still feel overdressed for the occasion.' Becky laughed.

Ben made to say something, but he appeared to hesitate.

Jen came out with a big box to put in the back of the jeep. 'Come on, guys. The food is amazing, and I have never seen fish cooked in a fire pit before.'

Sadie stood up, kicked off her high heels and wrapped her shawl around her. 'I'm ready,' she said. 'Lead the way.'

Iris harrumphed loudly. 'I'm not taking off these sandals so you might as well resign yourself to carrying me across the shingle beach,' she said haughtily, and Ben bowed low.

Becky and Sadie piled into the jeep, and Iris got into Brian's car with Jen.

'This has got to be the most unusual dinner I have ever been invited to,' Sadie said as they made their way past the lane leading to Coolnamona House, and drove the long way around to Orchid Bay.

At the beach, Sadie tried to walk across the shingle strand, but she gave up after a few strides. Ben came up behind her, and carried her to where they had a table and chairs set up and a small fire was throwing up smoke. Iris said dramatically that maybe they should drop her home – it was way too chilly to be beside the water – but Ben got out a wool rug and wrapped her in it, before carrying her across to her seat at the table.

Becky skipped on behind enjoying the freedom of being at Orchid Bay, where time didn't matter so much.

Jen helped Brian put out the plates and the crystal wine glasses.

'All we need now is for Maisie to see this carry-on,' Iris

hissed as she grabbed a small canapé from a plate. 'Delicious, but how I would love to be back in the restaurant,' she said.

'Give it a whirl, Iris. Wait until you taste the fresh salmon on a bed of spinach with cubed garlic potatoes,' Ben said.

Iris huffed a little, and poured herself another glass of prosecco. Becky sat beside Ben as he piled warm coals on the fish packets.

'This is so perfect. You should offer such an adventure to your guests,' she said.

'No, picnics are for friends and family. It puts the fun back into the sharing of food. It's something I lost when Rachel died, but thanks to you lot, I feel it is returning,' he said.

Slightly embarrassed, Becky looked out towards the sea where a dog was swimming out deep to retrieve a tennis ball.

'That's Maisie's old dog. No doubt she will come over for a snoop,' Iris said.

'Well if she does, we will offer her a plate,' Ben said firmly as he took the salmon from the pit, and placed it on the table.

'I don't think I have ever had salmon like this,' Sadie said.

'Wild Irish salmon. I am hoping that my fish dishes will become my signature dishes. It is fitting considering we are so near the sea,' Ben said.

Iris raised her glass. 'To the chef and his wild Irish salmon. A wonderful combination,' she said, and they laughed, clinking glasses.

The labrador bounded over to them, scooting between their legs and nearly throwing Sadie from her chair.

'Apologies, I hope we haven't interrupted your soiree,' Maisie shouted as she ran after the dog.

'You're in time to have some food with us,' Ben said.

Iris snorted loudly, and turned her back to Maisie.

'Oh I couldn't possibly intrude like that. You all look to be enjoying yourselves,' Maisie said, eyeing each woman up and down. Tightening her cardigan around her, she called Ronnie, and snapped on his lead. 'I'm afraid I might be underdressed for the occasion, but thank you all the same, Ben,' she said as she walked away with her dog.

'Good riddance,' Iris muttered, but Ben told her to hush.

'She only meddles because she's lonely,' he said, and the others fell silent.

The sound of the waves filled the air as the group sat quietly. Everyone had seconds of garlic potatoes, and said they couldn't eat another thing. They sat, sipping prosecco, following the late evening sun as it cast shadows across the sea. Jen and Brian added a sparkler to the lemon Sicilian cheesecake before cutting it. Everybody managed a small slice. Ben took out his old harmonica from his pocket, the musical notes drifting over the waves.

When he stopped, Sadie clapped loudly, and the others joined in.

'This has got to be the best dinner party ever,' Sadie said, and the others shouted, 'Hear, hear.'

Becky wanted a soft opening for the café, especially now that it was a little rushed. Best to make all the mistakes of a start-up before they came to any prominence in Coolnamona or further afield, she thought.

'If Hilda were here, she would shout at you. We are already in July, and the sunny weather is not going to stick around until you are fully ready,' Sadie said, the exasperation clear in her tone of voice.

Becky wanted to question how Sadie would know how Hilda would react, but she stopped herself. Sadie had enough on her mind right now without Becky causing any friction.

Iris felt done out of a party, and had made a big deal about trying not to show her disappointment.

When Ben arrived, Becky turned to him. 'You might as well have your say. Everybody else has,' she said despondently.

'We were much the same when we opened the restaurant, but it gave us an opportunity to iron out any kinks. Stick to your guns,' he said.

'You make it sound like a battle,' she laughed.

'With Sadie and Iris involved, I'm sure it feels like war.' He grinned.

Iris rapped on the back door, and came in with a bundle of napkins. 'Linen is much better than paper,' she said, plonking them on the table. 'And I'll tell all the ladies in my watercolour class, and everyone at my bridge club is dying to visit the revamped café,' she said.

'Well then, we know at least somebody will come,' Becky said brightly.

'The ladies love to gather, and this café, I mean location, was always first choice.'

Becky looked from Iris to Sadie. 'See, the locals are going to support us. That's as much as I need right now.'

'Of course, you're forgetting Maisie. That's free advertising right there,' Iris said, making Becky chuckle.

'I need to bake my cookies, and figure out how many we need,' Sadie said.

Becky was flummoxed, but Iris, sensing her predicament, stepped in. 'Going on the way things ran in the past, I think a few flyers around the town and down at the harbour wouldn't go amiss. Plan, and pray for about fifty, two cookies per person. That's one hundred each day and a falling-off after that,' she said.

'That's not very many. Have you done the figures, Becky?' Sadie said.

Becky felt so stressed. She had presumed that all fifteen tables and sixty covers would be full most of the day in summer, and she suddenly felt very silly that she had not fully considered the financial side. Jen, who had been sitting at the table scrolling on her phone, said a mum of one of the girls she knew from Greystones had a show on local radio, and maybe she could interview Becky.

'Do you think you can set it up?' Becky asked.

'Sure, I'll text her now.'

Sadie sighed heavily. 'Can we please give up this dumb idea of a soft opening?'

Becky didn't answer, but hopped up to switch on the kettle. They all listened as the water in the kettle worked up to boiling point. She spooned coffee into the mugs before filling them with the water, and handing them out.

'I know everybody was looking forward to a party. Just give me a few weeks, and then maybe we can have a get-together,' she said as Sadie took a mug.

'Now I know why Hilda ruled the business side of things,' Sadie said.

'And look where that got her. Let's get back to the opening. What about flyers?' Iris asked.

'Jen has designed one. We can distribute it today,' Becky said.

'Which leaves Maisie. I will have a private word with her. If I ask her to keep it to herself for the moment, it will be too irresistible, and she's guaranteed to tell the town.' Iris guffawed.

Becky wanted to chastise Iris, but before she had a chance to say anything, Iris pushed her chair back, and stood up. 'I don't want to be rude, but now that all that's finalised, I have things I need to do. Don't worry, I will make fifty or so scones, and I can whip up more here for you if there's a rush,' she said, heading for the front door.

Becky saw Sadie frown. 'Is there something the matter?' she asked.

'Did you ask her to make scones? I thought it was drinks and cookies,' Sadie said.

Becky shrugged. 'So did I, but what do I know?' she said, heading off to the sitting room.

She needed to escape from the others. All the work was done, and Ben would call around tomorrow to put up the old sign over the front door. Opening up the china cabinet, she took out Regina's teapot and the light green note, which had the words *The Café* written in capitals at the top.

My dearest Laura,

I had a silly dream that someday an important writer or reviewer would come to my humble café, and feel so moved by the place that he or she would give the café a stunning write-up. I imagined you coming across the review. What would you do, I wonder? In my silly dream, you dropped everything to come back to Coolnamona. I would see you walk up the path, I'd throw off my apron and run to greet you.

Too Hollywood, I guess.

How I wish life could be like that, but I still dreamed that if there was a review or a write-up that it would somehow find its way to you, and arouse your interest enough that you might make contact.

There were too many variables, and the first hole in my dream was who the hell would want to write a review of my little café over Orchid Bay? I love the café. God knows I would die of loneliness without it. There are those who say it is the best café in these parts, and I have to be happy with that. It was never destined to feature on the international stage, which is probably my only hope of straying across your path.

That time soon after you left when you penned a note from England, I travelled across in the boat. I went to Manchester, Birmingham and London. I thought those big cities sounded like a place a young woman would go looking for work. I must have appeared to be a mad one, clutching a little photo of you, and tramping the streets, asking anyone I could if they had seen you.

I stopped at Trafalgar Square and had my picture taken among the pigeons. Did you do the same at any time, I wonder?

There are days I stand inside the sitting room window and

watch people throng to my little café. I hope against hope that one day you will come up the path. Disappointment and despair are my only companions now.

We don't need to go back into the ins and outs of our difference of opinion. I know I did wrong. I have tried hiring private investigators to find you, but so far there have been no positive leads. I have used up the last of my savings, and I'm pinning my hopes on the latest private detective I have employed to help find any lead as to your whereabouts.

You have been gone so long, I wonder sometimes would I know you if we passed on a street anywhere but Coolnamona. I want to believe that years, nay decades could have passed, but I would know you, my daughter.

Until we can meet, my sweetheart.

All my love,

Mam

XX

Jen rushed into the room, her face red with excitement. Becky scrunched the note in her hand, and tried to regain her composure.

'What's wrong?' Jen asked.

Becky stood up. 'I suppose I'm a little nervous about the café opening. What if nobody comes?'

'I may be able to help there. Sophie's mom says can you do an interview over the phone tomorrow morning, and I said yes.'

The last words came out as a loud screech making Sadie rush into the room. 'What the hell is wrong?' she said.

'Mom is doing a live interview tomorrow morning on local radio.'

Sadie and Jen punched the air in their excitement, but stopped when they saw Becky's face.

'What's wrong?' Sadie asked.

Becky swallowed hard. Her head hurt, and her mouth was drying up at the thought of a live radio interview. 'I can't do it. What am I going to say? It's live, for heaven's sake.'

'You'll be fine. Just chat on about the café and how wonderful it is, and be sure to tell everyone where it is. This is so good,' Sadie said.

Becky gripped her hand. 'I have never done anything like this. What if I clam up?'

'Stressy, stressy Becky. Seriously, you're going to be great.'

Jen hugged Becky. 'I'm so proud of you, Mom. Now, I have to go and meet Sophie and the girls for a swim at Orchid Bay.'

On opening morning, Becky was up early setting up the coffee machines, and getting the crockery ready. Her stomach felt sick, and she wondered why she was putting herself through this. Sadie was downstairs soon afterwards. She handed a cash-box to Becky.

'I got Jen to get it for me in Bray yesterday, and I have added a cash float, but where will we keep it?' she said.

Becky held up the small white machine which was on the kitchen table. 'I sort of presumed everybody would pay by card,' she said.

'Maisie won't.' Sadie laughed.

Becky pointed to a shelf behind the kitchen door. We can put the cash-box and machine there and maybe a notebook to record sales.'

'Hopefully we'll be run off our feet,' Sadie said, and Becky felt queasy to think they would soon be open.

She jumped when there was a knock on the front door.

'It's only me,' Iris called through the letterbox, and Becky rushed to let her in.

Iris, carrying a large rectangular box, walked through the hall to the kitchen. 'Scones just out of the oven. You should put them out on a cooling rack,' she said, placing the box on the table.

When her phone rang, Becky ignored it.

'Aren't you going to get that?' Sadie said, handing the phone to Becky.

'What if it's the radio station?'

Sadie reached over, pressed the button and put the phone on loudspeaker. Becky wanted to shout no at her friend, but when the radio station researcher introduced herself, she stayed on the call. When she had finished, she walked straight out into the backyard. Sadie followed her.

'What was that all about? I hope you're still going to do the interview.'

Becky didn't answer,

Sadie, her voice softer, asked if Becky was OK.

Becky turned around, her eyes full of anxiety.

'What are we doing here, Sadie? I think I've made a huge mistake, and what if nobody comes? Or what if I don't know what to say on the radio?'

'Slow down, girl, let's take it one step at a time.'

Becky moved away, and began to pull tea-towels off the washing line. 'I should never have been talked into this madness of opening a café,' she said, walking back into the kitchen, and throwing the tea-towels on the table.

'Girl, you have to get your shit together. Everything about coming to Coolnamona was good, and opening the café is, too. Cop on, and as for the interview, the adrenalin will kick in,' Sadie said.

Bella called through the front door letterbox to let her in.

When Becky opened the door, Bella thrust a big bunch of flowers at her.

'You'll find little table vases in the back shed. A single rose at each table gives such a lovely look,' she said.

Becky didn't know how to answer, but Sadie scuttled off to find the vases and wash them.

Bella put her arm around Becky. 'You were good to me, so I'm returning the favour. You can't open this café without the support of the Reilly family, and here I am.'

'That is very kind of you,' Becky said, beginning to cry.

'Enough of that. Maisie is coming up the lane, and there's a gaggle of women with her. Best foot forward, and all that,' Bella said firmly.

Becky hastily wiped away her tears. Pulling on a new apron Iris handed her, she rushed to the front door.

'Thank goodness, you're open. I know we're early, but there's four of us, and another six joining us in a bit. Where do you want us to sit?' Maisie said.

Becky showed them to a table near the viewing rock and was taking their order when a different group strolled in, and took over two tables near the front bay window.

Iris took the orders, and Sadie and Jen offered to help with the clearing of the tables. Bella took a table near the gate because she said it was good if the café looked busy, and she ordered an Earl Grey tea and a choc chip cookie.

Becky greeted all the visitors and hovered, a fixed smile on her face. There was the happy hum of conversation, and she allowed herself to relax a little. When her phone rang, she disappeared to her bedroom. She was surprised to find that she enjoyed the radio interview, but felt it was over too soon. Lingering by her bedroom window, she looked down at the café where about thirty people were chatting and laughing, and Ronnie was sitting on the viewing rock. At this moment, she thought life was good here at Coolnamona House.

Becky, when she came downstairs, slipped quietly into the kitchen, but Sadie came in after her and said she was needed out front. Worried, Becky followed her out the front door, where Ben, Jen, Bella and Iris were standing waiting.

'What's wrong?' she asked nervously.

Sadie took a teaspoon, clinking it against a china teacup.

'Ladies and gentlemen, the star of radio and proprietor of this wonderful café, Becky White,' she said, and everybody applauded.

Ben popped open a bottle of champagne while Jen and Iris delivered glasses of bubbly to each table.

Sadie called for quiet again. 'Please raise your glasses to The Café over Orchid Bay, phase two,' she said, and everybody cheered.

To the cries of 'speech, speech', Becky stepped forward after Bella nudged her with her elbow. She swallowed hard, and tried to pick a point high in the branches of the apple tree so she wouldn't be distracted as she spoke.

'Thank you all for being here today, and to everybody in this community who has taken us to their hearts. I would like to remember the Reilly sisters, Regina and Bella, who first opened this café many decades ago. It is our honour to now continue the tradition,' she said, and everybody clapped once again.

People stood around chatting and laughing, exchanging stories about the café in the past. A local travel agent asked if she could direct a few tour buses a week in the summer to the café, and Becky could have hugged her, she was so happy.

After a while, Ben took Becky's hand and led her out to the backyard. There, he had a table set up with two glasses and a bottle of champagne.

'I thought you might enjoy a little quiet time,' he said, pouring her a glass.

'You know me so well.' She giggled.

'Congratulations! You have done it. Regina would be so proud of you,' he said.

'I hope so,' she said, holding her face up to the afternoon sunshine to feel the warmth.

Ben wandered over to the pink rambling rose and plucked a few. 'For you,' he said.

She was laughing when she took them. 'How kind of you to gift me my own roses,' she said.

'You're so welcome,' he said, his eyes twinkling. 'You know, when Sadie and Iris are gone, myself and Brian will help out as much as we can.'

'I don't know what I would do without you,' she said, taking his hand and standing up.

Ben was about to say something, but there was a knock on the back door, and Bella stepped into the backyard.

'I hope I'm not disturbing anything,' she said.

Ben stepped away, letting Becky move towards Bella.

'Thank you, Bella, it means a lot that you came today.'

'I would have helped with the prep as well. All you had to do was ask. I don't like imposing myself on anyone,' Bella said, her voice tight.

'You're always welcome here,' Becky said, and she saw Bella's shoulders relax.

TWENTY-TWO

Becky ducked upstairs where Sadie was hauling her suitcases out onto the landing.

'I'm going back to my hometown, and I feel so nervous,' Sadie said.

'You should be proud of yourself. We're all rooting for you. Just make sure to come back to us.'

Sadie smiled. 'You and Jen are staying on past the summer, aren't you?'

'I would like to think that, but I will have to wait to hear what Jen thinks, I guess.'

Sadie sighed. 'I have to confess, there's something about this place. I always thought that there was nowhere like Manhattan, but now there's Manhattan and Coolnamona on Orchid Bay.'

Bella, who had dropped in for a cuppa, called up the stairs that Iris had arrived. 'You should bloody see her,' she hooted, and they heard Maisie laugh out loud.

Sadie led the way downstairs, stopping halfway. 'Does the woman realise how long the flight is? Does she think this is the golden age of travel?' she muttered.

Becky leaned forward to see Iris approach the front door,

and she suppressed a giggle. Iris was wearing a royal-blue trouser suit and high heels and was carrying a wide-brimmed hat.

'Is it over-the-top? I was trying for the smart casual look,' Iris said anxiously as she stepped into the hall.

Becky couldn't answer.

'You look superb,' Maisie said.

'Airlines give us such a small baggage allowance. I could only bring four hats and this one in my hand,' Iris complained.

Bella eyed Iris up and down. 'You look a picture,' she said.

Becky smiled and nodded. Maisie stepped out of the kitchen, and made to say something, but Bella stood on her toe.

'We had better get going,' Sadie said, and they all walked out to the path where Ben was waiting in his car for them. Jen and Brian were also there to say goodbye.

Ben told Iris she looked like a glamorous model – she was only missing the dark sunglasses.

Iris whipped a pair of sunglasses out of her handbag. 'Everybody will think I'm a celebrity,' she said.

'Sadie, dear, you're going to have to make a little time for me. We have to walk the High Line together.'

She turned to Becky. 'It's such a pity you couldn't come. You could have got Maisie to run the café. She could change the name to *Coffee and Gossip*,' Iris cracked.

'I'm quite happy to be here in Coolnamona,' Becky said.

Sadie, coming up behind her, hugged her friend. 'You don't know how long I've waited for you to say that. In Coolnamona, Becky, you're such a happy person, and so is Jen.'

'Shit, don't say anything. I still have to sound her out. I'm hoping she'll feel the same,' Becky said urgently.

'She wants to stay here too,' Sadie said.

'I hope you're right.'

'You look a different person. Still stressy, stressy Becky, but a happy, different type of stressy, if you know what I mean. It makes sense to stay in Coolnamona,' she said.

As she got in the car, Sadie pulled Becky close, and whispered in her ear. 'And you're some pal to leave me all on my own with Iris and her itinerary.'

'You're so welcome.' Becky laughed.

'I'll miss you, but I have Ninja Iris,' Sadie said as she shut the car door.

Becky stood in the lane, and waved them off until the car had turned onto the main street and out of sight.

Jen took a large white envelope from the postman, who was passing on his bicycle.

'It's addressed to Regina. Shit, didn't she die years ago?' Jen said, examining the envelope.

Becky took it from her hands. 'Maybe I should give it to Bella.'

'Mom, just open it. It might be junk mail. If it turns out to be anything, you can give it to Bella then.'

'OK, but not right now,' Becky said, walking up the path. In the hall, she tossed the envelope in a drawer.

Jen looked at her phone. 'Brian's here. You know I will be back late,' she said, bolting down the lane.

Becky heard Jen talk to somebody at the front of the house, and she rushed to put on her apron.

When she got as far as the garden, four people were already sitting down, and looking at the menu. Stepping out into the garden, she stood for a moment to watch the robin as it flew between the tables pecking, diligently checking for crumbs. The waves tapped against the distant shore, the sound intermingling with the cries of the children playing loudly on the beach at Orchid Bay. One of the tourists was standing on the rock, scanning the horizon with his binoculars. He jumped off when he saw Becky.

'It's a clear day, but I can't see Wales, not even through these things,' he said, his voice low and disappointed.

Becky smiled sweetly, ignoring his tone, and he went back to the table.

'Are you the lady from the States who has brought this place back to life?' a woman asked.

'I suppose I am,' Becky said. She felt a thrill of excitement that here she was in a strange country, and she had managed – with a lot of help – to resurrect this café.

Becky was worried she would have to handle the lunchtime rush on her own. She set up the coffee machine, and put some scones in the microwave to heat them up. Clattering the plates down in a row, she placed them on a tray along with homemade jam and marmalade she'd spooned into little bowls, before making two mochas and two cappuccinos.

Becky was on her way to serve the guests at the front garden table, when Maisie came in the front door.

'I came back to help. I can see you're swamped, and Mademoiselle Jen is gone to Dublin. Let me lend a hand,' Maisie said.

'I would be very grateful,' Becky said, but had to break off to take a phone call. 'Shit, there are two tour buses due in the next hour. They say Sadie took the booking last week,' Becky said as she put away her phone.

'Didn't she say?'

'I guess she had a lot on her mind.'

'Well we had better get to work. We have a lot on our backs now,' Maisie said.

Becky started her deep breathing exercises.

Maisie walked purposefully into the kitchen. 'How many people am I baking for?' she asked.

'Two tour buses, about sixty people,' Becky said feebly, flopping down at the kitchen table, her head in her hands. 'We don't have enough cookies, and what if they don't all want scones? What the fricking hell are we going to do?'

Maisie, her head bowed, cut out the scone shapes, and put them on two baking trays, shoving them quickly in the oven. 'I rang Claire. She's only back a few days at the deli, but working hard.'

'I didn't realise Claire was coming back to Coolnamona and reopening the deli.'

'She says since Edith died she's going mad, and must work to keep her sanity. She quietly opened her doors yesterday.'

'I have been so wrapped up in this place, I didn't know,' Becky said.

'She has a freshly baked batch of cookies, choc chip, all of them, about fifty biscuits. She'll drop them up shortly,' Maisie said, shutting the oven door gently.

'But doesn't she need them today?'

'She says most customers are looking for her sambos and baguettes. She'll just take the cookies off the menu for the day.'

'I hope you told her we'll pay her.'

'That's between you and her. She's here. I see her car pulling up on the lane.'

Claire lingered to talk to the group of tourists at the outside tables. When she walked in carrying a large basket, Becky jumped up to thank her.

'Warm choc chip cookies. Best to put them out on a cooling rack,' Claire said.

Becky looked under the tea cloth. 'Hey, these smell so wonderful. You're a life-saver.'

'No bother.'

'I will pay you. We can't have you taking a loss on this amount of cookies.'

'No need.'

'I insist,' Becky said firmly.

Claire swung around sharply. 'You helped myself and Edith when we needed it most. I owe you, so here I am with a basket of cookies. Edith would have wanted me to do this.'

'I didn't help much, just listened.'

'You did more than that for Edith. You made us realise we needed to spend time together. I will never regret those precious last weeks, just the two of us. Thanks to you, we didn't waste the important last days and weeks together immersed in silly disputes and bitterness.'

Becky reached over, and took Claire's hand. 'I was happy to help, and I hope we can be friends now,' she said.

Claire, her eyes cloudy with tears, nodded.

There was a loud honking noise as a tour bus attempted to come up the lane. Maisie went out to tell the driver to back away, and park on the main street, while Becky switched on the kettles, and checked the coffee machine.

Claire said she had to get back to the deli, dashing out the front before the tourists descended on the café. Becky checked her appearance in the hall mirror, and she wished she had put on make-up that morning. Sadie usually did the meet and greet, but now Becky had to do everything.

Maisie helped get most of the first tour bus seated. The others were happy to sit on benches Ben had only a few days earlier placed around the side walls.

Ronnie trotted into the kitchen, and curled up in front of the Aga, even though it wasn't lighting. Becky hadn't the heart to push the dog out.

'Maisie, can you please go around the benches at the side and take the orders. You know our menu, don't you?'

'Like the back of my hand. Don't you worry. I'm on it,' Maisie said, her face beaming with delight.

For the next few hours, they worked side by side, Maisie taking orders as well as emptying and stacking the dishwasher in between chatting to the tourists and customers. Ronnie went out to the front garden where customers delighted in feeding him the leftovers. Maisie concentrated on the teas and coffees.

When they had waved off the last customer, Becky invited her in for a drink.

'I don't know about you, but I need a long drink with alcohol,' she said, reaching for a bottle of white wine and two glasses.

'I don't usually partake of alcohol during the day, but in this case, I will make an exception,' Maisie said excitedly.

Becky put up the closed sign on the front window, and they shut the front door, moving to sit in the back garden.

'Regina never let me in here. I never got past the hall and dining room. I have no idea why. What a huge garden, and so beautifully tended. I didn't know you were a gardener, Becky,' Maisie exclaimed.

Becky sat down, holding her face up to the afternoon sunshine. She always loved this time of the day when the work was done. These days, after the café tidy-up, she exulted in the quietness of Coolnamona House. Maisie though, liked to babble on. When Becky hadn't answered promptly, she enquired again about gardening as if this were a question that required an immediate answer.

'You must be joking. That has nothing to do with me. Ben and Brian are the gardeners,' she said, heading back to the kitchen to prepare a plate of cheese and crackers, with a bowl of olives and sundried tomatoes on the side.

'Things at Coolnamona House have got very fancy,' Maisie said, crunching a cracker and cheese.

Becky smiled to think what Maisie would tell the whole town by tomorrow. 'We will have to call you our PR person, Maisie, because you're singing our praises around town.'

'I like to know what's going on. It's all harmless,' Maisie said.

Ronnie sat beside them, and began to push Maisie's elbow, and paw at her skirt.

'He's so bold. It's his feed time, and he's not going to leave me alone until he gets his bowl of chicken or beef. You know, Becky, what he can get up to when he doesn't get his grub,' she said, standing up and clipping a lead on the dog.

'Don't get up. I will see myself out,' she said.

Becky remained in the sunshine, listening to the bees as they moved across the bank of oriental poppies at the bottom of the garden. She felt content, or as content as she could ever be. There was no doubt their lives had changed for the good, but always lurking in the background was the reason she had fled Manhattan. While that remained unresolved, could she ever say she was truly happy?

TWENTY-THREE

The next morning, Jen knocked on Becky's bedroom door shortly before eight o'clock.

'Mom, can we talk?'

Becky sat up in bed, rubbing her eyes. 'Is there something wrong, sweetheart?'

'Nothing bad, but, and I know I'm early with this, we're coming to near the end of our time here. It's mid-July already, and I want to know what we're doing next,' she said, sitting at the end of Becky's bed.

'We agreed the next step will be decided by both of us.'

'Can we do that now?'

'Sure, but what's the hurry all of a sudden? Is it because Sadie has gone back to the States?'

'I just want to discuss our options.'

Becky got up and pulled on Regina's dressing gown. 'Every talk is better over breakfast. Why don't we go downstairs ? I'll make pancakes.'

'Just let me get a hoodie on,' Jen said, taking one of Becky's.

In the kitchen, Becky got out the eggs, milk and flour, and

Jen set up the frying pan, and cut some butter, plopping a cube in the pan to melt.

'Remember when we used to make pancakes every Saturday morning, and Granny Hilda always said it would put pounds on our hips?' Jen laughed.

'And she would never join in, but always had her say. She was so stubborn,' Becky added. It was good, she thought, that they were remembering all sides of Hilda White.

Becky whipped up the mix, and poured some onto the pan.

'So what's on your mind, Jen? Is it Brian by any chance?'

Jen pushed her mother affectionately. 'No, it's not about Brian. I wanted to talk about what's next. Are we going back to Manhattan?'

'Do you want to?'

'Does it matter what I want?'

Becky fake-clipped Jen about the ears. 'Seriously, baby girl, we need to talk, and no sweeping statements about my bad parenting. That doesn't sit well with me.'

Jen slid the pancakes out onto two plates, and doused them in maple syrup. They sat down together.

'I don't want to go back and live in Manhattan, I want to stay here,' Jen said quickly.

Becky looked at her daughter. She had grown up so much in the last few months. Her face had changed too. She looked more like Hilda now, with the long nose and the big hazel eyes accentuated by her kohl eyeliner.

'Are you sure? Why the change of heart?' Becky tried to sound as normal as possible.

'I like it here, and I can finish off school, too. I've checked.'

'Steady on, girl. You do know Brian goes to boarding school near the city?'

'He comes home on the holidays and some weekends. Anyway, I would like to go to school with the girls in Greystones.'

'It's a big step, Jen. You can't base everything on one boy.'

Jen put down her fork and knife. 'Mom, I would never be that stupid. I like Coolnamona House. It just feels right, and I have more friends here than I ever did back in the States. Iris says I should think about art college.'

'You certainly have the talent.'

'Does that mean you're seriously thinking about it?'

'Yes, I like it here too,' Becky said tentatively.

'Mom, you're the best. I'm going to get dressed, and go and tell Brian.'

'We need to talk about this some more.'

'Yeah, but can we do that later?'

Becky called Jen back. 'Are you sure you don't just want to stay because of Brian? You know you can't change your mind in a few weeks. If we're staying, it's very much for good.'

'Mom, it's like you said, Coolnamona House is home. I don't know anyone in Manhattan any more. I don't even bother following the girls on Snapchat or Instagram.'

'As long as you're sure.'

Becky needed to think about this permanent move to Coolnamona, but for now she had to prepare for Bella arriving. It was time to give Bella the note with her name on it, and she had invited her to call up before the café opened.

Rummaging in the cabinet, Becky pulled out Regina's china teapot, and opened it to fish out the envelope and notes. She had already scanned Bella's note, but she sat down, and read it through now in an effort to assuage her worry that maybe she wasn't doing the right thing by showing it to Bella.

My dearest Laura,

I've had so many years to mull over my actions towards Bella. She tried to help you, and now I realise, far too late, she tried to help me. Life is full of decisions and the consequences of those decisions. How I wish I had an opportunity to rethink the two bad decisions I made about you and Bella.

A while after you walked out, I banished her from my life. I said dreadful things I bitterly regret. I blamed her for everything when it was my intransigence, my pigheaded stubbornness which brought everything to a head.

I am totally at fault, and if there was any hope of meeting you, I would tell that to your face, and I would say I was sorry over and over until you were tired of hearing it.

I am sure you would ask why didn't I walk up the lane, take a right and go as far as Bella's little flat and sort this out. She certainly tried to communicate with me. She came around here on my birthday every year, also on your birthday and at Christmas. All she asked of me was to sit and talk, and I denied her that.

I won't try to explain why I refused her, ran her from the door, and even banged it in her face. I have no credible explanation. I could not bear to talk to Bella, and yet I so wanted to confide in my sister. I was so unsure, so upset and so alone, but my doubts, my worries and my shame paralysed me and incarcerated me. It is a lot easier to stay indignant, to believe that you are wronged, than face the truth and ask for help.

I am ashamed of my actions towards you, and to Bella. To use your type of language, I messed up big, and instead of putting up my hands, and asking my sister to forgive me and help me to find you, I turned her away.

Please do not pity me, but pity Bella, who did nothing, only help her niece when she needed her most, and when her mother had turned away from her.

My hope is that Bella, if she ever reads this, will be set free, and the rage and indignation in her at the way I treated her, in time, will dissipate.

I pray that Bella will forgive me, and that you at some stage can remember me kindly. Know this: I have loved you, and will continue to love you and Bella to my dying breath.

Mam

XX

'Yoo hoo, anybody home?' Bella called out in a sing-song voice as she walked up the path.

Becky swiped away the tears from her face before opening the cabinet, and hastily stuffing the note and envelope back in Regina's teapot.

'What's going on? You still have the sign at closed,' Bella said as she stepped into the hall, and pushed a box of freshly made scones into Becky's hands.

'Did you switch the sign around to open?' Becky said as she carried the box into the kitchen.

'I did. Now, I must get something off my chest. Maisie Ryan is telling the whole town she's going to be taking over from Iris now she's gone to the Big Apple, and baking her scones for the café. If you take my advice, you'll only use them when you run out of my Reilly scones. Maisie's offerings are far too dry. The Reilly scone recipe was much sought-after, and sealed the high reputation of this café. Regina stuck to the recipe, even when I was no longer involved with the business.'

'I didn't mean to cause any rift. You both bake such lovely scones,' Becky said, but she knew immediately she had said the wrong thing when she saw Bella scowl. She sat, and waited for the next eruption, but the sound of the garden gate opening meant she could bolt from the kitchen to the front garden.

There was the happy chatter of a group of six women dropping in for a cuppa after their yoga session at Orchid Bay.

'Can you give me a hand, Bella? I didn't expect such a big group so early,' Becky called out.

Bella beamed with delight. 'I am only too delighted to help out. Maisie Ryan can put that in her pipe and smoke it. What does she know about Coolnamona House, anyway?'

Becky felt nervous, but she tried not to show it. She had asked Bella to help out, but she got the impression that Bella thought what was on offer was a permanent job. She needed Sadie here to talk straight to both Bella and Maisie.

Bella threw off her jacket, put it on the hook at the back door, and took an apron from the worktop. 'I will go out and persuade these ladies they need to eat after the walk up the hill,' she said as she bustled outside with a notebook and pen.

Becky put on the kettle because she knew they would all order mint tea. When she heard Maisie coming up the path, she groaned.

'Reporting for duty,' Maisie called out as she came through the front door.

'You'll have to do without an apron. There aren't enough to go around,' Bella snapped as she pushed past to get her order ready.

Maisie plonked her box of scones on the table.

'I hope Bella can be professional about this, but Becky, I'm disappointed you didn't tell me she would be working here as well.'

'It's all hands on deck while Sadie and Iris are gone. Becky has more to be doing than informing you about every decision she makes,' Bella said as she edged past Maisie with a tray of tea for the table at the front window.

'I couldn't get that lot to pick anything to eat. Better to run tea-and-scone specials. It works every time,' she muttered to nobody in particular.

Maisie confined herself to the clear-up, and Becky knew she was staying out of Bella's way. At one stage, Bella complained that the dishwasher wasn't stacked properly, and Maisie barked that she could walk out, that Bella was good at that.

By the time it came to close the café, Becky had a headache from navigating the tension between the two women. After Maisie had left, she asked to speak to Bella in the sitting room.

'I have elbowed my way in here, haven't I? I'm sorry, it's just I couldn't bear to think of Maisie lording it all over the place. I hope this doesn't put us back on bad terms.'

'Don't be silly. I wanted to talk to you about Regina.'

Bella hesitated. 'I don't want to talk about my sister. It's a subject that is off limits, please,' she said, her voice strained.

Becky saw the scowl on her face, and put her hand out to gently steer Bella into the sitting room. Nervously, Bella sat down on the edge of the sofa, her hands clasped together on her lap.

'Becky, we are getting on fine. Let's not spoil it,' she said.

Becky didn't say anything, but reached into the cabinet, and pulled out the teapot. She took out the pink note, and handed it to Bella.

'What is this?' Bella said.

'I found it with this letter concealed behind the painting.'

She handed the letter to Bella, who took it, her hand shaking.

'That's Regina's handwriting. She won't want me reading this.'

'The pink note is for you.'

Becky saw the pain flash across Bella's eyes.

'No, I can't. Too much time has passed. There's hardly a point.'

'Trust me, you're going to want to read the note. The letter, too. Will I leave you on your own to do it?'

Bella grasped Becky's hand. 'Can you stay with me, please?'

'Of course.'

Becky, as she sat beside Bella, felt her tremble, and heard her gasp as she began to read. She sat quietly beside her, concentrating on the portrait. When Bella began to sob, she squeezed her hand.

Bella took out a lace handkerchief from her pocket, and blew her nose.

'We were so close once. We were sisters and best friends. She could have posted it to me. I would have come knocking on the door,' she sobbed.

'Can I offer you tea or would you like something stronger?' Becky asked.

Bella slowly stood up. 'Thank you for this. You will never know how much it means to me, but at the moment I am feeling overwhelmed, and I cannot talk about it. I need to go for a walk, and think about this, contemplate on the years lost. If only Laura had come back, we could have sorted everything out.'

Becky linked arms with Bella to the front door.

'It was a good day when you took over Coolnamona House. I would never have found this note but for you, Becky.' She made to give the pink note back, but Becky pressed it into her hand. 'I will read and reread it,' Bella said before making her way down the path. Becky watched her walk up the lane, slightly staggering as if she were carrying something heavy.

TWENTY-FOUR

Becky was in the kitchen preparing for the café opening the next day, when Ben came around to the back door.

'I was afraid of waking you up, but Bella insisted I come at the crack of dawn. Don't tell her I waited until a civilised 8 a.m.'

'Is she all right?'

'I'm not sure. Did something happen between you?' he said, stepping into the kitchen.

Becky handed him a mug of coffee, and he sat at the table. 'I gave her a letter Regina wrote to her. I found it at the back of the painting. There were other notes too. Regina was a very sad and lonely lady. Did you know her?'

Ben shrugged. 'She was just a dear old lady. Sometimes we talked at the gate. I didn't really frequent the café. She felt I was the competition, when in fact we were geared towards different markets. Regina saw enemies everywhere. She seemed an unhappy person.'

'And Bella?'

'I think most people took Regina's side. Not that anyone really knew what had happened, only that Regina was so upset by what Bella did, she threw her out of the house. Bella became a little contrary, and Regina liked playing the innocent old lady who had been wronged.'

He reached into his pocket, and pulled out a letter. 'She called me around last night, and gave me this letter for you. She said I was to apologise on her behalf, but she can't help out at the café any more.'

Becky took the light pink envelope. Quickly, she opened it, and pulled out a lilac-coloured note, butterfly drawings at each corner.

'Who thought Bella was such a girlie girl with her fancy paper?' she said. She read the letter aloud.

My dear Becky,

Thank you for your kindness to me, but I'll not be able to help out at the café any longer. I apologise if this inconveniences you in any way. I am sure in my absence Maisie Ryan will do a satisfactory job. However, I enclose the Reilly scone recipe. Please feel free to use it so you don't have to depend on the dry offering from Maisie Ryan.

Kind regards,

Bella Carter

'She didn't need to write such a formal letter,' Becky said, her voice low with disappointment.

'You know Bella, she does everything right. I know Maisie can only give you two or more hours in the morning. It's my day off from the restaurant. I would be happy to help out.'

Becky sighed. 'I'm sure the last thing you want to be doing is serving tea and coffee in a café on your day off. Jen said she and Brian will help out too.'

'Get me to work. I might as well be helping as we're chatting,' he said, standing up and waiting for orders.

'If it's not too much to ask, could you do about twenty scones? Bella's recipe.'

Ben took it and read it. 'Regina always said that she could win hands down with the Reilly scone recipe, that it had been passed from generation to generation, and she could never reveal the secret ingredient. What a load of bullshit. There is no extra ingredient.'

'Maybe it was the Reilly light touch.'

Ben laughed out loud. 'That's a joke, isn't it?'

Jen and Brian started getting the outside tables ready.

'I think it's going to rain. Have you a contingency plan?' Ben asked.

Becky, who had been on the phone to the tour company just before Ben arrived said no, and a group of tourists were going to be dropped off in about an hour.

'Can't people sit under the parasols?'

'You're forgetting that it's a bit chilly this morning. Nobody is going to want to sit outside if it rains.'

'The sitting room is too small, and I haven't got the dining room ready.'

Ben walked up the hall, and peered into the room. 'It's tidy and clean. I will get a few chairs from the restaurant, and put them around the side walls, and you can have a buffet. They can help themselves.'

He left to get the chairs, while Brian and Jen lit a fire in the grate, and dusted the chandelier.

Ben, fifteen minutes later, pulled up in the jeep, and called out for the others to help with the chairs.

Everybody pitched in, and they had everything in place and the warm scones on plates when the tour group came to the front gate. Becky called the tour guide aside, and agreed a set price, as everybody piled into the house and began helping themselves to the buffet. Ben walked around with a large coffee pot and teapot filling cups and mugs, and Jen answered questions. When Maisie arrived at her usual time, she was surprised to see that they had opened early.

'You should have told me, I could have helped,' she said, disappointed.

Ben said he would call back later for the chairs, and he left by the back door.

'That man is trying to get his legs under your table. You want to watch that. I'm sure he would love a property like this to expand his business,' Maisie muttered.

'Let's just get on with the work. I think Ben is a very good neighbour, and the café is no competition to his restaurant,' Becky said.

'Don't mind me, I'm only making conversation. Where is Bella this morning?'

'She wasn't feeling well. I told her to take a day or two off.'

Becky saw Maisie frown.

They all worked side by side until the tourist group left. Maisie said she would do the clear-up if Becky wanted to take a rest.

Jen went outside to dry off the tables and chairs. Becky, feeling at a loose end, said she was going for a walk, and asked her to do the lock-up at four o'clock.

Becky would have liked to walk down by the sea, but she found herself going to the right towards the bakery and Bella's flat. When she got there, she dithered on whether she should push the intercom button. She had decided to leave it, and was turning to the park across the way, when a window opened up above her, and Bella stuck her head out.

'Do you want to come up, or do you want to continue loitering in the doorway?' Bella called out.

At the same time, she buzzed her in. Becky stepped into a light-filled hall. Bella came out on the landing as Becky slowly climbed the stairs. At the top, Bella led her into a large sitting room with a wide window overlooking the street and the park.

Becky took in the modern furniture, art deco lamps and the old mantelpiece where a modern painting had been placed.

'You expected me to be living in a sad old place with a faded carpet and thrift shop furniture, didn't you?' Bella said.

Becky felt uncomfortable.

'Go on, admit it.'

'OK, yes. It's not what I expected.'

Bella looked satisfied that her assessment was correct. Becky stood in the middle of the floor, not sure what to say. Bella pointed to a chair, and told her to sit.

'I needed time to think, Becky, and I couldn't face Maisie Ryan this morning. I hope you're not cross with me.'

'I just wanted to make sure you were OK.'

Without asking, Bella took out a bottle of brandy, and poured some into crystal glasses. 'You deserve an explanation, and this is too much for a mere cup of tea or coffee.

'You don't have to explain anything to me.'

Bella handed Becky a brandy glass. 'I haven't been OK for a long time, but I'm used to this type of existence. Now, let's toast to our friendship, please, before I get all maudlin.'

They clinked, both looking to the park in the distance.

'I'm just going to start because you deserve to know what all this is about,' Bella said.

Becky made to protest, but Bella told her to hush. 'You have only one chance of hearing this, so please let me tell you why Regina and I came to this awful hiatus.

'I lived in Coolnamona House with Regina, her husband and Laura, and when Regina's husband died, it was the three of us against the world. Regina went back to the Reilly name; we were the Reilly household, strong and united. We had a happy existence running the café, and making our designer dresses. Laura was our sweetheart. We lived our lives through her. She went into the teenage years and like all teenagers, she became a little difficult. She began seeing a boy in another town. She confided in me, and I guess I covered for her at times. Young love is such a precious thing.

'There was a change in Laura, and Regina, because she did not have the backup and support of a husband, felt it very deeply. When she finally discovered Laura was seeing the boy, she went mad. She went to the local priest for help, and I get the impression he sort of ran operations from there. All I know is Regina was on a mission to save her daughter from the clutches of this boy, and she even suggested sending Laura away on retreat for a while. You have to know, Regina was a devout woman and I think at that time, we all thought the local priest knew best.

'Regina insisted that Laura, who was just eighteen years of age, give the boy up and go immediately on retreat to the west of Ireland. Poor Laura was no match for Regina, though she tried her best to fight her mother. There was an awful lot of shouting, and it went totally out of hand. Regina said Laura would forever regret that she did not listen to her mother. Regina contacted the boy's family, and his father sent him away. After that, she and Laura had a big fight.'

Becky reached for the bottle of brandy, and topped up both their glasses. 'It is hard to listen to this story; and even harder to understand,' she said.

Bella shifted in her seat, and almost as if she had not even heard Becky, she continued.

'Laura came to me, and said she wanted to see her young man one last time, and she asked me for money to go and visit him. They planned to meet in Dublin. I gave her quite a bit of money. I didn't think it was right that the two of them had been so brutally separated. The next day, she got the train to Dublin, but when Regina found out, she went mad all over again.

'When Laura walked back into the house that night, Regina

was waiting for her. Terrible things were said on both sides, and Laura stormed out of the house into the darkness. We thought she would come slinking back, but she never returned. And there you have it, the sad story of the Reillys.'

Becky gulped her brandy.

'You know the worst part,' Bella continued. 'A week later, Laura wrote to Regina, and said she was OK, but was not coming back. There was an English postmark. Regina couldn't understand how Laura had the money to get the boat across the water. I didn't tell her then. It was years later when I blurted out that I had given Laura the money. I couldn't keep it to myself any longer. Regina's reaction was immediate. There was no talking to her. She ordered me out.'

Bella's voice faltered.

Becky moved towards her, but she pulled away.

'If you don't mind, I can't talk about this any more. Regina was right. I should never have given Laura the money. She would never have gone away if I had not done that.'

'You don't know that,' Becky whispered.

Bella looked at her. 'I do know it, and it is my cross to bear every waking moment,' she said, her tears choking her voice.

Becky reached out, and pulled Bella to her. They stood, their arms around each other, until Bella pulled away to get a tissue to blow her nose.

TWENTY-FIVE

The next day was Sunday, and the café was closed. Becky loitered about the house, but couldn't focus. She tried to relax, but the story of Bella and Regina kept interrupting her thoughts. A part of her wanted to be able to rewrite their chapter, but this late, she knew nobody could.

Stepping out into the front garden, she headed for the rock. Standing on it, she scanned across the sea, hoping to see Wales, the mountain peaks just visible on the horizon. A thrill of excitement flashed through her, but also a deep regret that Hilda never told her about Coolnamona or Orchid Bay. Loneliness crossed over her heart that she could never share Coolnamona with Hilda. She wasn't sure exactly how Hilda White would have fitted in here, and she certainly would not agree with them opting to stay past the summer. Hilda always said it would be impossible to catch up if you missed a season on the social circuit in Manhattan.

Becky needed to get away, so she sent a quick text to Jen that she was going for a walk, and would see her later. Easing the gate open slowly, she quickly walked up the lane to the main street. The street was quiet but she thought she saw somebody loitering by the railings of the courthouse. She didn't think much of it until she saw it was a man, who, when she turned right, began to walk behind her. Her hands stuffed in her hoodie pockets, she walked purposefully along, fear creeping through her. In her head she tried to rationalise that it was a coincidence that this man was walking behind her, and any minute, he would overtake and relief would flood through her.

She tried to glance behind, but all she could make out was a hooded figure with his head down. She nipped across the street, making sure to look in his direction. She thought he quickly adjusted, and she could only make out his back and his sneakers, golden-brown, which she thought were alligator-grain sneakers. It made her even more uneasy, and she scanned up the street to see if there was anybody who could help. The man turned down a side street, and she stood watching him get into a car with a Dublin registration, and drive away. She thought she recognised his gait and the whip of his shoulders as he hurried along to the car. There was something different about him too; the way he dressed was big city. Fear prickled on her back, and she began to perspire.

Becky continued on, not sure what had just happened. When a woman outside the church waved to her, Becky rushed over.

'What's the matter? You look as if you have seen a ghost,' Bella said, her voice full of concern.

'It's probably nothing. I thought somebody was walking too close.'

'You've spent too much time in New York. This is Coolnamona. Come on, let me buy you a cup of coffee,' Bella guffawed.

'I don't know, I felt scared,' Becky said.

Bella linked Becky's arm. 'Since Coolnamona Café is closed on a Sunday, one of the ladies from the church opens up her front room, and serves beverages and lemon drizzle cake. It's quite cosy.'

'OK.'

'Well, let's sit and have a cuppa together,' Bella said, leading the way down a narrow street lined with red-brick houses. Halfway down, they stopped at a terraced house, where there was a homemade sign on the window which said *The Sunday Café*.

Bella leaned over to Becky, and whispered in her ear as they knocked on the front door. 'The tea is a common breakfast variety, but the coffee, I'm told, is good, and her lemon drizzle is divine.'

Bella walked ahead of Becky into what looked like a small carpeted sitting room at the front of the house. A woman bustled over from behind a makeshift counter, and greeted them.

'The Yank who has resurrected the café at Coolnamona House. Wouldn't it be grand if Regina was still around to see it? I am honoured. I am Denise,' she said, shaking Becky's hand.

Bella said she would have her usual, and Becky would have the cake and coffee. Denise pulled Becky to one side before they sat down.

'Stick with Bella, and you'll be all right. She's all bluster, that one, but she has a heart of gold,' she said, calling out loudly to Bella to take the seats by the open fire.

Bella fussed, rearranging and fiddling with the table setting until Becky put her hand out, and rested it on hers. 'It's silly, but I'm nervous,' Bella said.

'I'm not here to interrogate you.'

'I just don't understand why you're so interested.'

Becky smiled. 'I'm not really sure why, but I feel a connection to Coolnamona House and Regina's story just cuts me up. What happened to you, Bella, left me feeling so sad.'

Bella sighed heavily. 'Pardon me, if I don't share your enthusiasm for the topic,' she said.

'I'm just trying to fit the pieces of the jigsaw. There is something so special about Coolnamona House, and yet what happened there was tragic and so desperately sad.'

'It's life, Becky, just family life,' Bella interrupted, her voice deflated. Becky thought Bella was going to cry but instead, she shifted in her seat to look at Becky directly before speaking again. 'Our life was great, and then it wasn't. End of story,' she said firmly.

'I didn't mean to upset you.'

'I have said all I'm going to say about my sister. All these years after her death, people still only want to talk about Regina. They don't ask how Bella is doing. Regina was the beautiful one, the popular one. I was always in her shadow, and I still am. I have to live my life in the long shadow of a ghost.'

Becky didn't know what to say.

Bella leaned back when she saw Denise come with a tray, and she waited until the tea, coffee and cake had been put on the table before she spoke again. 'Tell me, why exactly are you so interested in Regina and Coolnamona?'

'I own the house. I feel the weight of the story, I suppose, especially after finding the envelope, and there is something so, I don't know, I can't quite put my finger on it, but something so innocent about Regina in that portrait. I feel somehow life passed her by.'

Bella clattered her cup on the saucer before she spoke, her voice hushed, but urgent. 'What nonsense! She was a sad old bat at the end, but in her day, she was a good sister, wife and mother. Time eroded all the kindness and goodness in her, and she became everything she would have previously frowned upon: a bitter old woman who couldn't take the first steps towards forgiveness and reconciliation. Hers is a sad case, for sure,' Bella said, taking her spoon, and stirring her tea so fast, some sloshed onto the saucer.

Becky watched as Bella slowed down the spoon movement,

first stirring in a clockwise direction, before changing and stirring in an anticlockwise direction.

'I didn't want to talk about my sister. It makes me agitated,'
Bella said, replacing the teaspoon on her saucer.

Becky cut her lemon drizzle cake into bite-size pieces before
tasting one. 'I wish we could serve this at our café,' she said,
making Bella snort in derision.

'You know, Denise makes it all from a packet. You hardly
want that.'

'It tastes delicious.'

'The real test is would you think the same next Sunday and
the Sunday after that?' Bella snorted. 'You're a good person,
Becky, and I appreciate your kindness yesterday. I would like to
be able to visit Coolnamona House from time to time.'

'Sure, you're welcome any time.'

'That is kind of you, but do you think we could move on,
leave the past behind, if you get my drift?'

'Yes, if that is what you want,' Becky said uncertainly.

Bella leaned closer so that her face was almost touching
Becky's. 'Can I offer some advice?' she said in an unusually low
voice.

'Sure.'

'Feel free to tell me to piss off, that I'm not wanted. God
knows I have been told that often enough at Coolnamona
House.'

She paused, but when Becky didn't say anything, she took a
deep breath and continued. 'I just wanted to say, forget about
what came before about Regina and all that stuff. Let Coolnamona House enter its next phase. You're the new owner, but
don't let the previous one dominate your life.'

'I'm not doing that.'

Bella shrugged. 'If you say so. I had to learn the hard way,
my dear, that the past can pull you down. If you're not careful,
the house and café will dominate your life. Enjoy Coolnamona

House as it is. Clear it out, and don't get dragged down by the past.'

Becky shifted in her seat.

'You think I'm sticking my nose in where it's not wanted, don't you?' Bella said.

'I don't, but I want to know the past. The house is so beautiful, and Regina's presence is everywhere.'

'Darling, it's time to put your own stamp on the place. Otherwise, you'll be constantly looking over your shoulder, second-guessing yourself, wondering what would Regina have done? That's no way to live.'

After she had made her speech, she gestured to Denise to bring the bill.

'I am off for my Sunday walk now. I go the long way round to the old cemetery at the far side of town. If I come across your stalker, I'll give him an earful. I visit my sister's grave where I sit and chat for a while. It's about the only time I have ever had of speaking without Regina interrupting.'

Becky walked out with her, stopping to thank Denise on the way. Bella, at the end of the street, paused to lightly embrace Becky. 'I'm glad we had this chat,' she said.

Becky continued back towards Coolnamona. In the sitting room, she pulled the second to last note from the teapot.

It was a note written on lilac paper.

My dear Laura,

Today, I was told by the private detective to expect some news soon. Their investigations are seemingly going well. I could hardly breathe when he said it, and I wondered if he was just trying to fob off a silly old lady who rang him once a week for the last six months.

There were so many at the café today, and I wanted to run from table to table to tell them I might soon know what happened my Laura. I didn't, of course; you know me, I never let anyone know what I'm feeling. I wanted to tell my best friend, Iris, but I didn't.

I know you're thinking how could I have a best friend. There was a time when I let nobody into our lives. I know that was wrong now. I was torn up after the death of your father. I took Bella in, but in truth, I was jealous of how you and her got on. I let that petty jealousy take me over, and I let my stupid pride and fear of being shamed ruin our lives.

I am going to stop now, and instead, I want to remind you and myself of when times were good for us. Remember when we would skip down the lane to the sea, and we would pick pebbles on the shingle beach?

You once found one in the shape of Australia, and you insisted it was a sign that you were going to travel far. Have you travelled far, Laura? It's my wish that you are having a good life, and my greater wish that you have not let my stupidity pull you down. My hope is that you have carved out a big life for yourself, and I hope against hope that you have found love. Love sustains us when the rest of the world has gone mad.

My world has gone mad. Inside, my head has gone mad. I pray that the private detective has news, any news for me. I want to be set free of this longing in my heart, to be given the freedom of knowing about you. Imagine if I got your address. It wouldn't matter where in the world you were, I would go to you.

I have declined, and I don't have much time left as myself. I can write the following because at this juncture, I hardly think that anybody will read this letter, and if you do, which is only a remote possibility, well, I want you to know I have always loved you, and will until the end of time. My mind is going, Laura. There is a long official name for it, but to even say it frightens me. I refuse to recognise it, but I am not stupid enough to ignore it. It is one of the reasons I am constantly writing these letters. There is a great need in me to remind myself of what has happened, good times and bad.

However, I dread losing this feeling of longing for you. I dread that I won't be able to apologise to you in person, but my biggest fear is that they will find you, and by the time they do, it will be too late for the both of us, and I won't recognise you. How sad is it to think that you would be confronted by an old lady with a blank mind?

I still have enough stupid pride to not let that happen. My time is near, and all I can think of is that I love you, Laura, and dementia is not going to steal that love for you. Laura, remember I love you always. It is my intention to cheat dementia of taking my love for you away. It is a cruel disease, but I will beat it my way. When I take my last breath, I will know I have a daughter called Laura, and that I love her so much.

All my love,

Mam

XX

Becky pushed the note back in the teapot. She couldn't look at the portrait; she knew too much.

She went upstairs to sit at the dressing table. Opening the drawer, she took out a dark navy velvet box. Snapping it open, she saw a delicate gold necklace with an opal stone in a yellow-gold setting. A vintage piece, she held it up to the light, marvelling at the soft blue-pink colours of the opal. Instantly, she recognised the piece. It was the necklace that Regina was wearing in the portrait. She could never get away from Regina; it would always be her house. Reaching over, she picked up an old cardboard box and started to stack the velvet boxes in it. One, two and then ten boxes; many she had not even opened. She took one last look at the opal. It was so small and so exquisite, it took her breath away. She pushed the box under the bed, and closed the empty drawer. She wished she could box Regina away as easily.

TWENTY-SIX

Becky was cleaning off the outside tables when a taxi pulled up at the gate. Iris waved, and walked up the path dressed in jeans, sneakers and a hoodie.

'My God, look at you,' Becky said.

'Isn't it fantastic? It's the new me. I'm a New Yorker now, Becky. How could you ever have left the place?'

'Where's your baggage?'

'Just one case. Who needed all those hats, anyway?' Iris stepped up on the rock, and took a deep breath. 'Smell that sea air. I missed it, and bizarrely I missed Coolnamona House. There is nowhere like Orchid Bay in August.'

'We're so glad you came back. Sadie just said everything worked out, but she was in such a rush when she rang. What happened exactly?'

Iris continued to look out to sea. 'She went over there, and kicked ass. Your friend is one strong woman.'

Becky put her hand out to help Iris from the rock, but she pushed it away.

'I'm so fit. There's something about walking in that city, pounding those pavements. I feel so young. Becky, this old broad feels so relevant all of a sudden. I'm going back as soon as I can.'

Becky laughed, and told Iris to sit down. 'You've got to tell me what happened. Sadie was so tired, she said she would fill me in later, and you were on the way home.'

Iris plopped down on one of the café chairs. 'Your friend is some damn woman. She went over there, and faced them down. They have all pleaded guilty to some sort of embezzlement. She's going to stay over there to see them sent to jail. And she made sure that all those who had been dumped on get richly compensated.'

'I am so glad it has worked out, but Iris, you're so different. So—'

'Happy,' Iris interjected. 'I have realised, dear, I can walk up the steps of the Met as bold as brass, and look at Singer Sargent's *Madame X* for as long as I want. I can stride out on the High Line. I know where to sit to get the best view of the Empire State Building and where to get off to visit Chelsea Market. I can sit early morning on the edge of Central Park and sketch. Nobody thought I was odd, nobody looked my way, and yet when I went for a coffee, I was called ma'am. I loved every minute of it.'

'Sounds like you didn't miss Coolnamona one bit.'

Iris slapped her knee, and laughed. 'Around here they see me as the mad lady who paints. In the Big Apple, nobody really cares what I look like or what I want. It has been so goddamn liberating.'

'I'm not sure Coolnamona will be enough for you any more.'

'Are you kidding me? I even missed Maisie. There must be something wrong with me. What I need now is life balance, and that is Coolnamona with a big dollop of Manhattan every six months. My Bert left me well provided for, and it's high time I spent some of it. I'm thinking of buying some real estate there.'

Becky stared at Iris.

Iris laughed out loud. 'Your face right now. I know I don't look like a moneybags, do I? Sadie and I are going to get a place together. It's not likely we'll have much of a crossover; she plans to travel a lot too.'

'Is she coming back here?'

'You know, that gal needs to find herself. Travel will do her good. She excelled over there.'

Becky said they should move to the kitchen, where she made black coffees.

'You should update your machine. I got used to skinny lattes,' Iris said, making Becky giggle.

'Iris, you should hear yourself.' Becky chuckled.

'I know, but when you're my age, it's so exciting to have an opportunity to be re-energised.'

'So tell me about Sadie,' Becky said in a poor attempt to steer the conversation away from Iris's favourite topic: herself.

'She got stuck in from the start. Gave a deposition on the ins and outs of the fraud, and how they had tried to buy her off – well, bought her off. You know she got millions of dollars? Those businessmen folded like a cheap suit. They are looking at jail time, and thanks to Sadie and the negotiation she chaired, people who had lost money they never thought would be returned, are walking away with sizeable compensation.

'The negotiation took hours, and she advised them every step of the way. Before she came on board, there had been so much muckraking, everybody was exhausted and broken. Sadie helped put them back together again.'

Iris began to tear up, and Becky pushed a plate of cookies towards her.

'Oh dear, I want a plain scone please, with butter and jam. I've had my fill of cookies. I'm sorry to be such a nuisance.'

Becky laughed, and carefully picked one from the oven, and put it on the plate.

'Aw, I have missed this,' Iris said. She slathered butter on it, and took a big bite. 'There are some things that New York can't give you. Cookies and muffins are no replacement for this simple fare,' she said, making Becky chuckle.

Once she had eaten, Iris put her cup and plate in the dishwasher. 'Oh, I nearly forgot. I met someone who knows you. A young dress designer; such a lovely fellow. He brought me for afternoon tea at Tiffany's. It was such a treat.'

'Who was he?' Becky asked, anxiety rising inside her.

Iris giggled. 'Brad, of course. I told him that I had tried to book the afternoon tea, and I was so disappointed I couldn't get a booking. Would you believe I even went along, and checked if they had a cancellation? I told Brad the story, and he was such a dear about it.'

Becky reached out, and grabbed her friend's hand. 'Are you sure it was Brad?'

'Yes, he said he did an internship at your design house, and he was so grateful because he has just gone up and up from there.'

'How did you meet him?'

'He came to the courthouse. Said he recognised Sadie. I think he offered to take me off her hands so she could focus on the serious business.'

Becky got up, and pretended to concentrate on stacking the dishwasher.

'Do you remember him then?' Iris asked.

'Barely,' Becky said.

'Well, he was very taken by you. Said he always wanted to come to Ireland, and when I told him about the café, he said he will have to visit.'

Becky, who was holding a cup and plate, let them fall from her hand.

'Are you all right, dear?' Iris asked.

'Just clumsy. I'm a little tired,' Becky said, switching on the dishwasher.

'I had better get home to my bed. I've been on a bit of a high, and now the fatigue is kicking in,' Iris said, gathering up her things, and heading for the door.

After Iris had left, Becky sat outside. The sky was grey, and it was chilly; the wind from the sea was cold and damp. There were no customers yet this morning, and she didn't feel like working either. Her head hurt, and she could barely think about what Iris had said. She felt angry at Sadie for letting that weasel worm his way into their lives.

She needed Sadie back here now, but it didn't look as if she was going to return any time soon. When Ronnie pushed the gate open, she waited for Maisie to follow behind. Maisie was out of breath as she reached the house.

'That bloody dog nearly knocked down an old lady on Main Street. He was pulling me so much I had to let go of the lead,' she said.

Becky shrugged as if she didn't want to hear, making Maisie stop.

'Is there something wrong?' she asked.

'It's OK, but can you hold the fort? I have to run a few errands,' Becky said.

Maisie stood tall, and told her not to rush. 'Everything here is under control,' she said.

Becky thought Maisie liked it too much running things on her own at Coolnamona House, but she didn't want to dwell on that, and grabbed her rain jacket, setting off for the secret path. Her head down, she pushed past the brambles, droplets of water which had pooled after the rain overnight spraying over her. Her canvas shoes were damp, and she felt shivery and cold. Her head hurt even more. What was she going to do? Would she have to leave Coolnamona? Surely he would never find her on this path to the sea? It was her one place of solace. She checked behind her, but there was nobody about.

She wanted Sadie back. Sadie was a New Yorker through and through, and they understood each other. When Sadie was around, she felt that she still had some of her old life with her. Without her, she felt a stranger all over again. She felt the loss of Hilda more keenly, too. She felt the loss of shared experience and memory when a friend is out of touch. Jen was caught up in her own life, and she knew that was right, but Becky felt so lonely.

Tramping across the headland, she watched the grey clouds roll over the sea, the white-capped waves crashing to the shore. Maybe she shouldn't be out on her own, but what was she going to do? Should she hide away every time that bastard raised his ugly head? She had no answer, but she fixed her gaze on the waves. Scanning the horizon, she thought there was no hope of seeing Wales today. In a strange way, she liked this weather when there was nobody else around and the cold mist clung to her cheeks and hair.

Her head down, she made for the stairway down to the shore. The wind had whipped up stronger, and she had to tread carefully. She took her time making sure to hug the cliffside. As she stepped onto the beach, the rain bucketed down, and she pulled up her hood, and trudged across the heavy sand. When the seal lurched out of the water and onto the beach, she stopped in her tracks. She didn't know what to do; whether she should race for the steps or whether she should stay still, and wait for the seal to leave. It flapped and rolled over on the sand, creating a big indent which it seemed to manoeuvre into and lie in, its eyes all the time on Becky. Trembling with cold and fear, she started to talk to the seal so she didn't appear a threat.

'Hello, Seal. Nice to see you today. I hope you're having a good day,' she said, feeling somewhat foolish. The seal made a funny noise, and nosed at the sand.

'Seeing you has been the best part of my day,' she said, and she thought the seal chuntered an answer.

Becky's phone rang. She looked at the seal. 'Excuse me, I have to answer this,' she said as she said hello into the phone.

'So you're chatting to seals now,' Ben said.

'How do you know?'

'Look behind you.'

Becky twisted around. Ben was leaning against the entrance to a cave, and waving to her.

'Oh my God, this is so embarrassing. I just didn't know what to do, whether to run or back away, so I started talking to the seal.'

'Why don't you walk over to me?' he said.

'I don't know. What if the seal decides to lunge at me?'

'Becky, take a step.' His voice was soothing and calm, and she stepped back. 'Good, now turn around and walk towards me.'

She felt so stupid, and she began to laugh, and run. She heard the honking of the seal as it crashed back into the water, but she kept running until she fell into Ben's arms.

He swung her around before stopping to put her gently back on the sand so they could watch the seal together as it swam out against the waves, before diving deep in the water, disappearing.

'I have never experienced anything like that before,' she gasped.

'No seals on the mean streets of New York?' Ben laughed.

Becky burst into tears.

'Lord, what have I said now?'

'It's nothing you said. It's just a bad day.'

'Is that why you're out here so early, and in this weather?'

'Jeez, give me a break.'

Ben put his hand up. 'Why don't I stop asking questions?

But can I just say, Becky White, you're amazing. I bet you run from a mouse, but stop to chat with a big seal.'

'You talk to the seal.'

'From a distance.'

'Shit, was I in danger?'

'No, that great big seal is a sweetheart, really,' he said.

'You're making fun of me.'

'I am, but I still think you're great,' he said, taking her hand, and kissing it lightly. 'Becky, I think you're amazing. Are you interested in tramping up to the headland, and heading back into Coolnamona with me?'

'I need to check on the café.'

'I passed it on the way here, and it was definitely closed.'

'I left Maisie in charge. It shouldn't be shut.'

'Why don't we walk by that way? Maybe something came up, and she left a note.'

'Do you have her number? I could give her a call.'

'Maisie only has a landline, and she never gives out the number. She says that she likes to get out and walk every day and meet people. That it is much better than the phone, and it keeps her from getting old.'

'Can we get to the house? I'm a little worried.'

They struggled up the steps. When they got to the top, Ben took Becky's hand, and they walked across the headland together. At the bramble patch, he went ahead and pushed them out of the way. The rain beat down heavier, and they ran across the lane arriving at Coolnamona House laughing and drenched.

Bella stuck her head out the front when she heard the laughing. 'You will catch your death. Get changed immediately,' she commanded.

'What are you doing here?' Becky asked.

'Maisie had an emergency. The stupid dog was playing with

a stick, and it got caught in the roof of his mouth, and she had to rush him to the vet's.'

'I don't understand,' Becky said.

'She locked up the place, but she was expecting a party of ten, so she came and got me. I sat the group in the dining room. It's all good. There's a party of thirty due in about fifteen minutes, so we should just about turn around in time.'

Bella eyed Ben and Becky up and down. 'Ben, you need to go home, and Becky, can you get upstairs? You're both wetting the floor with the drips,' Bella said.

Ben bowed to Bella, and said he would be back to help in a while, and Becky ran upstairs to change.

She was brushing out her hair a little while later when she saw his jeep pull up at the gate.

She checked herself in the long mirror before going downstairs, stopping to put on some lip gloss on the way.

Bella had baked a fresh batch of scones, and was sitting at the kitchen table.

'It was very good of you to step in,' Becky said.

'My pleasure. It's rather nice to know Maisie owes me one,' Bella said, putting on a clean apron.

Ben arrived just as the group walked up to the gate. They served teas and coffees, and set up the buffet table with Becky's cookies and Bella's scones. At one stage, Ben disappeared out into the back garden to sit quietly, but Bella ticked him off. When the group were gone, Becky said she would tidy up, and Ben offered Bella a lift home.

'Don't be silly, man, you should stay here and help Becky,' she said, a gleam in her eye.

Gathering up her umbrella, she headed down the path, but Becky ran after her.

Pushing a box of cookies into Bella's hands, Becky, her shoulders hunched against the rain, said thank you. 'I know you don't like anyone else's baking, but I know you like the cookies.'

Bella beamed with delight. 'I might just have a little nibble,' she said.

Ben had set up some music, and had poured two glasses of prosecco when Becky came back in the house.

He handed her a glass. 'To Coolnamona on a grey day, and getting to know each other better,' he said.

She had only taken a sip when he took the glass from her hands. 'Let's dance, Becky White,' he said. He pulled her gently into his arms, and they slow-danced across the kitchen.

Reluctantly, she pulled away, and told Ben he should go home.

'I don't understand the mixed signals,' Ben said.

'I really like you, but I can't do this right now,' Becky said, her voice shaking.

'Has something happened to you?' Ben asked. When he reached out to her, she shivered. 'You can tell me. Maybe I can help?'

Becky shuddered. 'Nobody can help me.'

Ben took her hand, and led her to a chair where he told her to sit down. 'I'm not leaving until you tell me, Becky,' he said.

She shook her head. Her heart was racing, and there was a stabbing pain inside her head.

'Has this something to do with you thinking somebody was following you on Sunday?'

'How do you know about that?'

'Bella rang me. She was worried.'

'I thought he had come here from Manhattan.'

Ben pulled up a chair beside her, and took Becky's hands in his. 'Do you know this man?'

'I think so.' Becky stopped, pulling a hand free to tug hard on her hair.

'Go on,' Ben said.

'Iris met him in Manhattan. She didn't know I wanted nothing to do with him.'

'Is he an ex-partner?'

She shook her head, and tried deep breathing because she was so angry at the situation. When she spoke, her voice was firm. 'No, he attacked me as I left work one evening,' she whispered.

'What can I do to help?' Ben said.

'I don't know. Iris had no idea, but she gave him every little detail about my life here in Coolnamona. He said he must visit.'

She jumped up, and began to frantically tidy the kitchen. Ben leaned over, and put his hand out to stop her. 'Give me his name, and I will have my friends in the police check him out. Find out if he is in the country.'

'Would you do that for me?'

'Of course. In the meantime, I think it's a good idea if I bunk down in the house. Nobody need know; I will come late at night, and leave before dawn.'

Becky wanted to collapse into his arms, but instead, she slumped down as relief washed over her that Ben would be nearby.

TWENTY-SEVEN

Sadie rang in the early hours.

'I'm sorry, Becky. Things have been so hectic here. Can you talk now?' she asked in a rush as Becky sat up in the bed, and glanced at the clock on the dressing table, which said midnight.

'Iris says you were fantastic.'

'You're pissed, aren't you? That I didn't ring you straight away?'

'Honestly, I don't know what I feel. I'm glad everything went to plan.'

'You don't sound glad. Is there something wrong?'

Becky took a deep breath. 'The intern is now a designer, and you introduced him to Iris, and now he knows where I am. What am I going to do?'

'Shit! What? Who?'

'Sadie, he's the one who attacked me.'

'Oh shit, Becky. What have I done?'

'He was an intern, and now he is a big shot designer, I hear.'

'You never said his name. Oh crap. What can I do to fix this?'

'You can't, Sadie. Iris told him everything, and even invited him to Coolnamona.'

'What are you going to do? What can I do?' Sadie said.

'I think he's here. I thought I saw someone following me on Sunday.'

'Crap! Have him arrested.'

'I haven't seen him again. If I go to the police, they will think I'm crazy.'

'Talk to Ben. He will know what to do.'

'When are you coming back, Sadie?'

Becky heard somebody speak in the background, and she heard Sadie clear her throat.

'I've news, Becks. I swore Iris to secrecy. I hope she hasn't told you.'

'Told me what?'

'I've been offered a job here. A new firm. It's starting small, but we think we can make a difference.'

'In Manhattan?'

'Yeah, why?'

'You said you would never be able to practise there again.'

'I know this is crap timing, darling. I should come back to Coolnamona, be with you.'

'No, it's an opportunity you can't let pass. I'll be OK.'

'I am only a phone call away, Becks.'

'I wouldn't be in this situation, Sadie, if...'

'I honestly didn't know. He was so charming and so grateful for the opportunity you and Hilda gave him.'

Becky felt tears surge inside her, but she tried to hide it. 'We're going to miss you terribly,' she said, her voice faux jolly in an effort to hide her hurt.

'Please tell me you forgive me,' Sadie said.

'I do, just give me some time,' Becky said quietly.

'I'm sorry. This is such shit timing,' Sadie said.

'What am I going to do with the café?' Becky said.

'From what I hear, you're doing an amazing job.'

Becky sighed loudly. 'This is a lot to take in.'

After Sadie rang off, Becky stayed in the dark. She had no idea what to do next. Turning on the light, she grabbed the dressing gown from the back of the door, and went downstairs. She was sitting at the kitchen table drinking a cup of coffee when Jen came down about an hour later.

'I needed a drink,' she said.

'Sadie rang. Everything is fine. She sounded happy, but she's not coming back.'

'I thought she liked it here.'

'So did I, but she's going back to the law.'

'You sound upset,' Jen said.

Becky tapped the chair beside her. 'I guess I'm a little jealous. Practising law in Manhattan sounds so much more exciting than running a café in Coolnamona.'

She saw Jen take a step back. 'No, Mom, I don't want to leave Coolnamona. You can't do that to us.'

'Who said we are? I was just talking,' Becky said.

'I don't want to leave,' Jen said.

'And neither do I. I thought this was settled.'

Jen shrugged.

'I just worry.'

Jen peered out the window. 'It will be dawn soon. Can we go to the sandy beach for a swim?'

'Everybody will think we're crazy.'

Jen laughed. 'As long as we dodge the paparazzi, we'll be fine.'

Becky couldn't refuse her daughter. 'We can go in our dressing gowns. There won't be anyone around so early.'

Jen, who was halfway up the stairs, stopped, and eyed her mother up and down. 'You can if you want, but I'm getting dressed,' she said.

Becky followed her upstairs, and put on her bikini before

pulling on a yellow sundress belonging to Sadie, with a long cream cardigan. She had to try and have as normal a life as possible. She tied her hair in a bun on top of her head, and rifled through the laundry basket for some clean bath sheets.

'We should bring snacks for when we get out of the sea,' Jen said when Becky got back down to the kitchen.

'We can pack some scones and cookies, I guess.'

'Mom, we're not having a tea party. All we need is some soda and chips,' Jen said, filling up her holdall from the food larder.

They left by the front door, but were quiet on the lane, lest they wake up any of the residents. It was a still, chilly morning, and Becky pulled her cardigan tight around herself, and knotted the belt. A blackbird was singing in the hedgerow. A few other birds joined in sporadically, but Becky felt it was a little too early even for the birds.

'Do we have to go down the secret path that's not so secret, and which everybody knows about?' Jen said.

'We don't want to go the long way around. It will take ages. We only have two hours max. I have to get back to make a fresh batch of scones for the café opening,' Becky said.

Jen took her by the hand. 'Brian showed me a new way. You'll love it, I promise.'

Becky let herself be dragged past the opening for the secret path to an old gateway further down the lane. Jen manoeuvred past the gate and around a bank of fuchsia, almost disappearing.

'Come on, Mom, you're slacking,' Jen said urgently.

A thrush scuttled past her on the ground as Becky made to follow, and a blackbird flew out of a nearby tree, its warning call filling the air around them. Pushing past the fuchsia, she saw Jen standing at a stone stile waiting for her.

'Sweetheart, the gates are padlocked for a reason. We don't want to be arrested for trespassing.'

Jen giggled. 'Are there even cops in Coolnamona, Mom?'

Becky saw the happy, open face of her daughter, and she followed through the stile.

'Brian showed me this way. There is a boarded-up old house and a path down to the sea.'

'Doesn't anybody live there?'

'Brian says the family moved away a long time ago, and it had been for sale, but nobody wanted to buy it.'

They walked on up the old driveway, sticking to the centre where grass and daisies grew. On all sides they were surrounded by wide meadows where Becky could see drifts of daisies and poppies growing.

'There are daffodils all over the place in spring. Brian's mom used to bring him here when he was young, and they picked armfuls of different yellow and cream daffodils. We can do the same for the café and restaurant.'

Becky hurried along to a bend in the avenue. Jen went off to the side, but Becky said she would catch up. She didn't want Jen to go out of her sight, but she allowed herself a moment to take in her surroundings. The sun was rising out at sea, throwing rays over the long, low house, glinting gold off the side conservatory. The conservatory glass was broken in places, the windows and doors of the house boarded up. Some-where, a door was creaking in the light breeze coming in from the sea. Becky could see there was a walled garden to the far side, and she pledged to come back on her own some day and explore. The roof appeared intact, but she saw the swallows dive around the house as if they had nests there. Surrounded by the birdsong of the dawn chorus, she felt as if she were transported to a different world. If she lived here, she knew she would never want to live anywhere else. She knew that for sure.

'Mom, let's get going,' Jen said as she walked back to see where she was.

'Isn't this the most amazing place ever?'

'Dunno. It looks haunted to me,' Jen said, leading the way through the thicket of rhododendron.

They plodded on for about ten minutes until they came to a fence. Jen jumped over, and Becky followed, landing where an old sign that said TRESPASSERS WILL BE PROSECUTED lay on the ground.

'Jen, we shouldn't have come this way,' she said.

'Chill, nobody worries about that around here,' Jen said as she headed off across the field to where the steep steps led down to the sea.

Becky sauntered slowly through the field, the wind making her sundress billow out around her. The sky over the sea was streaked pink and gold, the sun a ball of gold resting on the horizon. She stopped to examine a small purple flower, and was bent over it when Jen came back.

'It's an orchid. There are loads in this field,' she said.

'They are so delicate, such a deep purple. It's like a teepee of purple on a stem. Is that why this region is called Orchid Bay?'

'Who knows?' Jen said.

Becky, hearing the impatience in her daughter's voice, tugged her on the arm and bolted off towards the steps. 'The last one to the top of the steps has to empty the dishwasher,' she shouted as she thundered across the grass. Jen, shouting back that it wasn't fair, bolted after her, only just missing out on first place.

'You cheated,' Jen complained as she set off down the steps first. They concentrated on their footing, not talking again until they got to the beach.

'The last one in the water has to stay until café closing time,' Jen shouted, stepping out of her shorts, and tearing into the sea, her T-shirt still on over her swimsuit. Becky threw off her cardigan, dropped the straps of her sundress, and raced to the water, but Jen was already swimming.

They swam out far before changing course to swim parallel to shore. The sunshine sparkled across the water, and they both floated so the rays didn't dazzle their eyes.

'This is my favourite spot in the whole world,' Jen said, and Becky had to agree that at that moment, she felt happy and content. She closed her eyes, and let the water lift her back to shore, the sunshine at times flashing silver across her eyes.

When she heard Jen call her name, for a moment she didn't realise the urgency of her voice.

'Mom, what are we going to do?'

Becky opened her eyes. The sky was almost pressing down on her, and she heard Jen shout again. Splashing the water hard with her arms, Becky looked all around her. Jen was closer to the shore, but there was a seal between herself and the beach.

'Stay calm. Don't frighten it,' Becky said urgently.

Jen dived into the water, emerging beside Becky. 'What do we do now?' she said.

'I'm not sure, but I know if we talk to it, it may not see us as a threat.'

'What the fuck do you say to a seal?' Jen said.

Becky gripped her daughter's hand, and they moved towards shore, until their feet hit the sandbank.

'Maybe if we wait, it will just move off,' Jen said.

'What do I say to the café customers? Sorry, I was trapped at sea by a seal.' Becky guffawed.

The seal swung around, and dipped into the sea, disappearing.

'Mom, where is it? Is it going to attack? You shouldn't have shouted,' Jen yelled.

'Which is what you're doing right now,' Becky said, grabbing Jen around the waist, and holding her close.

'Do you think it will attack?' Jen said, her voice shaking, her body trembling.

'Seals don't attack humans,' Becky said, her voice deliberately strong to hide her uncertainty.

'Mom, there's a baby seal on the beach.'

'That can't be good. We need to swim away from the seal pup, and hopefully the big seal won't get worried.'

'I'm too scared to swim,' Jen said.

'Come on, we can wade over to those rocks,' Becky said, and they set off the short distance ploughing through the water. They helped each other over the slippery rocks, and sat down.

'Our stuff is too near the baby seal. Can we stay here until it goes?'

'We can stay and catch our breath, but we are eventually going to have to leave,' Becky said.

They squeezed out their hair and relaxed, letting the early morning sunshine warm their bodies.

When, after about half an hour, they saw the big seal pop its head out of the water, they froze, all the time watching it as it moved towards shore. At one stage, it called out to the seal pup, which appeared to be crying and grunting, but moving slowly towards the water.

'I want to go and help the poor thing,' Jen said.

Becky put her hand on her arm. 'We stay where we are. They don't need our help,' she said.

The big seal moved across the sand, trampling everything in its path, including Jen's shorts and Becky's sundress. They watched as the seal nuzzled the pup, nudging it gently towards the shore until both of them let the water pull them out.

'Wow,' Jen said.

When they were sure the seal and her pup were far away, they crossed over the sand to shake out their clothes before they headed for home.

'Mom, that was the coolest time ever.'

Becky smiled. Jen was right. She had felt so exhilarated and so free, and a million miles from the worry that had consumed her brain every waking moment this last while.

TWENTY-EIGHT

The sound of hammering woke Becky up. Groaning, she stuffed her head under the pillow. It was like the walls were shaking. Getting up, she yelled from the landing, 'What's going on?'

'Did we wake you? We're just putting up some of Jen's superb works,' Iris shouted up the stairs.

'But I thought we still had to get frames,' Becky said as she made her way to the hall.

Jen stuck her head around the bottom of the stairs. 'Iris knew somebody, who knew somebody, who gave her a good deal for these cool frames. Come and have a look.'

Becky stepped into the hall.

Iris, the hammer in her hand, had already fixed three frames to the side wall and was measuring a space for an extra-large one.

'You have to see this one. It's Coolnamona House from the sea.'

Becky stood in front of Jen's pastel work. The sea was calm with only a hint of surf as the waves hit the shore. The cliff was sheer, the colours showing shadow and light. The terrace of houses was set back, but Coolnamona House, light pink in colour, wider and just slightly taller than the rest, stood out as if it were holding the others up.

'I can't believe that quick sketch has turned into this amazing scene, sweetie,' Becky said.

'She's a real talent,' Iris said proudly, as she stuck a price sticker on the frame.

'You can't sell it. It has to get pride of place here,' Becky declared.

'But the whole idea is to bring in the "bucks", as you call them,' Iris said.

'But this is so beautiful. I can't bear to let it go.'

Jen picked up the picture. 'I think Mom gets first dibs on this one,' she said, handing it to Becky.

Iris reached over, and took it back. 'You're not taking it anywhere,' she said.

'But Mom deserves it,' Jen said.

Iris put the picture up on the wall, and slapped a red sticker on it. 'It's an old trick in the galleries. It fuels a buying frenzy.'

'But I haven't paid for it,' Becky said.

'Hush, not a word. It's a successful exhibition already,' Iris said, and Jen beamed.

Becky bent down to examine the frames stacked on the floor. 'Jen, these are amazing.'

'I love the ones of the café. They will sell like hot cakes,' Iris said.

Becky slipped by to make some coffee. Jen followed her into the kitchen. 'Iris says I'm doing well building a portfolio. It may get me into art college. Mom, I'm going to save the money towards my fees.'

Becky hugged her daughter. 'We have a bit of time yet. Don't be worrying about money,' she said.

She watched Jen go back to the hall, and she envied her innocent enthusiasm. Becky put her head in her hands. The thought of her attacker knowing where she lived had really rattled her. And Sadie not coming back was a blow. Ben came and stayed each night, but he was gone by the time she got up.

Just at that moment, she saw Ben in the garden moving between the vegetable beds and filling up a basket. Ducking to the side so he couldn't see her, she watched him bend down, and pull lettuces and scallions from one bed and pick courgettes from another. When he was finished, he walked towards the house, and she wondered whether she should go back upstairs.

When Ben knocked on the back door, she dithered. He glanced through the window, and waved to her. Reluctantly, she opened it.

'Hi, I wondered if you were free later?' he asked.

'It's a busy day. I don't think so,' she said brusquely.

Ben loitered in the doorway. 'I need to talk to you about Manhattan man.'

'I woke up to hammering in the hall, there are two tour groups due this morning, and this cup of coffee hasn't hit the sides.'

'Let me cook dinner, and we can talk afterwards,' he said.

Becky sighed. 'I'm slammed all day so I don't think I'll be very good company.'

He moved towards her, and she sidestepped out of his way, concentrating instead on gathering the steel bowls so she could start the cookies.

'I just have a lot on my mind. I really can't think beyond the next tour buses. Sadie's not coming back, and I have a lot to think about.'

Ben reached out, and caught her by the shoulders, but she yanked herself away.

'You have been so good to me, Ben, but I need a little space. My life is very complicated right now. I can't think of anything else, only keeping the café going, and hoping that myself and Jen have made the right decision staying here.'

'You sound very stressed.'

'You figure.'

Ben put his arms out to comfort her, but stopped when he saw Becky's anguished face.

'I can't give anything right now, Ben.'

He stepped back, and she saw his face cloud over.

'Let's talk later,' he said, taking her hand and kissing it gently. When he left by the back door, she kicked a chair so it fell over.

'What's wrong, sweetheart?' Iris said as she tidied up the hall.

'No, Iris, I can't talk about it,' Becky snapped.

Iris stepped into the kitchen. 'This has something to do with me. I feel I have done something wrong. Spit it out, girl, for heaven's sake.'

'It's not your concern, Iris.'

'Jesus, Becky. I can't bear this. What have I done? You're the last person I would want to hurt.'

Becky leaned against the sink, and began to cry.

'Lovely lady, please tell me what is wrong.'

Becky snorted back her tears. 'I don't blame you, Iris. You weren't to know.'

'Know what? What have I done?'

Becky reached out, and gripped her friend's hand. 'You didn't know, Iris, but back in Manhattan, that bastard attacked me. I think he has followed me here to Coolnamona.'

'Mother of divine Jesus, who?'

Jen called that she was off out. Becky ran into the hall after her.

'Sweetie, you're supposed to help. Iris and I can't do this on our own.'

Jen made a face. 'But Mom, I told you I was going out with the girls. They're waiting at the gate.'

'OK, go, we'll work something out,' Becky said, trying to hide her upset.

Iris came up behind her. 'We've got this,' she said, gently leading Becky back to the kitchen.

Becky shook her head. 'I wish I could believe that.'

'Let's get the work done, and we can figure out what we will do afterwards. We'll go out in the boat,' Iris said.

Becky concentrated on making the cookies, while Iris walked between the dining room and the kitchen, carrying trays of crockery and scones in for the tour buffet.

After Becky finished putting the trays of biscuits in the oven, she disappeared upstairs. She knew she had been unfair on Ben, and on Iris too, because Iris hated long silences. She walked to the window, and scanned the sea to the horizon. What was it that had brought her to this place? She felt she had lost focus somewhere along the way. Maybe she should return to Manhattan, face up to the reality of life, and stop pretending that she and Jen could forge something new here. Maybe Coolnamona House was a real estate opportunity Hilda had left her, and nothing else.

Opening the window, she leaned out to listen to the sea. Closing her eyes, she let the sound of the distant waves fill the space around her, and she felt her body relax. Why was it in the very moment she hated being here, and questioned everything about her life here, she also felt that this was where she was meant to be?

She opened her eyes when she heard a lot of chatter on the lane. A group of about thirty were making their way to the café gate. One person waved, and Becky waved back before going downstairs. Iris was already on the front path greeting the visitors.

'I rang Bella. She's on the way to help out,' she said to Becky as the visitors trooped into the hall, huddling around Jen's work.

'Is this all you have? We all want one,' one woman quipped, making Becky beam with pride.

Becky stayed in the kitchen sending out the teas and

coffees, while Iris floated about selling Jen's pictures, and chatting. Every time Iris made a sale, she gave Becky a thumbs up, and made a big deal of taking the buyer's details before wrapping the frames in brown paper.

Bella arrived as the first tour group left.

'You took your time,' Iris said.

'I may be an older woman, but that doesn't mean I don't have a life, and can drop everything to rush to Coolnamona House because the neighbour called me,' Bella said, putting her nose in the air.

Becky giggled as she handed Bella an apron. 'You know I'm very grateful for your help,' she said.

'And so you should be, my dear,' Bella said in her hoity-toity voice.

Iris called out that the next tour group were coming up the path.

'They're early. What will we do?' Becky grumbled.

'I think a little walking tour of the garden for the first tour group on their way out. That will give us a bit of space to seat the second group,' Bella said.

'There's hardly enough for a walking tour. It will only take a few minutes to walk around the front garden.' Iris said.

'Not when you are Bella Reilly and you know every story and every plant in the front garden along with the local history, which of course is heavily intertwined with the family history.'

'All that guff should go down fine with the visitors, but please spare the rest of us,' Iris murmured.

In an effort to dissipate the tension, Becky handed a large plate of cookies to Iris to bring to the dining room, and asked Bella to take her group out to the front garden. Bella clapped her hands and asked the first group to follow her out the front, where hopefully they would be able to see across the Irish Sea to Wales.

'Free of charge, and a wealth of information about our

outstanding Orchid Bay and the role of the Reilly family, one of the foremost families of Coolnamona and surrounding districts,' Bella said.

Iris shook her head, and went off muttering to herself. Becky lingered in the hall, where there were no more framed pictures on the walls, except for the one she had asked to keep earlier that morning.

She needed to move Jen's picture to a better location, where the light would pick out the fine charcoal work up in the cloudy sky over Orchid Bay, and highlight the curl of the waves as they made their way to shore.

Bella was in full flight on the front lawn, and Iris was busy stacking the dishwasher. Becky set about clearing the dining room. When she carried a tray of crockery through to the kitchen, Iris switched on the dishwasher.

'Please don't tell me we have to invite Bella with us on our little boat trip,' she said.

'I heard Bella say she is off to Dublin this evening to go to the theatre, unless she was saying it to sound fancy,' Becky replied.

Becky went out the front when Bella called her to say goodbye to both tour groups.

'I'm going to fly off as well. I have to get a train from Greystones, and my cab will be here shortly,' she said.

Bella called into the hall to Iris, 'Don't worry, dear, I won't be going on the high seas with you. I have far too busy a social calendar,' she said, and darted off before Iris had a chance to reply.

Iris, when she came to the front door, was scowling. 'I know we're back talking, but that woman knows how to push my buttons,' she said, before wandering down the path to the door leading into her own garden.

'See you in ten,' she said, before disappearing.

Becky ran upstairs, and changed into jeans and a hoodie, and was sitting at a café table when Iris came back.

'So glad you dressed up for the occasion,' Iris said.

They drove down to the harbour where Danny was waiting to pull the yacht out of the harbour.

Becky took up position at the back, enjoying the breeze as they chugged slowly out of the harbour, and into Orchid Bay. The cool breeze lifted her hair, and she shut her eyes, the chugging sound of the engine a balm to her soul as the boat cut through the water.

'How are you feeling?' Iris said.

Becky opened her eyes. They were miles away from Coolnamona, the boat bobbing on the sea with the swell of the water.

'There is just us and the fish out here. Talk to me,' Iris said.

Becky kept her eyes on the sea.

'Before I came here, I was attacked and raped. It happened as I went to my car in an underground car park after I finished work.'

'Mother of God, you poor thing,' Iris said.

Becky swallowed hard, and let the light breeze ruffle through her long hair, and brush against her face. 'That guy you met in New York. It was him,' she said quickly.

Iris, who had been fiddling with an old lobster pot, stopped what she was doing. 'Brad, who brought me to Tiffany's?'

'Yes.'

'Jesus Christ, I didn't know. He was always talking about you and Hilda.'

'How many million people live in New York, and you met that one man?'

'Jesus Christ, Becky, I told him everything about you, and this place.'

'You weren't to know.'

'I was so full of myself, I let my tongue run away with me. How do I make this right?' Iris said.

'You don't have to.'

'I bloody well do,' Iris said.

When they docked at the Orchid Bay harbour, Ben was waiting.

'Boy, am I glad to see you. You have to help Becks,' Iris said.

'You know?' Ben asked.

'I am bloody responsible for a lot of her stress. How can I help?' Iris said.

Ben ushered them to the café on the seashore, and ordered three coffees. 'Becky, this guy is in the country, and he's staying in a Dublin hotel.'

She felt the blood in her veins go cold. Pains shot through her, and she couldn't speak.

Iris shovelled extra sugar in her coffee. 'What do we do? she asked.

Ben leaned forward. 'I will make a few calls, get this guy checked out.'

'And what if he rocks up to Coolnamona House before you have your ducks in a row?' Iris said.

'Becky is not sure if it was her attacker she saw in Coolnamona. We should take this step by step.'

'Somebody send the memo to Brad that this is a step-by-step process! We need him caught and incarcerated,' Iris snapped.

'It's not that simple, Iris.'

Becky put her hand on her friend's shoulder to calm her down. 'Ben knows about these things.'

'We need to be clever on this one, and in the meantime, I will stay overnight at Coolnamona House to make sure Becky and Jen are safe,' Ben said.

'What can I do?' Iris asked.

'I think you should leave it to the police.'

Iris straightened in her seat. 'You are a chef, Ben, and while I respect you and your former profession, and I am glad you're helping Becky, she needs more.' She turned to Becky. 'With your permission, I want to tell Bella, Maisie and Claire, and we will all be with you. You will never be on your own. We can work a rota.'

Becky made to protest, but Ben said it might be a good idea.

'That's settled then. I will meet the ladies later, and we will work everything out.'

'I don't want Jen to know yet,' Becky said.

'It will only take a day or so before we get word back from New York as to who we are dealing with. The local detective unit will also keep an eye out,' Ben said.

'And what should I do?' Becky asked.

'Behave normally. Try to project a business-as-usual attitude,' he said.

TWENTY-NINE

Iris asked Becky to join her in the sitting room. There was something about her voice which put Becky on edge. When she got to the front room, Jen was already there loitering by the fireplace.

'Is something wrong?' Becky asked.

Iris, who was fidgeting, and running a handkerchief through her fingers, said maybe Becky should sit down.

'What the hell is going on? This is my sitting room, but I feel I'm being treated like a person who has been invited in for a grilling. Just tell me what's up,' she said, looking from Iris to Jen.

Jen, her face red and her forehead creased in a frown as if she were in pain, gestured to Iris to speak.

'Shit, you're not pregnant, are you?' Becky said.

'Nothing like that, just sit down please,' Iris said, her voice agitated.

Becky sat on the edge of the sofa. She thought Iris was enjoying her role too much, and noted how she took her time arranging her skirt after she sat in the leather chair opposite. It was the polka dot skirt she'd bought in Target, and Becky thought it looked vaguely ridiculous on her.

'Jen here has news.'

'You didn't run off and get married, did you?' Becky interrupted, her voice booming across the room.

'Give me some credit, Mom,' Jen snapped.

'Would somebody please spit it out? This is so unfair,' Becky gasped.

Iris reached forward, and placed her hand on Becky's knee. 'Bear with us.'

Becky wanted to push her hand away. Panic streaked through her, and her head began to thump. Hadn't she put up with enough the last few months, and now this?

Iris patted Becky's knee smartly. 'Jen did a DNA test, and sent it off a while back.'

'What? Like Brian did? Why would you do that?' Becky said, staring at her daughter who was slumped over on the other chair by the fireplace.

'Brian was doing it, so I thought—'

Becky jumped up. 'What has got into you, Jen? Would you jump off a cliff as quick?'

Jen made to answer back, but Iris raised her hand to stop her before standing up, and placing herself between the door and the fireplace.

'The thing is, whether you agree or not, Jen has come up with a match,' she said.

'What – what are you talking about?'

'The DNA. There's a promising match.'

'What do you mean?'

'A relative.'

'You're kidding, right? I don't believe this.'

Iris sat down beside Becky. 'Just hear us out, please,' she said.

'This is so crazy. I was an only child and so was her father. I don't have a family. Don't you think I would know? I'm not listening to this crap any more,' Becky said, pushing Iris out of the way, and stomping out of the room.

When Jen followed her, Becky glowered. 'We have a café to open, or has nobody noticed?' she snapped, making her way to the kitchen. She was carrying a tray of cookies to the counter in the dining room when Jen stood in front of her.

'Mom, can't we just follow this up? DNA doesn't lie.'

Becky shoved the tray at Jen. 'Can you please set up the coffee machine, and open up the front door? I have to take more cookies out of the oven.'

'Mom, you have to listen.'

Becky banged her hand on the table. 'Can you just leave it Jen, please? I can't take this right now.'

'I knew you would be like this; so closed off to new ideas. You are so like Granny Hilda,' Jen yelled, before hurrying up the stairs to her room.

Iris stuck her head around the door of the sitting room. 'Permission to speak, please,' she said quietly.

'What now?' Becky snapped.

'Give the girl a chance. She's very excited by the development.'

'What bloody development? I'm trying to keep this café going, and I need to concentrate on that. I will go up to her when it gets quiet.'

'Lucky for you, that's never in this particular café. I can hold the fort while you two talk.'

'Maybe later,' Becky said, returning to the kitchen to take the cookies out of the oven.

'It might be worth listening to her,' Iris said tentatively.

Becky banged down the cookie tray, making them jump and two fall on the ground. 'Iris, forgive me, but this is none of your business. Please stop interfering.'

Becky knew she had said too much when she saw a red

colour rise up her friend's neck like ink seeping into a paper towel.

'Iris Jones knows when she's not wanted. I suppose this resentment goes all the way back to New York and that bloody designer fella. Why don't I open up the front door on my way out?' she spat out as she pulled off her apron, and threw it on the table.

Becky stepped back as Iris thundered down the hall. 'Please, there's no need for this,' Becky called out as Iris stopped to pick up her handbag from the banister.

'What a hullaballoo. I am reporting for duty,' Maisie said stepping into the hall and making her way to the kitchen. Becky pretended to be looking in the fridge as she tried to compose herself before Maisie realised something was up.

'What's eating Iris? She was in a fierce hurry,' Maisie said as she tied her apron strings.

'Something at home, I guess,' Becky said, closing the fridge, and trying hard to act normal. She saw Maisie get the crockery out of the dishwasher, and she hurried out into the front garden hoping to catch up with Iris. There was no sign of Iris, and Becky hesitated, wondering if she should follow her.

'She seemed a bit high. She'll simmer down and be back. Iris was always the hothead,' Maisie said as she carried a tray with little vases of flowers to the front garden.

Three customers came up the path, and Becky decided to worry about Iris later. Maisie complained that the morning rush was too much for the two of them, and she enquired several times if they should go over and get Iris or if Jen might be able to help out. Each time, Becky shrugged her shoulders, and smiled, which she knew annoyed Maisie even more.

Just ten minutes to go to her knocking off, Becky asked Maisie if she could stay on for the lunchtime rush.

'I'm happy to help, but Ronnie will chew the sitting room to bits. I can't leave the dog in the back garden or the kitchen any more. He has taken to howling when he doesn't get his own way. The only place he's quiet is the sitting room couch. He's a spoilt brat.'

'Do you want to nip home and get him?'

'Would you mind? He loves lying in front of the Aga in the kitchen, even when it's not fired up. He's such a silly sausage,' Maisie said, grabbing her jacket, and making for the door.

Becky was organising three trays when she saw Ben in the garden, and waved to him. He waved back, and walked towards the house, sticking his head around the back door.

'Do you need a hand? You seem short-staffed today.'

'Something like that. It's a long story.'

'I can help. Brian and Jen are doing the restaurant prep anyway.'

'She must have stolen out when I was busy.'

'Did you two have a disagreement? She seems a bit down in herself.'

Becky was about to answer when she saw a group of six come through the gate. 'I could do with your help right now.' She stopped to look at Ben. 'It's not that I don't want to tell you, it's just I don't want to get upset. I just need to get through the shift. Maybe later, OK?'

'Teenagers. We love them, but they do cause a lot of strife,' Ben said, grabbing an order notebook.

'It's more than that. I really need your advice,' Becky said.

'OK, I will help in any way I can,' he said, touching her gently on the arm before going out the front to take the orders.

Becky and Ben worked easily beside each other. When Maisie came back, Ronnie stretched out on the kitchen floor beside the door to the hall, and they had to step over him each time they passed in or out with a tray. Eventually, he strolled out to the front garden where he wandered from table to table begging for food. Becky made to whoosh him inside, but several customers objected, and said he was one of the best things about the café.

'I may have to hire old Ronnie out to you,' Maisie said, and Becky wasn't sure if she was joking or not.

When everybody, including Ben, had left, and Maisie had snapped a lead on Ronnie to walk him home, Becky opened the side gate, and stepped into the garden next door. Making her way around to the back door, she tapped lightly on the glass panels. Iris, who had been painting, called out her name from above.

Becky saw her stick her head out the window of the attic room.

'Can we talk, Iris, please?'

'The key is under the mat. Come up to my studio,' Iris said.

Becky let herself in, and walked up the three flights of stairs. Iris, her paintbrush in her hand, was waiting on the top landing.

'The light is just right, and I don't want to leave my canvas. What is it?' she said gruffly.

'I came to apologise.'

Iris gave Becky a severe look. 'I accept your apology, but really it's Jen you should be talking to.'

'I messed it up, didn't I?'

'That you did, girl. But if you eat humble pie, it should work.'

'I'm sorry I didn't hear you out, but this sort of stuff frightens me.'

'I was only there to help Jen. She suspected you wouldn't be happy.'

'Am I that predictable?'

'When it comes to our kids, we are all pretty predictable in wanting to protect them no matter what. There's nothing wrong with that.'

'I just never seem to get it right with Jen.'

'At her age, I'd be more worried if you did,' Iris said.

'I know she hates that I was an only child; her grandmother was, and she is. We have no relatives, really.'

'I saw the evidence with my own eyes. It's a high familial match. The percentage they use to judge these things was high, which means it's a relative of some sort.'

Becky walked to the window. From here she could see all the way to Orchid Bay and across the ocean. 'I am the only child of Hilda White, Brooklyn, New York. Hilda didn't have any other children. My father died when I was just a few weeks old. Don't you think when I was Jen's age, I would have jumped at this sort of thing? I just don't want her to be setting herself up for a fall.'

'Your Jen is a bright young woman. You're not going to thank me for this, but you need to start trusting her and her judgement more.'

Becky sat down, twiddling the worn tubes of paint laid out on a table.

'You're a good mother, Becky. Jen knows that too.'

'I suppose, but she's growing up so fast, and I never seem to be able to please her any more.'

Iris didn't say anything.

Becky looked at her in alarm. 'I'm worried she will get hurt, and what if this thing is a scam?'

'Lots of people these days trace ancestors this way. I think you owe it to Jen to follow it up.'

'For what? Tell me, for what? I know I was the only daughter of Hilda and my father who died when I was only a few weeks old. He was working in some sort of pit on a construction site, and the side caved in, trapping him underneath. He was buried under a pile of rubble on the Manhattan site. It took a long time to dig him out. Some skyscraper is there now.'

'That's tough. I'm sorry,' Iris said.

After a few moments, she continued, 'Look, I don't want to

raise old ghosts, but this is relevant, and it might help Jen. She's pretty devastated by her grandmother's death.'

Becky stood up. 'I'll talk to her, but I need to know, are we good?' she said.

Iris smiled. 'What's a little row between friends? Of course we're good.'

Becky leaned over, and kissed Iris on the cheek. 'I don't know what I would do if we weren't friends.'

'That's not going to happen. Now, let's find Ben Evans and pick his brains to get an update on this bigger situation of yours,' Iris said, shooing Becky downstairs.

Becky and Iris went straight to Ben's place, and knocked on the side door.

Ben, in shorts and a T-shirt, shouted to come in. When they stepped into the back garden, he was bent over the barbecue scrubbing it clean. 'I'm catering for a garden party, and they're insisting on a barbecue, so I'm sprucing this up,' he said, straightening up, and mopping his brow.

'I was hoping you had a few minutes now,' Becky said.

'If it is about Jen, my advice would be to let her simmer down. She can help out at the garden party, and I will make sure she gets home safe.'

Seeing Ben was so busy, Becky decided not to bring up anything else, and kicked Iris in the ankles to stop her talking. They left, but on the lane to Coolnamona House, Becky hurried ahead of Iris. Right now, she wanted to be on her own. At the house, she dashed up the path and straight to the kitchen. She had cookies to make for the café tomorrow. She pulled down the stainless steel bowls and the flour, but suddenly stopped. She couldn't do anything. The thought of a rift between herself and Jen was just too much. What was happening to her? Was she turning into Regina, and pushing her daughter away at the time she needed her most?

When Iris came in and made a cup of tea, Becky bristled.

'You take a break. Go home please, Iris,' she said.

'Not a chance, dear.'

'You can't camp out here forever,' Becky said fiercely.

'Who says?' Iris threw back.

Becky couldn't handle it any more and she bolted upstairs. She so needed to talk to Hilda right know. Loneliness snaked through her. There was still one long note from the teapot left to read, and she took it from her jeans pocket. Pulling up the bedroom sash window, she stood, the sea breeze ruffling around her, before she climbed into bed. Lying listening to the birds singing and the faraway sound of the sea, she felt so uncertain and afraid.

THIRTY

Becky had read Regina's final letter to Laura hoping to distract herself, but it had only heightened her anxiety about herself and Jen. She couldn't bear when they had a falling out, and this situation worried her deeply.

She picked up the letter, and read it again.

My darling Laura,

I can only hope that someday you will want to spend the summer months here. Remember when you were young? You always said, don't worry Mother, I will be back every summer. Where would I be but Orchid Bay, during the summer months?

I have waited all these summers for you, my darling. Starting in May when we used to put a makeshift May altar in the hall, and then June when the weather can be so bright; and July and August when the tourists drown out our own voices here, and we hear the laughter coming up from the bay. And at long last September, when we always had Orchid Bay to ourselves.

Every summer, I have yearned for your return, my girl, and every summer has passed without you coming back to Orchid Bay. I will wait until my dying day for you to return to Orchid Bay. I know I did wrong, my darling. I just wish I knew where you were to tell you in person.

Being a mother at times is not easy, and I am afraid I have not stepped up to the mark. I turned my back on you, and I tried to control your life. I thought at the time I was doing what was right for you. I know I was an interfering old bitch who was too afraid of what people would think. I took advice from the priest, and I thought I was doing the right thing. I blame myself for letting myself be swayed, and letting the church influence me. I have not gone back to church since then, and when I die, I do not want a church service. They can throw me in the sea. I have told them, don't even bless me.

I should have been your mother, full stop, and I should have turned my back on the interfering church. I let my fear of being turned away at heaven's gate, and my fear of people talking about me, and my standing in the community get in the way of supporting you.

I will regret what happened for the rest of my life, and my only hope is that someday we can meet, and I can bow my head in front of you, and ask for forgiveness.

I guess if you are reading this letter, that hasn't come to pass. All I can offer is my sincere regret, and these letters are my small way of trying to cope. Every year I added to the letters, a line here and there. It made me feel closer to you somehow.

You may never be able to forgive me, Laura. God knows, I can't forgive myself. But I hope you will read the letters, and realise how loved you have always been.

All my love,

Mam

XX

Becky turned over in the bed, and closed her eyes. She would never understand how Regina could have lived with so much pain all her life. She was determined to talk to Jen when she got home, and to tell her how much she loved her.

Becky was dazed when a few hours later Jen shook her awake.

'Mom, are you OK?'

Becky sat up in bed, rubbing her eyes. 'Yeah, why?'

'You never take a nap.'

'I don't think I intended to, but...'

'Iris is downstairs, and she says she's your new bodyguard.'

'I thought she would go home.'

'Are you ill?'

'No, why?'

'Iris said I have to be strong for you, and stop giving you grief, and Ben said he would pay me a full shift even though he sent me home super early. I'm sorry for arguing.'

'Sweetheart, I flew off the handle. I'm sorry, too. I just have a lot on my mind right now, but I'm not ill.'

Becky thought her daughter looked upset, and she moved to reassure her. Getting out of bed, she pulled on her jeans, but changed her course, and began to close the windows when she saw Jen turn away to hide her distress.

'Let's wander down to the harbour, and have an ice cream,' she said.

'Why can't we talk here?'

Becky felt exasperated, but tried not to show it. 'I checked earlier. The ice cream van is down at Orchid Bay, and we can have whatever you like. Maybe best to chat on neutral territory. We will tell Iris she can take the evening off.'

Jen shrugged, and Becky felt a flash of frustration, but

stopped herself saying anything further, and instead started to make her way downstairs. Jen said she had to change, and would follow her down. Iris was reluctant to leave, but was persuaded that Jen would look after her mother.

Becky sat at a café table, and waited for Jen. The air was still, the only sound the soft rhythmic thud and pulling of the waves against the shore at Orchid Bay.

When Jen came downstairs, she sat opposite Becky. 'Mom, can we be friends?' she said.

Becky smiled. 'Sweetheart, we're always friends. Maybe if we reverse a little, and start all over again?'

'Yeah, but over ice cream. You promised.'

They set off down the lane, holding onto each other on the steep parts going down the hill, giggling when they went too fast and stumbled.

'We don't do this often enough,' Jen said, and Becky felt a tinge of guilt.

At the harbour they ordered 99s, and decided to sit on the harbour wall, their legs dangling over the water.

Jen took out her phone, and took a selfie of the two of them, but then continued to scroll on TikTok.

'Jen, we really need to talk. Can you put it away, please?'

Becky was surprised when Jen immediately pocketed her phone.

'Mom, please don't get cross, but I have made contact with this person who is a DNA match.'

Becky stared at Jen. 'When did you do this?'

'After our row, but, Mom, I've got a reply back, and she wants to meet.'

'You're not seriously going to meet this stranger?'

Jen crunched into the cone of her ice cream. She swallowed hard before speaking. 'I want you to meet her too. She is staying not far from here, and she is calling to the house tonight.'

Becky stopped eating the chocolate flake from her ice

cream. 'What the hell, Jen? What am I supposed to do with that?'

'I was going to meet her in Bray, but Brian said that Coolnamona House would be better.'

Becky shook her head. 'Why is it that you have discussed this with the whole village before me?'

Jen giggled. 'Slight exaggeration, Mom.'

'The hurt isn't so slight, baby.'

Jen dipped her head as Becky continued.

'It just hurts. I imagined with Granny gone that it would be the two of us against the world. I don't want that to change.'

'Me neither,' Jen said, shuffling closer to her mother.

'Well then, you had better tell me how all this DNA stuff came about,' Becky said gently.

Jen sighed. 'I didn't mean to cause trouble, Mom, honest. I just tried it because Brian was doing it.'

'Did Brian get a hit?'

'It's so unfair. He didn't, so he didn't tell Ben about it at all.'

'Go on.'

'I had forgotten about the results, and then I was informed there was a DNA match with a high probability of it being a relative. Next thing, I got an email from a woman, and she said we should meet.'

'This sounds so crazy.'

'But if we meet her together we can judge.'

'I don't know, Jen. Do we need this? I don't know if I can take something like this right now. Think, what would Granny Hilda say?'

'Mom, she's dead, and I loved her, but can we stop trying to think what Granny Hilda would have done?'

There was some sort of sense in that, Becky thought, but she was worried that they were going down a rabbit hole which would eat up their time and their hearts.

Jen jumped off the wall and called her mother to follow.

'She is due in an hour, and we have to walk up the long hill,' Jen called out as she quickened her step.

Becky followed at a slower pace, not entirely sure what was going to happen next. She lingered halfway up at the bank of foxgloves, watching the bees burrow into the petal bells before flying away laden with pollen, and the butterflies dance between the blooms of the purple buddleia. Jen twisted around, and gestured to her to hurry, and she reluctantly continued up the path past the ferns and the thick-leaved plants with yellow flowers, where a host of small blue butterflies rose up, flitting off in all directions. It was hard to believe that this peace she treasured so much could soon be under threat, not only by her attacker but also by this DNA match mystery.

THIRTY-ONE

'That must be her,' Becky said as she watched a young woman stop and loiter at the front gate. She saw her look up and down the lane-way, before holding the gate open for an older man wearing a linen suit and a Panama straw hat.

'Should we go out to meet them?' Jen said.

'No, let them knock. We don't want to appear too keen,' Becky said, her head beginning to thump.

'The man has stopped. Maybe it's just some people looking for the café,' Jen said from her vantage point behind the sitting room curtain. Becky was about to answer, but Jen told her to hush, the woman was coming to the door. They heard somebody reach for the knocker, and gently tap it. Becky and Jen stood very still, and waited. The person called out to somebody not to leave, before she rapped the door with the knocker again.

Becky and Jen didn't move. Becky would have been quite happy to let the visitors wander off, and forget the whole thing, but Jen jumped on the door handle, and opened the door wide.

The woman, who was in her twenties, stepped back a little.

'Hi, I'm Nicola Long,' she said, holding out her hand.

Jen shook hands, and introduced herself and Becky. They

stood for a moment until Becky nudged Jen to invite their guest inside.

'This is all a bit strange, but I brought along my passport so you can see I am who I say I am,' she said, fishing it out of her handbag.

Becky took it, and examined it. 'I apologise, but this is obviously the first time we have done anything like this.'

'My grandfather is supposed to come in, but...' Her voice trailed off, and Becky felt for the young woman who was among strangers.

'He is very welcome,' she said.

'Thank you. I understand he knows the house, and he's worried he may not be welcome. I'm so sorry to have inconvenienced you,' the girl said, making to go back out the front door.

Jen gave Becky a pleading look. Becky called on the woman to stop. 'He may not know the house recently changed hands. Let me talk to him,' she said.

The man, who had a walking stick, was leaning against the garden wall, his eyes closed, when Becky got as far as the gate.

'Pardon me, you're welcome to come in. Nicola is at the house,' she said.

The man flinched, but quickly recovered his demeanour, and tipped his hat. 'I was listening to the waves at Orchid Bay,' he said by way of explanation.

'I never tire of it,' Becky said.

The man straightened up, and she noticed how tall he was. 'Thank you for your kind invitation, but I don't think the Reilly family would be very happy with me coming on the property,' he said.

'You knew them?'

'I knew Laura. She doesn't by any chance still live here, does she?' he said, his voice shaking.

Becky stepped out onto the lane, and held out her hand. 'I

am the new owner, and from what I know, Laura left many years ago, and has not been back since.'

'You're from the States?' he asked, shaking her hand gently.

'Yes, New York.'

'I have been in Boston most of my life,' he said.

His granddaughter called him from the front door, and he waved to her.

'Do please come in. I'm Becky. I take it you know about this DNA search result?'

She saw him hesitate.

'I promise, you're very welcome,' she said softly.

'The old lady must be dead,' he said.

'Regina? Yes, she is.'

'Pardon me, I'm Tom Little. I knew this house a long time ago, and the old lady wasn't very nice.'

'I don't know about that, but the house has changed hands,' Becky said, holding the gate open for him.

She followed him up the path.

He stopped at the rock. 'Laura always boasted it was the best view in Coolnamona,' he said.

Becky slipped by him, and led the way to the house. 'How did you know Coolnamona House?' she asked as they stepped into the hall, and she showed him into the front sitting room.

'I lived in the next town. It is very strange to be invited in here. Do you know anything at all about the whereabouts of Laura?' he asked.

Becky shook her head. 'I only know she left, and never came back.'

The man stopped when he saw the portrait of Regina. 'She looked so beautiful there,' he said, his voice harsh.

Nicola rubbed her grandfather's arm lightly in what looked like a bid to calm him down. 'They need to hear your story,' she whispered.

Becky showed Tom to the armchair, where she noticed he

angled himself so that he didn't have to look at the portrait. She offered a drink, but could see he only wanted to tell his story.

'My granddaughter, quite a long time ago, persuaded me to do a DNA test, and now, two years later, there's a match. I was shocked, and now I am excited. Whether it was a good or bad idea, Nicola persuaded me to fly to Ireland, and now all of a sudden I am here in Coolnamona. I have not been back in this country for decades. The last time I stood in this house, that woman, Regina Reilly, told me I had no right to fall in love with her daughter, and she would ruin everyone belonging to me.'

'I don't understand what this has to do with us,' Becky said uncertainly.

Tom seemed lost in his thoughts until Nicola leaned towards him, and softly spoke in his ear, suggesting he go back to the beginning.

'I apologise. I am feeling a lot of raw emotion being back here,' he said, before taking a deep breath, and starting his story. 'I lived in the locality outside Coolnamona. I was eighteen years old when I met Laura, and she was barely eighteen herself. We had a wonderful summer together here at Orchid Bay. We cycled and swam together. The sandy beach off the beaten track was our private strand. We loved each other so completely. On that beach we exchanged vows, and pledged undying love to each other. On that beach, the last night I met her, Laura told me she thought she might be pregnant.

'I had a job with a jewellery designer in Bray. That's how I managed to give Laura a beautiful ring: gold with a red stone which was a tiny pink ruby. Laura allowed me to put the ring on her left hand, and she said she would never take it off. We planned to get married as soon as possible.

'We were young, and thought our families would be happy for us once they realised how much we loved each other. Frankly, I have never felt a love like it, and it is my greatest regret in life that I let others step in our way.'

Becky sighed, and Tom put his hand up to stop her speaking.

He stood up in front of the portrait.

'That woman ruined my life, and I can hazard a guess that she ruined Laura's too; though I will never know that because after a perfect day at the sandy cove at Orchid Bay, our whole world fell apart. We kissed at the bottom of the hill, and Laura dragged me up here to meet her mother, show her the ring and tell her our plans.

'We had no idea that others would not be happy for us. After Regina Reilly threatened me, she manhandled me out that door,' he said, pointing to the front. There was silence as he stopped to catch his breath.

'She was a bitter, vindictive woman. By the time I had retrieved my bike down at the harbour and cycled the few miles home, she had already been to my family's house. She had made outrageous allegations against me.' He stopped for a moment, and his granddaughter sat on the floor beside him.

When he continued, his voice was low.

'I was the eldest of a large family. My father ran a pub and shop combined. Regina Reilly went to my family home, and that woman handed over a wad of cash in an envelope, and said they were to put me on a plane to America as soon as possible. If they didn't, Mrs Reilly said she would make it her life's mission to ruin my family and our business.

'She was well in, and she made it clear she would get the cops involved and have me arrested. She told my mother that she believed I had known Laura since before she was eighteen years old, and to use her words, "God knows what he has done to her".'

'This is dreadful, but can we discuss the DNA connection,' Becky said, her voice tight with tension. Tom smiled at Becky, and continued his story.

'I don't blame my parents. Regina Reilly and the Reilly

name had some weight back then. My father said it didn't matter what I had or had not done. The danger was that the whole family would be dragged through the mud. He said I had to go for the sake of the family. My mother held me close, and said first love was just that, and while it hurt immediately, it would ease, and I would have a great adventure in Boston. I remember, through her tears, she said it would be the making of me.

'My father cycled to the post office the next morning to ring my aunt who lived in Charlestown, Boston. He just told her I was coming on holiday because he knew the postmistress was listening to the call. It was arranged I would fly out the following day.

'That night, I got out of the house, and was halfway to the train station at Bray when my father drove up behind me in his delivery van. I intended to meet Laura in Dublin the next day. We always said if things got bad we would wait for each other outside the GPO. Dad ordered me to get in the van, and said I wasn't going to bring shame on my family for any girl.

'It sounds harsh, and it was. I never saw Laura again. I flew to Boston where my aunt met me, and brought me to her house. The next day, I was set up as an apprentice to a jewellery designer at a fancy store.'

He looked around the room.

'It is so hard for you all to understand now, but there was nothing I could do. I tried writing to Laura, but there was no reply. I wanted her to have my address in case she could make it to the States. After three months, I did get a letter postmarked Coolnamona. It was signed in Laura's name, but I knew it wasn't her writing. It said she was getting married and to refrain from any communication, that she wanted to give her marriage a good start.'

Tears rolled down his face as he placed a hand on his grand-daughter's head. 'I pined for so long, but it was my lucky day when I met Anna Davis. We went out for two years, and then we married. I told Anna about Laura, and she knew I would always love her, too. I eventually took over the jewellery business, and I did well, opening more shops outside my county. We had four children and ten grandchildren, and we were very happy. Anna often suggested Ireland for a vacation, but I couldn't face it; the pain would have been too great. I had my parents and siblings over to us in Boston instead. All they knew was Laura had left Coolnamona, but they didn't know anything else.

'Before Anna died, she told me to find Laura, that she wanted that for me. She said I had to find out if she had our child. She said I had to meet this lost child. My Anna was a wonderful woman,' he said, his voice high with emotion.

They sat in silence. Becky wanted to ask a direct question, but she didn't know how. In her heart, she was afraid of the answer and why Hilda had led her to Coolnamona House. Beside her, Jen sat silently, her head dipped. After a few moments Tom stood up.

'I have said too much. You didn't need to hear all that. We must get back. We're staying above Spring's Restaurant for two days. I don't have any family in these parts any more,' he said.

Becky stood up, and walked to the door with Tom and Nicola.

'Would it be OK to call down to visit you before you go?' she said.

He smiled at Becky. 'Maybe we can sit in the garden, and I can tell you all the good things about Coolnamona,' he said.

She watched him walk down the path, stopping at the rock to show his granddaughter the view, and she wondered what she should do next. Jen said she was off to meet Brian.

When she saw Ben rush up the path, she knew there was something wrong, but she was so glad of the distraction.

'Good, you are on your own. Can we talk inside?' he asked urgently.

For some reason, she felt the meeting deserved the formality of the sitting room.

'I got a friend of mine who is pretty high up in the force to check on this designer character, and the news is not good from NYPD, I'm afraid,' he said.

'Oh God, I'm not the only one, am I?'

'This character is a suspect in multiple rapes in New York City all around the same time as your attack.'

Becky felt her legs buckle, and she fell onto the couch. Her stomach was heaving, and her skin was burning. Ben reached out to her, but she pushed him away. He disappeared, and she heard him open the fridge door in the kitchen before he came back with a glass of orange juice. He handed it to her, but she ignored him.

'What happens now?' Becky asked.

Ben sat opposite her. 'We need to get this guy out of the country and into the hands of the police over there.'

'I am frightened, Ben. Maybe I should leave Coolnamona. Where is Jen? We have to get away.'

'Let me ask you a question, Becky. Do you trust me?'

'Yes,' she said softly.

'I have a plan, and for it to work, I have asked a number of people I trust to help out.'

He went to the window and waved. Becky heard a group of people scurry up the pebble path, and Bella, Iris, Maisie, Jen and Claire, along with Brian, came into the room.

Becky threw her head in her hands. 'Does everyone know what happened?' she cried.

Jen sat on the couch beside her mother, and held her hand. Iris sat on the sofa on the other side.

'None of this is your fault, dear. That designer lad is the bastard, and he's not going to come into this town and frighten our great friend. We're here to put a ring of steel around you, and snare him.'

'I can't expect all of you to do this for me. We don't even know if he will come back to Coolnamona.'

'If he does, he will have the A team to contend with,' Bella said, and the others murmured in agreement.

'I, for one, owe you,' Claire said.

Becky shook her head. 'I don't know what to say.'

'You don't need to say anything. Nobody is going to hurt you again. We will all make sure of that,' Bella said.

THIRTY-TWO

'Mom, what do you think? Isn't this almost unreal?' Jen said, standing beside her mother.

'I don't know what to think.'

'Tom's so nice, and he's American. Imagine all of us coming here to this small place, and meeting up. Totally.'

Becky was looking out the front window at a figure who was standing beside the oak tree on the lane, and appeared to be staring at Coolnamona House. She didn't know if she should ring Ben, and was debating whether to make the call when she saw Iris march across and remonstrate loudly until the man ambled away. Becky reached out to her daughter, and hugged her tight.

'Let's leave it for now,' she whispered.

'But this is so unreal. Imagine if Granny Hilda were here. She would be so buzzed by the whole thing.'

Becky kissed her daughter's head. 'Let's talk about it later,' she said firmly.

'OK. Me and Brian are off to Greystones after we do some prep in the restaurant,' Jen said as she made for the door.

Becky went back, and sat in front of Regina's portrait. She

didn't even know if she wanted this painting in the house any more. How could this woman with the gentle eyes and the enigmatic smile have turned into someone so harsh? Yes, she had lived with a lifetime of regret. Maybe that was her penance. Somehow, her portrait no longer held the mystery and allure it once did.

Becky jumped up from the couch, and ran upstairs to find the ring she had brought from America. It was still in the velvet pouch the jeweller had given her after Hilda had died. Rifling through her old case, she found it under a pile of clothes she had never worn here along with Hilda's old passport. She didn't know why she had included the passport in the possessions she had decided to haul across the world, but the navy booklet seemed somewhat ironic now. She opened it. There Hilda was: just two years ago when she renewed her passport, her haughty eye to the camera. Her place of birth was Brooklyn, New York.

Frustrated, Becky flung it across the room. Opening the velvet pouch, she took out the ring. A simple gold band with a tiny pink ruby surrounded by a thicker gold band. She had never known a time that Hilda didn't wear it. She asked her once, when she had so much expensive jewellery including an emerald ring gifted by an admirer, why she continued to wear such a simple piece. The answer seared through her heart now, and she doubled over.

'Darling, before you were born, your father gave me that ring, and told me he would love me forever. I wear it because he is the only man I have loved, or I ever want to love.'

Pain flushed through Becky, and she couldn't move. What was she going to do? Her whole life was a sham. She didn't even know who she was any more.

When she heard a gentle tapping on the front door, she froze. She waited for the person to go away, but there was another knock, this time a little louder. Crawling to the window, she managed to peek out. Tom was standing there, leaning on his walking stick. She didn't know what to do. She wanted to run from the house, and go to the sandy beach, and talk to the seal. She wanted to be back to days ago when all she had to worry about was how they could keep the business going at Coolnamona. She was cross at Jen for landing this on her, and furious at Hilda. Who was Hilda White anyway, and who was Becky White? She peeped out again. Tom was sitting down now at one of the café tables, and she felt sorry for him that he was being yet again locked out of Coolnamona House.

Quickly opening the window, she stuck her head out, and called out Tom's name. He didn't hear her as her words were whipped by the wind out to sea. She saw him get up, and make to leave. Desperate to stop him, she bolted from the room, and down the stairs. Hitting hard against the door, she yanked it open.

'Don't go, please,' she shouted.

When he turned around, Becky began to sob.

'Hey, what's wrong?' he said, quickening his pace until he was beside her.

'I came back so we could talk some more. I couldn't wait in the apartment hoping to see you; this time round I don't want to make any silly mistakes.'

Becky opened her fist, letting the ring slide out onto the palm of her hand. 'Is this the ring?'

She saw him go pale, staggering a little as he leaned over to peer at the ring. 'Where did you get this?' he asked, his voice low and rasping as if he were finding it hard to breathe.

'It was my mother's.'

The old man reached out, and picked up the gold ring. 'The ring was made here in Bray. The designer himself was experimenting with a design, and because I knew his son, he said I could have the prototype at a fraction of the cost. He said there wasn't another one like it.' Tom's voice shook, and he began to tremble all over. Gently, Becky led him to the sitting room, but he pulled away. 'I can't be under Regina Reilly's gaze. I can't, not now,' he said.

Becky diverted him to the kitchen, where Tom bundled into the first chair at the table inside the door.

'We have a lot of talking to do,' Becky said.

'Is there any chance Laura is alive, that we will meet again?' he said, and Becky thought he may be speaking to himself, his voice was so low.

'My mother was Hilda White, and she died not so long ago; a heart attack.'

'This Hilda had the ring?'

Becky got two mugs and a bottle whiskey from under the sink, where she had hidden it from Maisie's eye. She sloshed the whiskey into the mugs, and pushed one towards Tom.

'My mother wore the ring almost every day of her life. She only ever took it off to have it professionally cleaned at the start of May every year. She said it was the start of summer, and she wanted the tiny ruby to sparkle. She said it was a beautiful reminder of the summer when my father gave her the ring, and she knew she would love no other.

'It was on 31 May at Orchid Bay we pledged ourselves to each other,' he said quietly.

'Are you my father?' Becky asked, her voice so low, Tom had to lean closer to hear her.

She could barely get the words out. She wanted to throw her arms around Tom, and she wanted to run away all at the same time. Confusion and excitement raced through her.

'I gave Laura that ring. I don't know any Hilda White,' he said.

She pulled away as she saw concern flood across his face.

'This is all happening so fast. I'm not putting enough thought into my words. It would be my honour to be your father, but I don't understand how Hilda got that ring,' he said.

'There is the DNA test result, but I also have to tell you

Hilda left me this house in her will. I had never heard of Coolnamona House or Orchid Bay before this.'

Tom reached for his wallet in the inside breast pocket of his linen jacket. Opening it up, he took out a strip of black and white photographs which was creased and browned at the edges from spending too long tucked into a plastic slot.

He didn't at first show the strip of photographs to Becky, but held it close as he explained how he and Laura had gone down to the seafront in Bray one summer evening, and had posed in a photo booth.

'She got a colour strip, and I kept the black and white. I didn't know then it would be the only photograph I would have of my lovely Laura. When you're young, you don't think of all the bad things that could happen. The beauty is the living in the now, and the freedom that brings. When I look at our happy faces in these photographs, I am back at the seafront kicking stones on the beach, and running into the waves, twirling through the sea water together. It was a precious time,' he said, before putting the strip into Becky's hands.

Becky stared at the photographs. It looked like Jen and a boy, making silly poses, their heads comfortable touching, the love in their eyes apparent. She knew every silly twitch and face they made because she knew these photographs by heart. Carefully placing the strip on the table, she said she had to get Tom something. Dashing to the sitting room, she pulled her handbag from behind the couch. Fishing inside, she took out a small wallet, where she held an old colour photographic strip of Hilda, and the man she believed to be her father.

All the times she had looked into her father's eyes, and wondered what he would have been like if he had lived. Shaking off the anger which was rising inside her that Hilda had kept the truth from her, she walked smartly back to the kitchen, and handed the colour strip to Tom. He was silent as he ran his fingers over the photos.

'I was trying to remember if she had her blue or green coat on that day, and now I know,' he said quietly.

Becky took the colour strip, placing it on the table beside the black and white one. 'That's my mom, Hilda,' she said.

'That is my Laura,' Tom whispered.

They sat in silence together. Outside, a wagtail landed on the kitchen windowsill pecking at the loose paint. It stood still, listening and watching all around it, before pecking at the glass. Becky moved, and the bird launched into the air, flying into a fuchsia bush at the side. Tom smiled, reaching out to take Becky's hand in his.

'What do we do now, Becky?' he asked.

She shook her head. She had no idea. There was a large gap, and she didn't know how to bridge it. Hilda had left her completely in the dark. Was the man who had died on a Manhattan building site just a story? And was her father this man sitting at her kitchen table sobbing into his linen handkerchief?

There was no doubt that Laura was Hilda, but why had she changed her name? Was she so afraid of Regina finding her that she deleted Coolnamona from her life, and made up a Brooklyn heritage?

'I visited Manhattan a lot. I never looked in the crowds for Laura. I never thought to,' Tom said sadly.

When he asked her date of birth, and she gave it, she saw pain flash across his face.

'Why didn't she make some effort to contact my family? Why did she do all of this without me?' he asked.

'I don't know. All I remember was my mother was a very independent woman with a drive to succeed, and she did. Hilda, or Laura, or whoever she was, always felt she had to be better than everyone else. She was a strong, forceful and eccentric woman, who never took no for an answer.'

Tom drank down the last of his whiskey. 'My Laura was a

quiet, gentle young woman. I imagine what Regina Reilly did trying to snuff out our love had some effect on what she later became. I am glad she left here, and forged her own life. I just wish she had reached out, or even tried to. What a life we could have had together.'

Becky didn't say anything.

'I want to believe more than anything that I am your father. All the evidence points there. The fact that we are sitting here in the kitchen of Coolnamona House and so happy to be in each other's company is, I believe, proof that love can win out in the end.'

Becky was about to answer when there was a sound at the front of the house, and a quick knock as Ben walked in. 'Hey, have you forgotten we are supposed to go up the mountains?' he called out as he walked through the hall.

Becky jumped up when he came into the kitchen. Ben put on the brakes, looking from Tom to Becky. 'I seem to have a knack of picking a bad time. Have I interrupted something?' he asked.

Becky didn't answer, but Tom, taking his photographic strip from the table, reached for his walking stick and said it was time for him to leave. Becky walked to the front door with him.

'Maybe we should take time to think, and see where we go from here, no pressure,' Tom said.

'How long are you staying in Coolnamona?'

'I will stay for as long as it takes,' he said, reaching over and kissing Becky on the cheek. 'This is a good day for us both,' he said.

'Will you come by tomorrow?' she asked anxiously.

'I will be the first customer knocking on the door.'

'Come before opening, and we can have something together in the kitchen.'

'I would like that very much,' he said.

As she stood by the door watching Tom make his way down

the path, Ben came up the hall. 'I feel bad, but I just wanted to see you,' he said.

'Can we go? I need the mountains right now,' she said.

'Your carriage awaits,' he said, and she followed him to the jeep.

They drove in silence, away from the sea and up the narrow roads to the mountains. Ben turned on some classical music low, and she appreciated that he wasn't expecting her to talk. Her head was a muddle, and she needed time to think. As glad as she was to think that Tom was more than likely her father, she was so angry that Hilda had left her to deal with this on her own. She had to come to terms, too, with the fact that Hilda never intended to tell her of her true heritage, but had copped out by leaving Coolnamona House to her in her will.

Another part of her felt for the young girl, Laura, who lost the man she loved, and never again gave love a chance to come back into her life. There was a time she thought Hilda had the best life, and now she wasn't so sure. She let her brain rest, and concentrated instead on the mountains as Ben drove up a narrow steep road hugging the side of one gigantic mountain and looking across the valley to the peaks of another range.

She was watching the cumulus clouds pressing into the space between the mountains when Ben gently stroked her cheek.

'Everything will work out fine,' he said.

'How do you know that?'

'Because I know you, Becky. You're a good person with a good heart.'

'I'm not sure who I am any more,' she blubbered.

He pulled over into a parking bay overlooking the mountains and a lake.

'Let's get out and walk,' he said, and she followed him as he set off on a narrow path across the bog. 'Let the wind blow away the cobwebs,' he said.

She smiled at him, and she liked that he didn't quiz her about Tom.

Tramping along the mountain path, she concentrated on the horizon. The light glossed over the mountains, the clouds scuttled between the rays, and she breathed in the clear air. Ben pointed out two rabbits busy nosing through the heather, and she stopped to watch them as they stalled to listen before bolting for what she thought looked like a tunnel underneath the growth. Ben smiled at her, and took her hand, and she felt safe. High above them, a red kite dominated the sky, gliding low near them to view the ground for prey.

'Thank you for bringing me here,' she said.

'Does that mean we're friends?'

'Always,' she said.

THIRTY-THREE

Jen and Becky walked down to Tom's apartment early the next morning. When he answered the door, he was still in his pyjamas.

'I think I've been running on adrenalin since I landed in this country. With the raw emotion of yesterday, the jet lag took over. I just slept and slept,' he said.

He invited them out to the balcony, and brewed some coffee. Jen went to help him, and Becky heard them chatting easily together in the kitchen. She remembered back to the time she and Jen had stayed here. It was only a few months ago, but it felt like a lifetime away.

When Tom carried a tray through, she thought he looked happy.

'Does Jen know?' he asked.

'That you might be my grandad and Granny Hilda might really be Granny Laura? I know,' Jen said, picking up her phone to scroll through Instagram.

'There was I thinking I was big news.' Tom laughed.

Jen drank down her orange juice and said she had to dip.

'Would you like to come back to Coolnamona House?' Becky asked Tom.

'So nice to get an invitation. Careful, or Regina will come back to haunt you,' he said, before excusing himself to go and get changed.

As she waited for Tom, Becky leaned over the balustrade hoping to get a glimpse of Ben. He had looked after her so well on their mountain trip, and before she left the jeep, he said he would like if they could be more than just friends. When she didn't react immediately, he seemed upset, and started up the engine, saying brusquely he had to get back. There was an awkward silence between them, and she had excused herself and thanked him for the mountain drive before jumping from the jeep. She wasn't entirely sure where that left their friendship. She felt sad, and a little stupid because she liked Ben so much.

Stepping back from the balcony, she shook herself. Who was she kidding? When she was around Ben, she felt complete. When she wasn't with him, she missed him. He was exasperating and lovely all at the one time. She had never felt like this before, never felt such a powerful emotion. She was in love with Ben Evans, and yet she had pushed him away.

'Hey, why so serious?' Tom said as he came onto the balcony.

Becky grinned, but didn't answer.

They walked down the main street, and were about to turn up the lane to Coolnamona House when the labrador, Ronnie, scooted towards them at high speed, Maisie calling him, and trailing far behind.

Tom stood in the path of the dog, and managed to grab him, holding him until Maisie caught up.

'That silly dog will be the death of me. You're so kind,' she said as she quickly snapped the lead on Ronnie's collar.

Becky dithered when Maisie asked if Tom was a friend.

'I'm a relative from the States,' he said, taking Maisie's hand, and kissing it. Ronnie barked, and tried to jump up, but Maisie ignored him.

'You Americans have such good manners,' she said, giggling like a schoolgirl.

When they reached the lane, Tom stopped at the first oak tree. 'I often stood here, and waited for Laura. It was just out of sight of even the top windows at Coolnamona House.'

He rummaged around underneath the tree, pushing past nettles and stepping on brambles, and Becky wondered what he was doing when he called out, 'It's still here. Come have a look.'

Becky picked her way through the undergrowth, and around a young butterfly bush where Tom was bending down, and looking at the trunk of the tree.

'Laura was terrified Regina would see if we put it at normal height, so I had to bend down with my penknife to do the inscription.'

Becky reached down and traced the initials T and L encased in a shaky line, the shape of a heart.

'I know it has young love written all over it,' Tom said, taking out his handkerchief, and dabbing his eyes.

'You really loved her,' Becky said.

'I still do. Don't get me wrong, I loved my wife dearly, but the love I had for Laura was that young love that hasn't been tainted by the usual everyday drudgery. There was the pain of our separation, but our love was left untainted by all the normal strife of a relationship. Silly to think this engraving has stood the test of time.' He choked up, and pushed his way back through the brambles which had blanketed the base of the tree. 'At my age you would think I could handle this, but I'm finding it over-whelming,' he said.

'Snap,' Becky said, and they continued up the road to Cool-namona House.

At the front door, Becky opened it wide, and invited Tom in.

'Thank you, but could I ask for a glass of water?' he said.

He sat at the kitchen table, and took a small framed photograph from his jacket pocket.

'I usually have this on my mantelpiece. My children used to call it my special friend, which raised a few eyebrows, but Anna was an understanding woman,' he said, handing the picture to Becky.

'We were in Dublin on O'Connell Bridge. There was an old guy with a camera around his neck, and he took the photograph. Laura was excited. She said it was the thing to do. I got him to send it to the jewellery shop for me. I had it framed, and was going to give it to Laura, but I never got a chance.'

Becky looked at the photograph closely. Laura was wearing what looked like a mid-length Dior dress belted at the waist, her hair tied back in a ribbon.

'You both look so young,' she said, walking to the window to peer closer at the picture.

'That necklace; is that an amethyst?'

'How did you know? I made it for her. I saved and saved to put down a deposit on that rock. Before I was sent to Boston, the jeweller told me I was square. I think the man felt so sorry for me, he let the rest of my debt slide.'

Becky examined the photograph closer as Tom continued. 'Laura could only wear the necklace once she was out of the house. Before the old man took the photograph, she took it out of a special compartment in her handbag.'

Becky's eyes filled with tears. 'An amethyst rock on a silver and pearl chain.'

'Yes.'

They both stared at each other. For a moment, too overwhelmed to speak. Tom broke the silence. 'Amethyst to ward off negativity. I don't know if it was very successful at that.'

'Wait here,' Becky said, and shot upstairs.

In the bedroom, she pulled open the dressing table drawer, and took out a silk pouch. When she got downstairs, Tom was in the sitting room gazing at the portrait of Regina.

'Regina looked so innocent and beautiful there. Laura inherited her good looks, and you, but particularly Jen, who has Regina's eyes,' he said.

'Life was hard on Regina, I guess.'

'Maybe, but...'

Becky took the necklace from the pouch, and held it up so the amethyst swayed back and forth.

Tom reached for it.

'I made it with my own hands for her. See this pearl? Laura asked for that. We said it was our secret sign to say we loved each other.' He lightly rolled the pearl through his fingers. 'Laura wore it at night as she slept because she wanted it close to her, and she didn't want Regina to see it.'

'It was my mother's necklace,' Becky said.

Tom got the necklace, and opened the clasp. Pointing to the inside, he took a small magnifying glass out of his jacket pocket. 'Occupational hazard. I always have one of these nearby.'

He hovered the magnifying glass over the clasp, and invited Becky to have a look.

There was a tiny capital T and L intertwined.

'We don't even need a DNA test,' Becky said.

Tom took the necklace. 'May I?' he asked, and Becky nodded, letting him tie it around her neck. 'Beautiful, so like your mother,' he said, tenderly touching her cheek.

Becky heard a sound on the path outside. 'I asked somebody to come along, and meet you,' she said, walking to the front door to let Bella in.

Bella stopped in the hall, and pulled Becky aside. 'Do you really think I should be here? That man is not going to want to meet me,' she snapped.

'You helped Laura, and I think he will want to meet you. There's also something else I need to tell you. Come on.'

'I was so nervous. Now, I'm worried as well.'

Becky took Bella's hand, and led her into the sitting room. Tom got up when they entered the room.

'Bella Reilly Carter, Regina's sister for my sins. Laura told me you were so lovely to her. I am sorry how everything turned out.'

'It is nice to finally meet you,' Tom said, standing up, cupping Bella's hands in his.

'Laura always did say you were charming, and she was right. What in the name of God are you doing back here? Tell me you know what happened to our Laura?'

Becky asked Bella to sit down. She did, on the edge of the couch.

'Why do I get the impression that there is bad news lurking in this room?'

Becky stood under the portrait at the mantelpiece. 'Laura was my mother,' she said.

Bella looked at her. 'What did you say?'

'My mom was Hilda White, but we now know Laura emigrated to New York. She became Hilda White, and we lived in Brooklyn. She was a successful designer, and we ran a clothing company, and moved to Greenwich Village.'

'Whoa, one step at a time, please. You said your mother died, and left you this house?'

'Hilda died earlier this year. She had a heart attack.'

Bella cried out, and put her head in her hands. 'Jesus Christ, I always thought she would come back,' she sobbed.

'I know this is hard to hear,' Becky said.

'Somebody just got a pin and burst the stupid bubble I have been living in all these years. I firmly believed she would come back.'

'I'm sorry,' Tom said.

Bella spoke as if she were talking to herself, and hadn't heard anything else beyond the fact that her niece was dead. 'As the years went by, I thought age would soften Laura in some way, and she would come back to Coolnamona House.'

Bella shook herself as if she were trying to shake off the bad news, and stood up in front of Becky. 'What am I thinking? There is one great thing to come out of all this.'

'We're related,' Becky said.

Becky opened her arms, and the two women hugged.

'What will Maisie do with this?' Bella said, and Becky couldn't help but giggle.

'How did Laura, I mean Hilda, get the deeds of this house?' Bella asked.

'I don't know,' Becky said.

'It's all a matter now. Coolnamona House is in the family,' Bella said, a smile of satisfaction on her face.

Tom clapped, and got up. 'You two have a lot to talk about,' he said.

Becky put her hand on his shoulder. 'All three of us have stuff to talk through,' she said.

Bella pushed past her, and grabbed Tom's hand. 'I know you don't know me, but we're family now. This is what Laura would have wanted,' she said.

'If you're both sure.'

'I know my sister did a terrible thing to you and Laura. I would like to hear your side of things, and to express how sorry I am.'

Becky excused herself to make tea. She took her time getting the good china cups and saucers down. She arranged fruit cake and cookies on a plate, stopping often to savour the hum of conversation coming from the sitting room. When Iris came to the back door, Becky opened it before she had time to knock.

Gently, she pushed Iris back into the yard.

'Bella is here, and she's in a meeting in the sitting room. Can I explain it all to you later?'

'How intriguing! I love a mystery,' Iris said, trying to peep over Becky's shoulder.

'Please, Iris,' Becky said impatiently.

'Fine, but you can't blame a gal for being curious,' Iris said as she turned to go back down the garden.

Becky made the tea, and carried a tray into the sitting room.

'Just in time. All that talk has left me gasping,' Bella said as she dabbed her eyes with her lace handkerchief.

Becky poured the tea, and handed around the cups and saucers.

'Earl Grey. You're a good girl,' Bella said, and Tom nodded in approval.

They sat in silence for a few moments until Bella purposely replaced her teacup on the saucer, and delicately put it back on the tray.

'I think Tom here has every right to see those letters you found, Becky. In the absence of Laura, he deserves to read them to know of my sister's remorse and agony.'

'I agree,' Becky said.

Bella straightened up in her seat as if rooting for a fight, but just as fast, relaxed. 'I will drop my own letter over to the apartment later, Tom. Maybe we should all meet again in the afternoon.' Bella stood up. 'Does after the café shuts at four suit?'

Becky looked at Tom, who nodded.

'I think I'll leave too. There is so much to think about,' he said.

Becky went to the cabinet, and took Regina's envelope and notes from the teapot, and handed them to Tom.

'They are all from Regina to Laura. It's tough reading,' she said.

'All of this is tough,' Tom said, reaching over, and kissing Becky on the cheek.

Becky watched as Tom and Bella made their way down the path, and out the gate, all the time chatting to each other. Turning from the door, she went back into the sitting room, but sat with her back to Regina's portrait, because she couldn't bear to look at her grandmother.

THIRTY-FOUR

At four o'clock on the dot, Tom, with Bella on his arm, walked up the path to Coolnamona House.

'We have to decide what to do with these letters,' Bella said.

'What do you mean?' Becky asked.

Tom walked through to the kitchen. Bella bustled in after him, and sat down at the table.

'Do you mind if I have my say, Becky?' she said.

'Go ahead.'

Bella took out her letter along with the bundle from the teapot.

'Do you want to keep them?' Becky asked.

'Good lord, no. Can we burn them in the fireplace? We have all read them. They have served their purpose, though I now realise I owe Iris Jones an apology. She insisted Regina wanted to be cremated, and not to have any religious involvement, and I completely ignored her. I know now, I was wrong.'

Becky looked at Tom.

'I honestly don't know. They were so painful to read. I no longer hate Regina. I think I feel very sad for her,' he said.

'It hardly matters what we do with the letters, does it?' Becky asked.

Bella sighed. 'Regina herself put most of her letters on the fire. I don't think we want anyone else reading these. It's time to let Regina rest in peace, and setting these letters alight will do that,' Bella said.

'I don't have a problem with it, if it means so much to you,' Becky said.

Bella turned to Tom.

'I told you, she's some girl. Can we do it in the sitting room fireplace?'

Becky looked around for a box of matches. Opening the drawer, she rummaged, the letter addressed to Regina falling into her hand.

'This came ages ago. I should give it to you, Bella,' she said, putting it on the table.

Tom pointed to a box of matches on the windowsill.

'Let's do it,' Becky said.

They followed Bella to the sitting room, where she placed the stack of letters in the grate.

Becky struck a match, and held it to the paper. Blue flames curled through the little pile, crisping the paper edges, and eating up the words. They stood in silence. Every now and again, Bella reached in with the poker, and lifted the mound of burning notes to let air fuel the flames.

When the fire died down, all that was left was smoking ashes.

'It was the right thing to do,' Bella said.

'I hope so. I just wish my mom knew how awful Regina felt about what she had done,' Becky said.

Tom stood up, his hands clasped together in front of him. 'I have an idea, and maybe it's a bit crazy, but I think Laura would have liked it,' he said.

'Get on with it, man. I can't bear any more suspense,' Bella snapped.

Tom took a deep breath. 'I know you have Laura's ashes with you, Becky. This may sound a bit impertinent, but could I suggest that we scatter the ashes from Regina's letter along with Laura's, I mean Hilda's? It would be a symbolic gesture...'

Bella gasped. 'What a great idea! I know Regina would approve,' she said.

Becky didn't know what to say. She had dithered over whether to scatter Hilda's ashes in Manhattan, which Hilda loved, and only brought them to Ireland in her suitcase because she didn't know what to do with them.

'Would my mother have liked that?' she asked.

'I apologise if I have overstepped the mark, but I know my Laura did love her mother, and if she had read those letters, I know she would have forgiven Regina. She loved Orchid Bay, maybe...' He stood up, and walked to the door. 'I have gone too far, I apologise.'

Becky shook her head. 'I think it's a good idea, but I will have to talk to Jen.'

'Orchid Bay is the perfect location. We could ask Iris to bring us out on her boat,' Bella said.

'Let me think about it,' Becky said, scooping up the ashes from the fireplace into a crystal glass bowl from the china cabinet.

'It might be silly, but I think it could give us all some closure,' Tom said.

Bella said she had to go, and Becky told her to hang on, she had post for her. Becky went to the kitchen to get the envelope.

'It's addressed to Mrs Reilly, maybe you should open it,' she said.

'Can I open it here? It's probably junk mail,' Bella said.

She ripped open the envelope, pulling out the two sheets of

paper. Becky asked Bella what was wrong as she saw her stagger, and lean against the wall as she scanned the letter.

'Read it out loud,' she said, shoving it into Becky's hands. Becky took the pages from Bella and read them aloud.

New Jersey

Dear Mrs Reilly,

My name is Paul Hofstra, the new owner of Boulevard Private Detective Agency.

It has come to my attention that you employed Mr Alan Hopkins to investigate certain matters. That case was closed several years ago, and it has only now come to my attention that you may not have been briefed on the outcome.

Unfortunately, while the file to locate Laura Reilly was indeed closed our end, I regret that you were not informed of such at the time.

Mr Hopkins was suddenly taken ill, and there was a period of adjustment, until on his death the agency was taken over by myself. We have been sifting through files to make sure everything is up to date, and that is how your case has come to light.

I wish to apologise on the part of the agency, and I hope this has not inconvenienced you in any way. As a token of our esteem, I return here the $5,000 fee which was the last instalment sent to the company.

I have set out the information we unearthed below, and can confirm that the house deeds were passed on as requested. We are sincerely sorry for the delay in conveying the information to you.

If I, or the company, can be of any further assistance, please do not hesitate to reach out.

Yours sincerely,

Paul Hofstra

Becky rushed to the second page.

Dear Mrs Reilly,

We are pleased to inform you that we have located your daugh-ter, who now lives in Manhattan, New York. She travelled to London, and from there moved to Brooklyn, New York. She took on the name of Hilda White and is a successful designer. She gave birth to a girl and is now also a grandmother of one.

I have forwarded the information about Coolnamona House to Ms White along with the deeds of the house. I have also supplied her with your contact details as per your instruc-tions. I also include the address and business phone number of Hilda White.

If I can be of further assistance, do please let me know.

Yours sincerely,

Paul Hofstra

'So Regina found her but never knew. This story gets sadder by the hour,' Bella said.

Becky nodded. 'At least I know now it was my grandmoth-er's tenacity that brought me to Coolnamona.'

Bella patted Becky on the shoulder. 'I need to go home. This has all been too much,' she said.

Tom hung back as Bella left. 'Are you OK?' he asked.

'I don't know,' Becky said.

He held her hand, and kissed it. 'Becky, you have some answers. Laura, or Hilda, had her reasons for not wanting to come back. Maybe it was too hard for her to share her story, but she wanted you to know your true identity. She need not have left Coolnamona House to you. Be happy that you now know you were meant to be here.'

'It hurts, that's all,' Becky said.

'There are decades of hurt in this story, but we're here together now, Becky, and that means something,' he said quietly, before kissing her on the cheek, and making his way down the path.

When Tom had gone out the gate, Becky went into the sitting room, and sat on the couch to look once more at the portrait of Regina, her grandmother. She marvelled at the beautiful young woman starting out in life, and felt an overwhelming sadness for the lonely life she had.

THIRTY-FIVE

Maisie was supposed to be on duty at the house, and Becky was so glad she was delayed. Her head was bursting with all the new information, and she needed time to process it. Tom was right; Hilda wanted her to know her true identity, but right now she felt an overwhelming sadness that Hilda and Tom never got to meet, talk or communicate again.

Regina suffered unbearably for her interference too, and there was a certain poignancy that if the PI agency in the States had not messed everything up, there was a window where mother and daughter's paths may have crossed.

The pain of that thought seared through Becky as she made her way to the kitchen.

As she crossed the hall, she heard a scuffling at the front door, and she opened the door to let Ronnie in. The dog ran past her, his tail wagging, and she smiled because these days he was always a good ten minutes ahead of Maisie. She let the door swing shut because Maisie had a key.

Ronnie sat eyeballing the tin treats box Jen had left on the table. Becky opened it and threw one for the dog to catch, because she knew afterwards, he would settle down in front of the Aga.

Maisie always liked to have what she called a machine-made coffee and a gossip before she started her protection shift. Becky didn't know how she would react to having Maisie come by for the evening shift until Ben came back, but she had come to like the hapless chatter of Maisie. It meant she didn't have to think of Brad or what he might be planning to do. She was hopeful he may be about to return to the States; the last report was that he had a return ticket for the day after tomorrow, so maybe he would give up on her.

When she heard the door open and shut again, she called out that the coffee was nearly ready.

Ronnie usually didn't bother moving but slept through most of the evening, but this time, Becky noticed he was up on his four feet staring at the hall door. When he let off a deep growl, she put down the cup of americano coffee. Her back straightened, and she moved her hand across the worktop hoping to find something, anything she could use as a weapon.

Fear surged through her as Ronnie advanced to the doorway and growled, barking loudly. Becky reached into her jeans pocket for her phone, but just as quickly she realised she had left it on the couch in the sitting room.

Picking up the old wine bottle she used as a rolling pin, she held it high. If she ran to the back door, she may not make it.

Somebody called Ronnie by his name, and the dog wagged its tail.

Confused, Becky hesitated.

When he walked into the room, Brad put his hands in the air.

'Whoa, is that the way to welcome a visitor from the States?' Brad said as he strolled into the middle of the kitchen.

Throwing a piece of chicken to the dog, he sat down at the table.

'So, I was on vacation, and I thought, let's drop into Beck's. She was a such a sweet lady, and we had such a lovely time together.'

'Get out of my house,' Becky said, brandishing the bottle high.

'What are you going to do, hit me with it? Crash it over my skull? That's not a very nice welcome, is it, Becky?'

'Leave me alone.'

'You're not going to have much of a business if that's the way you treat new customers.'

Becky took a step, and she wanted to hit him. Her arm hurt from holding the bottle aloft, and she had begun to tremble all over.

'You have a nice place here. I think I would like a coffee while we wait for Jen. I always did think she was a beauty,' he said as he took the cup of americano from the counter. 'Where do you keep the sugar?' he said as Becky felt her knees go weak.

'You leave my daughter alone,' she shouted.

At least she thought she shouted. Her head hurt so much, she didn't know if the words actually came out because Brad laughed, and said he would like one of the famous café cookies.

'Tension really works up an appetite.' He laughed. Slowly, he walked over and took the bottle from Becky's hands. 'Now, that's better. That bottle wasn't a good look,' he said.

He grasped Becky's hand, fondling it and running his fingers up her arm. 'Why don't you come over beside me and we can talk, Becky? We have so much catching up to do.'

'Get away from me, and get out of my house,' she spat out, but his grip on her arm now became tighter.

'Remember, you're only garbage to me,' he snarled in her ear.

She began to shiver violently, and his tone changed.

'I am not happy with you, Becky. From what your friend,

Iris, told me, you're a very nice person who would welcome me with open arms. I'm getting the opposite vibe, and I don't like it.'

'Please leave. I don't want any trouble.'

'You have a funny way of showing it, Becky. I have made my way in the world now, and I won't have somebody like you make unfounded allegations against me. You had a cop friend warn me off. That wasn't cool, Becky. It shows you have been telling tales. I'm not happy, Becky.'

She saw Ronnie go as far as the front door, and sit down.

Brad's hand pushed up towards her neck. 'We can do this the easy way or the hard way, Becky. I obviously would prefer the easy way.'

She heard Maisie put the key in the lock.

Becky didn't know how, but she felt a strength course through her body, and she shouted out loud. Pain consumed her as he slammed his fist into her face, and punched her in the stomach. As she fell to the floor, the dog ran down the hall and began to bark loudly. She tried to drag herself away, but Brad pulled at her legs and laughed loudly. The dog, unsure what to do, ran around in circles, barking. When Brad slumped down on the floor in a pool of blood, Becky screamed and screamed.

A hand reached out to pull her up off the floor. She saw Ben's face and heard him say she was safe now.

Shivering, she let herself fall into his arms.

Maisie was sitting at the table, sobbing. Uniformed gardai and detectives were swarming around the kitchen as Brad, who was bleeding from the back of the head, was rolled onto a gurney.

'What happened?' Becky asked so quietly, she thought nobody had heard her.

A uniformed garda turned around, and pointed at Maisie. 'Ms Ryan here saved your life. That's what happened.'

Maisie was brought to another ambulance for a check-up.

Iris, Jen and Bella ran up the path, and shouted to be let in the house.

'Can I go outside to Jen?' Becky asked, and Ben led her to the front door.

Jen threw herself at her mother. 'Mom, I couldn't bear it if anything happened to you,' she cried.

'Loath as I am to say it, but it's thanks to Ronnie and Maisie we don't have a much worse situation,' Iris said.

'Is Maisie OK?' Becky asked.

'She is just getting a check-up. What will the rest of us do? She will be insufferable after this,' Bella said.

Ben stepped forward.

'She happens to be right. If she had not contacted the rest of us, and gone in there only armed with a sweeping brush, it could have been a very different story.'

He turned to Becky. 'She ran in and hit your attacker on the head with the sweeping brush.'

'The yard brush, I forgot to put it back in the shed,' Iris said.

'So now you're trying to claim credit,' Bella sniffed.

Tom arrived at the gate. A garda made to stop him.

'That's my dad, please let him through,' Becky cried out, and Tom rushed up the path.

'I should have been here,' he said as he stroked Becky's hair.

'You're here now,' Jen said, and the three of them had a group hug.

Bella told Iris to show the way to her house. 'We all need a cup of tea, and they won't let us near the kitchen for quite a while,' she said.

Ben put a blanket over Becky, and they trooped over to the house next door.

Bella doubled back to get Maisie. When she walked in, everybody clapped. Maisie, her hair bedraggled, and looking unusually pale, smiled, surprising everybody by not saying anything at all.

Iris led her to a comfortable chair. 'Sit down, dear. You've done your bit.'

Bella looked all around the modern, bright kitchen with the huge glass doors leading out into the garden. 'You've a nice pad. Can somebody please give some whiskey to Becky and Maisie?' Bella said.

Iris pointed to a drinks cabinet. 'There's a bottle of good whiskey in there. I was saving it for an occasion, and I think it might be appropriate to open it now,' she said.

Bella arranged crystal glasses on a silver tray, and placed it on the table with the bottle of Midleton Whiskey. She poured the whiskey and handed the first glass to Becky and the second to Maisie.

Tom stood up, and asked could he make a toast. 'To Maisie, who saved my daughter, and to this tight band of friends here in Coolnamona; you are all our family.'

Becky could barely hold up the glass she felt so weak and so emotional. Iris, realising her predicament, led her to the couch, and told her to put her feet up. Jen put a rug around her, and Bella handed her the glass. She closed her eyes. She needed to know this was finally over, that Brad wouldn't be released on bail, or something like that.

Pain shot through every part of her body. The paramedics said it was the stress and wanted to bring her to hospital, but she had refused because she couldn't bear being separated from Jen, and being away from Coolnamona House.

The others sat about the table chatting, and grilling Maisie on how she had the courage to go into the house.

'You do what you have to do,' Maisie said, and the others, for once, were disappointed that she didn't hold forth.

Becky must have nodded off because when she woke up, Ben was sitting across from her.

'Are you up to talking?' he asked.

Becky sat up, and tried to focus, but her head was thumping.

'Do you want to do this in private?' he asked.

Becky shook her head. 'We are all friends here.'

'OK, we have arrested this Brad fellow. He goes before the court tomorrow morning.'

'Will I be expected to be there?'

'We will go with you,' Iris said.

Bella grasped Becky's hands, and squeezed them. Maisie said she was sorry but she needed to get home to Ronnie, and Tom offered to accompany her.

'Maisie must be very rattled that she didn't stay,' Iris observed.

Ben took a deep breath, and Becky felt herself tense up.

'You don't want me there,' she said.

'There is no need. Everything is in train, and if all goes according to plan, and I have no reason to believe it won't, Brad will be on a plane to New York by tomorrow night with a warning never to return to this country again.'

'But how does that help Becky?'

'Police will be waiting to arrest him when he steps off the plane in New York.'

Tears of relief streamed down Becky's face. 'Thank you,' she whispered.

The next morning, Iris and Bella insisted on opening up the café, and Becky had a lie-in.

Ben went off to observe in court, and when he came back they all sat at a table in the front garden.

'He flies out from Dublin Airport in the next few hours,' Ben said.

Becky reached over, and grasped Ben's hand. 'How can I ever thank you, and thank all of you?' she said.

'Just stay in Coolnamona. You and Jen are a big part of our world,' Ben said quietly.

The others murmured in agreement, and Becky felt safe and happy for the first time in a long time. She looked around at the faces of these, her friends. She was at home here in Coolnamona; she knew that now. This was her family, and it felt good.

THIRTY-SIX

It was a sunny Sunday morning in late August when they gathered down at the harbour to travel out onto Orchid Bay, and scatter the ashes.

It had taken a lot of planning to get to this stage, and there was a sense of excitement among the small group as they waited to be invited on board the yacht.

Iris, when Becky had asked her for help, had readily agreed and they had set about planning a special boat trip to scatter Hilda's ashes on the sea at Orchid Bay.

'I suppose Bella will be with us,' Iris said, her tone resigned, but kind.

'Actually, Bella has had a rather wonderful idea,' Becky said.

'Not another one. Let's be having it.'

'She wants us to wear Regina's designer outfits, and dress up for the occasion? Both women loved their style.'

'I didn't know Hilda or Laura, but Regina would certainly approve. Just no stilettos,' Iris said.

The day before the scattering, Becky, Bella, Iris and Jen met at Coolnamona House to pick out their dresses.

'I have asked Maisie to join us,' Becky said, and nobody objected. Ronnie flopped down in the garden as Maisie joined everyone upstairs.

'I have always admired Regina's talent,' she said, lightly touching the silk dresses which were hanging up at the bedroom window.

'I know which one young Jen should wear,' Iris said, taking out the pink Eugénie ball gown.

'You look so like Regina. It would be so fitting,' she said.

Bella, her eyes beginning to water, agreed.

Jen put on the dress, and twirled around the back bedroom. 'She must have been so happy to make and wear such a dress. This is so epic,' she said, and the others laughed.

Becky stood back, and looked at her daughter. It wasn't the Met Gala, but Jen was wearing the dress for a big family occasion.

'You need something at your neck,' Bella said.

Becky told them to wait, and she ran to her room to pick up the necklace Hilda had given her at the same age.

'Granny Hilda said I was to pass this on to you when you came of age, but this occasion seems the appropriate time,' she said, handing the silver and pearl chain with a large amethyst stone to Jen.

Jen fingered it, and smiled. 'Granny used to let me steal into your room, and wear it every now and again. She said it was precious because somebody very special had gifted it to her,' she said, taking the necklace, and putting it on.

Bella, her face crumpled with emotion, lightly touched the amethyst. 'So beautiful,' she said.

Becky selected a siren-red dress in a confection of tulle.

'I remember this too,' Bella said. 'She copied the Dior Zaire dress from the 1950s. I know we thought the colour was too out there, but it was such fun making it.'

Becky held the dress up to her. 'I am not sure about a strapless dress out at sea,' she muttered.

'You have to let go at some stage. I didn't know Hilda, but I think she would approve,' Iris said.

Becky slipped the dress on over her jeans and T-shirt. It was a perfect fit, and she could put her hair up in a messy bun.

Bella told her to hold on. 'I remember Regina had the exact same problem with that dress, and she said that on the catwalk there was a wrap of the same colour, so she made one in soft satin,' Bella said as she rifled through a box at the bottom of the wardrobe. Triumphantly pulling out the red wrap, she handed it to Becky, who casually threw it over her shoulders.

'It's beautiful, but will it be OK to wear my sneakers?'

'Of course, no silly footwear is allowed on board,' Iris said severely.

'And what are you going to wear, missus?' Bella asked.

'I know exactly,' Iris said, reaching into the back of the wardrobe, and taking out an outfit wrapped in what looked like black bin bags. Ripping off the plastic, she revealed a blue-grey brocade silk trouser suit along with a blouse, a pussycat bow over a collarless box jacket.

'Dior 1970s and so practical,' Iris said.

'It feels like you're cheating,' Jen said.

'Well I'm not. I just have more sense than the rest of you put together,' Iris retorted.

Bella snorted that it didn't have the wow factor.

'And what are you going to wear?' Iris said.

'All will be revealed. I will choose from my own collection,' Bella said enigmatically before she turned to Maisie. 'You can't be outdone. Pick something.'

Maisie looked very nervous. 'I am not sure anything will fit me. I am such a skinny minnie.'

'Nonsense, I know the perfect dress for your figure. The

baby-blue cap-sleeve Dior dress. It was always kept at the back of the wardrobe,' Bella said.

Jen dug into the back of the wardrobe, and pulled out a blue dress covered in a white sheet.

'With cap sleeves and a plunge neckline, it's perfect,' Iris said.

Maisie looked nervous. 'I'm not sure it's for me. I am more of a slacks and cardigan girl,' she said.

'Go on. You'll never know what it's like until you try it on,' Iris said.

Maisie sighed, and went to the other room to try on the dress. When she was ready, she stepped out on the landing. 'This dress is so wonderful, look at the way the skirt fans out. I feel beautiful.' She giggled.

'And you look it too,' Iris said kindly, and added, 'just bunch it up getting on the yacht. You don't want to trip.'

Becky asked Ben to do the catering for the small group, and a lunch was planned at Coolnamona House after the sea trip.

The night before, Ben and Brian had moved operations to Coolnamona House, and began preparing the menu for the next day. Jen and Brian got the dining room ready, and put out the best china dinner set and the crystal glasses from the china cabinet. Becky found two candelabra in an old cupboard, and polished the silver until it shone.

On Sunday morning, Ben and Brian were back at Coolnamona House at 7 a.m. to do the final preparations before they all went down to the harbour. Tom, in a freshly pressed linen suit and shirt and tie, arrived soon after.

Becky made a pot of coffee before she went upstairs to get ready.

Jen was the first to get her finery on. She called out to Brian to take a photograph and waited on the landing so he could get the perfect shot as she came down the stairs.

Becky watched from the first-floor landing, and she smiled that Jen was so happy here at Coolnamona House. She waited for a little while, listening to Jen and Brian as they took selfies and photographs and roped in Ben to take some of the two of them together.

When they moved to the front garden to take more photographs, Becky followed them outside.

Ben stood back, and stared at her. 'Beautiful,' he said.

She smiled at him, and moved towards him, but Jen came rushing up the path for a photograph.

'Mother and daughter at the front door of Coolnamona House, and then, Grandad, you must join us for the next photograph,' she said, and both Brian and Ben took out their phones and snapped a photograph. Tom handed his phone to Ben and asked him to take a photograph too.

'Grandad with his Irish/New York family, my beautiful daughter and granddaughter,' he said, his voice shaking with pride.

'Why don't I see anybody rushing to take a photograph of me?' Iris guffawed as she pushed the garden side door open, and stepped into the front garden.

'You look stunning,' Becky said, grinning when she saw Iris straighten up, and do a little twirl.

'Silk is so wonderful to wear,' she said.

They piled into the cars, and headed for the harbour. Bella was already there, standing by the yacht, her arms folded. 'Well, about time,' she said.

Becky eyed Bella up and down. 'Is that a Dior Bar jacket?' she asked.

Bella, running her hand down the contour of the jacket to the nipped-in waist, beamed with delight. 'I have still got it, girls. Myself and Regina made this from a pattern a long time ago. It's a little snug, but I don't even need to have the jacket open. Of course one doesn't let the jacket hang open. It would ruin the look.'

Jen fingered the tulle skirt. 'I just love it, Bella. Maybe I can borrow it some time, now that we're family.'

Bella shook her head. 'Sweetheart, there are some things one never shares, not even with family,' she said.

Iris ordered everybody on board.

Ben and Tom jumped on the yacht first, and helped each of the ladies.

As the boat was about to move out of the harbour, a car swept onto the far quay and a woman leapt out. Becky watched as the woman, who appeared vaguely familiar, danced about, waving at the yacht.

'Is that Ms Manhattan?' Bella asked.

Iris looked at the woman, who was shouting, and frantically waving.

'How did she know we would be here?' she said.

'I told her,' Jen said, and enthusiastically waved back.

Sadie, in high heels, attempted to run down the quay.

'Dear, we've got you,' Iris said through a loudspeaker, and everybody laughed.

'Our Ms Manhattan always has to make an entrance,' Iris muttered.

Sadie was out of breath when she reached the yacht.

'What are you doing here?' Becky asked.

'I can't let you have all the fun. This gig was too good to miss. I have a ball gown in my bag,' she said.

'And put something sensible on your feet,' Iris barked.

Bella ushered Sadie to the cabin to get dressed as the boat made its way out to sea, carving a trail through the water.

'Can we stop, and scatter the ashes from my favourite spot?' Jen asked.

Iris nodded, and shouted out the instruction to Danny, who was at the boat's wheel.

Bella told Ben to get a bottle of champagne ready and for Brian to get the plastic champagne flutes from her bag. 'Regina would like a bit of pomp and ceremony, and Laura too, I imagine,' she said.

Maisie, who was feeling a little nauseous, disappeared to the cabin.

The yacht lowered anchor where they had a view of the whole of Orchid Bay and the sheer cliffs where Coolnamona House stood proud.

Becky took the box holding Hilda's ashes, and invited Jen to stand with her. Bella clutched a small tin box with the ashes from the burning of Regina's letters.

Iris told everyone to wait a moment as she got a bunch of red roses from the wheelhouse. 'Let's do this,' she said.

'Shouldn't we say something?' Tom said.

Becky turned to him. 'Why don't you say a few words for Laura, and I will for Hilda?'

'I will draw up the rear with a few words about Regina,' Bella said determinedly.

They all gathered at the side of the boat.

Tom cleared his throat as Becky handed him a scoop. 'Goodbye, my beautiful Laura, until we meet again in a better place,' he said quietly, letting the dust fall to the sea, and a rose plop on the water.

Becky took the scoop from his hand, and gave it to Jen.

'You do it, Mom, for both of us,' Jen said, her voice wobbly.

Becky took a big scoop, and let the wind take it across the water. 'Fly, Hilda White, fly, and when you land, let the waves bring you back to shore at Orchid Bay. We love you,' she said as Jen dropped two red roses.

Becky tipped the rest of the ashes into the sea, and they watched as the water carried them away.

Bella opened the tin box and emptied it into the sea. 'My hope is that somewhere out there these ashes will mingle with yours, Laura, and somehow you will know that you were very much loved, and your mother deeply regretted what happened.'

The others threw in their red roses, and watched them float across the water.

They all stood in silence, surrounded by the sound of the sea as it lapped against the side of the boat. For a short while, the grey dust and paper ashes surfed the small waves before sinking into the deeper water as it made its way to the shore at Orchid Bay.

Sadie, who had changed into a soft-pink off-the-shoulder vintage Dior gown, broke off from the rest, and filled their glasses with the champagne before handing them around. 'To Laura, Hilda and Regina. May they finally rest in peace,' she said, and the others murmured, 'Hear hear.'

They were silent on the way back to shore and Coolnamona House, each lost in thought.

Becky led the way to the sitting room when they got back to the house. 'Before we eat, I have something important to say,' she said.

The others crowded into the room as she spoke.

'We have tried to make peace between Laura, Hilda and Regina, but I think I need to do something else. Bella, I would like to give you this painting of your dear sister and my grand-mother. You loved her, the good and the bad. You still love her.'

'Are you sure?' Bella asked.

'I have a new work of art I would like to place in this prime position,' she said, pointing to Jen's framed pastel picture on the hall wall. 'It deserves pride of place at Coolnamona House. It is a reminder to us that while there can be disputes in families, all roads lead to home. Coolnamona House over Orchid Bay, I am proud to say, is our home, and it is out there on Orchid Bay that hopefully Laura, or Hilda, whatever you want to call her, but my mother and Regina are finally laid to rest.'

Bella reached out, and pulled Becky into a tight hug. 'You have a way with words, girl,' she said.

Sadie popped a champagne cork, and poured the bubbly into the vintage champagne glasses which Becky had polished specially for the occasion.

'To a new chapter at Coolnamona House over Orchid Bay,' Becky said, and they all cheered.

A LETTER FROM ANN

Dear reader,

I want to say a huge thank you for choosing to read this novel. If you did enjoy it, and want to keep up to date with all my latest releases, just sign up at the following link. Your email address will never be shared and you can unsubscribe at any time.

www.bookouture.com/ann-oloughlin

I am so excited to present to you Book One of the Orchid Bay series. I so loved each day sitting down to write this novel.

I adore writing about women, and how when they band together, they can overcome anything. The group of women at Orchid Bay certainly show that.

The exciting thing about this crew is that there is plenty more to come. I am so looking forward to bringing you more stories from Orchid Bay in another two novels.

For me, to be able to return to Coolnamona on Orchid Bay is an exciting opportunity to follow these women, tell their stories and write about their adventures, ups and downs.

My wish is that you all enjoy visiting Orchid Bay and dipping into the lives of Becky, Sadie, Ben, Iris, Bella and Maisie. If you enjoyed reading the novel, I would be very grateful if you could write a review. I'd love to hear what you think, and it makes such a difference helping new readers to discover one of my books for the first time.

Remember, I love hearing from my readers – you can get in touch on my Facebook page, or through X, Instagram or TikTok.

Thanks,

Ann

facebook.com/annoloughlinbooks

x.com/annolwriter

instagram.com/authorannoloughlin

tiktok.com/@authorannoloughlin

ACKNOWLEDGMENTS

I felt very lucky when writing this novel to spend time at Orchid Bay and the beautiful Coolnamona House. I live by the Irish Sea and often, I opened the window, the sound of the waves hitting the shore as a backdrop to my writing.

When I needed a break from the words and the plot, I brought my dogs for a walk by the sea.

It's when I forgot to take the breaks that my family stepped in with cups of tea and sympathy.

I want to say a huge thank you to my husband, John, and family, for their unwavering support and words of encouragement at exactly the right time.

I am also so lucky to have Harriet Wade as my editor. Her wise words and encouragement, and her eye for detail, made the editing process so rewarding.

Bringing a book to publication is a team effort, and I must thank everyone on the Bookouture team who worked so hard to get this novel over the line.

As always, thank you to my agent, Jenny Brown of Jenny Brown Associates, who for a decade now has championed my work.

Special mention must be made of all the readers out there who have enjoyed reading an Ann O'Loughlin book, and have taken the trouble to write a review or have got in touch to say how much they loved the novels. To all of you, dear readers, I say thanks a million for spreading the word, and I hope you enjoy this novel, Book One of the Orchid Bay series.

PUBLISHING TEAM

Turning a manuscript into a book requires the efforts of many people. The publishing team at Bookouture would like to acknowledge everyone who contributed to this publication.

Commercial
Lauren Morrissette
Hannah Richmond
Imogen Allport

Cover design
Emma Graves

Data and analysis
Mark Alder
Mohamed Bussuri

Editorial
Harriet Wade
Sinead O'Connor

Copyeditor
Helen Hawkins

Proofreader
Jenny Page

Marketing

Alex Crow
Melanie Price
Occy Carr
Cíara Rosney
Martyna Młynarska

Operations and distribution

Marina Valles
Stephanie Straub
Joe Morris

Production

Hannah Snetsinger
Mandy Kullar
Nadia Michael
Ria Clare

Publicity

Kim Nash
Noelle Holten
Jess Readett
Sarah Hardy

Rights and contracts

Peta Nightingale
Richard King
Saidah Graham

Dear Reader,

We'd love your attention for one more page to tell you about the crisis in children's reading, and what we can all do.

Studies have shown that reading for fun is the **single biggest predictor of a child's future life chances** – more than family circumstance, parents' educational background or income. It improves academic results, mental health, wealth, communication skills, ambition and happiness.

The number of children reading for fun is in rapid decline. Young people have a lot of competition for their time, and a worryingly high number do not have a single book at home.

Hachette works extensively with schools, libraries and literacy charities, but here are some ways we can all raise more readers:

- Reading to children for just 10 minutes a day makes a difference
- Don't give up if children aren't regular readers – there will be books for them!

- Visit bookshops and libraries to get recommendations
- Encourage them to listen to audiobooks
- Support school libraries
- Give books as gifts

There's a lot more information about how to encourage children to read on our websites: **www.RaisingReaders.co.uk** and **www.JoinRaisingReaders.com**.

Thank you for reading.